FOR
THE MOST
BEAUTIFUL

FOR THE MOST BEAUTIFUL

A Novel of the Women of Troy

EMILY HAUSER

PEGASUS BOOKS
NEW YORK LONDON

For the Most Beautiful

Pegasus Books Ltd
148 West 37th Street, 13th Fl.
New York, NY 10018

First Pegasus Books hardcover edition January 2017

ISBN: 978-1-68177-301-8

10 9 8 7 6 5 4 3 2 1

Printed in the United States of America
Distributed by W. W. Norton & Company, Inc.

For Oliver, always

Contents

Prologue 13

PART I

Before the War 23
Helen's Tale 41
The Princes Return 47
On Olympus 65
In Love 71
Rise of the Greeks 85
Over the Plain 95
The City Falls 99
Into Captivity 113

PART II

The War Begins 133
Lying with the Enemy 141
In the Hands of Fate 155
Battle of the Gods 177
Dead Men 185
The Parting of the Ways 201
Prayer to Apollo 209
Plague 215
Taking Leave 229
Goddesses 239

PART III

Changing Camps 245
Fateful Words 257
The Gods Prepare 265
Embassy 271
The Camp Sacked 287
Change of Plans 301
Duel 307
Appeal to the Prince 321

PART IV

Death of a Hero 331
Final Acts 341
The Last Song 359
Epilogue 371

Author's Note 375
Bronze Age Calendar 379
Glossary of Characters 381
Glossary of Places 386

Further Reading 390

FOR
THE MOST
BEAUTIFUL

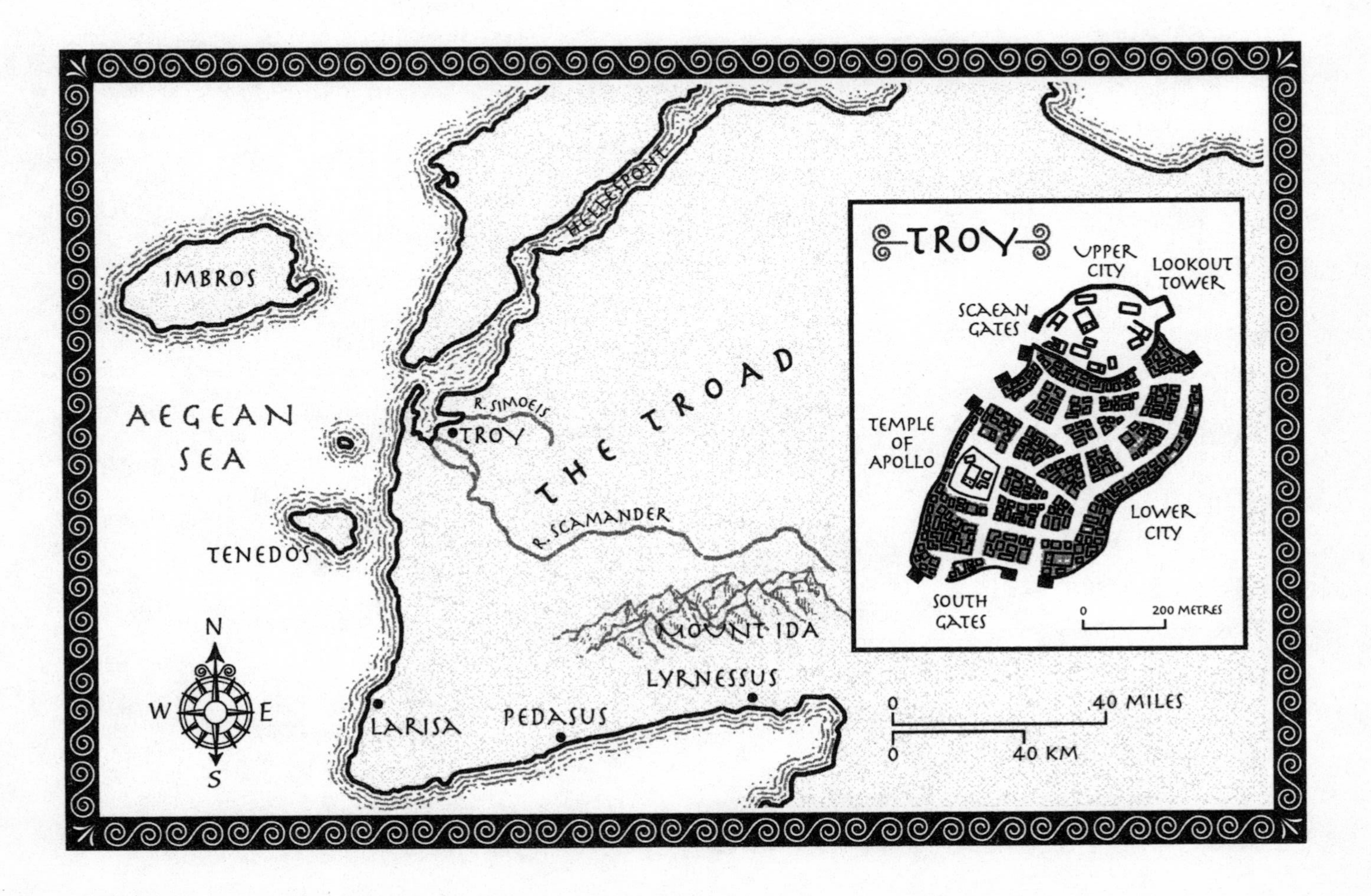
IMBROS
AEGEAN SEA
TENEDOS
HELLESPONT
R. SIMOEIS
TROY
THE TROAD
R. SCAMANDER
MOUNT IDA
LYRNESSUS
PEDASUS
LARISA
N
W
E
S
TROY
UPPER CITY
LOOKOUT TOWER
SCAEAN GATES
TEMPLE OF APOLLO
LOWER CITY
SOUTH GATES
0
200 METRES
0
40 MILES
0
40 KM

Prologue

High summer on the slopes of Mount Ida. Sweat trickling down his forehead, flies buzzing around his herd with their incessant thrumming, the stench of the goats thick in his nostrils mixed with the salt of the sea air from the north. He pushes the hair back from his brow and looks up to the sky. The sun, Apulunas' chariot, is at the height of its course.

The middle of the day.

He moves to the shade of an olive tree, his dog following at his heels. The cool darkness beneath the shimmering leaves envelops him and eases the heat on the back of his neck as he picks up a loaf of bread wrapped in stiff linen and his leather pouch, filled with wine. Though he is a prince born of the line of the kings of Troy, he has tended the goats on Mount Ida since he was a boy. The king hopes to show his people that his sons are not afraid to work the land which provides Troy with its famous wealth; yet Paris has always preferred the soft whisper of women's robes swishing through the painted corridors of the palace to the hollow clang of the goats' bells. He unties the thong around the neck and lets a few drops fall to the parched earth as a libation, an offering to the gods who make and destroy all things. The wine hisses on the ground and disappears, soaked into the thirsty soil.

His dog begins to growl behind him.

'What is it, Methepon?'

He turns. The dog's hackles are raised, his snout quivering. He bends to grasp Methepon's leather collar, but the dog snarls and barks, sending saliva flying.

'What—?'

There is a sound of movement, a rustling as of leaves upon the wind. Methepon is growling and barking ever more insistently, long teeth bared, eyes fixed ahead.

Paris looks up.

Three women are standing in the sunlight just beyond the shade of the olive tree. How they came to be there he does not know; neither, in this moment, does he care – for they are women of breathtaking beauty, with rich hair falling over their shoulders in waves, soft, shining skin, and robes of the finest gauze that brush against their slim waists and thighs. He feels the tension in his muscles relax. What in the names of all the gods is Methepon so afraid of? And then he smiles, thinking of his brother Hector, whose wife Andromache is as plain as the Trojan fields in winter. There are some men, true, who would fear to be before three such beauties.

But if there is one thing he, Paris, of all the princes of Troy, knows above all others, it is women.

One of them beckons to him, smiling. He bends down to pull at Methepon's collar again, but the dog is still snarling fiercely, paws dug into the dirt. 'What's wrong with you?'

Methepon lies down on the ground, whining, refusing to move.

Paris frowns. 'Very well,' he says, shrugging his shoulders and picking up his pouch of wine. 'Stay here, then.' He strides out of the shade towards where the women stand. 'I apologize,' he says, bowing deeply. 'My dog is not normally so—'

'Mortal.'

The voice rings in his ears. It seems to come from within his own head. He stops where he is and stares at the women, and they smile back at him, eyes glinting. There is a hardness to them, now that he is closer – as if they were sculpted of marble or stone with a sharpened chisel, not soft and made of flesh. He swallows. 'Who – what – who are you?' he says, trying to ignore the renewed growling and snarling of his dog behind him.

'Goddesses,' comes the reply. 'The three great goddesses: the ones you pour wine for. Goddesses of Ida.'

'Goddesses?' he says. 'Goddesses of Troy?'

He thinks of Arinniti – his favourite goddess – the one he worships with rose petals and pomegranates, whose statue he keeps in a shrine in his chamber. Era, queen of the gods, the august patron to whom his mother Hecuba lays a fresh-woven robe each night as an offering. Atana, the goddess of war and wisdom, whose high temple graces the upper city of Troy and whom the priestesses worship with almost as much reverence as Apulunas himself.

'You cannot be,' he says. 'It is blasphemy to say so. The gods appear only to their chosen priests within Troy.'

The women smile, and the air shimmers slightly. 'Look again.'

He looks up. He sees Era with her crown of golden oak leaves and the sceptre in her hand, her bearing infused with easy command, and even through his fear he sees in her the deep allure of a woman who knows that the world is hers for the taking. Atana has a burning intelligence in her grey-green eyes, and as he turns to her he feels the urge to plumb the secrets of the earth with her, to fly to the tops of the mountains to steal eggs from the eagles' nests and dive into the depths of the oceans. And the third . . . The third has skin paler than ivory brushed by roses in full bloom, shining hair that falls in waves to the curving swell of her breasts and a mouth as red as apples at the height of summer.

'What do you want of me?' he asks, his voice shaking.

The last of the three smiles, a smile that promises everything – and he knows, from the rush of desire that channels through his veins, that she truly is Arinniti, his Arinniti, to whom he prays each morning and each night. She extends a hand. In it is an apple, an apple of gold, glimmering in the sunlight, some words he cannot read etched into the surface.

'Choose,' she says, reaching out towards him. 'Choose to which of us the apple most belongs.'

He stares at her. 'You are goddesses,' he says. 'How can I choose?'

Arinniti smiles again, revealing white teeth. 'Because we have chosen you.'

He hesitates, then stretches forward a trembling hand. She drops the apple into it.

He brings it closer to his face, gazing at the sheen of its skin, the impossible perfection of its surface.

And then he sees the inscription etched into its flesh.

ΤΗΙ ΚΑΛΛΙΣΤΗΙ.

'For the most beautiful,' he whispers.

The goddesses are staring at him, their faces hungry, their eyes dark and wild.

'If you choose me,' Atana says, in a low voice, 'I will give you victory. You will win every battle you choose to fight. Everyone will come to you to beg you for the secret of your fame. Kings and gods will look up to you. You will fail at nothing.'

She draws a hand through the air, and at once his vision is obscured with golden light. Cities form before him – cities besieged by warriors whose brazen armour glints in the sun, stretched across the plain beneath the cities' walls in a sea of sparkling weapons, led by a prince with his own fine features and curling hair. He sees palaces toppled, their golden ramparts dissolving like sand, and ahead of him, an empire stretching as far as the eye can see – innumerable cities, countless lands, all his for the taking . . .

The apparition vanishes as quickly as it came.

He blinks, turns to the ox-eyed beauty with the oak wreath. 'Choose me,' Era breathes, 'and you will become king of the world. You will have power beyond your wildest dreams. You will sit on thrones and carry jewel-clustered sceptres. The sky itself will bow down to touch the earth at your command. Who needs to win a war, when you can force the peoples of the earth to do your bidding?'

His vision changes. Now he sees gold-clad kings kneeling at his feet, a jewelled sceptre in his hand and a crown upon his head. He watches as the kings raise their sceptres to him as their ruler, and hundreds upon thousands of warriors and slaves bow to him, acknowledging his power . . .

He cannot see Arinniti through the vision spread before him, but he knows she is speaking from the sound of her voice – something like the froth of ocean foam caressing the shore.

'I offer beauty,' she says, and, for a third time, the golden image shifts. He is looking now into the eyes of a woman – a woman so beautiful that he feels as if the breath has been drawn from his body at the very sight of her. Her hair is soft, like fine-spun silk, her eyes deep as liquid honey, her skin the colour of

virgin oil, her breasts round and firm as pale-skinned apples, just visible through the long gold-spun veil she wears draped sheer over her naked skin. He hears a soft groan of desire, and knows it has come from his own lips.

Arinniti laughs – sensual, confident. 'My gift,' she says, 'is nothing less than the most beautiful woman in the world.'

He reaches his fingers forwards, trembling, the tips brushing the woman's veil, but as he does so, the vision disappears.

He hesitates, gazing at the goddesses, the image of the woman filling his mind.

He cannot know that a war hangs upon his choice, the tale of which will be told for a thousand years and more. He cannot know that heroes whose names will echo through the ages will fight and live and love and die because of the words he will say now. All he knows is that Arinniti is looking at him, and as he gazes back into her face, her eyes are blue, like the clear shallows of the sea, and her breath is like roses in summer upon his face.

'Arinniti,' he breathes.

Her lips curl into a smile.

'Helen is yours,' she says, and her fingers close around the apple he is holding out to her.

There is a scream of rage from Atana and Era. A pillar of flame rises up around the three goddesses, casting their skin into shadows and turning their eyes a burning orange, their hair flying around their faces in the fire. The air around him grows hot, unbearably hot, as if it would melt, and the goddesses' forms shimmer before him, dissolving into the yawning chasm of chaos. He falls to the ground, his eyes aching, his palms covered with sweat. A sharp breeze whips across his forehead.

He looks up.

The goddesses are gone. All is peaceful once more. The sound of goat bells echoes across the mountainside, interspersed with the occasional rustle of leaves as a lizard skitters across the rocks, and the cries of the eagles circling overhead. The city of Troy is just visible on the horizon, its sturdy walls and upper city rising above the mud-brick houses of the town, and, beyond it, the plain, the meandering rivers lined by tamarisk trees, and the shimmering sea.

He stands up, shaking.

He is hardly sure that it happened. A mirage of the summer heat, he thinks. He wipes his sweating forehead with his arm. But if it did . . . If it is true . . .

His thoughts move back to the golden woman, the vision still shimmering before his senses. Helen . . . *The name whispers in his mind, like a faint breath of wind in summer.*

He smiles in spite of himself.

Helen . . . The most beautiful woman in the world.

Hermes, god of trickery and thieving, turns away from where he has been watching, hidden from Paris and the goddesses behind the thick trunk of the olive tree. He shakes his head. What a fool Paris was not to run away as soon as he heard what the goddesses wanted him to do. And Helen will create a problem, he thinks. She already has a kingdom in Greece over which to rule, and a husband, wedded and bedded – did the goddesses not think of that? If Paris is to receive his prize, it will mean war: a war that will rage across the world from the walled cities of the Greeks to the gold-filled treasuries of Troy . . .

Hermes pauses. A slow grin spreads across his face.

Of course the goddesses had thought of everything. Of course they had known what would happen.

That must have been why they had wanted to come.

He begins to pace up and down, his thoughts whirling as he puts the pieces together. They must have known that Paris would choose Helen. They must have realized that Paris would choose to seize her from her husband, Menelaus, and that Menelaus, in turn, would summon the Greek armies to avenge his loss in the greatest battle the world has ever seen. Why else would they have bothered with a paltry piece of golden fruit? Why else would Zeus have told him to bring them here, to Paris, an idiot if ever there was one? What god ever cared about an apple compared to the chance to start a war?

He cocks his head, his excitement rising, like the foaming crest of a wave before the shore. He can almost hear the sharpening of the weapons – the delightful scraping of bronze on stone that means the mortals are at it again.

Definitely time for a war, he thinks. It's getting far too pastoral around here. A little blood to stain the plain, a few heroes fighting and dying, a couple of cities burnt, the columns of soot and ash curling up to heaven, like the smoke of a sacrifice . . .

He glances at Paris, who is sitting on the mountain slope, his head in his hands and his mind full of Helen. Hermes grins. Helen will not cause the war, he thinks. It will be the gods, as it always is, who do that. It will be the pride of the lords of Greece when they fight over a beautiful woman. It will be the greed of a prince who steals her to have her beauty for his own.

But Helen won't be the only beautiful woman in this war.

Hermes turns to gaze out over the green and black Trojan plain, the battlement-crowned towns of Lyrnessus, Pedasus and Larisa dotting the pale blue line of the coast all the way to Troy.

The contest for the most beautiful has only just begun.

PART I

Before the War

Χρυσηίς
Krisayis, Troy

The Hour of Prayer

The First Day of the Month of Roses, 1250 BC

'Three – four – five . . .'

We scattered. Like a flock of pure white birds frightened by a barking dog, we skittered away from Troilus, flapping, chattering, fluttering with the thrill of the chase.

'Twenty-seven – twenty-eight – twenty-nine . . .'

Feet clattering against the cobblestones, hearts pounding against our ribs.

'Fifty-two – fifty-three – fifty-four . . .'

Down a flight of stairs. Past a garden surrounded by a high wall, the ripe fig trees bursting with fruit, a grape vine climbing the wall. Pluck a grape, feel the juice on your chin, run on. Round a corner, across a courtyard. Avoid the old man selling fish and the group of women carrying water on their heads in large clay pots.

'Cassandra – come on . . .' I laughed and took her hand – after all, she was not as fast a runner as I, and she did not know where I wanted to hide. I felt her fingers close around mine, and we kept running, whispering and breathless, as excited as if we were children once more and not almost women grown.

'Krisayis . . .' Cassandra panted. 'Krisayis, where are we going?'

I took a turn to the right into a long, narrow street, its name scratched into the cornerstone of one of the houses. A large stone slab was planted in the paving-stones beneath, roughly hewn from Mount Ida where the gods lived, its very crevices numinous with the presence of the divine. These slabs were scattered throughout the city, one for every sanctuary, and several for the gates in the walls and King Priam's palaces: markers, if you knew where they led, as well as guardians – the eyes of the gods upon our city.

Cassandra's eyebrows creased in sudden recognition. 'We're going to the temple of Apulunas!' she exclaimed. 'But you *know* your father forbade you to set foot in the precinct until—'

'Hush,' I said, my voice thrilling with excitement. 'We're almost there. It must be near here . . . somewhere here . . .'

I skirted around the edge of a small shrine with a bronze brazier set before it, streaming cloying incense into the air, and nodded to the two slave girls who were cleaning the steps. I had never been to Apulunas' temple before, but had I not seen it a thousand times from the tower in the walls? It was the largest in Troy, for Apulunas was the protector of our city and the greatest of the prophecy-giving gods. It was certain to be close by. I grasped Cassandra's hand and took a turn to the left.

And there it was. At the end of the alley, blocked off on either side by two tall mud-brick houses, the sloping wall of the precinct of Apulunas: five layers of enormous limestone blocks, each block almost half the height of a man, and laid on top of each other in uneven rows to the height of two grown men. Unlike the city walls, where the blocks of polished limestone fitted seamlessly together, the gaps here at their rough-hewn corners were so large that I could see between them into the sanctuary itself and make out the columns of the temple set against the sky behind.

'We *are* going to the temple!' Cassandra exclaimed, as I started towards it. The street was empty, the windows of the houses covered with woven rugs to keep out the heat of the day, a stray cat curled up here and there on a front step. 'Your father, Krisayis – we shall be in so much trouble . . .'

But I had already reached the wall, and was testing the gaps between the stones. They were large enough to fit my hands and feet with ease. I pulled myself up, fingers gripping the rough-chipped surface of the stone between the blocks as easily as if I were climbing the rungs of a ladder.

'You can't mean to *climb* it!'

I shrugged my shoulders. 'It's the only way. We wouldn't be able to get past the guards at the main gate, would we? Come on, Cassandra – it's not that bad, and Troilus will never find us. We might even win the game this time! Look . . .'

I stepped up a layer of blocks, found purchase in the cracks between the stones with my foot, then reached up with one hand to pull myself higher, like the lizards I had seen climbing the palace walls on a hot summer's day. 'You see? It's easy!'

But Cassandra did not reply.

'Cassandra?' I asked, twisting around to look down at her.

She was facing away from the wall, standing still and staring.

'Cassandra, are you all right?'

And then I froze.

Three feral dogs the size of wolves had appeared at the other end of the alley, a hundred paces behind us, and were advancing down the narrow street, their sharp teeth bared, hackles raised. They moved stealthily, jaws curled in a low snarl, revealing sharp, pointed fangs, their wild, dark eyes fixed on us as if they would hunt and savage us as easily as hares caught in a thicket.

'*Quick!* Climb up!'

Cassandra did not need telling twice. Whirling around, her blue eyes wide with fear, she snatched up her skirt and started to pull herself up the wall. I was moving fast – there were only two more large stone blocks between me and the sky . . . One more . . .

I looked back, my heart racing. The dogs had started to run and they were gathering speed, teeth bared, snarling, spittle flying behind them. They were fifty paces away now and the distance was closing, and Cassandra was still within their reach . . .

Cassandra was breathing hard with mixed terror and exhaustion as she pulled herself higher. I stepped down a layer to help her and reached out my hand to pull her up. 'Come on, Cassandra! You have to keep climbing! Only one more – one more—'

And then we had reached the top of the wall, and the dogs were beneath us, snapping and leaping, jaws barely missing our heels as we scrabbled up and on to the broad rough stones that capped it.

'Oh, Krisayis!' Cassandra breathed, as she pulled herself up next to me, her words ragged and uneven as she gasped for breath. 'That was – *so* – *close*!'

I nodded, my heart hammering with fear and excitement. 'I know.' I looked down at the dogs, snarling and jumping only a few feet beneath us, white teeth bared, and shivered slightly; then I turned, lowered myself over the far side of the wall and climbed down, dropping on to the grass of the sanctuary.

'We didn't get hurt, though, did we?' I said, as Cassandra started down after me.

'No,' Cassandra said, 'but—' She faltered, looking over her shoulder at the ten-foot drop.

'Here,' I said, moving forwards. I held out my hand to help her jump to the ground.

We gazed around us as we got our breath back, taking in our surroundings.

The temple was set above us on a slight hill, a tall, imposing structure of dark stone with bronze doors fronted by painted columns and set above an open courtyard, with a flight of steep steps. Around it were clustered several smaller buildings – a white-plastered dwelling, perhaps the home of the priest and priestesses, a wooden storehouse set against the wall and a workshop from which a faint smell of sand and dust drifted towards us. A single stone-flagged path wound up the hill towards the buildings, lined on either side by twisted old oaks and the sacred stone slabs of the gods, scattering the precinct like relics.

'What now?' Cassandra asked. 'Can we not go back to the palace, Krisayis?'

I felt a twinge of guilt at the pleading note in her voice. I knew that Cassandra did not like to leave the palace grounds and that she disliked disobedience even more; she was happiest when she was in the palace, surrounded by her brothers, in her familiar element. But then, I thought, I simply could not let this pass me by. It might be the only chance I had to find out about the life my father was determined to force me into before he succeeded in his plans, and all was lost.

I brushed my long hair off my face, gathered my courage and started off across the precinct with determination. 'We are going to the temple of Apulunas.'

Βρισηίς
Briseis, Pedasus

The Hour of the Evening Meal

The First Day of the Month of Roses, 1250 BC

I was standing in the palace herb garden, surrounded by fragrant lavender in the shade of a pomegranate tree, waiting, tall and proud as a princess should be. But my heart was quivering in my chest, like a small, frightened bird.

He has to want to marry me, I thought, standing there, trying not to show my desperation. *He has to. I must fulfil my duty before it is too late. I have to be chosen. I have to show to my family that I can still be a good daughter and a good wife and, if the gods will it, a mother of princes.*

Above all, above everything, he has to want me.

I flicked back a stray lock of dark hair from my forehead, as my mother always told me to do, and tilted my slim figure slightly to one side, just like the statues I had seen of Arinniti, goddess of love. I could hardly remember a time when they had not told me I was beautiful. Indeed, my old nurse, Deiope, had sworn from when I was a child that I should make a great match and a great marriage. With my long, dark hair, pale skin and delicate features, she had often said I looked like the living embodiment of the women whose brightly coloured portraits decorated the palace walls, their black hair braided down their backs, their skirts tied tight around slim waists. If it had not been for the prophecy, no one would have been anxious at all.

But, because of the prophecy, nothing was certain any more.

I readied myself, drew myself up tall, like a queen, and tried to hide my quaking heart, which felt as if it had dropped all the way from my mouth to my slippered feet.

The small oak-wood gate of the garden creaked and I turned. It was my mother, the Queen of Pedasus, a woman known as much for the firmness of her hand in ruling our city as for her beauty. 'Now, Briseis,' she said, without preamble, as she always spoke and especially to me. She walked towards me down the stone-lined path, straight-backed and stern, her flounced skirt brushing the herbs at the path's edge and sending the soft scent of lavender and thyme into the evening air. 'It is my expectation that you do your best.'

I looked down at my hands, trying to be humble. 'I do try,' I said meekly. 'I did not ask for the prophecy. I did not want—'

'Briseis, please,' my mother said, folding her hands in front of her in her most regal stance and gazing sternly at me. 'Not this again. We each deal with the fate the gods have dealt us. You will be silent and let your beauty speak for itself. Perhaps this time, at last, the gods will bless us with good fortune.'

I touched my forefinger quietly to my thumb, sending a silent prayer to the goddess Luck that this might be so, then cast my eyes to the ground and tried to trust in my beauty and the gods.

There were sounds of footsteps on stone approaching the garden gate. I took a deep breath. My suitor was approaching – and, if he chose me, he would have the power to change my life for ever.

Χρυσηίς
Krisayis, Troy

The Hour of Evening

The First Day of the Month of Roses, 1250 BC

'Your father . . . High Priest Polydamas . . . he will be so angry . . . if he knows you are here,' Cassandra panted beside me, as we climbed up to the temple of Apulunas. A slave dressed in a plain white tunic was brushing the steps with a broom, and he frowned at us as we passed.

I swallowed. 'I know,' I said. 'But I simply have to see what it is like for myself. I have to know. I have to know what it is to be a priestess, what my father is trying to give my life to when I reach my sixteenth year.'

Cassandra was still breathing heavily with the climb and did not reply. The steps were steep and each of them very high, as if they had been worked by the monstrous Cyclopes themselves.

I gazed up at the sky behind the buildings: turning pink now and shot through with gold as, drawn by the horses of Apulunas in his golden chariot, the sun started to dip down towards the mythical Garden of the Hesperides in the far west. 'Oh, if only I were divine, like Apulunas,' I burst out. 'Then I should be immortal, and no one could tell me what to do, least of all my father. I could just knock him over with my thumb, like this.' I illustrated, flicking the tip of my forefinger against the soft pad of my thumb. 'He would never be able to force me to become a priestess.'

I sighed as the dream of immortality vanished before my eyes, and all that was left in front of me was the temple, its bronze doors glinting in the sunlight.

'There must be more I can do with my life than lay it on the altars of the gods,' I continued. 'Just because I am a woman, and the daughter of the priest, my father thinks—' I shook my head. 'I do not see why he cannot understand that I—'

'Indeed,' a disapproving, all-too-familiar voice interrupted me. 'I do not understand. And *you*, daughter, are disobeying my command.'

We had reached the top of the steps. Standing in the gloomy shadows of the portico beside one of the blue-painted columns was the last person in the world I wished to see: a tall, stooping, grey-bearded man with a shrewd look on his face, wearing a priest's long white robes, which carried with them the scent of incense from the temple. He was nothing like me, with my curling hair and honey-brown eyes, but however much I wished at that moment it were not true, he was my father.

'Good evening, my lord,' I said.

I did not need him to speak to know he was angry: the set line of his mouth and the single grim line across his forehead told me that. His dark eyes flicked to Cassandra. 'Princess,' he said, with clipped politeness, bowing deeply towards her so that his long robes brushed the ground, and his laurel wreath – the badge of honour of the High Priest of Apulunas, protector of Troy – tipped forwards slightly on his thinning grey hair. Then he turned back to me. 'What,' he asked slowly, in a voice of forced calm, 'in the names of all the gods of Ida do you think you are doing here?'

I looked up at him. 'I thought—'

'You thought nothing,' he interrupted me forcefully. 'I have told you again and again that you are not to enter the precinct of the Great God Apulunas before your sixteenth year. The rites forbid it. The customs of the god prohibit it. And yet, after all I have done for you, after all I have worked for, you choose to disobey me and the dictates of the Great God, whom I have promised you will serve for the rest of your life.'

I tried to bite my lip, to stay silent as a daughter should. I could not. 'But, Father,' I said slowly, trying to make him see sense, 'if you would only *listen* to what I am trying to tell you! I revere the gods as much as anybody, but – I do not wish to be a priestess!'

He looked as if he would interrupt, but I continued all the same: 'Who could lock themselves willingly into the temple when there is a whole world outside? The gods are to be found in daylight, not in darkness – isn't that what the prophet Huwashi himself said? I wish to *live* my life, Father! I want to laugh with my friends, to dance in the palace at night and spend my days helping the people of Troy, like the king and princes do! I promise you, if my mother were here she would have—'

'That is *enough*, I tell you!' my father thundered, cutting me off, his dark eyes sparking with rage. 'I have heard enough! Is this all that fills your foolish head, Krisayis? Princes and dances and palaces? There is more to life, daughter, than mere court foolery and gold! And, if your mother were here, she would tell you the same as I: that it is the duty of a priest to listen only to the voices of the immortal gods, not the tattling speech of foolish women. You *shall* accept the destiny I have granted you and be *grateful* for it!'

I could feel tears of frustration welling at the corners of my eyes and immediately I blinked them away, hard. I would not let him see that he had made me weep.

But then Cassandra spoke: 'High Priest Polydamas,' she said, her bird-like voice quavering a little – my father was a hard man when he was in a rage. 'It was not her fault, my lord. We were playing with my brother Troilus. We were merely trying to find a place to hide when some wild dogs chased us. We ran here and – well – we had nowhere else to go. Krisayis did not mean for it to happen. She was protecting me. We had no choice.'

Cassandra felt for my hand and squeezed it, tight.

I felt my heart swell in gratitude, and squeezed hers in return.

My father paused, his thin chest heaving, looking us both up and down with the air of a man who had been winded halfway through a running contest. It was clear that, even in his rage, he would not contradict a princess, a member of the House of Priam.

'Is this true, Krisayis?' he asked me at last, his teeth gritted, as if he begrudged every word.

I nodded vigorously. 'Yes, Father,' I said. 'We were only playing hide and seek and then the dogs came.' I stopped myself saying any more. We were outside the temple of a god after all, and I knew that the gods could hear a lie louder than a stone dropped in a still pool. At least I could say in all honesty that this much was true.

He stared at me as if he, too, like the gods, could discern the truth from a lie. 'Oh, very well,' he said eventually, holding up his hands in surrender, though I could tell from his face that he did not want to believe me. 'Very well, then. But you are *not* to enter the temple,' he said, stepping in front of me as I tried to peer around him.

I caught a glimpse of a couple of white-robed women and a dark hall behind one of the doors, an altar sending a spiral of smoke from the sacrifice towards the ceiling, before his robes whipped before my face and blocked them from view.

'You must both return to the palace before night falls – and most especially you, Princess,' my father said, inclining his head towards Cassandra. 'King Priam and Queen Hecuba would not want you wandering the streets of Troy at night. I shall send Eusebius with you to ensure you reach the palace safely.' He clicked his long fingers and, as if from nowhere, a eunuch with dark-lined eyes and curled hair appeared by his side, carrying a torch and with a long, shining bronze dagger at his waist. 'Eusebius,' he said to the eunuch, 'I am entrusting the Princess Cassandra and her companion to your care. Return them to the palace and ensure they come to no harm.'

The eunuch nodded and placed his right hand on the hilt of his dagger by way of an answer.

Cassandra and I gathered up our skirts and turned to leave.

But then my father placed one bony hand on my shoulder. 'Wait, daughter. I would have a word with you before you go.'

I felt uneasy. What new reprimands would my father think up for me? Was it not enough that he was doing his best to lock me away in a priestess's robes for the rest of my life? I turned to face him, making a show of my reluctance.

He firmed his grip on my shoulder and steered me around the corner of the portico, where Cassandra could not hear us. 'Daughter,' he said, after a small pause. 'I do not wish to quarrel with you.'

I looked up at him. 'No more do I with you. It is not *I* who keeps trying to force people to be other than they are.'

My father took a deep breath, then, apparently, decided to ignore me. 'I am glad that you are enjoying your position in the palace as companion to the princess,' he continued evenly. 'You were fortunate that she chose you when we were summoned here from Larisa. It is a source of great comfort to me that you are content and well cared for in the palace.'

I stared at him. 'But, if that is so, then why can I not simply—'

He held up a hand, and I spluttered into silence. 'I have not finished. I said that I am glad you are content, and that you and the princes and princesses are close to each other, as friends and companions should be. And yet,' he looked down at me, his face stern, 'I must tell you that I have heard your name mentioned by the temple-goers over the past few weeks, more than once, with regards to the Prince Troilus. I only hope, daughter, for your sake, that the rumours are not true, for half of them are more scandalous than I dare to repeat.'

'I do not know what you have heard,' I said, 'and if you will not tell me, then how can I deny it?'

His eyes sparked and he looked as if he would shout at me, but he mastered himself with some difficulty and said, 'Krisayis, this is no laughing matter. You must remember that you are merely the daughter of a priest. You must not let your position as Princess Cassandra's companion fool you! A priestess of the Great God—'

'But I am *not* a priestess of Apulunas yet!' I said, and I almost stamped my foot in frustration. 'There are still two months left until I reach my sixteenth year!'

My father took my wrists in his hands and shook me. 'Daughter, *listen* to me!' He lowered his voice. 'It is essential that you guard your reputation. It is essential that you live up to the purity of the gods, whose chastity is beyond compare. You will never,' he continued firmly, as I tried to interrupt him, 'be anything more than a priest's daughter. Nor should you wish to be. And there can be no higher honour than to serve our gods as I do – as you *will* do. Do you understand me?'

I was looking at my hands. I would not suggest by even a flicker of my eyes that I agreed.

He gave a sigh. 'I shall not warn you again, daughter,' he said, and there was a finality to his tone. 'There is nothing – *nothing* – more important than this.'

He did not allow me to reply but gripped me by the arm and led me as if I were a brute ox at the plough back to Cassandra, who was watching us curiously.

I shook my head to tell her I did not wish to talk about it now. 'Shall we go?' I said to the guard and, without looking back at my father, I ran down the steps and away from Apulunas' temple.

Βρισηίς
Briseis, Pedasus

The Hour of the Setting Sun

The First Day of the Month of Roses, 1250 BC

'Prince Mynes, son of King Ardys and Queen Hesione, rulers of the city of Lyrnessus and beloved by the gods,' the herald announced.

I bowed my head, trying not to let my fingers shake as I clasped them before me.

Beside me, my mother did the same. A retinue of at least six ambassadors and a herald was entering the herb garden through the gate. They were followed by my father, my eldest brother, Rhenor, and beside him, apparently deep in conversation with the king, a young man with a golden diadem sitting on his head of boyish, curled brown hair, and laughing brown eyes.

I looked quickly at my mother, but her face was serene, her expression calm. She was clearly not taken aback by the appearance of the prince. And yet I could not help my lips parting in surprise as I glanced at him. All of my other suitors – the long line of men who had contended for my hand only to flee, their hearts failing them when they had heard the words of the prophecy and fearing war with my father's formidable armies – had been kings. Men in their prime, not boys. I had expected a man for a husband, a king who ruled his territory with the wisdom of age and the strength of a seasoned warrior. A man who wanted a beautiful young bride at his side to demonstrate his power. Instead, here was a young prince, the beard on his chin still light and downy, barely older than I.

'He is – he is young,' I commented, under my breath, to my mother, as my father and the prince walked up the stone path towards us.

'He is strong,' she corrected me calmly. 'And, if the gods will it, you shall have many years together.'

'I was expecting a king,' I whispered, my eyes cast down to my feet.

My mother looked at the prince as he approached, her royal smile now fixed upon her face, her head slightly inclined in a perfect image of nobility. 'He shall be a king,' she replied, her lips barely parting as she swept her eyes to the ground.

I nodded. Of course she was right. He would be powerful, I reminded myself. Many kings died young, and left their thrones to their sons. Perhaps this young prince would soon come into his own. I collected myself and inclined my head, smiling like my mother, knowing that I must act the part of a future queen. I was a princess with everything at stake. I could not think to dictate the terms of my marriage, when any marriage, to any man, was the most I could hope for.

'We are here,' the herald announced, his voice carrying through the small herb garden, 'to discuss the betrothal of Princess Briseis of Pedasus to Prince Mynes of Lyrnessus. Before we begin the formal proceedings, however, I must tell you that the King and Queen of Lyrnessus have requested clarification on the matter of a certain prophecy.'

My heart sank. So we had arrived at it already. I fixed my eyes on my feet, trying to ignore the thudding of my heart.

'King Ardys and Queen Hesione require a full declaration of the prophecy, its terms, and the conditions of its annulment,' the herald continued smoothly, in the nasal tones of a palace official. 'They stipulate that they will be willing to consider an agreement on the marriage contract only should their ambassadors,' he gestured to the white-bearded men beside him, 'agree that the prophecy is no longer valid.'

I felt a cold dread as my father's herald stepped forwards and cleared his throat to speak. I had seen this happen so many times.

I closed my eyes in fear, my fingers clasped once more in the sign of the goddess Luck.

'Let this be the statement of the prophecy of the storm god Zayu, given to his servant the priestess of the said god on the thirteenth day of the Month of New Wine, in the fifteenth year of Princess Briseis' birth,' my father's herald recited in a dry, sharp voice, like chipped stone.

I knew the words so well I could almost say them from memory.

The herald cleared his throat. 'The prophecy reads, "He who seeks Briseis' bed shall then her brothers three behead."'

There was the usual moment of ringing silence as the words of the prophecy hung on the air. I felt numb with fear as I always did when I heard those words. I wanted, as I always wanted, to forget my formal stance, to run over to them and tell my suitor and his ambassadors that it was not true. *Why would the gods have set such a sentence on my head?* I wanted to say. *What have I ever done, in my short life, to wrong them?*

But then my father's herald continued, and I was forced to listen on, in silence, as I always did, as my sentence was passed by others.

'For five years Princess Briseis was kept in her father's palace without suitors or admirers of any kind, in the fear that the prophecy might indeed prove true, and that her suitor should kill her three brothers and my king's sole heirs. But then, six months ago, on the twenty-fifth day of the Month of New Wine, and in the twentieth year of Princess Briseis' birth, King Bias returned to the sanctuary of the storm god Zayu. King Bias was told that the gods have decreed the prophecy holds no more. That is, that the prophecy is now no longer true and that Princess Briseis may marry without consequence.'

My breathing was coming very fast and shallow. I risked a glance at my father, but he was looking at the herald, and my eyes came to rest instead on Prince Mynes.

Our eyes met.

He was a handsome young man on closer inspection: olive-skinned, strong, smiling, the ease of his bearing and the honesty of his smile making up for what he lacked in years and stature. I could imagine being married to such a man. He was not what I had thought he would be, but I could imagine being by his side, and being happy.

But then I caught myself. It was for this very reason that I should neither look nor hope.

I could not give myself away so easily when the gift might still be scorned, as it had been countless times before. I looked away quickly, a slight heat in my cheeks.

The ambassadors of Lyrnessus were conferring in a small group, their white-haired heads bowed and foreheads creased in a uniform frown. My father and elder brother were conversing in low tones. My mother, by my side, was a paragon of wooden formality, her eyes veiled, her expression unreadable.

I saw Prince Mynes join the ambassadors, speaking to them in a low voice and, occasionally, glancing towards me.

At last, one of the ambassadors, the eldest to judge by his straggling white beard and rheumy eyes, turned slowly to face my father. 'We have come to our decision,' he said, his voice thin and quavering.

I held my breath, my eyes fixed on the old man, the nail of my forefinger digging hard into the soft flesh of my thumb in the sign of the goddess. Everyone in the herb garden seemed to be fixed absolutely still as they waited to hear the sentence the ambassador would pronounce upon me.

'The word of the storm god is law,' he said slowly.

I caught my breath. What did that mean? My heart was pounding against my ribs so fast it felt like the beating of the drums at a festival of the gods.

The ambassador cleared his throat and continued: 'If the prophecy is declared null, then we, the ambassadors of Lyrnessus, think it so. The prince and I,' the ambassador gave him a slight smile and a nod, 'have no fear that the prophecy shall be fulfilled, or that there shall ever be war between the kingdoms of Pedasus and Lyrnessus, between whom there has ever been only friendship.'

He paused and glanced at me, his head slightly bowed. 'I therefore announce that Prince Mynes and Princess Briseis are henceforth to be considered betrothed. The wedding will take place on the next day declared favourable by the gods.' He turned away.

I let out my breath slowly. It had happened. *It had happened.* I was to have a husband at last.

Helen's Tale

Mount Olympus, Greece

If Briseis thought the gods were watching over her as she stood in the herb garden, she was wrong.

On Mount Olympus, where the seven peaks stretch to the sky and the gods make their homes in the clouds, the fragrant gardens of heaven are dotted with eternal beings enjoying the evening sunshine, with not a thought for the mortals below. The sky is a deep forget-me-not blue, making the view on earth from the clouds particularly spectacular. The fountains in the gardens of the gold and ivory palaces are glinting and sparkling in the light of the setting sun, the peonies and poppies in the flowerbeds bending their delicate dewed heads, black swallows spiralling through the lines of cypress trees. Hera and Zeus are engaged in one of their favourite pastimes, arguing fiercely about nothing in particular as they pace the stone paths of Poseidon's apple orchard, past Poseidon himself, who is napping on a hammock strung between two apple trees. Athena is polishing her armour in an alcove shaded by a large oak. Hephaestus is sitting next to her, whittling at a figure of a wooden horse and humming to himself. Artemis and Aphrodite are taking a cooling bath in the pool before Artemis' palace, surrounded by pomegranate trees and jasmine blossoms, and Apollo is sitting on a bench nearby, surrounded by fragrant roses, snatching glimpses of the two goddesses while trying to pretend to be occupied with the piece of ambrosia in his hand.

The only one of the gods who is looking at the mortals at all, in fact, is Hermes. 'There,' he says to the youngest of the cupids who is sitting at his feet, and he points through the clouds towards the distant garden in Pedasus where

Briseis stands. 'The one with the dark hair and . . .' he allows himself a grin '. . . that ravishingly captivating smile. Can you see her now?'

The cupid nods and settles back upon the grass. Hermes adjusts his lyre, made from a hollowed-out tortoiseshell with four strings and inlaid with ivory, on his lap. He is seated in the fragrant garden of his father Zeus' palace. Around him are gathered several young cupids, staring up at him wide-eyed, their little wings fluttering like those of the butterflies on the box hedges. Nearby, a fountain tinkles as it sprays nectar from a golden dolphin's snout. Pure white roses nod in the breeze, sending wafts of scent over the young cupids, but they have eyes only for Hermes for they love to hear his tales.

Hermes looks around to make sure he has his audience captivated. 'Where was I? Oh, yes. We move now from Briseis, in Pedasus,' he waves a hand again towards the gap in the clouds, 'to the tale of Helen, who is about to enter our story and who needs – how shall I put it? – a little explanation.' He clears his throat. 'Helen is a princess of Sparta, the daughter of Lord Tyndareus – and she is also, if we are to believe the mortal bards, the most beautiful woman in the world.'

At once the cupids twist around to look through the clouds towards Sparta, the older ones elbowing the younger out of the way. Hermes chuckles. 'A few years ago, when Helen reached marriageable age, suitors began to flock from every corner of Greece to try to win her hand. More and more lords arrived in the palace, desperate to take Helen as their wife, and as their numbers increased their gifts became wilder and more extravagant. One brought a whole herd of calves, a year old and prime for sacrifice, another a chariot built of polished olive-wood from the slopes of Mount Taygetus. Lord Menelaus of Mycenae, trying, so the more outspoken of the suitors claimed, to compensate for his ugly red face and pot belly, brought with him a chest filled to the brim with precious stones and a whole harem of young Nubian slave-girls, each weighed down with necklaces of gold and bearing heavy golden tripods in their arms. The atmosphere in the palace of Sparta grew heated as calves jostled nubile young women, and hostile lords, set on proving their manhood, rubbed shoulders in the packed Great Hall.

'It was Lord Odysseus – he had come all the way from rocky Ithaca – who stepped in to calm things down. What he offered was a simple proposition. Let Helen decide whom she wished to marry – what plan ever went well that

didn't keep the women happy, after all? But, first, all had to swear a solemn pact to defend Helen's chosen husband, in case,' his eyes glitter, 'anyone should try to steal her for their own.

'It was an elegant solution. The lords, each short-sighted enough to believe that they would be Helen's choice, rushed to make the oath. Then came the decision.'

The cupids gaze at Hermes, their eyes as round as libation bowls.

'Helen, her grey-blue eyes sparkling with the reflection of the jewels laid before her, was beguiled by the extravagant gifts and wealth of the greatest of Greece's kingdoms, Mycenae. She chose Menelaus. They were married within the month, nearly two years ago to this day.

'Unfortunately for Helen and for Troy, however, Menelaus really was as ugly as the other suitors said.'

There is a pause as the cupids take this in. Then—

'I can't see Helen anywhere,' one of the older cupids says impatiently, craning his neck. 'And,' he shoots back at Hermes, frowning, 'I don't understand how this has anything to do with Troy.'

Hermes grins. 'It has everything to do with Troy, my dear cupid, because when a young Trojan prince with scented golden hair turned up in the palace on an embassy to Menelaus a few weeks ago, well . . .' He glances through the clouds. A single white-sailed royal ship is ploughing the seas from Sparta towards Troy, its prow just rounding the headland of the isle of Cranae.

'Hector and Paris,' Hermes says casually, and the cupids lean over the clouds, wings fluttering, trying to get a look, 'returning to Troy after their visit to Menelaus, an embassy of peace between the two wealthiest kingdoms in the world.'

'But what of Helen?' the cupid insists, crossing his arms, still frowning.

'Yes,' says another, 'what has Helen to do with it?'

Hermes looks around to make sure no one else is listening. Then he leans forwards to the cupids and lowers his voice, a mischievous glint in his eyes. 'Something tells me they're bringing back more than just gold.'

The Princes Return

Χρυσηίς
Krisayis, Troy

The Hour of the Rising Sun

The Eleventh Day of the Month of Roses, 1250 BC

Fifty-four days left until my sixteenth birthday.

I rolled over on the thick, soft woollen covers of my bed, so much richer and more comfortable than those of my father's home in Larisa had been, and into Troilus' arms.

Fifty-four days left to determine my destiny.

I moved closer to him, drawing the covers with me and pressing my cheek against his chest, letting my hair flow loose down my back as I knew he liked. He gave a muffled snore and drew me towards him, wrapping me around with one arm, his fine black beard grazing the top of my head. I took in the scent of him, like leather and sweet grass.

It had not always been thus. I had lived the early years of my life in Larisa, a small town half a day's ride away, with nothing much to speak of but a temple of Apulunas and a few lowly huts and outbuildings where the priests and farmers lived. My friends had been the children of temple slaves, mostly – Melaina, Heron, Palaemon, Lukia – and we had played together in the sand and longed to go to Troy, where princes ruled and merchants traded and wealthy women learnt to write and read; a world we had made in our imaginations, where we could be who we wished, not who we had been born to be. When a courier had arrived one day in my tenth year, the dust of the Trojan plain hot upon his heels, and had told my father that he was summoned to the city as High Priest of Apulunas, I had gone with him.

In that moment, my world had changed.

But I had never forgotten where I had come from.

I glanced at Troilus, the handsome youngest son of King Priam, sleeping soundly by my side in my bed. He shifted in his sleep on to his back and his eyelids fluttered. My heart leapt at the realization that he had chosen me – me, above all the other women of the city – to take to his bed. And that perhaps, just perhaps, in time, he might desire something more.

That he might wish to take me to his bed always.

I shivered and shook my head. I could not think such things.

But then I paused. *Surely*, a small voice said in the back of my mind, *surely it could not do any harm, just for a moment, to imagine what can almost surely never be: that, even in spite of my low birth, he might choose me to be his wife.*

I took a deep breath as visions floated up before my eyes. I would become a wealthy woman, just as I had imagined all those years ago in Larisa, and even more than that: a princess. My father's plans to make me a priestess would be foiled as I rose far higher than he could ever command. We could rule together, Troilus and I, the handsome prince and his beautiful princess, meting out justice to the slaves and poor among whom I had once counted myself.

I smiled, my skin prickling, as I moved closer into the warmth of my lover's embrace. These days, my desire for Troilus and my love for Troy were so closely intertwined that I could hardly separate them.

'Krisayis?'

It was Cassandra. I heard the door to her chamber, the larger room, the princess's bedroom to which my chamber was only the entrance, open quietly.

'Are you awake?'

Her footsteps padded noiselessly over the stone-tiled floor as I sat up, one finger to my mouth, then pointed at Troilus.

'Oh,' she said, stopping and pressing her hand to her mouth to stifle a giggle as her eyes came to rest on my bed. 'Good morning, brother.'

Troilus started and his eyes flew open. 'Who's there?' He sat up quickly, drawing an inlaid bronze dagger swiftly from beneath his pillow.

'Hush,' I said, under my breath. There were guards outside the door, and if they heard a man's voice inside the princess's chambers they were bound to come in, and then what would I do? King Priam might have me thrown out of the palace – or worse – for lying in secret with the handsomest of his royal sons. 'It's only Cassandra. Go back to sleep.'

Troilus replaced his dagger and fell back on to the pillows.

Cassandra tiptoed over and seated herself carefully at the edge of the bed beside me, lifting her night-robe and placing it gently to the side so it did not crease. She smoothed the beautiful white linen with one hand, then looked at me. 'Oh, Krisayis,' she said with a sigh, 'you know how glad I am for you and Troilus, but you *must* be more careful.' She took my hand in hers to show there was no ill-feeling, then lowered her voice to a whisper. 'You know how many people around the palace already suspect you. Do you really think the slaves have not noticed you and Troilus stealing into each other's chambers every evening these past few weeks? This cannot stay a secret much longer. Nor shall I be able to hide it for you, however much I wish to.'

I lowered my eyes. 'I know,' I said. 'I know all you have done for us, Cassandra, and for that I thank you. I cannot say how much—'

I stopped short. Both of us sat suddenly alert and upright, like hares in the field, our eyes turned to the door. We could hear heavy footsteps marching down the corridor outside, growing louder.

'Who requests permission to enter the chambers of the Princess Cassandra?' I heard one of the guards outside ask in clipped, military tones, as the footsteps halted right outside the door.

'I come bearing a message from Queen Hecuba for her daughter,' the herald announced, as clearly and loudly as if he were in the room with us.

Cassandra and I looked at each other, wide-eyed.

'*Quick!* Hide!' Cassandra whispered frantically.

We jumped up from where we were sitting, half scared, half giggling, and prodded Troilus awake as hard as we could. In a moment all three of us were running, stifling our laughter as we pushed him towards the large, hollowed-out oak chest in the corner of the room where I kept my skirts and shifts.

'*Quick!*' Cassandra murmured again in anguish, as we bundled Troilus into the chest and tried to close the heavy lid. 'Quick! You have to *move*, Troilus!'

We had just hidden him, and were trying to appear innocent, when one of the guards opened the door and entered, accompanied by King Priam's old herald, Idaeus. He was dressed in the deep purple tunic of the Trojan court, dyed with the purple shells of the murex found in the Trojan bay, and I saw his eyes flick around my chamber, taking in the intricate paintings of larks darting between lotus flowers on the walls, the large wooden chest in the corner, and the simple pine-wood frame and tumble of woollen covers that was my bed.

'Princess Cassandra,' he said, kneeling to the ground and bowing his head.

Cassandra was still in her night-robe, her red hair dishevelled, and had her hand to her mouth. She looked as if she were exerting every effort she possessed to stop herself smiling.

I could feel the laughter bubbling in my throat, and forced myself to look down at the floor.

'I come with a message from your mother, Queen Hecuba,' Idaeus said. 'The ship of Prince Hector and Prince Paris has just been sighted. It is your mother's wish and her command that you attend her on the walls to welcome your brothers home after their long voyage from Sparta.'

'My brothers have returned?' Cassandra asked, her hand dropping away from her mouth and a rare tinge of pink appearing on her usually pale cheeks. 'Hector is home?'

Idaeus nodded. 'The queen awaits you on the lookout tower,' he said.

'Very well,' Cassandra said. 'You may go. Tell the queen I shall be with her as soon as I am dressed.'

The herald stood and bowed himself out of the room.

The guard bowed then and left, closing the door behind him.

I moved to let Troilus out from the chest. He was a full head taller than I, and I gloried in the muscular firmness of his arms and chest as he climbed out, his clear hazel eyes, his fine profile and dark hair. He was a catch any girl in the cities around Troy would be proud of. And yet I could not help but feel a little shiver of fear run up my spine as he bent to kiss me full on the lips and I felt the warmth of his mouth on mine. It was such a great risk, such a very great risk, that I was taking.

'Good morning, my love,' Troilus said, straightening up and giving me his sideways smile as if nothing had happened, as if we had not nearly been caught and my life put on the line. 'And what message does our mother send us this morning?' he asked, turning to Cassandra and throwing his tunic over his head.

Cassandra was still flushed as she replied. 'Our brothers are returned from Sparta, as you very well heard,' she said. 'We are to go to the walls to greet them.'

Troilus lifted his silver-studded sword belt from a nearby stool and fastened it around his waist. 'Hector and Paris home at last,' he said, smiling with us. 'I have missed having Hector around the palace, and I cannot deny I am curious to see how Paris fared on his first diplomatic mission.' He bent down to fasten his sandals, then looked up at Cassandra and me.

He grinned at me. 'I hardly wish to encourage the habit, but you'll need to dress,' he said, his eyes dancing as he took in my hair tumbling loose over my shoulders and thin linen shift. 'I want us to be the first on the walls to welcome my brothers home.'

Βρισηίς
Briseis, Lyrnessus

The Hour of the Stars

The Eleventh Day of the Month of Roses, 1250 BC

By the time I arrived in Lyrnessus on the day of my wedding, my old nurse Deiope in the chariot beside me, as custom dictated, my father and brothers riding ahead, I was half torn apart by nerves, quite certain that the meeting in the herb garden had been but a dream and that none of this would happen at all.

'What if he changes his mind?' I whispered to Deiope for the hundredth time.

She laid her old, worn hand on mine and smiled at me, the wrinkles around her eyes creasing so that she resembled a dried brown walnut fallen from the trees of the Troad in the autumn months. 'He won't,' she reassured me. 'You have been as beautiful as the goddess Arinniti since you were a child, and on this day more so than ever.' She turned to adjust my flounced red-dyed skirt, tied tight around my waist with a saffron girdle and topped with a scarlet bodice edged with blue, then fussed over my hair, which was bound back in a mass of dark curls and covered with a saffron-yellow veil. 'No man in his right mind could refuse you.'

'But what if he listens to the prophecy?' I said, still uneasy, ignoring Deiope as she straightened my gold necklaces and checked the heavy gold earrings, shaped in delicate double spirals. 'What if he has become afraid that he will kill my brothers and incur my father's wrath? What if he decides he doesn't want me, like the other suitors?'

'I'd sooner swear there are no gods in the sky than that he'll do that, you mark my words,' she said, gently placing gold rings on my fingers. She gave my hand a little squeeze. 'Doves nest with doves, just as crows with crows. Trust me, child, all will come right in the end. And when he sees you, there'll be nothing he won't do to have you as his bride.'

I did not have to wait long to see Deiope proven right for, at that very moment, our gold-embossed chariot was pulling up the long road into Lyrnessus, the musky scent of rock-rose and warm bay leaves heady on the evening air, the shadow of Mount Ida – the home of the gods, where Apulunas, Zayu, Atana and the other deities reigned – stretching over us and a deep purple sky receding into blackness in the west.

'Welcome to Lyrnessus.'

Our procession had ridden through the gates and the main street of the lower city and come to a stop before the palace, a spreading expanse of buildings, columned porticoes and courtyards, surrounded by waving juniper trees. I could hardly have expected it, but Prince Mynes was standing there, his hand outstretched to help me from the chariot. He was quite as real as he had been two days before. I felt a sudden heady rush of dizziness as my hand touched his, as if I were on a ship on a stormy sea, not stepping down on to a well-paved road. I murmured a word of thanks, my cheeks warm under my veil.

He gestured into the palace. 'The ceremony will take place in the courtyard,' he said, as we walked through the gate and down the long, winding corridors, the procession of my mother, father and brothers, their nobles and slaves, streaming out behind us, the torchlight flickering on the brightly painted walls.

Mynes placed his hand on my arm, his touch gentle, and I felt a sudden thrill at the feel of his skin on mine. I could hardly believe this was happening, that I was to be married at last. I turned aside and gave Deiope a small smile, as if to say, *Perhaps you were right*, and saw my old nurse smiling back at me.

The courtyard of the palace, a long, open area at the centre of the buildings where ceremonies and games were held, was filled with priests and nobles and clouded with heavy incense when we emerged from the dim corridors. Oil-lamps and torches flickered everywhere in the open space beneath the light of the emerging stars.

Mynes led me over to the sacrificial altar, a large, square block of stone that stood at the courtyard's centre, and we stood there, he and I, as my three brothers, my mother, father and all our attendants filed around us to witness the ceremony that would mark my transition to womanhood.

The priest of Hymen, god of marriage, held his arms up to the skies, his robes shining white in the light of the moon.

And then our wedding began.

A few hours later, I was lying in our bed, waiting for Mynes to return from the anteroom with goblets of warm red wine. We had been escorted to our chambers by a dancing procession of girls singing hymns, carrying torches and scattering barley meal and rose petals to bless the consummation of our marriage. I smiled up at the dark blue canopy above, held up by four carved juniper-wood pillars, as I remembered how Mynes had taken me in his arms, so gently, how my lips had trembled as he kissed me and the pain mixed with soft, sweet pleasure as he took me for his own.

I am a woman now and a wife at last.

Mynes entered the room. I heard him set down the goblets of wine, then felt him lie beside me on the soft covers. He drew me towards him and kissed me deeply, and I felt once again the thrilling touch of his naked skin on mine.

'What are you thinking?' he asked, smiling down at me, his arms around me.

I hesitated. I did not wish to spoil this most beautiful moment after our first love, and yet, I felt there was something I must ask, to make sure. To make absolutely sure.

'You saved my life, choosing me,' I said, rolling over on to my belly on the bed and looking up at him. 'There are not many who would have done the same. If you had not chosen me, I would have lived out my days in Pedasus, alone and barren, useless to everyone.'

I hesitated again, and then the question I had to ask spilt out of me, like wine from an overfull cup, before I could stop myself. 'I don't understand – why did you choose me? Are you really not afraid of the prophecy? Don't you – don't you worry, that you will be forced to fulfil its terms, in the end?'

He considered me for a moment, and there was no trace of anger or fear in his honest brown eyes. The fires of the torches set on the walls in bronze brackets crackled beside us, a warm and comforting sound. 'No,' he said at last. 'It does not trouble me. It is not that I would deny the existence of the gods,' he added, 'but why would they make us suffer? It is my belief that we make our own fate, and there is no one else who decides it for us.' He paused. 'And as for choosing you, Briseis,' he said, and bent to kiss me again, 'as soon as I laid eyes upon your beauty, I knew that you were my destiny. We shall, neither of us, worry about the prophecy any more. We shall make our fate together, my love, whether the gods are on our side or against us.'

I looked up at him, and it was as if all my cares, all the troubles I had ever had, dropped from my back, like the disappearance of a heavy load. And, as I melted once more into his passionate embrace and we whiled away the long hours of the night in love, I felt that, at last, I had come home.

Χρυσηίς
Krisayis, Troy

The Hour of Music

The Eleventh Day of the Month of Roses, 1250 BC

I helped Cassandra to dress, tying her long, flounced purple-dyed skirt around her waist with a dark blue girdle woven with gold thread, fitting her embroidered bodice over her linen shift and tightening the slim ribbons behind her back. Her hair had been dressed for her by her slave Lysianassa with elaborate threads of pearls and covered with a fine veil scattered with beads of gold, and two curls of red hair framed her face. I stepped back to admire her.

'You look lovely,' I said. 'Your brothers will hardly recognize the beauty you have grown into while they were away.'

She shook her head. 'I am nothing to you, Krisayis – I never have been – but you are kind to say so.' She smiled at me, the companion she had chosen above all others, to sleep in her rooms, to work with and to play with, almost as a sister, though I was only the daughter of a priest and a Larisan at that. 'Here,' she said, and she handed me her burnished bronze hand mirror with its intricately carved ivory handle.

I stared at her. 'I – may I?'

I had hardly ever seen my reflection in a mirror before: only the wealthiest people in Troy could afford them, and Cassandra's little hand mirror was kept carefully guarded by Lysianassa. I held it back a little, marvelling at how clear the reflection was in the polished bronze, far better than the water in the clay basin I used to wash my face. I smiled, and saw my eyes warm, turned my head and saw my curls falling down my back and the way my simple yellow bodice pressed invitingly against my breasts. Then I twirled a little on the spot, laughing at the way my pale blue skirt swayed about my hips.

At that moment, Troilus pushed open the door to Cassandra's chamber. 'Are you ready?'

I stopped twirling, a little out of breath. Cassandra giggled and took my arm to steady me.

Troilus raised his eyebrows and smiled, then turned to leave. 'We shall miss my brothers' return entirely if we do not hurry.'

The way to the lookout tower was long, through the winding corridors of the palace and up, up the stairway in the walls to the tallest tower on the northern wall of Troy that looked out over the two bays of the sea, one to the north beneath the cliff on which the upper city stood, the other further to the west, sweeping in a wide curve of blue. When we finally reached the top of the narrow stairway and climbed out on to the tower, we saw that Queen Hecuba and King Priam were already there, seated on two ornately carved wooden thrones, decorated with gold and blue-glass images of leaping dolphins under a shaded canopy of purple Assyrian silk that fluttered slightly in the faint breeze. They were accompanied by two of their five sons, Prince Aeneas and Prince Deiphobus.

Troilus and Cassandra walked quickly over to their parents and knelt at their feet for their blessing, while I touched my head to the ground behind them, as someone of lower rank should.

'Son,' King Priam said, inclining his white-haired head towards Troilus' dark one. 'Daughter,' he said, to Cassandra.

Cassandra and Troilus stood, and moved into the shade beside Aeneas and Deiphobus. Reluctant to leave, I gave Cassandra a little smile and a shrug, then moved to the side, as I knew I must, to join the small crowd of favoured nobles and chosen companions of the princes and princesses.

It was hot in the beating rays of the sun, and I peered out over the edge of the parapet, trying to catch a cool breeze coming up from the sea. I had always loved the view from the lookout tower – the highest point in the city, set at the edge of the high cliff on which the Trojan citadel lay. To the west, the tamarisk-lined Scamander river meandered out of the woods and through the rich plain of fields and olive groves, a woven blanket of rich green and black soil threaded with blue, before emerging on to the shore to join its waters to the western bay. To the north, the sea curved in towards the city to form the second bay, and beyond it, over the ridge of Rhoeteum, I could see the strait of the Hellespont, trading ships moving up and down on their way to the Black Sea, white sails spread like wings. When the Great God Apulunas had founded the city, he could not have chosen a better place in all the world. As I stood there, I smiled and thought, with a sudden flood of happiness, *I never want to leave Troy.*

Suddenly one of the lookouts positioned on the battlements gave a cry. 'The princes' ship is making land, my king!' he shouted, shading his eyes from the blinding sun and pointing out to the bay across the plain to the west.

I squinted in the same direction, trying to ignore the stinging salt of the sweat in my eyes and the pounding beginnings of a headache, until I found the royal ship among the fleet of trading vessels making for the beach, the gilded figurehead of Apulunas, protector of Troy, just visible at the prow. Little figures had jumped out and were splashing through the waves, carrying ropes to pull the ship up on to the sand. They began to furl the sail, which flapped loosely in the wind as the ropes slackened. Then we could see slaves unloading the vessel. The crowd on the walls applauded.

I turned to Cassandra, wishing to congratulate my friend on her brothers' safe homecoming. The air before me seemed to shimmer in the heat-haze, and it was a few moments before I found her. My hands faltered mid-clap as I caught sight of her under the royal canopy and I saw the expression on her face. My smile died before it had formed.

Cassandra looked as if she were being subjected to the most exquisite torture. Her eyes were stretched wide in horror, her fingers clenching and unclenching, her body heaving with bone-racking pain.

'Cassandra!' I shouted, terrified. I tore away from the battlements and pushed my way through the crowd of nobles until I reached the royal canopy, rushing over to her side and taking her stiff white hand in mine.

Troilus was staring at her with his mouth slightly open. Aeneas and Deiphobus were frowning.

'Cassandra, what is wrong?' I asked. 'What's happened?'

She could not speak. She was gurgling, spluttering, choking.

I whirled around to summon one of the slaves for help. 'Please – someone – anyone – we need help for the Princess Cassandra! Some water, at least! Quickly!'

But my words were drowned by an ear-splitting scream.

'No! No! *Noooooo!*'

I stopped still in shock.

The sound was coming from Cassandra's mouth, but it sounded unearthly, like the shrieks of the Harpies: foul monsters with the bodies of eagles and the grotesque, twisted faces of women. Her whole body twisted as she let out repeated, agonizing screams as she gestured towards the parapet at the edge of the tower, the beached ship and the figures moving on the shore.

I stood transfixed, horror-struck, my fear mirrored upon the faces all around me. I had no idea what to do or how to act, except to listen to that awful, piercing voice, which was not her voice at all.

'Cassandra . . .' I faltered.

'Troy will fall!' she screamed, her beautiful red hair blazing over her shoulders, like flames, as she shook her head wildly from side to side. 'I see fire – burning – people screaming – dying—'

The nobles near her were backing away, muttering and glancing over their shoulders.

King Priam and Queen Hecuba were like statues sculpted from marble as they stared at their daughter.

'The prize that is not theirs will be our ruin,' Cassandra continued piercingly, tears leaking from the edges of her eyes. Then, without warning, she stood up straight and pointed towards the sea, her hair fluttering down her back, her eyes wide. 'Turn back! Take her back! The prize of Troy that is not Troy's shall be its ornament and its ruin! Troy will burn – burn—'

Her hand wavered like a leaf in a breeze, and then, slowly, gracefully, her legs folded beneath her and she fell to the ground. I tried to catch her, but it was like trying to lift a pine tree fallen in a storm.

'Cassandra!' I shouted, shaking her, but she was as still as death. 'Cassandra – wake *up*!'

She did not move.

I covered Cassandra's limp, faint body with her veil and summoned a few young slave-boys to pick her up and carry her further into the shade of the canopy. I followed them, fanning her face, watching her eyelids for any signs of consciousness. *Let her be alive. Please, Apulunas, let her be alive.*

I knelt beside her, as they laid her gently on the ground, and covered her forehead with my hand. It was blazing hot and covered with sweat. Thank the gods, it was not cold in death. I let out a sigh of relief and bent down to stroke the damp hair from her face.

'Cassandra,' I whispered in her ear, as if I were calming a frightened horse. I took a cushion from one of the nearby stools and set it beneath her head. 'Hush, it's all right, Cassandra. I'm here. Everything will be all right now.' I picked up a goblet that one of the slaves had brought, and tried to pour water between her parched lips.

There was a loud bang of a door being thrust open, and sounds of commotion by the entrance to the tower. A messenger had burst on to the walls, wearing a deep blue tunic, the colour of Hector's servants. He was panting hard, clutching at a stitch in his side, but he ran straight to King Priam, half bent over, until he was standing before the king's throne. Then he knelt on one knee and touched his forehead to the ground in a deep bow.

He drew a deep breath. 'My king,' he said, in a loud, clear voice. 'I bring news from Prince Hector and Prince Paris.'

The murmuring of the nobles quietened to a low buzz, then died away.

'The princes have arrived,' the messenger continued, 'but they do not come alone.'

King Priam gazed down at him. 'Whom do they bring?' he asked. 'An ambassador from Sparta, come to return our pledge of friendship? Lord Menelaus himself, perhaps?'

The messenger bowed. 'No, my king,' he said. There was a long silence. It seemed he was struggling to find the words. 'They have brought . . .' The messenger swallowed. 'My king, they have brought Lord Menelaus' wife, Helen of Sparta.'

There was a sudden low buzz, like the humming of a swarm of angry bees.

I could see Troilus standing very still, gripping the arm of his father's throne, his knuckles white.

'I do not understand,' Queen Hecuba said, looking from her husband to the messenger. 'What queen travels without her husband? Is this some foreign Greek custom? Why would she come to pay her respects alone?'

King Priam held up a hand to silence his wife. 'Go on,' he said to the messenger, his voice deep with foreboding.

The messenger bowed again. 'Helen of Sparta is Helen of Sparta no more,' he announced, his voice ringing in the deep silence on the tower. 'Prince Paris begs that you accept her into the Trojan royal household. Helen has come, my queen, not to pay her respects, but to stay. She is Prince Paris' chosen wife.'

The crowd of nobles erupted into exclamations of shock and surprise.

I stared at the messenger, one hand still tight around Cassandra's limp fingers, the other still clasping the goblet.

Queen Hecuba leant back on her throne, her lips pressed tight together, her eyes on her husband.

King Priam looked as if he was still trying to take in the news, to understand the enormity of what had just happened. 'She comes with Paris?' he asked slowly. 'She comes as his wife? Does her husband, Lord Menelaus, know of this?'

The messenger opened his mouth to speak, but the hubbub around him was still too loud for him to make himself heard. Slowly, the nobles muttered themselves into a scandalized silence, waiting to hear what the messenger would say.

'My king, I have not yet told you all,' the messenger said. 'We stopped at Athens on our way from Sparta. We had news from their ruler that Lord Menelaus has sworn to burn the city of Troy to the ground and to take Helen's life with his bare hands. The Athenians told us that every one of the Greek lords pledged a binding oath of protection to Menelaus and his wife, and that Menelaus' brother Agamemnon, king of all the Greeks, has already sent out the summons to muster their forces. They say he is gathering the greatest expedition the world has ever seen. There is word of a thousand ships being called to his command.'

There was a stunned silence.

King Priam sat forwards on his throne. 'When was this?'

'About two weeks ago, my king.'

The king leant back, frowning. The crowd of nobles was as hushed as the sea before a storm.

The messenger took a deep breath. 'My sovereign king, we have it on good authority that Achilles, the most fearsome warrior alive and son of a god, has agreed to join them.'

On Olympus

Mount Olympus, Greece

'I don't care what you say, Hera. A thousand ships is far too many.' Zeus sips at his nectar with supreme nonchalance. He has had his throne moved out into the garden of his palace to get a breath of fresh air, and he must say he is enjoying it. He watches, amused, as a butterfly flits towards him, lands briefly on his hand, and then, unaware that it has just communed with the divine, flies off again. 'Pass the ambrosia, Hermes. You're taking it too personally.'

'Personally?' snaps Hera. 'How am I supposed to take it, when Paris gave the prize to that tart?'

Aphrodite, who is reclining near the rose bushes on a chaise longue forged from golden cloud, raises one arched eyebrow, but says nothing. She does not need to. No man, not even a god, would let a goddess so beautiful go undefended.

'I really don't see what the problem is,' Hermes says, popping a bunch of ambrosia into his mouth, then passing the remainder to Zeus. 'You asked Paris to judge, and he did. I'm afraid you may just have to admit, my dear stepmother, that Aphrodite won the contest fair and square.' He grins at Aphrodite, who gleams a smile back at him.

Hera ignores Hermes and continues. 'I'm the queen of the gods,' she thunders at Zeus. 'I'm your wife! And look at Athena – your own daughter!' She motions to Athena, who is sitting beside her, her arms crossed over her breast-plate. 'Don't you want to teach the Trojans to show us a little respect?'

Zeus sighs and turns his goblet round in his hands. 'It's not that simple,' he says. 'We can't just burn down the city of Troy because of a slight to your beauty by one Trojan prince.'

Hera puts her hands on her hips. 'And why not?'

'Because there is more to it than just you, my dear wife. We are supposed to be looking after the mortals, in case you've forgotten. This is a job we're doing. Do you remember the last time I had a holiday?'

Hermes starts muttering something about a summer trip to the Ethiopians, but Zeus silences him with a single gesture.

'Exactly. We look after them, answer some of their prayers, and in return we get honour and praise and the fat from their sacrifices. In short, we need them, they need us. We can't just wipe them out.'

'Who said anything about wiping out?' asks Hera. 'It's just one city, not the whole race of men. All I want is Troy.' Her eyes flash. 'And I might remind you, Zeus, that you're not so holy either. Remember the flood? When you tried to wipe out the whole earth because one man didn't pay you enough respect?' She snorts. 'And you say I'm overreacting.'

Zeus passes over the reference with regal indifference.

'It might be "just Troy" to you,' he says. 'You'd batter down the gates single-handed, given the chance. But you know how much I love that city. Priam and his sons are good people. They never leave my altars empty. I won't punish them, not even for you.'

She hesitates for a moment, thinking. The fountain at the centre of the garden – a dolphin spraying nectar from its snout – tinkles in the silence. Then she glances at him from the corner of her eye, a sly look on her face. 'Maybe not for me. But would you do it for a city?'

Zeus' head jerks up, so that his beard ripples like the River Styx. 'What do you mean?' he asks.

'I'll do a deal with you,' says Hera, leaning forwards. 'Give me Troy, and I'll give you three of my most beloved cities in return. How does Mycenae sound? And Sparta, and Argos? Imagine – whenever you feel like it, I'll step back without a word, and you can smash them to the ground. The three biggest cities in Greece,' she adds seductively.

Zeus is clearly tempted. Everyone knows that Mycenae and Argos worship Hera more than any other goddess, and he can't deny that a change would be nice. A few more altars to Zeus here and there couldn't hurt, could they? Besides, three of her cities for one of his? It sounds like a pretty good deal. But he has a reputation for reasoned deliberation to uphold – the mortals call him 'Zeus, the far-seeing' and 'god of counsel', after all – so he pauses for a long moment, just for appearances' sake.

Hermes, Athena and Aphrodite watch the twitch of his eyebrows in anticipation.

Then, after a suitable interval, he nods.

Hera smiles triumphantly.

'Troy is yours,' he announces. 'Do as you want with it. Troy . . .' he gazes down through the clouds at the hundreds of Greek ships already blackening the seas of the Aegean as they sail towards the east '. . . will fall.'

In Love

Χρυσηίς
Krisayis, Troy

The Hour of Prayer

The Eighth Day of the Month of Threshing Wheat, 1250 BC

A few weeks after the princes' return, I was walking with Troilus through the gardens of Troy's lower city, towards the western circuit of the walls. It was a perfect summer's day, the sky a calm, unruffled blue, the sun warming the stones beneath our feet, fountains splashing in gardens hidden behind high mud-brick walls, and the smell of burning wood from the bakers' ovens mixing with the sweet scent of rock-rose and ripening figs. We looked for all the world like a young couple newly wed, except for the absence of a golden ring on my finger and a diadem on my head, and the fact that every time we saw a palace guard or a slave in royal livery, we had to leap into the shadows and press ourselves flat against the walls to prevent them seeing us together. Today, however, was a day to send our cares to the skies on the breeze that played with the apples hanging over the orchard walls.

Except that I could not.

'Troilus . . .' I said, turning towards him. 'Troilus, I can't stop thinking about what my father said when I was at the temple of Apulunas. About my becoming a priestess.'

He sighed deeply. I had told him of this days ago, yet still the fear of my father's threat had hung between us, like a cloud, on these balmy summer days.

'Yes, I know. I have tried speaking to my father, but he always turns me away. I shall try again, soon. And besides—'

A sudden low booming sound bellowed over the town and drowned his words. I stopped in mid-stride, startled, and looked back to the upper city, the palaces and temples all enclosed within their own ring of thick walls and the high lookout tower to the north.

'What's that?' I asked. 'Why are they ringing the bell? I've never heard them do that before.'

Troilus was standing still, a small crease between his eyebrows. 'It is a warning,' he said at last, in a low voice. 'A warning of attack.' He caught my hand. 'Come,' he said, and he pulled me forwards. 'Come, we must see for ourselves. The West Gates are closest and look over the bay. We can see from there.'

It was cooler up on the walls, a strong sea-breeze blowing over the city and bringing the smell of the salt sea on the afternoon air. Troilus ran to the battlements. After a few moments, I followed him, standing several paces away so that no one could suspect us, though in truth the tower was empty of guards. They must all have gone to the lookout in the north when they heard the bell toll. I watched the waves whiten as they beat the shore of the Trojan beach and the blue horizon of the ocean melt into sky beyond the Hellespont.

And then I saw them.

It was like a thin line of grey cloud at first, emanating from the island of Lemnos to the west, to the other side of the headland of the bay. Nothing definite. Just a gathering mist on the horizon. But as the moments slipped by, and the cloud rolled gradually closer, it began to billow out into shapes. Keels cutting into the water. Sails held taut against the wind. Masts pricking up into the sky like the points of swords. Oars stabbing in rhythm into the waves. And as the cloud rolled on and on, it brought them closer – a thick black stripe that covered the horizon and spread slowly, so slowly, over the surface of the sea, like a tempest.

I turned to Troilus but, for once, he was not looking at me. He was staring out to sea, his expression full of foreboding as he took in the threatening dark mass of ships on the horizon.

'The lookout tower,' he said to himself, his voice hoarse. 'I must go to the lookout tower. My father—' His throat seemed to constrict. 'My father will need me.'

We ran, together, along the walls, breathless and silent, past the Scaean Gates and the old fig tree growing on the plain that had stood there a hundred years and more, towards the lookout tower, following the tolling of the bell. As we emerged on to the open space of the battlements I saw one of the lookouts strike a wooden battering ram against a huge bronze bell on the tower's corner, sending those deep, vibrating explosions of sound bellowing through the city, like the rumble of an earthquake.

Prince Hector, the eldest of King Priam's sons and leader of his armies, was already standing by the battlements, and Troilus strode quickly over to join him, leaving me in the shadows by the tower door and the guards. Together, the brothers studied the dark outlines of the ships growing clearer, and took in the size of the fleet – thousands of ships, tens of thousands of men, darkening the ocean, like a storm sent by Zeus. I watched Hector's expression with growing dread. There was a frown there, a concern that I had never seen before in all the years I had lived in the palace. Hector knew Troy, its walls, its armies, its horses, better than anyone in the city – he lived for Troy, he always had – and the worry drawn in lines upon his face as he contemplated the Greek fleet was a worse omen to me than any number of ships. He turned, saw me and gave me a brief nod. I tried to smile.

A teeming crowd of confused people had gathered at the bottom of the walls by the Dardanian Gates into the upper city, shouting over the noise of the bell that was still sending out its low, resounding knell. I could hear their buzzing chatter, the clamour of their voices, as they called up to find out what was happening. I watched as Hector stood for a moment, taking in the ships one last time, and Troilus laid a hand upon his shoulder, saying something in a low voice. He nodded again, and walked to the edge of the tower facing south, towards the city.

'People of Troy!' Hector shouted, his voice carrying over the noise and the hollow echo of the bell's last toll.

Gradually the crowd in the city below fell silent.

'You ask to know what is happening. I shall tell you. The Greek fleet is even now,' he gestured towards the horizon and the gathering mass of ships, 'sailing towards our shore. And yet we did not ask them to come. We did not ask for war.'

I felt myself shudder at the very sound of the word. I glanced at Troilus, standing by the battlements. It was a fear beyond anything I had ever known, to think that he might go to war, that the high walls of Troy might be battered by arrows and spears and that the shining towers might fall, as the old widows had told us they feared would happen when Hercules came to the city all those years ago. I felt a wave of pity for Hector, standing at the tower's edge, straight-backed, like the general he had been raised to become. In truth he was a gentle man, who loved to ride swift horses across the plain and play at swords with his little son, Astyanax. He had only ever wanted to rule his city in peace, like his father did.

A loud, coarse voice shouted from the back of the crowd down in the city, up to the tower, interrupting my thoughts. 'And what about Paris? What about how he stole Helen?'

The crowd took up the chant: 'What about Helen? We don't want Helen! Send back the adulteress!'

The chant spread and was getting louder.

Hector motioned at some of the soldiers down by the gates to control the crowd as they shouted, punching their fists into the air to the rhythm of the words. But the shouting was growing ever louder, and the soldiers were calling up to Hector, asking for orders, reluctant to turn on their own people and powerless to do anything as more and more took up the chant.

At that very moment, the door to the tower beside me flew open and a trumpet fanfare sounded over the cries and shouts of the people. King Priam and Queen Hecuba emerged on to the tower with their retinue, followed by their fourth son, Paris, and, behind him, Helen.

A sudden hush fell over everyone on the tower and in the city below, as if by some enchantment, as Helen stepped out on to the walls.

So *this* was Helen of Sparta.

I stared at her as she passed me, the first time I had seen her since she had come to Troy. She had spent weeks hidden in Paris' chambers. She was not beautiful as such, I thought, weighing the words as I watched her walk towards the battlements. It was not enough to call her beautiful:

it did not do her justice. She was simply, irresistibly, desirable.

Indeed, I could not stop looking at her. No one could. We all just stood there, gazing, as she made her way towards the tower edge, hand-clasped with Paris, leaving behind her the scent of summer roses, sweet myrtle and the musky fragrance of jasmine. Nothing about her was absolutely perfect, and yet – I could not have said how – everything was arranged in such a way that she was infinitely, hopelessly alluring.

You wanted to touch her, to test if her silvery-blonde hair really was as soft and rich as it seemed. You wanted to trace the slim curves of her hips with your hands and feel the silken material of her dress slip through your fingers. You were desperate just to be looked at by those smoky grey-blue eyes, deep and clear as the pool Narcissus gazed into when he fell in love with his own reflection, just to catch a little of their lustre in your own.

And her breasts – her ripe, full, creamy breasts . . . I forced myself to look away. I could not help but feel a little nagging jealousy. Would Troilus still call me his most beautiful girl, now Helen was there for him to compare me with? Who would look at Krisayis, when there was Helen to be had? Surreptitiously, I tried to rearrange my dress a little, pulling the neckline of my bodice lower so the plump curves of my breasts showed, like Helen's, and I tied my girdle a little tighter around my waist.

The people down in the city were elbowing each other now and whispering Helen's name, eager to catch a glimpse of the woman who had brought the Greek fleet to the shores of Troy. They were paying no attention to Hector and the glare he was casting at Paris.

But then old King Priam stepped forwards, holding his sceptre high in the air, and the crowd in the city below calmed, like the waves that grow silent after a storm when the god of the sea holds up his trident.

'My people,' King Priam said, his voice filled with authority, 'what madness is this that Apulunas has sent down upon you?'

The last few loudmouths muttered themselves into silence as he surveyed the crowd.

'Have you forgotten the duty we owe to Zeus, king of the gods?' he thundered. 'His laws demand that we care for any fugitive or traveller who begs for assistance within our walls. You all know this. And yet you would turn Princess Helen over to the Greeks, when you know as well as I that she will be slaughtered like carrion for the birds. My people, what has come over you?'

The crowd seemed almost to cower before the anger that sparked in his eyes.

'In Troy, we are known for our hospitality,' he continued. 'We are not barbarians, to hand over a fugitive – a woman, no less, and my son's chosen wife – to her captors. We are not savages, to turn away a guest from our walls. We are men, and we are men who righteously fear the gods, whose strength and justice oversee all. Princess Helen has claimed our protection, and she shall have it.'

He paused to allow his words to sink in, and then he spoke again, this time in a lower, gentler tone. 'My people, I am not ashamed to confess that my son may have done wrong when he disregarded the honour of his host, Lord Menelaus,' he said, 'but it is not his youth that is to blame. It was by the gods' will that Princess Helen was brought to our city.'

People began to mutter, craning their necks to peer at Paris, some shaking their heads, but most gazing up at the king, waiting for what he would say next.

'The high priest of the Great God has informed me that our holy goddess, Arinniti, daughter of the storm god Zayu, blesses us with the beauty of Princess Helen as the richest treasure to crown our well-built city,' he continued, bowing graciously towards Helen. 'Prince Paris has been awarded Helen as a gift, a sign of the gods' favour towards Troy. They have appointed us the protectors of Princess Helen by the eternally binding laws of hospitality.'

Helen's blushing lips arched into a smile as King Priam turned to her. I felt my stomach turn over with a terrible fear, and it was almost as if I could feel the sweeping of some unavoidable doom over the walls as the king looked directly into Helen's grey-blue eyes.

'The gods and your king have spoken. Helen has our blessing. She shall stay.'

The crowd erupted into shouts and cheers as King Priam lowered his sceptre. One of the young lords standing beside me thumped his neighbour on the back and shouted in his ear, 'And I wager the gold Helen brought with her doesn't hurt either, eh?'

'Nor does the king's liking for a pretty face,' the other replied, and they both spluttered with quiet laughter.

Hector stepped slowly back on to the platform at the tower edge to take his father's place, accepting his spear from the page who carried it for him. His wife, Andromache, stepped out of the king's retinue to join him, their young son in her arms, her eyes turned up to Hector in a silent plea, but he was unable to meet her gaze, like a man swept away in the current of a sea he cannot fight. He took a deep breath. The crowd fell silent, waiting to hear what Hector would say.

'My father the king speaks the truth of Zeus. Whatever my young brother has done, he did it by the will of the gods.'

The people in the crowd were murmuring among themselves now. Prince Hector cast a look at his father, who nodded, smiling. Hector took a deep breath. 'Now that the Greeks are here, are we going to run, or are we going to fight?'

They were shouting more loudly now: 'Fight! Fight for Troy!'

Hector drummed the end of his spear into the ground. 'Do we see the forces of the enemy and weep like girls?'

'No!'

Hector brought his spear down again. 'Do we turn over a gift given to us by our gods, a guest who claims our protection, to be torn apart by those Greek unbelievers with their false gods?'

'No!'

The spear came down once more. 'Then, Trojans, *what do we do?*'

The reply came back at him, as inevitable as an echo: 'Fight for Troy! Fight for Troy! *Fight for Troy!*'

Hector raised his spear into the air and shook it, the sunlight flashing off the sharpened blade. He looked at Helen for an instant, spear held in mid-air, and their eyes met.

And Helen's lips curved again into a smile.

Βρισηίς
Briseis, Lyrnessus

The Hour of Evening
The Eighth Day of the Month of Threshing Wheat, 1250 BC

Those first weeks passed in peaceful bliss: the warm wedded delight of a young couple newly married, and the joy that flooded my veins every time I looked at my young, strong husband, and knew that I would no longer be alone, or feel the blame of my brothers' impending death and the wrath of the gods hanging over my head. The prophecy had vanished, and with it my doubts and fears.

And, of course, I was in love.

It seems improbable, and yet, from almost the first moment that Mynes' hand had touched mine, I had loved him. He was not the king I had imagined, true, but he had believed in me when no other man had. He had taken me and promised to care for me and, to a girl who had been shunned by her family and suitors for five long years, this was worth the promise of the world. More than anything, I had learnt to thrill with joy at his touch and the sound of his voice. I felt complete, whole, finished. For the first time in my life, I felt that I was loved, and it was like the touch of sun on my skin after a long imprisonment.

A few weeks after the first joy of our wedding night, I was going into the evening feast when Mynes came out from the men's quarters. He had just taken a bath, and his skin was scrubbed and scented with cedar-wood oil imported from the mountains in the south, his face glowing from a day spent in the sun. He came up to me and caught me from behind in his arms, nuzzling into the nape of my neck.

I wriggled free and gave him my most dignified, regal look. 'And what do you think you are doing, accosting the Princess of Lyrnessus?' I asked, in mock outrage.

His brown eyes danced as he leant towards me, the heat of his skin deliciously close to mine. My whole body yearned to fall into his arms.

'I simply cannot help myself,' he whispered into my ear, 'when she is so beautiful.'

I let out a deep, shivering sigh of excitement and desire, then looked around to see if anyone was nearby. They were not.

'Well,' I said, lowering my voice, 'if that is the case, then I suppose the princess may consent to being accosted again.'

He laughed, then took me by the hand. 'Come, Briseis,' he said. He pulled me away and down the corridor towards the south gate. 'There is something I wish to show you.'

'Wait!' I called. 'Where are you taking me? What about the feast?'

He did not look back but kept pulling me by the hand, laughing and saying, 'You'll see.'

We ran around the palace to where the slaves' quarters and kitchens were. Hot air was billowing from the bread-ovens, and the warm, delicious smell of roasting meat on the kitchen spits floated from the windows. I could see the slaves through the large, open windows, their faces shining with sweat as they turned the meat above the fire.

Mynes led me to the kitchen door. Set in front of it was a large wicker basket, neatly covered with a snow-white cloth. He lifted it and handed it to me.

I drew back the cloth and saw a small feast packed inside: a jug of red wine, slices of cold boar, a loaf of warm bread, a flask of olive oil and a handful of figs surrounding a honey-walnut cake. I reached for a slice of bread, but he caught my hand.

'Not now,' he said. 'Just wait – you'll see.' He took the basket and pulled me on again.

We were running away from the palace now, through the grape-laden vineyards and down towards the steep cliffs and the sea. A storm seemed to be gathering on the horizon. Thick, dark, rolling clouds were massing up from the sea, dragging a veil of rain behind them across the lowering sky. We came to the gate at the top of the steps cut into the stone of the cliff, and Mynes pushed it open, lifting me through and on to the steps. And then, gloriously, without warning, the summer rain burst over our heads and we ran, slipping, sliding and laughing, down the steps, the smell of water heady in the air, our clothes damp and clinging to our wet skin.

'This way!' Mynes shouted, over the hiss and splash of the rain, jumping the last few steps and lifting me down on to the beach. He pointed to an old tree a few feet away, its silvery leaves dripping water, like strings of white agate. I held my arms over my head and ran, following Mynes' shadowy figure through the slanting rain that splashed in my eyes and ears, slipping on the slimy-wet sand.

Mynes ducked under the leaves of the tree and pulled me, half sliding in my wet slippers, with him.

We were inside the hollowed-out trunk of a gigantic ancient olive tree. I settled down on the floor and looked around. It was warm and dry in there, and dark like the inside of an old chest. The withes of the living wood twisted around us, winding up into the sky, like a knotted sailor's rope. Outside, beyond the canopy of leaves waving and dripping in the wind, the rain slanted down from stormy grey clouds, and the sea was stirred up into great waves.

Mynes put his arm around my shoulders. 'What do you think?' he asked softly, resting his head on mine and looking out into the storm. 'Was this worth missing the feast for?'

'Almost,' I conceded, smiling. 'But you are forgetting, husband – we had other things in mind than the feast.'

He laughed at that and took me in his arms, then pulled me gently down to the ground so that we were lying side by side on the warm earth. He gazed deep into my eyes, and I found myself silenced in the warmth of our love. There was a long pause as we looked at each other, and the rain dripped against the roof of wood.

'What are you thinking?' I asked, smiling as I remembered how he had asked me the same question on the first night of our marriage.

Mynes did not answer, but picked up a small sharp stone that was lying on the ground and weighed it in his palm. 'Hold my hand.'

I cupped mine around his. He started scraping into the wall of bark, small movements at first, nothing legible.

'What is it?' I asked, as he guided my hand back and forth over the bark.

'Wait . . .'

Shapes seemed to be materializing even as I watched: a series of lines coming together into a triangle crossed by another line . . .

'B . . . M,' I read, as he finished, scraping away the last few grains of bark with the edge of the stone. Then I saw it. 'Briseis and Mynes.'

He turned to nod and, before he could do anything else, I had caught him in my arms and was kissing him, fully, passionately, my hands on his neck and in his hair.

His fingers uncurled instinctively and he dropped the stone to the ground as he responded, his hands and fingers exploring the skin of my body, pulling the brooches and pins from my wet dress and soaking hair. As one, we rolled together, the basket tipping to one side as Mynes pushed it away, all thoughts of food forgotten.

And there, in the warmth of the olive tree that night, with the rain pouring down over our heads, we made love for the last time.

Rise of the Greeks

Χρυσηίς
Krisayis, Troy

The Hour of the Rising Sun

The Ninth Day of the Month of Threshing Wheat, 1250 BC

The day after the Greeks arrived I went to see Cassandra. My friend had taken to her rooms ever since she had collapsed on the walls when Paris and Hector had come home. I had visited her and sat by her bed every day since, telling her what was happening in the city, and wondering what the Fates would send upon us next.

Cassandra was lying on her delicately ornamented maple-wood bed as I opened the door and looked in. Lysianassa was busying herself by one of the chests, folding blankets.

'Are you awake?'

Cassandra nodded and I came across the room towards her, my feet sinking into the soft pile of the woollen rugs laid across the floor. 'How are you?' I asked tenderly, as I reached the bed and seated myself beside her. Cassandra seemed in far better spirits than I had seen her lately, and her blue eyes were lively and warm in her pale face as she sat up against her pillows.

'Krisayis,' she said, taking my hands, 'it is good to see you again, and I am well, better than I was. Tell me, what is the news?'

I laid beside her the sprig of rock-roses I had brought her from the shrine of the goddess Arinniti. 'The Greek ships have arrived,' I said quietly, not wishing to be the bearer of bad tidings, though I could not deny her the truth. I tried to keep from my voice the terror I had felt ever since the bell had first tolled across the city.

I saw Cassandra's cheeks whiten.

'They arrived yesterday. I was on the lookout tower, I saw the ships on the horizon – hundreds of them, Cassandra. Your father the king and Prince Hector are determined to keep Princess Helen within our walls. And Troilus says he cannot see any way out of the war that the Greeks seem intent on bringing against us.'

Cassandra did not reply. It seemed she was struck dumb with fear at the news I had brought, and I remembered her words on the walls that day: *The prize of Troy that is not Troy's shall be its ornament and its ruin . . .* Perhaps she was remembering too.

'There is something I must tell you.'

I looked at her in surprise. A pink tinge was blossoming on her cheeks and her eyes were strangely bright. She took a deep breath, then said in a rush, 'I have to tell you what happened on the walls when Paris and Hector returned home, Krisayis. I cannot bear it any longer. I have to tell someone.'

She looked excited and scared at the same time, the flush on her cheeks deepening. 'Only – you promise you will believe me?' she continued, the words tumbling out of her mouth. 'You won't doubt me? No matter what it is?'

'Of course!' I said, taking her hand. 'Of course I shall believe you. You are my dearest friend, my sister almost. How could you doubt it?'

She gave me a small smile, then took a deep, shuddering breath. 'It began on the day my brothers came home,' she said. It was as if she were trying to say everything at once, and that now she had begun she could not stop. 'I was standing on the walls, under the canopy, where you saw me. It was hot that day, and I felt dizzy. I was standing there, trying not to faint, when I realized there was someone behind me.'

I stared at her.

'I turned,' she continued, her voice shaking, 'and – and I saw—'

'What? Cassandra – who was it?'

She looked me straight in the eyes. 'Apulunas.'

It took me a moment to register what she had just said.

'Apulunas?' I breathed. 'The Great God Apulunas came to you on the walls of Troy?'

'Yes,' she said.

I stared at her. 'What did he look like?'

'He was invisible. He told me I was the only one who could see him. And he – he . . . He wanted to have me,' she whispered, so quietly I could hardly hear her. 'He told me I was beautiful, and he – he asked me to come to the home of the gods on Mount Ida with him. And when I refused . . . he cursed me. He cursed me with the gift of prophecy. He – he said that I would always tell the truth, but that – that –' she began to sob, and then she looked up at me, her eyes overflowing '– that no one would ever believe me.'

I gazed at her in horror, my hands over my mouth. 'Cassandra, no – do not say such things – it is blasphemy—'

'That is why he forced me to make the prophecy that day,' she whispered. 'It was true, Krisayis. It was all true. Troy will fall. We are all ruined.' She paused. 'Can you believe me?'

I looked at her, my hands still to my face, and she looked at me. There was a moment's silence.

'Do you mean – are you saying he desired you?' I asked slowly.

She nodded.

'And you refused him?'

She nodded again.

My mind was reeling with shock. For Cassandra to say that she had seen a god was one thing. But to suggest he had wanted to lie with her – a god, with a mortal, just like that, and not any god but the god who was the highest of all the divine beings, the god who was above all others in his goodness and purity, who guarded Troy with an ever-wakeful eye . . . It was impossible!

And yet Cassandra was my friend. And I had sworn not to doubt her.

'I – I believe you,' I said, trying to put enough conviction into my voice to satisfy her.

Her eyes still shone with tears. 'You do?'

I hesitated. 'Yes.'

Great God, I thought, *if you are listening, I pray you do not hear my lie.*

Βρισηΐς
Briseis, Lyrnessus

The Hour of the Evening Meal

The Ninth Day of the Month of Threshing Wheat, 1250 BC

It was towards the end of the afternoon. Mynes had been out hunting again, and he was just about to return. I was in our quarters, my hair wound up around my head with a swathe of dark blue cloth, preparing a bath for my husband when he came home. The brightly painted clay tub had been set up in the bedroom, surrounded by piles of linen towels, large pots decorated with black spiralling patterns for pouring the steaming water, and small jugs of fragrant olive oil. Wild rose petals had been scattered on the water to float on the surface.

I rubbed scented cedar oil into my hands to make them smooth, and then I knelt beside the tub at the foot of our bed, waiting for him to arrive home.

I waited.

And I waited.

But he did not come.

After an hour or so I stood up, my back and legs stiff from kneeling. I caught one of the slaves by the arm as she came in from the wash-rooms, her arms laden with fresh linen.

'Phryne, have you seen Prince Mynes?' I asked. 'I am afraid he may have been injured on the hunt. I expected him at least an hour ago.'

She looked at me, her eyes wide. 'Have you not been told the news, my lady?' she said.

'What – what do you mean?' I asked quickly, my voice faltering. 'What news?'

'An urgent message arrived from Troy about an hour ago,' she said. 'Prince Mynes was summoned directly to a council meeting as soon as he got back. The king and his councillors are still in the Great Hall.'

I frowned. 'Do you have any idea what the message was about?'

'No, Princess.'

I let go of her arm and sank down on to the rugs on the floor. The rose petals on the water were still giving off a last memory of their pale, sweet scent. I rested my arm on the side of the tub, my fingers playing with the flowers, half submerged. The water was cold.

Χρυσηίς
Krisayis, Troy

The Hour of the Stars
The Ninth Day of the Month of Threshing Wheat, 1250 BC

'Do you love me?'

'More than anything else in the world.'

I rewarded him with a kiss.

'And shall we spend the rest of our lives together here in Troy, do you think?'

We were in the sleepy aftermath of love-making in Troilus' juniper-wood bed, cushioned on layers and layers of the finest woollen blankets and embroidered pillows in his private chambers in one of the large palace towers, as the dark veil of night fell around the city.

Troilus rolled languidly on to his back. 'And watch you grow old and ugly?' he teased me, poking at the softness of my belly with his finger. 'I'm not sure. I think I'd rather always have a beautiful woman by my side.'

I fought off the offending finger. 'Who says I'll be ugly?' I demanded, sitting up in bed. 'I – I might be— I will be the most beautiful matron you've ever seen, and then you'll be sorry,' I finished.

Troilus drew me back into his arms and caressed me. I smiled into his chest. 'That's better,' I said, as his fingers worked their way down my back. 'But it still doesn't make up for it.'

He laughed, then stopped, alert, his eyes darting over to the tower window overlooking the shore and the darkening plain. 'What was that?'

'What?' I asked, sitting up quickly. 'Is someone coming? Do they know I'm here?'

He shook his head. 'You didn't hear it?'

'No.'

He got up, threw a light tunic over his head and went to the window.

'What is it, Troilus?'

But Troilus did not answer.

I drew the woollen covers closer around my shoulders, slipped from the bed and moved over to stand beside him. I could just make out the ships of the Greeks beached in the Trojan bay to the west, silhouetted in the light of a thousand campfires, their prows sticking up into the night sky, like dark trees.

A river of dots of light – torches, probably, though they looked like fireflies from such a distance – seemed to stream away from the ships over the plain towards the forest in the south. They stretched as far as the eye could see; just audible, I could hear the dull, rhythmic tramping of thousands of soldiers' feet. 'What does it mean?' I breathed to Troilus.

He turned to me, frowning, and gathered me in his arms again in a protective gesture. 'It means,' he said slowly, 'that the Greeks are hungry.'

I did not understand. 'They're going hunting – at night?'

'Not hunting, no,' Troilus said. 'They are going to sack one of the cities of the Troad – Thebe, Arisbe, Percote . . . Who knows? Steal their gold, their women and their food.'

I felt a shiver of fear shoot up my spine. 'But they are not marching on Troy, are they?'

He gave me a grave look. 'Not yet, at least.'

'Have the cities been warned?'

He nodded. 'Oh, yes. The closer ones have been sent supporting armies, and my father sent messengers to those further from us to tell them to prepare for an attack, if it comes. But it is unlikely that the Greeks will go that far in a single night.'

He walked thoughtfully away from the window and climbed back under the covers. I nestled into his arms again, grateful for the closeness of him and the strong shield of him around me, and, though the rugs were warm, I shivered. I could not help thinking that somewhere, in a city out on the Trojan plain, there might be another pair of young lovers, just like us, innocently preparing for a night's sleep, not knowing. Not knowing that this was about to be their very last night of all.

Over the Plain

Mount Ida, Overlooking the Trojan Plain

Most of the gods are sleeping soundly in their palaces on Mount Ida, which looms large over the Trojan plain and is one of the summer haunts of the Olympian gods. They are snoring in beds plated with gold and cushioned with downy cloud; but there are two who cannot sleep. Hermes and Apollo are sitting at the edge of a gap in the wispy, moonlit clouds, looking north to the bright windows of the palace of Troy, the high walls ringed with torches and the flickering lights of the houses in the lower city.

'It simply isn't fair,' Apollo is saying, in a hurt voice. 'I offered her immortality – what more did she want?'

'Well, you didn't exactly choose the best time to ask her, did you?' Hermes points out reasonably. 'I mean, what were you planning to do? Whisk her away from the walls and hope that no one noticed?'

Apollo broods over the city on the plain below, and does not answer.

'Oh, come on, Apollo. Cheer up. Cassandra is only one Trojan woman. There are plenty more where she came from. Or then again,' Hermes gestures to a line of torches, trickling away from the Greek camp by the sea, heading towards Mount Ida, 'perhaps not. It seems the Greeks are missing female company quite as much as we are.'

Apollo does not remove his chin from his fist. 'What do you mean?'

'Well, they're on their way to sack a city, aren't they? Pity. So many pretty girls we could have chosen from, but . . .' he sighs '. . . we can't go down there tonight. Even I have some morals.' He pauses. 'All right, I don't,' he says, in

response to Apollo's raised eyebrows, 'but seducing mortals while their city's being destroyed – it's too easy. They'll be so desperate they'll practically be throwing themselves on us.'

Apollo mutters something under his breath, and Hermes chuckles.

'Oh, don't be so dramatic. There are plenty more fish in the Aegean. And speaking of which,' Hermes stands up, turning away from the city towards the southern slopes of Mount Ida and stretching lazily, 'I thought we might pay a visit to Sicily. Cheer you up a bit. Visit some of those wood-nymphs Ares was talking about the other night.'

Apollo perks up at once. 'I've always liked Sicily. The girls are much less highly strung there than they are around here.' He chances a glance back at Troy.

'Well, let's go, then,' Hermes says, clapping his hands.

Without further ado, the two gods leap together from the edge of the clouds, speeding gracefully over the shadowy foothills of Mount Ida and towards the coast, like two shooting stars.

Apollo pauses, hovering in the air as they turn west to follow the coast, gazing down at a small city nestled in a bay by the sea, at the bottom of the mountain's slopes. The line of soldiers from the Greek camp is pouring towards it and, even as they watch, the gates set in the outer walls go up in a blaze of orange flames. 'Which city is that?'

Hermes shrugs his shoulders. 'No idea,' he says.

And they fly off into the star-spangled veil of the night.

The City Falls

Βρισηίς
Briseis, Lyrnessus

The Hours of Night

The Ninth Day of the Month of Threshing Wheat, 1250 BC

I sat up in bed. It was the middle of the night, and the room was as dark as the bowels of Hades. Mynes was not there. He had not come to my bed the evening before – I must have fallen asleep waiting for him.

'Mynes?' I whispered into the silence.

I slipped out of bed and wrapped a blanket around my shoulders. The sky behind the window shutters was tinged with orange. Perhaps it was nearly dawn, and Mynes had not come to bed at all. I walked over and drew back the bars to let in the cool night breeze.

A roar of flames tore through the air. A woman's shrill scream, children crying, earth-shattering creaks and groans as buildings were swallowed by fire and fell to the ground. The lower city was spread out beneath the palace walls in a blazing carpet. I backed away in horror.

Lyrnessus was going up in flames.

I slammed the shutters and ran from the window, terror rising in my throat. I had to find Mynes.

There was a spiralling staircase from our bedroom, leading up to one of the tallest towers of the palace that rose above the fortifications of the upper city and overlooked the town below. I raced up it, my thin night-robes trailing in the wind behind me, desperate to catch a glimpse of Mynes somewhere in the frightened crowds in the streets below.

The lower city was laid out in a confusion of fire and frightened people. Soldiers in bronze breastplates, with shining helmets and greaves, were running through the streets and throwing torches at every house they came across. Men and women were screaming. The sea in the harbour, down by the south gate, was reflecting the flames of the lower city as if it, too, were on fire, like a slithering mass of black lava. The smell of burning wood and the bitter scent of smoke drifted up to the palace and caught at the back of my throat. Trumpets were shrieking on the air, men rallying and crying for battle.

Then, amid the crowds of terrified people, I spotted a group of Lyrnessan nobles by the front gates in the forecourt before the palace, arming themselves from a pile of weapons, preparing to leave the fortifications of the strongly walled upper city for the burning town. Perhaps they would know where Mynes was.

I rushed back down the stairs from the tower and a figure loomed out of the darkness, his arms full of wooden effigies of the gods, his white hair astray, eyes wide. It was the priest from our wedding. 'Run, Princess!' he called to me, his voice shaking, his face full of fear. 'Run, or die!'

He started to hobble away, clutching the statues of the gods to his chest.

'Wait – Panthus, wait!' I shouted after him. 'Have you seen Prince Mynes?'

But my question echoed down the empty stairwell, and he was gone.

I was weeping now. I ran down the stairs, along the dark colonnade, then burst through the great doors of the palace to the large forecourt, looking wildly around me. The Lyrnessan soldiers I had seen from the top of the tower were still there. I clutched at one, sinking to my knees with my hair tangled over my face, wet with sweat and tears.

The soldier turned away from me, instinctively on his guard, and another drew his sword. Then I heard the sound of brisk footsteps, and a hand turned my face up by the chin.

'Briseis?'

It was Mynes.

'What in the name of all the gods are you doing here?' he asked fiercely.

I could hardly speak through my tears and the fear, thick in my throat. 'Mynes!' I gasped. 'Mynes, what is happening?'

He crouched low so that he could look directly into my face, and took my shoulders in his hands. 'We had news earlier today that the Greeks might attack,' he said. 'But we did not expect it so soon, and the city has been taken unprepared. I have to help. I cannot let Lyrnessus fall. I must protect my people.'

His mouth was set in a firm line, and my blood ran cold at the glint of war reflected in his eyes. For the first time I realized that, whatever he was to me, my husband was a leader of his city and a fighter: a man born to wield a spear before he was anything else.

'But what about me?' I sobbed, and a wave of grief crashed over me with a strength that shocked the breath out of my lungs. 'What will happen to me if you die? You cannot go. You are all I have! You are everything to me, Mynes. I cannot lose you!'

'I cannot leave my people,' he repeated, but this time his voice cracked with pain. 'What would they say if I ran away from battle, like a coward? It is impossible. I have to go. But, Briseis,' as I started up, about to interrupt him, 'I shall not leave you unprotected.' He clasped my hand in his, and his face was filled with anguish. 'You know you mean more to me than any of the people of Lyrnessus,' he whispered. 'More than my parents, even. I shall come back for you, I promise.'

I swallowed. 'And if you do not?' I said, my voice barely more than a whisper. 'If you cannot?'

He gave me a long look. 'Come here,' he said. He took my hand and led me away from the group of soldiers, some of whom glanced up curiously from arming themselves, strapping their greaves to their shins and tying their breastplates over their tunics.

Mynes stopped when he reached the line of juniper trees beside the gate, sending their heady scent on to the air, out of earshot of his men. 'Briseis, you must know the truth. The Greeks have taken the lower city. Most of our soldiers are dead, and I do not have enough left to fight the enemy.'

His face was bleak, his forehead creased with pain. I stared up at him. 'You think we will be defeated?' I whispered.

Very slowly, he nodded.

'Then we must flee!' I said urgently. 'Come back with me to Pedasus! My father has a great army – he will take care of you and provide you with reinforcements so you can return—'

He shook his head. 'No, Briseis,' he said firmly. 'I have already said I will not run. My men need me here – now, more than ever.' He lowered his voice and pressed my hand. 'I swore when we married that I would protect you with everything I have. But if my luck is against me and I am killed—'

'Don't say it!'

He gripped my hand more firmly. 'No, Briseis, listen to me – *if* I am killed, you must not grieve for me. You must learn to live your life without me. I will have Lygdon take you to Pedasus where you can live in safety with your family and—'

I gasped, my eyes filling again with tears. 'I will not leave you!'

'I cannot allow you to defy me on this,' he said, his voice uncharacteristically sharp. 'I will not be able to fight if you are in danger, Briseis. Do you understand?'

A scream rang out from somewhere nearby, piercing the still night air, and I shuddered. At last I nodded. I knew well enough from listening to my father and his soldiers at the feasts, when wine had loosened their tongues, how fatal it could be in battle if a warrior did not leave his cares behind him.

'And I will not,' he swallowed and lowered his voice once more, 'I *cannot* bear the idea of your grief.'

The light of the flames upon the sky was growing ever stronger, as he leant towards me and kissed me, dyeing the heavens blood red. 'We shall be reunited in the Underworld, whenever the gods take us from this earth. Whichever of us leaves the land of the living before the other – we will wait. We will wait for each other, Briseis, as we waited for each other in this life, and we will welcome each other on the banks of the Styx, to be together always.' His voice broke, and he swallowed again. 'But until then – if anything should happen – will you swear to stay in Pedasus and learn to forget me, Briseis? To protect yourself?'

I shook my head again, the tears streaming down my cheeks. 'You cannot ask this of me.'

'I must,' he said, his voice urgent, full of pain. 'Briseis, please – *promise me.*'

I looked up at him. He was gazing at me, his eyes eloquent with hope and anguish. I felt my heart break at the sight. 'Yes,' I said at last, as tears rimmed my lashes again. 'Yes, very well. I promise.'

I felt the muscles of his hand relax in mine. Then he stood up, pulling me with him to the crowd of men who stood, ready armed and gleaming with spears and swords, in the forecourt.

'Lygdon!' he called to one of the soldiers, a burly man who carried a double-headed axe forged from bronze and was Mynes' personal guard.

'Yes, Prince?'

'Take the Princess Briseis,' he said, leading me to the soldier and placing his hand on my shoulder. 'Take her through the hidden gate from the back of the palace and lead her straight to Pedasus without delay. Do you understand?'

He saluted. 'Yes, Prince.'

Mynes turned towards me. 'Will you be all right?' he asked gently.

I wiped the tears from my eyes with the sleeve of my robe. 'Of course I shall,' I said, with as much conviction as I could muster. Then, with a brave attempt at courage: 'I have faced worse.'

He laughed and kissed me fully, his hands on either side of my face. 'Now there's the girl I married,' he said. Then he turned away, his mind already on war.

'Men – are you ready?' he shouted, and the soldiers shook their spears and shields in reply, roaring and grunting.

'Are you ready to give your lives for your city?'

They shouted even louder.

'Then let us go and fight for our gods and for our kingdom!' he thundered, then bent to pick up his oval shield and bronze-tipped spear from the ground.

'Wait – Mynes!' I said, darting forwards and laying my hand on his arm as he began to hoist the shield on to his back.

'Not afraid, Briseis?' he asked, smiling.

'No,' I said. 'I just – I love you.'

'And you know I love you too. But I must go.'

He kissed my forehead, then straightened to put on his bronze helmet, topped with a waving horsehair crest of red and gold. He lifted it, fitted it easily over his head and fastened the cheek-flaps in place. Then, with a brief smile to me and a call to his men, my husband disappeared through the large wooden gates of the upper city into the burning town.

I wished I could stand and gaze after him for as long as the impression of his blazing armour lasted on my eyes. But I felt a hand heavy on my shoulder, and heard Lygdon's gruff voice say, 'We'd better get you to Pedasus, then, Princess.'

There was a moment of silence as he waited for me to walk towards the palace. Then—

'Lygdon,' I said slowly, 'do you think the gates of the upper city will be strong enough to hold the enemy back?'

Lygdon paused. 'Of course,' he said at last. 'Lyrnessus has never been captured before. It's the Greeks' good fortune they came upon us by surprise.' He smiled grimly at me. 'But their fortune will not last long enough to lead them into the upper city, of that I am certain.'

The gods knew I did not want to break my promise to Mynes, but I could not bear to run from him, like a child to her mother's skirts. I kneaded my knuckles against my forehead in frustration. 'The prince told me he believes we will be defeated . . .'

Lygdon shook his head. 'We shall win, Princess, you can be sure of that.' His voice was steady, confident. 'Most likely the prince only said so to persuade you to flee.'

I thought this over. 'And do you wish to leave the battle?'

He shook his head again. 'I would rather stay and protect my home,' he said honestly. 'I have a wife of my own, Princess, and three young children, one newly born. I'd rather not leave them.'

'Then we shall stay,' I said, making the decision in a moment. 'You will take me to the Great Hall, where I shall wait for the prince to return. I shall show the Lyrnessans that their princess does not flee in terror at the first sign of danger.'

There was a pause, then Lygdon bowed his head, his face impassive. 'As you wish, Princess.'

Together, we hastened towards the doors to the palace. They were open and Lygdon heaved them shut behind us, with a great creaking of hinges, then led me quickly down a long corridor, through the open courtyard, the sky above it tinged with a blazing red glow, and into the empty Great Hall. It was dark in there, and only a few rays of moonlight drifting through the high slit windows illuminated the four red columns around the hearth, the washed-out paintings on the walls and a stone altar to Apulunas, bearing a small ivory statue of the Great God and some food offerings.

Lygdon placed me beside the altar, trusting to the sanctuary of the gods. Then he walked heavily to the double bronze doors, and stood, feet planted, in front of them, holding his massive two-headed axe before him. 'It shouldn't be long before the prince returns,' he said.

The palace around us was eerily quiet. The sound of my breathing was heavy in my ears, and the scent of incense and smoke hung around the altar from the last offering to the gods. Time moved slowly. I watched a moonbeam approach me slowly across the painted tiles of the floor.

Suddenly a loud, echoing crash resounded through the halls of the palace.

'What was that?'

I started up. Lygdon was staring at the closed doors of the Great Hall.

The sound came again – a shuddering, bellowing crash, like an earthquake.

'Lygdon – what is happening?' I demanded again, clutching at the edges of the altar.

He turned back to me, gripping the handle of his axe. 'It sounds – it sounds as if—' He shook his head.

'Yes?'

'It sounds as if the Greeks are ramming the gates of the upper city.'

My mouth went dry. 'What shall we do?' I whispered.

Before Lygdon could answer, a splintering blast of breaking wood split the air, then a creaking, shuddering, heaving sound as the gates were forced open, followed by cheers and roars and the pounding of feet against earth.

'They're in,' Lygdon said, stunned. 'The Greeks are through.' He turned to me. 'Come with me, Princess, quickly – we have to get you to the back gate.'

I could hear Lyrnessan soldiers in the corridors beyond the Great Hall regrouping, interspersed with sounds of clashing metal that sent a chill of terror through my entire body. I prayed with all my heart that one of them was Mynes, that he was still alive . . .

I slipped from the altar, numbly, my legs barely moving beneath me.

Lygdon placed his hand upon the bolt of the door and held out his other arm towards me. 'Come, Princess, quickly!'

I could hear fighting, the clash of swords and spears ringing through the echoing halls of the palace, nearer and nearer. I half ran, half stumbled towards Lygdon . . .

And then I froze.

The whole palace was suddenly deathly silent.

And the silence was more terrifying still because it meant there was no one left to fight. None, except Lygdon.

Then came the sound.

Boo-oom.

The hall reverberated with physical shock. Something had struck the double bronze doors with enough force to make a visible dent in the moulded metalwork.

Lygdon leapt away and raised his axe, tightening his grip. I fell back towards the altar, my fingers white as I clung to the riveted edge.

Then it came again.

Boo-oom.

The dent was larger, hollow, caving in.

Boom. Boom. Boom.

And then—

A fist punched through the door with impossible strength, and the metal gave a shattering, booming sound like the crashing of a wave on to the shore as it split. Two hands thrust through and pulled away the bronze, ribboning it into curving folds of shining metal as easily as if it were soft clay. And in the hole there stood a man.

And yet it was not a man. His eyes glittered in the dark, the skin of his arms and chest tight over smooth muscles, like a shining young snake. His strangeness was painfully gorgeous, his slim height framed by the gap in the door.

There was a second of silence in which Lygdon took in the full impact of the man before him. Then he let out a whisper, like the slice of a blade on the air: 'Achilles.'

The man reared towards the ceiling as Lygdon charged – and it was so fast I did not even see it, beyond a flash of steel and the spurt of blood from Lygdon's neck. Achilles was past him before he had even hit the floor.

My skin was wet with the cold sweat of fear, my fingers slipping against the stone of the altar, every instinct screaming at me to run, yet I knew I had nowhere to go. The beam of moonlight filtered down from the circular opening in the roof above the hearth directly on to the altar top, and caught my thin white robe in its glow.

Achilles saw me. I felt his dark eyes lock on to mine and I knew that the end had come, and I prayed for death. Death over slavery. Anything over becoming a Greek slave.

'Apulunas, god of the Trojans, our protector,' I whispered, through the dry spittle on my lips, and I made the sign of the goddess of luck again with my fingers, my hands trembling violently, 'help me now. Help me. *Help me*.'

There was a sudden sound of battle cries and clashing bronze, and then, the next moment, a loud crash.

I looked at the entrance to the room. The bronze doors were being pushed from the other side, bulging with the weight of the warriors pressing against them, and then, at last, with a loud *crack*, their hinges snapped, pressed through by the men spilling into the room. The last of the Lyrnessans were pouring into the Great Hall, fighting ferociously even as they were being driven back by the overwhelming forces of the Greeks.

Slowly, Achilles moved towards me. My heart was racing in my throat. I could not move.

There was nowhere else to go.

'Apulunas,' I whispered again, my voice hoarse and strangled, '*help me now*.'

Achilles was walking faster, his black eyes boring into mine. The sound of the battle was terrifying, metal scraping on metal, the hard tang of blood on the air and the strangled cries of the wounded. Lyrnessan soldiers were attacking him from every side, but Achilles swatted them away, like flies, with a single sharp thrust of his sword, not moving his gaze.

I stared panic-stricken into the mass of fighting bodies. 'Help,' I muttered, my voice shrill with fear. '*Help.*'

A figure in the crowd flashed into view behind Achilles. He was forcing his way through the soldiers with almost demonic ferocity, hacking right and left with a sword and an oval-shaped shield.

Achilles was weighing his sword easily in his hand.

Behind him, closer and closer, I saw the other figure slashing and thrusting, diving through the mass of bodies, blood running down the nose of his helmet, the red and gold crest dyed crimson with gore.

Red and gold.

My heart leapt to my mouth.

It was Mynes.

He was only a few feet from Achilles now. His sword was raised high above his head, his eyes blazing with fury as he bellowed my name. A little closer, and he would bring his sword down and smash it through Achilles' skull.

Achilles did not even turn to look. In one moment he spun on his heel faster than a breath of wind and thrust his sword into Mynes' chest.

I saw Mynes ripple with the shock as it impacted on his breastplate, watched it pierce through his ribs and into his heart.

'*Mynes!*'

It cannot be true. Let it not be true.

'Mynes – *no*—' I jumped from the altar, my hair sticking to my face as I fought my way towards him, oblivious of the battle that raged ahead, the flash of swords and spears, the cries of the wounded. All I could see was my husband, the sword of Achilles sticking through his heart, and a pool of bright scarlet blood spreading on the floor around his feet.

He collapsed to his knees.

'*Mynes!*' I screamed again, and I pushed more frantically through the packed crowd of battling warriors, oblivious to the battle-axes swishing over my head and the clanking of metal hammering at my ears as sword struck sword. 'Mynes – don't die—'

Suddenly I felt a hand grip my arm, so strong that it almost wrenched my shoulder from the socket and punched all the air from my lungs.

'Let me *go*!' I screamed, thrashing wildly, struggling and kicking and biting like a wild animal, desperate to be free.

In front of me Mynes' face was deathly pale. Achilles tightened his grip around my arm so I could hardly move.

'*Mynes!*' I screamed, but my voice was lost in the din of the battle.

Mynes' eyes fluttered slightly.

'*Mynes!*'

But it was too late. He gave one last gasp, one last shudder, and then he fell forwards on to the floor.

He was dead.

'*No!*' I shrieked, my whole body racked with sobs, fighting to get free with every last ounce of strength I possessed. 'No – my husband—'

But Achilles had had enough.

I felt his hand gripping my neck, his fingers pressing agonizingly into my flesh, and I wondered for one moment if he was going to strangle the life out of me. But then I felt his muscles tense, felt myself flung back through the air towards the altar with more than mortal force. My skull slammed into the stone edge of the block, the pain seared through my head and into my eyes, then dissolved into nothing.

My world went black.

Into Captivity

Χρυσηίς
Krisayis, Troy

The Hour of the Stars

The Tenth Day of the Month of Threshing Wheat, 1250 BC

Cassandra and I were seated in her chamber on the seat beneath the window, looking out over the moonlit Trojan bay and the shore, where the watch-fires of the Greeks were glimmering before their ships' prows. We had talked ourselves to silence, wondering what the Greeks were planning, how long it would be before they attacked Troy and which other cities they were going to fall upon while they prepared. Now it was almost the hour for the evening feast. Cassandra was to stay in her rooms – she had the food sent up to her from the kitchens, these days. Since she had fainted on the walls she had preferred not to suffer the taunts and gossip of the court – but she had insisted, despite my protests, that I should not stay with her, that I was to go and enjoy myself.

Cassandra stood and took my hand. 'Come,' she said, turning away from the window. 'I cannot think any more about the Greeks. I will have Lysianassa dress your hair for you.' She led me over to her table and set me on the small carved stool, then beckoned to her slave.

Lysianassa moved over from the door and knelt at her mistress's feet.

'I want you to dress Krisayis' hair.' She glanced at me. 'And her eyes. And use my new Egyptian perfume – the one the pharaoh's ambassador brought.'

The cosmetics were laid out on the table in dozens of little alabaster pots, each so much more costly than anything I had ever owned. 'I cannot,' I said, twisting round to look up at my friend. 'They are lovely,' I picked up a small pot filled with powdered green malachite and gazed at the bright colour, 'but . . .'

Cassandra leant down to whisper in my ear. 'If you look your most beautiful at the feast, then perhaps Troilus will ask for your hand this very night.'

I stared up at her in surprise, my heart leaping in my chest. 'I never told you I was thinking of marriage!'

Cassandra grinned at me. 'Oh, Krisayis, it is written all over your face. Anyone who knows you would be able to see it.' She took my hand and squeezed it. 'And Troilus could not wish for a lovelier wife.'

'Do you really think so?' I breathed, as if I was afraid someone might hear us, though in truth there was only Lysianassa in Cassandra's chambers. 'Do you truly think he might consider marriage? Even – even though I am only the daughter of a priest? And with a war outside our gates?'

Cassandra gleamed a smile at me, her blue eyes dancing. 'I am sure it will make him even more certain of it.'

I took a deep breath. 'Very well,' I said, turning towards the mirror and meeting her gaze in the reflection. 'Then we had better begin, had we not?'

Lysianassa stepped forwards, her hands quick and deft with Cassandra's ivory comb.

I held the beautiful bronze hand-mirror to watch her as she pinned up my hair with white rock-crystal pins, then wound a golden ribbon around it and tied it at the nape of my neck. She set large spiral golden earrings inlaid with lapis lazuli from Cassandra's own jewellery box in my ears and draped a delicate gold necklace around my throat, then bent over me to outline my eyes with black kohl and paint my eyelids with blue azurite.

'Wait,' Cassandra said, running over to her chest and opening it. She drew out a flounced skirt and bodice, both spun from rich gold thread and embroidered all over with tiny golden birds and flowers.

'I cannot wear that!' I gasped. 'There are Greeks outside the walls,

Cassandra! I should be helping your brothers prepare for the war or – or pounding barley for the grain-stores, not dressing like a peacock. Besides, it is far too costly. I cannot wear your clothes as well as your cosmetics and perfume! They will think I am trying to look like a princess!'

She handed the gown to Lysianassa and bent down to the mirror so that our faces were both reflected in it, cheek to cheek. 'If all goes well tonight, you will be a princess, and my sister, no matter what happens outside the walls,' she said, with a smile.

By the time I approached the doors of the Great Hall it was well into the night, and the sounds of merriment and feasting could be heard from across the courtyard. I paused. I had never worn anything so beautiful in all my life, and Cassandra had further heightened my nervousness by refusing to allow me to see myself in her hand-mirror, saying merely, 'You will see soon enough.'

I reached down and smoothed the material, feeling the richness of the thread beneath my fingers and the tiny forms of the birds and flowers embroidered on it. My hair in its elaborate style was heavy on my head, and the scent of the perfume at my neck spicy in the evening air. I took a deep breath and stepped forwards, fear and anticipation bubbling up inside me, like a clear mountain spring.

The guards swung the brightly painted blue and red doors open and I entered the Great Hall. It was filled with low tables and cushions, benches and stools, each occupied by a noble dressed in a tasselled tunic or a white-robed priest. Slaves hurried past me, bearing gold-embossed platters loaded with roasted meat garnished with herbs, jugs full of iced pomegranate water and red wine, grapes, apricots and sweet, plump figs. The fire in the open circular hearth at the centre of the room was burning brightly, and above it a spit bearing a large boar was being turned by two young slaves.

I saw the king and queen seated on their carved stone thrones to the side of the hearth, and moved over to pay my respects. 'My king,' I said when I reached them, bowing and touching my head to the ground. 'My queen.'

I looked up to see Troilus sitting at the king's side with his brothers

Paris, Deiphobus, Aeneas and Hector, and beside him Hector's wife, Andromache, and their son Astyanax. Troilus was gazing down at me, at my tightly laced bodice, following the curves of my body and the forward tilt of my breasts, his eyes fixed upon me like those of a sailor staring at the stars.

'Daughter of Polydamas,' King Priam said, acknowledging me. 'You are welcome.' There was a pause as the king surveyed me, his eyes narrowing a little as he took in my gorgeous robes. 'Your father told me he has selected you for the position of priestess of the Great God Apulunas, and that you will be initiated in a few days,' he said.

I felt myself stiffen.

'You are a fortunate daughter, to have a father who cares for you so well,' the king continued drily, a small smile turning up the corners of his mouth. 'Few women are given the chance to become a priestess of Apulunas.'

I bowed my head, biting my lip to prevent myself saying the wrong thing. 'My father does his best to provide for me,' I said carefully, trying not to allow my dread at the king's words to show in my face, images of white-robed priestesses gliding in dark temples flooding my thoughts, large lonely halls and cold chambers where there was no Cassandra to laugh with before we slept, no Troilus to love, no life at all . . .

'The king and I will be delighted to have such a pretty priestess serving the Great God,' Queen Hecuba said.

I bowed again, then stood and backed away from them, unable to say anything by way of reply. I sat on a stool between a noble lord's daughter and the High Priestess of Atana, and accepted a platter of crisp bread, shiny dark olives, fresh-pressed cheese and roasted boar from a slave, but all the joy had gone from the evening. I could no longer bear to sit there and watch Troilus with the royals on their thrones, knowing that they thought so little of me – not when I had just been so forcefully reminded of the ordeal that lay ahead.

I glanced around. I had not eaten anything but, then again, I thought, remembering King Priam's words, I was only the daughter of a priest. I would not be missed. Plucking an olive from the platter in front of me, I slipped past the great central hearth to the far corner of the hall and through a side door that led out to the terrace and the palace's grape arbour.

I walked through the archway into the garden and around the little path between the thick withes of the vines, heavy with their ripe fruit overhead, my heart full with disappointment. The arbour was empty, the sounds of the feast – the clattering of goblets and the loud chatter of the nobles – just audible through the windows from the Great Hall. The scent of grapes, sweet like violets, drifted on the breeze. A nightingale was singing at the top of one of the vines, its little throat stretched up as it heralded the night. I walked over to the limestone fountain in the centre and sank down on to the stone bench beside it, watching the crystal drops of water leap and splash against a small bronze statue of Arinniti without truly noticing them.

'Krisayis.'

I gasped. 'Troilus?'

I turned to find him almost upon me. He looked around quickly to check there was no one who might see us, then swept me into his arms and kissed me deeply, longingly, full on the lips. At last he pulled back to gaze at me. 'You are so beautiful. The most beautiful woman in the world.'

'I thought you would not want to speak with me, after what your father said.' I lowered my voice. 'You know we cannot do this for much longer. We have only twenty-five days until my sixteenth year—'

Troilus silenced me with another kiss. 'Krisayis,' he said. 'I have to have you. I simply have to.'

I shook my head. 'Later, perhaps. You cannot be seen to be missing from the feast too long, and if someone comes into the arbour . . .'

'I did not mean that.'

I looked up at him, very slowly. 'What did you mean?' I asked softly.

He pulled me again towards him, his arms around me, his mouth deeply upon mine and his fine black beard grazing my chin. Then he broke apart from me and leant forwards to whisper in my ear. 'Meet me here tomorrow at the Hour of the Rising Sun. There is something I would ask you.'

Βρισηίς
Briseis, Greek Camp

The Hours of Night

The Tenth Day of the Month of Threshing Wheat, 1250 BC

We were walking, but I did not know where. My wrists were chafing under the knotted rope that bound my hands together. My feet dragged on the ground, my hair covered my face as my head lolled forwards with exhaustion and throbbed in pain. I could smell the ashes of Lyrnessus on the wind; I could taste them on the tip of my tongue. The smut and smoke of the ruined city poured black rivers of tears from my eyes. My city, my home, my love were dust and air and carrion for the birds: a pile of blackened ashes heaped on the plain, like an accursed sacrifice to the gods. My husband, the only person who had ever believed in me, the single shining light in the darkness that had been the prophecy, was gone. And now the blackness threatened to envelop me entirely.

I panted with effort, pulling my feet through the sand. Each breath I took was a curse. A curse, for as long as I lived, on the gods who sat upon Mount Ida and looked down on us while Achilles had destroyed everything I had ever loved. And I promised myself that every breath I took for the rest of my life would be a reminder of what the gods had done to me. What their son had done to me.

The night was clearing now, but I saw only one thing.

Mynes. Mynes, on his back, looking up at the canopy over our bed and his arms around my waist, smiling at me. Mynes, with his sword raised above his head, his lips still framing my name.

And I saw another person. A man with skin like a snake's and glinting black eyes that never left my face. A man who would kill to get what he wanted and who killed like a god. The man who sent a blade through my husband's heart, not even blinking as he did it. The man who had killed the man I loved.

Without warning, silent and deadly, a whip came flying through the air and made contact. My body buckled and I cried out with the pain. I moved unsteadily forwards, pushed and kicked by the slave-driver, my wrists pulled forwards by the rope. The line of prisoners continued across the plain and away from the burnt corpse of the city.

My breath escaped my lips, ragged and uneven, like a curse. And it had the sound of a name: *Achilles.*

It took us two nights to reach the enemy camp. Dawn was breaking over the horizon when we finally arrived. I was exhausted. Anger and grief seemed to have drained me of all energy. Now I did not even care, and it felt good to be numb. All I had to do was to keep walking, one foot in front of the other, and that I could do without thought. Much easier to have someone else tell you what to do. Much easier to ignore your shattered world and your rage and your pain if you could just keep walking.

At that moment, the woman in front of me, bent double and grey-haired, slowed and came to a halt.

The ropes around my wrists slackened. *No, don't stop*, I thought dully. *Just keep walking. Don't think, don't stand still. One foot in front of the other.* I tried to keep moving, but there was no way around. For the first time since that night, I raised my eyes from the old woman's heels.

I strained to focus. We were standing on a beach. Huge ships were lined along the shore, their prows ploughed into the sand for at least three thousand paces, like black, sleeping beasts. On the shore before them was a motley array of driftwood huts topped with thatched roofs and tents, made from ships' sails draped over stakes in the sand and tied down with rope. At the camp's edge a circular palisade of sharp-tipped wooden spikes had been driven into the beach, encircled within by a wooden walkway, which guards were using to patrol the gates. Warriors were wandering about, sharpening spears, laughing and talking, hardly glancing at us as they passed. Slaves stirred pots over open fires that sent steaming spirals of smoke into the air. Mules brayed, dogs barked, bronze armour clanked as it was thrown on to heaps for mending. A citadel grew out of the mist on the horizon to the east, its high walls glowing pink in the morning light.

'You there,' the slave-driver shouted. He was short and runty, with scrawny tufts of ginger hair patching his head and a leering, mocking smile, which he was directing at me. 'To the hut of Achilles.'

I looked at him coldly. 'My name is Princess Briseis, soldier,' I said.

His smile broadened as he capered towards me, and I noticed several missing teeth. 'Princess, is it?' he asked, jeering. 'Did you hear that, men? Apparently it's *Princess* Briseis to us unworthies.'

Several of the Greeks who were nearby, watching, waiting for their pick of the haul, laughed. There were catcalls and jeers of 'Your Royal Highness' and other, dirtier, variations.

'Do you think the princess will need an escort to Achilles' hut, boys?' the slave-driver shouted, prodding me in the back with his whip.

I kept my face impassive, though my whole body was riddled with pain, and a rage I had never felt before bubbled in my veins. I stood straight and did not flinch when he took a sharp dagger to the rope around my wrists and, with a swift movement, sliced through it so that it fell off. My skin was raw and red underneath, cut into bracelets of blood. He grabbed me by the arm and thrust me forwards, into the middle of the circle of soldiers.

'Come, men, where are your manners?' he called. 'An escort for the princess!'

The soldiers jumped to their feet and ran forwards, making mock bows, dancing around me in pretended servility. One darted out from the crowd, took my hair and dragged me towards him. Another pulled on my wrist, his fingers cutting into the weals from the rope. My eyes smarted in pain.

'Make way for Her Royal Highness!' taunted the slave-driver. 'Make way for the princess of the camp!'

The other soldiers roared with laughter and resumed their bowing and jeering.

The slave-driver was grinning, toothless maw gaping wide.

Suddenly there was a flash past my cheek. A spear, long and slim, had whistled past my face and buried itself in the slave-driver's chest, breaking through the ribcage. He stumbled back, the inane smile still spread across his face, eyebrows raised in foolish surprise. His grin faltered. Then, slowly, deliberately, his knees loosening beneath him, he crumpled backwards, and fell on to the sand.

At once the men around me stopped jeering. They stood still, taking in the slender ash shaft of the spear still quivering in his body.

Then a commanding voice thundered through the crowd. '*Leave my prize.*'

I turned.

It was the man who had murdered my husband.

Χρυσηΐς
Krisayis, Troy

The Hours of Night

The Eleventh Day of the Month of Threshing Wheat, 1250 BC

Early the following morning, I slipped from my chambers in the dark with a hurried farewell to Cassandra, full of excitement but also – my ever-present companion in these troubled days – fear. Troilus had sent a message the evening before with a young page of the court, paid for his silence, to change our meeting place to the South Gates of Troy. I was puzzled at his request. The South Gates were at the other end of the city, a fair walk from the palace. *I suppose I shall find out soon enough why he wants to meet me there, of all places.*

The city was still asleep as I set off through the palace grounds and down into the lower city. The roads beyond the upper walls were lit by sputtering torches hung in brackets on the walls of the houses, and a few bread ovens, set in the courtyards of the bakers' shops, still glowed with the embers of the previous day. Above me, the vault of the sky was a rich black, tempered only by a thin line of palest yellow along the horizon that announced the coming of the sun. I shivered a little in the cold air and drew my cloak closer around my shoulders.

As I neared the towers of the South Gates I could just make out Troilus' outline, standing a few feet from them. Beside him, two finely bred horses were curvetting and tossing their manes in the shadows, their reins held by the guard of the gate.

'Krisayis,' Troilus said, when I walked up to him. He held out his hands. 'You came.'

I glanced apprehensively towards the guard, but Troilus shook his head. 'We can trust Axion with our secret.'

I saw a couple of silver coins glinting in the man's palm, and I understood. Troilus had bought his silence, too. I turned back to him. 'Why have you brought me here? And why have you brought *horses*?' I asked, in a whisper.

'You have to follow me,' he said, and moved towards a side-gate.

'Wait,' I said, catching his shoulder. 'Wait, Troilus – what are you doing? You cannot go outside the walls! Not when the Greek ships are moored a mere two thousand paces away!'

Troilus looked back at me. 'We must,' he replied in a whisper. 'We cannot be seen together, not in the city.'

I felt a sudden chill go through me, and took a small step back. 'You are ashamed to be seen with me?'

Troilus shook his head. 'Of course not,' he said, frowning. 'But there are people who may think differently. We cannot risk being seen – especially not now.'

Again, I lowered my voice to a whisper: 'But what about the Greeks? You cannot afford to put yourself in danger, Troilus! You are a *prince*! If they find you outside the walls—'

Troilus spoke across me, silencing me. 'We will be safe. Axion has been on the tower watching the Greek camp since the sun set and all is quiet. We need only a moment.'

I could not think of anything else to say. I allowed him to lead me towards the gates, and tried to ignore the fear that seemed to have taken root in me ever since the Greek ships had arrived on our shores. But if the guard had seen that the camp was quiet then surely all would be well . . . And yet I could not help but feel a strange dread as Axion nodded to Troilus, handed the reins of the horses to him and unbarred the side-gate, pushing it open.

We stepped outside the walls, the arch of the dark sky above us, the yellow on the horizon shifting slowly to pink. In the distance, to our right, the tips of the prows of the Greek ships were silhouetted black on the horizon, like stark trees stripped of their leaves in winter.

'This way,' Troilus said, and he strode across the plain towards the forest of Trojan oaks that grew within fifty paces of the walls to the south, the horses following him at a trot.

'Troilus – what—'

He hushed me. 'I will tell you in a moment.'

We slipped into the woods, and I looked around, thankful for the thickly woven branches and trunks of the green-grey trees. At least we would be hidden from view there, if any hostile Greeks were upon the plain.

Troilus tied the reins of the horses carefully to a nearby branch, then turned towards me.

'Krisayis,' Troilus said. His eyes met mine in the dark shadows of the forest.

I remembered then why he had brought me there, the insistent pressing of his body against mine in the grape arbour and his words: *I have to have you*. My fear dissolved into a delicious excitement. 'Yes, Troilus?' I lowered my eyes to the ground, but I knew he would be able to see the trembling at the corners of my lips.

'Krisayis, I cannot marry you.'

It took a moment for the words to reach me. I looked up at him, not understanding. A crease had appeared between his eyebrows. 'I cannot marry you,' he repeated, his fists clenched. 'My father has forbidden it.'

I opened my mouth, then closed it, then opened it again. My heart was pounding in my chest as excitement turned to dread. I felt as heavy and as dull as new-felled oak. I could not think of anything to say.

'I asked my father last night for his blessing on our union. He refused it. He told me that I am to be betrothed to Princess Tania of Dardania,' he said.

'A princess,' I repeated. 'Of course.'

'He ordered me, before the whole court, never to speak to you again, and he has given instructions to your father to send you to the temple this very day for your initiation.'

I gasped. 'My *initiation*?'

Troilus reached for my hand. 'I will not allow my father to part us,' he said, his voice low and full of emotion.

I stared at him. 'How?' I breathed. 'You would defy the king?'

'We will leave Troy!' He was speaking faster now, his eyes shining, his face alive with adventure. 'I have horses – if we ride fast we can flee the city and my father's anger.' He lowered his voice again to a whisper. 'We can marry, Krisayis, once we reach the lands of the Hittites in the east, far from my father's kingdom. It will be just you and I, always.'

'Far from Troy?'

He nodded. 'As far as we can go.'

'And we would never come back?'

'Never. Your life would be forfeit – mine too, perhaps. We would be outcasts.'

I looked down at the ground, the thick bed of the forest floor carpeted with leaves and pale pink wildflowers among the grass.

He took my other hand. 'Krisayis, will you do this for me? Will you leave Troy and be my wife?'

'This – this was not what I had expected,' I said slowly.

'I know. I did not think my father would refuse me anything. I—'

I shook my head. 'No. That was not what I meant. I mean – I did not expect to spend my life running from Troy and the people I love.'

His forehead creased again in the slightest of frowns. 'But you would have me. Is that not enough?'

I gazed at him. His clear hazel eyes were filled with hope. I remembered my dreams of sitting beside Troilus upon our thrones, dealing out justice to the Trojan people. When I had thought of us together, I had always thought of us in Troy – seated upon the tower, helping the Trojan poor, walking the streets to meet the people and laughing in the palace with Cassandra.

And it was at that moment that I realized, if I had to choose between Troy and the young prince standing before me, I would choose Troy.

No matter what it cost me.

'I am sorry, Troilus,' I said, my heart breaking. 'I truly am. But I cannot live my life as a fugitive. I – I am meant to be here. My father, no matter what he has done – Cassandra – my city – I – I cannot simply leave them.'

His frown deepened, and he let go of my hands. 'Not even for me?' He swallowed. 'Not even to escape the priesthood?'

'No.' My voice broke as I said it. 'I am so sorry. I can't even explain it.

I feel as if – as if I am needed here, somehow. As if this is where I am meant to be.'

Troilus turned away from me. 'This is your final choice?'

I nodded. 'I—'

But then I stopped.

Somewhere within the woods, a twig had snapped. The *crack* echoed sharp in the air.

Troilus tensed and turned back to me, his hand on the hilt of his sword.

'What was that?' I whispered.

Troilus looked sharply up at the city gates, but all was silent. Then the sound of voices floated towards us on the still air: male voices. He motioned to me to crouch and I knelt down, trying not to make a sound, my mouth dry, fingers brushing the dry leaves.

'That's what I keep telling Nestor,' someone was saying in a low voice. 'It's not going to be long until the Trojans start snooping around the forest and find that the path into the camp is unguarded. It isn't wise to leave the forest unprotected. I say we go back to the king and tell him to send a permanent guard.'

Another snorted. 'So you say. I agree with Odysseus and Diomedes. The trees grow too close to the walls, and if the Trojan bowmen torch the forest while we are beneath we're done for. Safest to guard the camp and trust that they don't dare venture out too far.'

The first voice sighed. 'Well . . . if you think so . . .'

The voices were coming nearer now. The sound of twigs and dried leaves crunching grew louder. The first daylight was filtering through the trees, turning the tips of the leaves a pale gold and casting shadows through the wood.

'*Greeks!*' I mouthed at Troilus. '*They're Greeks!*' I could feel my heart throbbing in my ears.

'Quick – on the horse!' Troilus hissed, and he ran over to untie the grey mare from the tree where she stood tethered beside his stallion.

She was tossing her head nervously, her nostrils flared as if she, too, could sense the danger. I tried to get close enough for Troilus to help me up, but she shied away, stamping on the ground fretfully.

'*Hold – still!*' Troilus muttered, grasping her reins and stroking her nose as she tossed her head, trying to calm her.

'What about the lookouts to the east, then?' a voice said, as clear as if he were standing beside us. 'If you're all for guarding the camp, then why has King Agamemnon posted most of the lookouts on the southern side?'

One of the others gave an easy laugh. 'It's the main gates that need guarding, Acamas. The palisade will hold up to an attack well enough.'

'Krisayis, quickly!' Troilus took me around the waist and lifted me on to the horse's back. I grasped at her mane to keep my balance as she shied, then tightened my thighs against her flanks.

'Now go!'

'Wait!' I breathed, twisting around, 'Troilus, you have to come too!'

Then five black-bearded men rounded a corner between the trees not even forty paces away.

Our eyes met.

'*Go!*' Troilus shouted, slapping the mare on the haunches and running to untie the reins of his own horse.

The mare's dark eyes widened in fright at the sound of Troilus' voice and the slap upon her rear and she bucked.

The Greeks were shouting to each other and running through the trees towards us.

I clung on desperately, my fingers gripping the horse's mane as she reared. Branches swiped across my vision and I ducked forwards, trying to grasp the reins, now swinging around her neck. But she was tossing her head, whinnying wildly with fear, and they swung far out of my reach, tangling and knotting around a branch, swinging round and round, looping and knotting more tightly. And still, the mare was rearing, her eyes wide, her front legs kicking out in front of me . . .

I heard Troilus shout from somewhere nearby.

I looked around in terror and, as I did so, a branch swung out of nowhere and hit me full across the back of the neck. I cried out, let go of the horse's mane, and then I was falling, falling . . .

I slammed to the ground, the oak leaves carpeting the earth cushioning the worst of my fall, my bones splitting with pain and my lip bleeding. I could hear Troilus drawing his sword and the sound of the mare's hoof beats as she tore herself free and bolted into the woods.

Ahead, a dark-bearded Greek was approaching me. Before I could do anything, before I could even move, he had hauled me upright, grasped me by the wrists and tied them behind my back. Then a rag was knotted around my eyes and another pushed into my mouth. I tried to scream, but I could not make a sound. I could not see. The sounds of a fight surrounded me, confused shouting, and the thud of sandalled feet running over earth. Then I felt rough arms around me, and I was picked up, belly-down, carried and thrown over a horse's back, like a rolled-up carpet. I kicked and struggled, and someone slapped my face, setting my skin stinging with pain.

'Shouldn't you kill her?' a voice said nearby. 'She might have heard us talking. It would be safer to be rid of her.'

Another man, beside me, laughed. He was tying a rope around my legs – I could feel the knots tugging against my skin as I tried in vain to struggle against them. 'She's a woman, Teucer. What can she do? Besides, she's nice to look at. Even the king might want her in his bed.' He snorted with laughter. 'She would certainly find a warm welcome in mine!'

The other Greek laughed. At that I tried again to shout, but my voice was gone, muffled, and I could neither see nor move.

There was a jolt as the horse was urged into a gallop; and then there was nothing but dust.

PART II

The War Begins

Mount Ida, Overlooking the Trojan Plain

'You'll never guess what I saw.'

Hermes is standing behind Artemis' throne in the spacious entrance hall to her palace, lounging idly against the throne's back, twirling a golden rod in his hands.

Artemis does not turn, but takes another sip of nectar from her goblet in a weary sort of way. 'What, Hermes? What this time?'

He twirls the rod a little more, just to make sure she is listening. It is sensational news, after all – there wouldn't be any point in giving it away all at once. 'You know Aphrodite?' he asks, maddeningly superior.

Artemis sighs with an air of martyred patience, then sets down her goblet and turns to look over the back of her throne. 'We've only been living together for eternity,' she says, rolling her eyes. 'So what? What about her?'

Hermes smiles with the air of one dropping a bucket of pitch on an unsuspecting enemy. 'I saw her yesterday,' he says, pretending not to notice that Artemis has turned around. 'In bed.'

Artemis gives an unmaidenly snort. 'That's where she is most of the time,' she says, reaching for her goblet. 'And I don't need to hear your fantasies on what she looks like naked, Hermes. Zeus knows, we've all been treated to the real thing often enough.'

Hermes ignores her. 'Not alone, she wasn't. And it wasn't her husband, Hephaestus, either.'

A distinctly prudish expression comes over Artemis' face. 'What's new about that?' She sniffs. 'She's always in bed with some mortal or other. Who was it this time? Anchises? Adonis?'

Hermes shakes his head. 'Not a mortal,' he says, lowering his voice. 'A god.'

Artemis' eyes widen as she takes in the full implications of what he has said. It almost never happens that a goddess will dare to cheat on her husband with another deity. Everyone can excuse a bit of fooling around with mortals from time to time – they are hardly competition, after all, and they'll die soon enough – but to take a god as your lover? Now that is another thing entirely.

Hermes watches with barely suppressed delight as Artemis wrestles with her curiosity. Then . . .

'So?' she asks. 'Who was she with?'

Hermes grins. The virgin goddess, more chaste than the colour white itself, gossiping about a sordid love-affair. That's not something you see every day on Mount Ida. He saunters around from the back of the throne and comes to stand in front of her, bending down to pet the hunting hound lying at her feet. He is enjoying this. 'You might know him,' he says, as if he cannot quite remember the name. 'Big bloke. Calves like tree trunks, and buttocks the size of—'

'Didn't you see who it was?'

'Might have.'

Artemis sighs again and hands him the goblet. 'Do you remember now?'

He takes a deep draught and wipes his mouth on his arm. 'Ah, that's better.' He looks at her, watching him. 'What's that? Oh, yes – Aphrodite's little boy-friend. Yes, I remember. I don't think Hephaestus will be too happy when he finds out she spent the whole day canoodling with Ares, do you?'

Artemis looks shocked. 'Ares? Are you sure?'

Hermes takes another swig. 'Positive,' he says, full of glee. 'If there's one god she could have chosen to make Hephaestus mad . . . Let's just put it this way. Ares has everything that Hephaestus doesn't – if you grasp my meaning. And you know how touchy he is about his looks.'

'I can't believe it,' says Artemis, and she seems truly surprised. 'Just when I thought she couldn't go any lower. You heard about Helen and the beauty contest, I suppose.'

Even Hermes has enough sense to tread with caution here. 'Artemis, any man with eyes in his head would've chosen you for the contest. Zeus probably just picked the first three goddesses he could find. You remember how drunk he was that day – we all were! That was some party,' he adds.

Artemis is just opening her mouth to reply that she doesn't much care whether she was chosen or not when the sound of two voices raised in argument echoes sharply across heaven. 'Who's that?' she asks.

'Probably Hephaestus and Aphrodite,' he replies, with a cheerful smile, producing a bunch of ambrosia from his pocket and biting into it with enthusiasm. 'He must have found out.'

'No, I don't think so.' Artemis strains her ears, and the hound at her feet pricks his, too. 'It doesn't sound like Aphrodite.' She gets up from her throne and walks lightly through the colonnades of her palace towards the sounds of the commotion, followed by her dog and, after him, Hermes, wearing an expression that has 'I told you so' written all over it.

The gods are gathered in the area of heaven over Mount Ida that has been reserved for the meeting of the council. The clouds here are the brightest gold, and there are several large thrones ranged in a circle, like rows in a theatre, all facing a gap in the clouds that opens up on to earth – and the city of Troy – below.

'How dare you interfere?' spits Athena. She is standing on the arena facing the thrones, just in front of the gap in the clouds. 'How dare you spoil his first fight?'

Poseidon, who is lounging on a cloud, laughs so loudly that his beard ripples like waves. 'Sorry if I messed things up for your perfect boy,' he sneers. 'But Cycnus is my son. Hate to break it to you, Athena, but I think the claims of blood come over your fancy for a bit of Greek muscle.'

Athena is almost apoplectic with rage. 'It's got nothing to do with that!' she shouts, and the snakes on her breastplate hiss and dance. 'He's one of the best warriors in the Greek army. I pledged my protection! I promised him glory, and you come in and interfere, and make us both look like fools!'

Artemis bends down to whisper in her brother Apollo's ear. 'What's going on?'

Apollo glances over his shoulder at Artemis and twists around in his seat. 'War's started,' he says, grinning.

Artemis doesn't react. These things happen all the time, and if you're immortal, it's hard to keep track of everything. She wonders how Athena can still get so worked up.

Apollo continues: 'A few of the Greeks went on an expedition earlier to attack Colonae, just a few miles south of Troy. Ajax went straight for Poseidon's son, Cycnus – you know, the king of the Colonians? – so, of course, Poseidon gave him protection. Made him impervious to weapons. Ajax can't kill him – he's in a pretty bad state right now.'

He points towards the coast, just south of the city, where Artemis can make out a small town, two bands of warriors swarming over each other like ants and, in the centre of it all, a dark-haired figure throwing a rain of spears at his opponent with single-minded ferocity.

'And Athena isn't happy.' Artemis nods, straightening. That makes sense. Athena has become so devoted to the Greeks after Paris' slight to her beauty that Hermes often jokes she should give up immortality and go down to live with them. And Ajax is one of her favourites.

'You don't override me, Poseidon!' she's saying now, in a threatening voice. 'This isn't how the war is going to go. Don't think you'll have everything your own way.'

'Oh, really? How's that?' replies Poseidon, leaning back into the cloud and propping himself up on one elbow to watch Ajax, still striking out at the invulnerable Cycnus with every weapon he can lay his hands on. 'You'd do well to remember, niece, that I'm a good deal older than you are. Just because you're Zeus' daughter doesn't mean you can be rude to your elders.'

Athena seems to be struck dumb with anger. She stands there, her grey-green eyes blazing.

No one notices as Aphrodite and Ares sneak in at the back and take their seats just behind Zeus.

Then she says, 'Yes. Yes, you're right. You are older than I am.'

Poseidon smiles and settles back into the cloud. It seems he has won.

Athena bends down slowly towards the ground, where her helmet and spear are lying abandoned at her feet. 'But you're not faster!' In one quick movement, she picks them up and places the helmet on her head. Before anyone can stop her – before Poseidon even has time to move – she's gone, flying down towards the Trojan plain faster than the speed of her father's lightning.

Poseidon has hardly registered what's happened. He is still lying on his couch of cloud, the smug smile plastered to his face.

But the rest of the gods have stopped looking at him and are crowding quickly into their seats to watch. They can see Athena on the battlefield now. She has taken on the appearance of one of the Greek soldiers and seems to be shouting advice to Ajax.

'That's my clever girl,' says Zeus, proudly, eliciting a venomous look from his brother.

Ajax turns. Instead of picking up one of the many spears littered on the ground from his previous throws, he runs towards Cycnus, unarmed.

Cycnus hesitates, not sure what is going on. Isn't it dishonourable to kill an unarmed man?

Ajax feints to one side, runs past, turns and takes him from behind. He grabs hold of Cycnus' helmet straps in his enormous hands and tightens them around his neck.

A deep hush falls over the gods. It's a daring move. You rarely see it in battle, these days, not when there are so many different types of sword and spear to thrust through an opponent's heart.

Will Ajax be strong enough? Will he be able to hold Cycnus down as he kicks and struggles against the embroidered strap pressing at the soft flesh of his throat?

Finally, Cycnus stops kicking.

The gods let out a collective breath. Athena did it. The Greeks have won again.

All the gods – except Poseidon, who is busy sulking – start to applaud.

It looks like it's going to be a good show.

Lying with the Enemy

Βρισηίς
Briseis, Greek Camp

The Hour of the Middle of the Day

The Eleventh Day of the Month of Threshing Wheat, 1250 BC

I knelt on the damp, rush-covered floor of the hut. The scent of flowers drifted from the surface of the hot water of the bath and stung my nostrils. A raw clay jug of olive oil stood balanced on the packed earth. A slave appeared at the door and held it open. 'The bath you ordered, my lord,' he said, to a figure standing just outside, bowing deeply. 'And the girl as you requested.'

A shape moved across the frame of the doorway, and Achilles stepped into the darkness of the hut. His tall, lean figure was outlined with bright white light as he stood ringed by the sun. Then he closed the door, drew the bar across the bolts, and it was dark again, except for the dim light of the oil-lamps and their reflection on the water in the bath, and the thin slivers of sunlight between the stakes that made up the walls.

I turned my back to him, brushing my dark hair from my face and pretending to test the water with my fingertips. It was hot, hot enough to bathe, and there were white rose petals floating on the surface. *Roses*, I thought. *I scattered roses on the water for him.*

Achilles was moving around the hut, but still I did not turn. I was being disrespectful, but I did not care. After a few moments I heard a slight noise behind me, the sound of wine being poured into a goblet. Then I heard him walk towards me, and felt him crouch at my side. 'What's your name, girl?' he asked, taking a mouthful of wine.

I did not say anything.

He swallowed some more wine. 'I said, what's your name?' he repeated.

Still, I did not reply. I began to fold one of the white linen towels.

A hand gripped my chin with extraordinary strength and wrenched my face around, making me cry out with pain.

'You have a voice, then,' he said. He let go and stood up. He began to untie his breastplate, loosening the leather straps. When he next spoke it was with a quiet threat. 'I will not ask again.'

At last I spoke. 'Briseis,' I said, my voice breaking. 'Princess Briseis of Lyrnessus.' In my head I added, *And the wife of Mynes, Prince of the Lyrnessans, the man you killed with a sword through his heart.*

He looked at me. 'Briseis,' he mused. 'That's an old name. It means "the girl who wins", does it not?' He smiled. 'Appropriate for the slave of the best of the Greeks and a demigod.' He sauntered towards me, and bent over to tip my chin up to his face. His eyes glittered. 'My beautiful prize.'

My cheeks were burning as I looked into the shining black eyes, so close that I could see the pale lashes one by one. I could feel my colour rising and my stomach churning with bile. *What god put me here?* I thought. *What bitter god sent me as a slave to the man I watched kill my husband?*

I tried to pull my chin away. I could not bear his touch and the memory of what those hands had done.

He laughed and let me go, tossing me back with such strength and ease that I fell to the ground, my hair tossed beneath me and the robe slipping off my shoulders. Without thinking what I was doing, without even deciding to do it, I scrambled to my feet and slapped him, hard, across the face before he had taken his next breath. My palm and fingers stung with the contact, but I did not care. I drew my hand back to slap him again, anger burning in me so strongly that I felt as if I were going to be sick.

He did not laugh this time. Instead he caught me by the wrists, chafing the cuts around them so that I winced and tears started to my eyes. His fingers were pressing into my skin so hard that I thought the bones would break, and I sensed a terrible rage blazing from him, palpable as heat. His whole body was tensed, like that of a lion crouched for the kill.

Then, abruptly, he let me go.

There was a long silence. I stood still, paralysed by the raw power that seemed to emanate from every fibre of his body. My wrists were throbbing. A few soldiers passed the hut and I heard snatched words of their muted conversation. The fire in the hearth sputtered, sending acrid smoke through the hut and spiralling up through the hole in the rush roof.

At last Achilles spoke. 'Girl who wins,' he said. 'There is not a single man in this camp who would have dared to strike me as you did.' He surveyed me with a strange look in his eyes. 'Who would have thought it?' he said, almost to himself. 'A slave girl, a match for Achilles.'

Χρυσηίς
Krisayis, Greek Camp

The Hour of Offerings

The Eleventh Day of the Month of Threshing Wheat, 1250 BC

I stood in the Greek camp, exhausted, my dust-covered face streaked with the tracks of tears. The Greek who had taken me on his horse had left me on the shore of the Trojan bay in the midst of the camp of the enemy.

A short, filthy-smelling red-haired man had bound my hands and feet and pushed me into line with a group of smut-smeared girls in rags, despite my struggles and my attempts to bite and kick at every inch of him I could reach. I gazed up and down the long line, strung along the beach, and guessed at once, with a shiver of horror, why I had been brought there. The Greeks had taken all the women they could find from the surrounding countryside for their brute pleasure; I had heard it happened when men were so far from their homes. Then I thought back to Troilus and had to bite my lip to stop myself crying out in pain as I remembered him fighting in the woods, one prince against four Greeks. But it could not be – he could not be—

I heard voices and looked up. I could see a couple of Greek lords at the other end of the line, in simple beaten-bronze breastplates and greaves, nothing like the decorated cuirasses of the Trojans. Only one wore jewels, and he seemed to be their leader: a fat man, his tunic stretching around a large paunch, his eyes small and cross in his flaccid face.

I watched with growing dread as he walked down the line, panting with effort, occasionally turning up the chin of one of the girls with the end of his sceptre, stopping to squeeze her breasts and buttocks, then laugh with his men. But none of the girls seemed to be what he was looking for.

'Hah!'

The king was standing a few paces in front of me, his piggy eyes peering out of his fleshy face. He turned to raise his eyebrows to his men, and my cheeks flushed as their stares rested on me.

'Now, who is *this* pretty piece?'

One of the Greek ambassadors ran up to his side. 'We do not know her name, King Agamemnon,' he said, bowing deeply. 'She was found by the men you sent to scout the forest to the south of Troy, along with one of the Trojan princes.'

'What have you done to him?' I demanded. 'What have you done to Troilus?'

The ambassador did not reply, and the king merely bent down to take a closer look at me. His breath smelt rancid and he was missing several teeth.

Despite my efforts not to appear afraid, I felt myself flinch.

'Don't be shy, girl,' the king said thickly, placing one pudgy finger under my chin and lifting my face.

I tried to struggle as he turned my profile from side to side, sniffing my hair, like a boar grubbing for roots, but the ambassador darted forwards and forced my head up. I felt his fingers digging painfully into my collarbones. 'They always said old King Priam had a hoard of precious jewels in his coffers up in Troy,' he announced, to the crowds of nobles and soldiers around him, 'but they never told me he had such a jewel as this.'

They laughed, and King Agamemnon gestured to one of his slaves, who ran to unfasten the ropes around my wrists and ankles. The king took my hand, raised it to his lips and kissed it, his fat lips pressing horribly against my skin. 'You are welcome to the Greek camp, slave,' he said.

Βρισηίς
Briseis, Greek Camp

The Hour of Prayer

The Eleventh Day of the Month of Threshing Wheat, 1250 BC

'Out! *Get out!*'

I fled from the hut. A slim, brown-haired young Greek with a delicate chin was just outside the door and I ran into him, blindly, my eyes filled with tears.

He stared at me in surprise. 'What – who are you?'

I shook my head and tried to push past him, but he caught my arm. 'What happened?'

I struggled to free myself.

He pulled me with him and strode away from the hut down the shore towards the sea, still holding my arm, leading me around the sides of huts, shacks and tents, past soldiers sharpening swords and binding together bronze-tipped arrows, and slaves carrying clay jars full of water, until we were almost at the shore and the sea-wind made my eyes sting. Then he turned to me. 'What happened?' he said again, his voice urgent, his pale forehead creased with worry.

I looked up at him through my tears. 'Why should I tell you? I don't even know who you are.'

His expression softened. 'You are Achilles' slave girl? The one he took from Lyrnessus?'

I nodded, and a tear spilt down my cheek.

'I am Patroclus,' he said. 'Patroclus of Thessaly. I am Achilles' . . .' he hesitated '. . . companion. You can tell me what you have done to anger him. I wish you no harm.'

There was a long silence. 'I am no slave,' I said at last, my voice very low. 'My name is Princess Briseis, daughter of King Bias of Pedasus. And I did nothing to anger Achilles,' my voice broke, 'except bathe him, as I was ordered.'

Patroclus frowned. 'You must have done something.'

'I did not!' I protested angrily, my face growing hot. 'I bathed him and rubbed his skin with oil from the shoulders to the feet as my mother taught m—'

'You touched his feet?'

'Of course I touched his feet. Why should I not?'

He turned away so that I could not see his face. 'Tell me what happened.'

I considered, frowning as I tried to remember. 'I anointed his legs and his ankles with oil, and then – and then I touched his heel. He flew into a rage and threw me from the hut.' Tears were stinging my eyes again. 'I did nothing,' I said again.

Patroclus paused, his gaze distant over the sea. 'You – you would be best advised not to touch his heel again,' he said at last.

I raised my eyebrows in disbelief, my vision still blurred with tears. 'I slapped him across the face, and he said nothing – and now you tell me I cannot touch his feet?'

Patroclus nodded, his back still to me.

'Why?'

'I cannot tell you.'

'Is it some custom of the Greeks?'

'No.'

'Then why will you not tell me?'

He turned back to face me and a shadow crossed his face. 'I cannot. Let us leave it at that.' Then he said, under his breath, 'No man, especially Achilles, will admit his only weakness.'

I opened my mouth to speak, but he cut across me. 'You slapped Achilles' face,' he said, clearly trying to change the topic. His expression grew thoughtful. 'I must say, I am surprised you are still alive.'

I shrugged my shoulders. 'It seems I have a talent for staying alive.' My voice turned slightly bitter. 'Or perhaps it is a curse.'

He gazed at me for a moment. 'I do not know what you mean by that,' he said. 'But if you wish to live to see the dawn tomorrow, Briseis, I have some advice for you.'

'What is that?'

He took my hand, and I looked up into his face, startled at the gesture.

'Do not do the same tonight.'

I pulled my hand from his grasp. 'And what is that supposed to mean?'

He blushed again. 'Well – you know—'

'No,' I said, drawing myself up in height. 'I do not.'

His cheeks and ears were a brilliant red now. 'You must know why Achilles chose you as his prize?'

'He needed a woman to serve him, as all Greeks seem unable to perform their work for themselves.' Patroclus regarded me in silence. 'I know what you are thinking,' I said, slightly impatient. 'But it cannot be true. Not even *he* would dare to bed a princess of royal blood. It is against the laws of the gods and the customs of men.'

Gently, ever so gently, he took my hands again, his eyes filled with concern. And this time I did not pull away. 'Do you not understand?' he asked softly. 'Do you not know, Briseis?'

'Know what?'

Patroclus sighed. 'That is exactly why he wants you,' he said. 'He wants you in his bed because you are beautiful, but most of all because you are a princess. You are to him what all men want: that which they cannot have.' He took a deep breath. 'That is the only reason why you are still alive, Briseis.'

The silence stretched. 'Do not say such things, Patroclus. Do not say them,' I said, wrenching my hands from his and backing away several steps up the beach.

Patroclus moved towards me. 'It is the truth, Briseis,' he said. 'I am sorry.'

I turned and ran away from him along the seashore as if I could run from the horror of it: that Achilles should even think of defying the gods and taking a princess to his bed. That he wanted to touch me with the hands that had put the sword through Mynes' heart. I felt the sickness swell again in my belly.

'Briseis!' Patroclus called, running after me. 'Briseis, please stop!' He caught me by the shoulders and shook me, hard. 'You are bound to sleep with him. You have to. Achilles can be most . . .' he hesitated, looking for the right word '. . . most passionate – when he is hot, in rage or in love. You have seen so already for yourself. There is no other way.'

I tore myself from his grip and ran on. 'You tell him from me that he can take his passion with him to Hades,' I shouted back at him, tears welling, my whole body burning with rage and pain. I stopped and turned to him, my eyes blazing. 'I shall never, *never*, as long as I have a heart in my chest and a soul in my body, let Achilles have me in his bed. Do you understand me?' I took a deep, shuddering breath. '*Never*. Now, if you will excuse me, I have to return.'

I turned on my heel and ran back up the beach towards the hut, leaving Patroclus standing, open-mouthed, by the shore of the sounding sea.

My resolve was tested that very night.

Achilles was strumming on a tortoiseshell lyre, humming to himself, singing stories of his exploits and tales of men and gods. Patroclus was stoking the dying embers of the fire with his dagger, the smoke still curling up to the thatched roof, trying to find a last few moments of heat. It was hours before I would be weary, I knew. But I had to act now, or it would be too late.

I walked quietly to the pile of warm fleeces and woollen covers that marked Achilles' bed, and bent down. It was dark in the corner, away from the glowing fire, but eventually I managed to gather a few skins and rugs and dried herbs to scatter on the ground, enough to make a small pallet for myself.

Achilles was still singing in a low voice, and I could hear Patroclus rustling the dry ashes of the fire.

I turned and walked, without looking at them, to the other end of the hut. Then I set down the skins and started to make my bed.

The sound of the lyre stopped.

'What are you doing?' Achilles' voice cracked through the warm silence, like lightning, but I did not flinch.

'Making my bed,' I said, trying to keep my voice calm, scattering the dried herbs with deliberate care.

There was a tense silence. I heard Patroclus set down his dagger, and knew he was about to interrupt.

'I shall sleep here tonight,' I said, before Patroclus could speak. I continued scattering fragrant herbs and placing the skins. 'I do not see why I cannot make my bed where I wish.'

'Briseis—'

'Be quiet, Patroclus.'

It was Achilles. I heard the discordant clang of strings as the lyre was dropped to the ground, hurled by a hand with more than mortal strength. In spite of myself, I turned.

Achilles had stood up. His dark eyes were blazing. He was radiating heat and power and wrath, like an angry god. He seemed to fill the entire hut in his rage.

'Patroclus – get out,' he bellowed, and Patroclus stood up and ran, casting a single terrified glance at Achilles. The door banged behind him – and then, silence.

It felt like an eternity that I looked into those fathomless eyes. Achilles' face was unreadable, a mask. I could feel my heart beating fast against my chest, as if it knew it might be only moments away from death and would make up for lost time. And then—

'I shall not force you,' he said, in a startlingly low, quiet voice. 'No one should make love because they have to.'

There was a silence as I took in what he had said.

Achilles, murderer of thousands, slayer of my husband in cold blood, and he calls it making love?

He does not know what love is.

'But remember this, Briseis,' he said, bending down so that I could feel the heat radiating from his skin and his warm breath on my face. 'You *will* come to my bed. I shall not wait for ever.'

He straightened and stood there for a moment, tall and muscular, godlike, his eyes still dark, burning with passion. Then he strode to the door and slammed it, leaving me alone in the hut.

I had won again.

In the Hands of Fate

Χρυσηίς
Krisayis, Greek Camp

The Hour of Prayer

The Fourteenth Day of the Month of Threshing Wheat, 1250 BC

'You are certain?' King Agamemnon asked. 'Certain it was him?'

It was only a few days since I had been captured in the woods of Troy and brought to the Greek camp, though it felt like a lifetime. It was as if I had aged years for each night I had spent there, since I had first had to serve King Agamemnon in his bed, forced to please a foul-smelling boor of a man old enough to be my grandfather, to lie beneath the general who had brought his troops upon my home.

Now, on the third day of my captivity, I was pouring wine for the king and his favourite lords in his tent: his palace, my prison. Several ships' sails had been stitched together overhead as a canopy over the council room, the king's chamber and the kitchens, supported by a forest of poles – some of them driftwood, others oars that had been lodged blade-down in the sand. Tapestries woven in bright colours depicted the kingdoms of Greece over which King Agamemnon ruled, and a carved juniper-wood throne stood on a small dais before a large circular table covered with clay tablets and surrounded by intricately carved stools on which several of the Greek lords were sitting.

'Completely certain,' said another voice, younger, warmer, with a slight rustic twang. I recognized it as that of Odysseus, another of the nobles serving in Agamemnon's army, lord of Ithaca and renowned for his cleverness and honey-tongued speech. 'I can confirm it, my king. I saw the body myself in the healer's hut. There was no mistaking him from the descriptions our heralds have given us.'

Odysseus snapped his fingers at me. I walked over to him, as I had to do, and tilted the clay jug of wine to refill his goblet. He waited until I had done so, and I felt him watching me, his light brown eyes resting on my face with interest as I bent to pour the deep red wine.

I felt the heat rise into my cheeks under his stare and stepped back, taking care to wipe the rim of the jar, though no wine had spilt.

Odysseus raised his goblet to his lips and took a sip. 'Yes, the man we killed in the woods was certainly Troilus, Prince of Troy.'

My hand slipped on the wine jug. It crashed to the floor and shattered into hundreds of pieces, the wine splashing everywhere and drenching my tunic with red stains.

The lords began to mutter. King Agamemnon snarled at me as I stood there, rooted to the spot in horror: 'That was some of my best Attic wine, you clumsy fool! Well? Pick it up!'

I gasped and dropped to my knees to collect the broken fragments. I could hardly think. *Troilus was dead?* It could not be . . . Only a few days ago we had been lying together in his chambers in Troy. He could not be—

I bit my lip, my fingers trembling as I gathered the potsherds. *If he had not wanted to defy his father for me, if I had only said yes, we could have mounted the horses and outridden the Greeks* . . . Tears smarted painfully in my eyes and I tried to brush them away with my forearm, guilt and sorrow and terrible regret welling inside me, like a river threatening to burst its banks in the first melt of spring. *Troilus* . . . *dead* . . .

'But that is not all,' Odysseus continued, his eyes still upon me. 'The death of this man is of far greater significance than even the Trojans know.'

There was a murmur as the lords of the council considered what Odysseus had said.

I looked up quickly, my hands filled with potsherds and dripping with wine. What did he mean?

Odysseus rubbed his chin again. 'You must remember the prophecy that Calchas made when we landed.'

One of the warriors, a broad-shouldered man with a scrubby red beard, hit himself on the forehead with the palm of his hand. 'Of course! The prophecy!'

An old white-haired man, Nestor, raised his eyebrows. 'Would any of you care to explain what this is about?'

All the lords became quiet, waiting to hear.

'The prophecy, given to Calchas by the Lord Apollo himself,' Odysseus said, clearing his throat, 'was this. "When Troilus falls . . .' he paused, surveying the council, '. . . Troy shall be yours."'

I stared at him. This Apollo seemed to be a god – a prophecy-giver. Yet how could the Greeks think to pray to the gods when all the gods favoured Troy? They must be false gods – idols . . . and yet . . . and yet . . . how could they have received a prophecy from a false god, if that god did not exist?

Odysseus looked at the king and the gathered warriors, on whose faces a dawning comprehension was starting to register. 'Troilus, the son of Priam, was the object of the prophecy,' Odysseus said, 'and he has fallen at the hand of a Greek. His corpse even now lies in our camp. It is an omen – a sign! Troy will be ours! The gods have promised us victory!'

I knelt, frozen on the floor, paralysed by the words Odysseus had just spoken. I wanted to move, but my body would not respond. My heart was beating so fast it felt as if it was going to burst.

Troilus – dead – and Troy will fall—

My thoughts were scattering. I could not concentrate, could not think. Guilt and terror were flooding through my veins. Troilus had died trying to protect me, and now his death was prophesied by some god of the Greeks as the cause of Troy's fall. Panic gripped me as a terrible thought occurred to me. Was Apulunas punishing me for not wanting to become his priestess, as my father had foretold, by withdrawing his protection from us?

The lords around the table had burst into laughter, applauding, cheering and raising their goblets.

'He thought,' King Agamemnon boomed over the noise, as the men clapped Odysseus on the back and repeated the prophecy over and over again, 'that he could wander from his city and not suffer the consequences?' His tone changed to a derisive sneer. 'And instead, he played into my waiting hands and gave me Troy into the bargain!'

The men roared with laughter, clattering their goblets against each other, then drinking deeply from them.

I sat on the floor, the broken shards of the jug in my hands, wine seeping into my rough slave's tunic. Horror was flooding through me, my stomach heavy with dread. If the Greeks were telling the truth, they had powerful gods on their side who were able to prophesy the future – and their gods had promised them that our city, our beautiful, god-built city, would fall.

And I was to blame.

Βρισηίς
Briseis, Greek Camp

The Hour of the Evening Meal

The Fourteenth Day of the Month of Threshing Wheat, 1250 BC

I stood beside the rough wooden table in Achilles' hut holding a grey clay pot of boiled onion broth, while my own belly grumbled with hunger. Meals, these past few days, had been silent, and I saw no reason why this one should be any different.

As Patroclus reached out to ladle the broth into Achilles' bowl, Achilles held up his hand. 'Not now.'

It was the first time that Achilles had spoken that day since he had returned from ransacking another of the cities of the Troad: Thebe, the city of Eëtion. *A beautiful city, and not far from Lyrnessus*, I thought, with bitterness.

Patroclus frowned at Achilles. 'You have to eat. Starving yourself will not bring back the men you killed today.'

Achilles gave him a cold stare. Patroclus dropped the ladle, sat on his stool, then bent his head to eat.

'You do not have to fight. No one forced you to come and destroy people who have done nothing to harm you.' I heard my own voice before I realized I had said it.

Achilles' head turned towards me, and the crease in his forehead deepened.

Patroclus began to eat his broth as loudly as he could, clattering his spoon against his bowl, clearly hoping to distract Achilles from me.

I took a deep breath. 'You did not have to come,' I said coolly. 'You could have chosen otherwise. Your regret means nothing to the men whose lives you have taken.'

I expected another outburst of rage, as when I had bathed him and touched his heel that first day in his hut. But Achilles did not look angry. If anything, his dark eyes showed nothing but interest. He turned on his stool to face me. 'Is that what you think, Briseis of Lyrnessus?'

'Yes,' I said stiffly. 'It is.'

I could see Patroclus out of the corner of my eye. He was staring at us both with the attitude of one watching a lion and a mouse caught in a cage, half fascinated, half appalled.

Achilles was considering me, like a farmer weighing up the price of wheat. 'I would not blame you if you do not believe me,' he said, 'but I, too, think that we make our own choices.' He looked up at the ceiling of the hut. 'I believe there is no such thing as Fate, only the choice for greatness. I, like you, was forced into war by the dictates of my king and the will of the gods. But, since I am here, I intend to make the best of the lot the gods have given me.'

I stared at him, fingers still clutching the handles of the clay pot. His words sent a shiver down my spine. They were so like the ones that Mynes had spoken on our wedding night. 'You wish to achieve greatness?' I could not keep the contempt from my voice. 'And what is that?'

He smiled at me. 'I believe there is greatness in two things: the deeds of war, and love.'

I let out a laugh that had no humour in it. 'Love? And what do *you* know of that?'

There was a long silence. I stared into Achilles' eyes, determined not to hide my hatred and scorn.

He opened his mouth to speak.

Then Patroclus let his spoon fall to his bowl with a clatter, and Achilles turned to him.

'My apologies,' Patroclus said, his face flushed. 'I – I think I shall—'

He did not finish the sentence. Scraping his stool against the dried rushes on the floor, he picked up his bowl and strode from the hut, letting the door close behind him and leaving me alone with Achilles.

Achilles' mouth was set in a grim line, his dark eyes unreadable.

'Here,' I said, and thrust the clay pot with the broth on to the table. 'Eat, if you can bear it. If you are not too consumed with your guilt.'

Then I followed Patroclus from the hut, away from Achilles' silence and on to the shore of the Trojan sea.

Χρυσηίς
Krisayis, Greek Camp

The Hour of Evening

The Fourteenth Day of the Month of Threshing Wheat, 1250 BC

Think! I paced furiously up and down King Agamemnon's tent. The king and his war council had moved to Odysseus' hut to celebrate with some of his finest Ithacan wine, and I had been left alone, the torches in the brackets flickering as the day turned towards darkness. *Think what this means!*

Perhaps Odysseus had been bluffing about the prophecy. But, if so, then he was a skilled actor – and the other warriors had agreed with him, had remembered the prophecy from when they landed in Troy.

And who was this god of theirs? Everyone knew that the gods on Ida loved Troy above all other cities, that the gods blessed us alone with prophecies of the future. How could the Greeks claim to have gods of their own – gods who, according to Odysseus, not only spoke with their priests but promised victory to Troy's enemies?

I rubbed my aching temples in frustration. None of it made any sense.

I longed to speak to Cassandra, or – I closed my eyes in pain as I thought it – Troilus. He would have known what to do, I was sure. But then I shook myself. This was no time for weakness. The last thing Troilus would have wanted was for me to cripple myself with confusion and guilt. No: I had to *do* something.

But what?

I looked around the chamber, as if I might find the answer there. The clay tablets lay on the circular table where the warriors had left them. I eased my way towards them and scanned the surface. Lines and flourishes criss-crossed the tablets, pressed in with a stylus while the clay was still soft, strange symbols I could not understand, for I had never been taught to read more than the most elementary words. I gave an impatient sigh of frustration, then strode over to the chamber's entrance and past the guards, telling them I had been sent for by the king. I went out on to the shore.

It was a relief to be in the open air again. Grey clouds were caught along the line of the horizon under the darkening sky, and a slight wind whipped at the waves of the wine-dark sea, turning them white as they curled to crash on to the beach. I was about to walk along the bay, keeping the high walls of the city in view to the east, when a strain of sweet music reached my ears on the breeze. It seemed to be coming from one of the other tents, towards the line of the breaking sea, a series of wooden poles and one larger in the centre, over which a linen sail had been thrown, a flap cut roughly for a door. A moment later I saw the symbol embroidered across it, a rock and a goat, the sign of Ithaca, and realized it belonged to Odysseus. I stood still where I was.

I could not go closer. It would be a foolish thing to do, a reckless thing. If the king found me, alone, outside, listening to his private conversations . . . But the memory of the strange lines and symbols on the tablets came back to me. *If I do not listen, I shall not discover anything. And what if they are discussing the fate of Troy?*

Gathering my courage, I walked over towards the sounds and flickering lights, keeping my tread as soft as I could against the sand. I could hear a voice now, a sweet, low voice with a lilting Trojan accent, singing to the strumming of the lyre. That voice alone, after so many days in the camp, was music enough to my ears. I edged closer to hear the words of the song.

'Hecuba, mother of princes, once a beauty beyond compare,
Now sits on her regal throne, and is sobered by barren care.
Andromache, daughter of Thebe and by Cestrina given life,
Is hopelessly plain to look at, though betrothed as Hector's wife;

Cassandra, pale-skinned nymph with flame-red hair and deep blue eyes,
Is slim and blithe and bonny, though we hear she is most unwise;
But loveliest of all is Krisayis, Krisayis of the golden hair,
Whose glance is like the sun's, and of all she is far the most fair.

'Hesione, Queen of Lyrnessus, is a full-bodied beauty, 'tis true,
Whose husband is Ardys of Thebe, and whose love she did win through and through;
Briseis, wife of her love-child, and a daughter of Pedasus past,
Is faithful and loving and pretty, and blessed with a husband at last;
Laodice, mother of three sons and Pedasus' queen and king,
Seems more of a man than a woman, a quite indefensible thing.
But boldest of all is Helen, the woman who now sits in Troy,
Whose cunning escaped her from Sparta, and whose daring will see her destroyed.'

The sound of men laughing, slapping their thighs in merriment and shouting lewd comments across the small space to much jeering and whistling, could be heard clearly through the thin fabric; then wooden stools were scraping against the rough rushes on the sand and goblets clattered on to tables. The men were leaving.

Heart leaping, terrified of being seen, I moved swiftly to one side and pressed myself into a narrow opening made between the linen on one side and a hut of driftwood on the other. My hair had just whipped out of sight when the first man left. I could hear the swish of the flap as it was drawn aside, then the tramping of feet and more drunken laughter as the king and his lords departed.

I let out my breath slowly. I had not been seen. But I had also not overheard anything worthwhile, and now I was facing the very real danger that King Agamemnon would return to his tent and find out where I had gone.

I peered around, checking if all the lords had left. I could see the clear-cut outline of the singer left alone inside, his silhouette outlined against the linen, illuminated by the flickering light of the oil-lamps. He was moving around inside as he gathered up his pear-shaped lute and stool.

Quietly, very quietly, I took a step forwards out of my hiding place, hoping against hope that he would not hear me.

'Who's there?'

I stopped in my tracks.

'Who's there?' the singer asked again, not unkindly, his voice as clear and sweet as it had been when he sang, his Trojan accent soft on my ears.

'I – I'm no one,' I said quickly, to the shadow, keeping my voice low. 'Just a captive from Troy.'

'Ah,' he said, and I saw his outline nod against the linen. 'I come from Troy too, you know, or thereabouts – a small village on the slopes of Mount Ida. I would not expect you to know it.'

I looked up in surprise. 'A captive?'

The silhouette shook its head, and from the sound of his voice when he spoke he was smiling. 'No, a travelling bard. I journey between the different cities of the Troad, sometimes further, singing my songs for whoever will pay me to play for them.' He sighed, and his voice became grave. 'Though, of course, that has changed, with the war.'

I was shocked. 'You play even for the Greeks?'

'Even for the Greeks. They are men too, you know. They have need of song to lighten their cares, and I – I have need of silver to pay my keep.'

I pondered this. 'Those – those women you were singing of,' I asked, 'do you know them?'

The silhouette of the bard shook its head again. 'I do not know them,' he said, 'but I heard enough tales of the women of Troy around the royal palace. Why do you ask?'

'I – I am a friend of one,' I invented quickly.

'I see.'

There was a long pause.

'You tell stories of love and war, do you not?' I asked. 'Do you know anything of them?'

The bard shrugged. 'Of war, much. Of love . . .'

I waited for him to continue, but he said nothing.

'If one of the figures in your poems . . .' I was not entirely sure what I was saying, except that I was desperate to talk to someone, and the lack of Troilus' and Cassandra's counsel felt like an ache in my belly. 'Imagine one of the figures in your poems knew something. Imagine they were the only one who knew that their city might fall. What would you do? As the poet, I mean – even if it did not make any sense? Would you have them give up, or fight back?'

The bard was silent for so long that I began to regret what I had said. Had he understood what I had meant? Would someone who accepted silver from the Greeks take pay for more than songs? Or – my stomach turned over as I thought it – was Odysseus still there, perhaps? Had *he* heard what I had said? Then—

'I would have them fight,' the bard said, in a very low voice, so low that I had to inch closer to his shadow to hear him.

I swallowed. 'Even if they were only a slave? Lower than a slave, perhaps?'

'Even then. The most powerless slave is as powerful as a king – more so, perhaps – if they can understand what it is they truly most desire, and fight for it.'

I frowned. 'This is not about desire. It is about saving people's lives, and . . .'

'And?'

'And – and knowing that the gods would not willingly destroy a city they loved above all others.'

The silhouette of the bard nodded. 'This character you imagine – if they did what you said, and fought for what they knew was right, they would indeed be worthy of song.'

I found myself smiling. 'And what of the women you sang of to the Greeks?'

'I repeat only what I think others may take pleasure in listening to,' the bard said, in a serious voice. 'I do not always say what I believe. And I should be a fool if I thought beauty were simply to be seen with the eyes.' He paused. 'You should remember,' he added, with a laugh, 'that I am a poet, after all.'

I laughed, too, my heart a little lighter.

'I am afraid I must leave,' he said.

'Yes,' I said, 'yes, of course.' There had been something strangely comforting about his words, like the smile of a kind friend in the midst of all the doubt and fear of the last few days. But then I saw his silhouette move, not away from me towards the tent's entrance, as I had expected, but towards me. I watched in surprise as he stepped closer. Then he held his palm against the linen, the dark outline of his hand as clear as if he were standing right beside me – which, of course, he was.

I held up my hand, too, not knowing what he meant by it or why I did it. But I pressed my hand against his palm all the same and was surprised to feel the warmth and solidity of his touch through the linen. We stood there for a few long moments, two Trojans in a hostile Greek camp, hands pressed against each other, offering some comfort that seemed beyond words.

Then his hand dropped, and the moment was broken.

I gathered up my rough-spun tunic and turned to leave.

'Goodbye, Krisayis,' he said.

Βρισηίς
Briseis, Greek Camp

The Hours of Night

The Fourteenth Day of the Month of Threshing Wheat, 1250 BC

I dreamt that night of Achilles.

In my dream, I lay with him. I knew, in the deepest, most secret parts of my flesh, what it felt like to be kept awake by the unstoppable desire of a demigod. His skin was dappled with white moonlight as we rose and fell together again and again, tangled and hot, mingling lust and sweat.

All was a confusion of desire as he touched me, and I felt the brush of his lips upon mine, so real that it was almost . . .

I awoke with a start, my forehead damp with sweat, and sat up on my pallet on the other side of the hut from Achilles' bed, heart beating very fast, horror pumping through my veins. All was quiet. Achilles lay asleep on his woollen covers, his naked belly rising and falling with his breath, a shaft of moonlight from the hole in the rush roof shading his chest with the same perfect clarity as in my dream. I hugged my knees to my chest, my mind a whirl of shock and fear. Achilles was my mortal enemy. I had sworn never to lie with him. How could I have dreamt of making such passionate – such very passionate—

I shook my head to clear it as my mind filled with images of Achilles: his lips, his tongue . . . I looked up at the meadow rushes of the darkened ceiling, willing myself to think of something else, anything.

Mynes, I thought furiously. *Think of Mynes. Remember what it felt like to be with him, to love him.*

I tried to remember every detail of the first night we were together. The blue canopy above our bed, his arms around me, the moonlight filtering in through the roof of the hut . . .

No! Not the hut. We were in the palace. The palace of Lyrnessus that Achilles sacked.

I felt my anger flicker, like a kindled flame. *You hate Achilles*, I reminded myself fiercely. *You hate him.*

It was just a dream.

I tossed around my bed in frustration and anger and brought the covers up under my chin, holding them tight in my fists. I should not even be thinking of this. To think such things was a betrayal of Mynes' soul as he wandered, unburied, in Hades.

You are Mynes' wife and his love, always.

I paused.

And yet you promised him, a small voice said in the corner of my mind, *you promised that you would live your life without him.*

I shook my head. *No*, I told myself, *no. I didn't mean it. He should not have asked me.*

But as I stared up at the thatched ceiling, trying to will myself to fall asleep again, I could not help but wonder if Mynes had known what small comfort the dead could bring to those who were left behind, with cold beds and broken hearts, to live the war alone.

Χρυσηίς
Krisayis, Greek Camp

The Hour of the Evening Meal

The Sixteenth Day of the Month of Threshing Wheat, 1250 BC

'Idaeus, the herald of the Trojans, has arrived, my king.'

I was standing at the corner of King Agamemnon's council chamber beneath the largest of the decorated tapestries, the stools that were usually occupied by the Greek lords empty, the large round table cleared of tablets and maps for the king's evening meal, lighting the oil-lamps in their bronze stands as the day darkened towards evening. One of the Greek heralds, Talthybius, had drawn aside the tent flap to reveal a stooped old man, his dark hair patched with grey. I half gasped as I recognized him: he was the messenger who had delivered Queen Hecuba's early-morning summons for Cassandra to attend her on the walls of Troy, only a few weeks before. But he did not look at me. Who, after all, would notice a slave? His gaze was directed at the king, who was seated as usual on his throne.

King Agamemnon raised a hand heavy with gold rings in acknowledgement. 'Ah,' he said, clearly unsurprised by the presence of a Trojan in the camp. 'Herald. Yes. You have come for the body of Troilus, I take it?'

Idaeus nodded. 'I have the treasure in a cart at the gates of the camp.'

King Agamemnon leant forwards. 'You had better make sure you do not go back on your word, Trojan,' he said, his eyes boring into those of the herald. 'We have King Priam's assurance that he would send the prince's weight in gold in exchange for the right to bury him.'

Idaeus looked evenly back at the king. 'We have kept our side of the bargain.'

King Agamemnon leant back again and glittered a smile at him. 'And we ours,' he said smoothly. 'You will find the corpse laid out in the healer's hut.'

Idaeus inclined his head.

'You can go now,' King Agamemnon said, waving a hand again. 'Talthybius will escort you to bring back the ransom and ensure it has been paid in full.'

'Wait!'

The king turned slowly to me, and Idaeus exclaimed, 'Companion to the princess! But we thought you were . . .'

I ignored him and moved towards Agamemnon, then forced myself to kneel at his feet. 'Will you allow me to accompany Idaeus and ensure that Troilus' body is prepared in the proper way?' I asked, the words tumbling out of my mouth in my nervousness.

Talthybius started forwards, as if to silence me, but the king shook his head, the corners of his mouth turned up in a slight smirk. 'The body has already been prepared in the proper way, slave.'

I dared to look up at him, and my eyes met his. 'No, my lord. It has been prepared in the Greek way.'

There was a long silence as Agamemnon stared at me, his eyes narrowed, and I held my breath, wondering if I had gone too far. Then the king let out a short bark of a laugh. 'Very well,' he said. He motioned towards the two heralds. 'Talthybius, take her with you. Ensure she has what she needs.' He smiled, his eyes cold. 'We cannot be seen to treat the Trojan dead without respect, can we?'

Talthybius gave the king a deep bow, and I rose to my feet and moved quickly towards him before the king could change his mind.

The two heralds stared at me as we left, Talthybius' glare full of disapproval, Idaeus' expression one of barely concealed surprise.

The healer's hut was only thirty paces or so from King Agamemnon's and we made the walk in silence, the heralds' sandals crunching on the dry sand.

'You can't come in.'

We had reached the hut. I moved to stand before the door, arms crossed over my chest, holding the Greek herald's gaze.

Talthybius' eyes narrowed. 'And who are you to tell me what I can or cannot do, slave?'

I shrugged. 'The king told you to give me everything I need, did he not? Idaeus and I must be alone. Only Trojans may witness the rituals for the Trojan dead.'

Talthybius gave an impatient grunt of annoyance, but said nothing.

I turned with a smile and pushed the door open. 'Idaeus? Are you coming?'

The herald nodded and bent to follow me. I caught a last glimpse of Talthybius, standing with his back to us, foot tapping irritably on the sand, before the door swung shut and we were alone.

The hut was small, dingy and smelt strongly of myrrh and incense. I bit my lip as I caught sight of Troilus in the opposite corner and almost faltered. I had known, of course, but . . . it was different seeing him. I blinked streams of salt tears from my eyes, and steadied myself against one of the wooden pillars that supported the roof. His beautiful body had been embalmed with sticky scented oils and laid out on a wooden bier, the wounds washed clean, and a wreath placed around his head. For a moment all I wanted was to throw myself upon his body and give in to my grief, but I knew I could not. There were other things to be done.

And time was short.

'Idaeus,' I kept my voice low as I turned to the herald, who was gazing at the body of the prince with tears in his eyes, 'you know you can trust me, do you not?'

The herald sniffed. 'Princess Cassandra always used to say she would trust you with her life,' he whispered, 'and she believes you were not to blame for Prince Troilus' death.'

I gave him a long look. 'And you?'

'I am but a herald, daughter of Polydamas,' he said in a low voice. 'I am in no position to say. But if I were to venture an opinion . . .' He shrugged his shoulders. 'The prince was always a hot-headed young man, the gods bless him. And the king's refusal of your marriage shook him greatly.'

'You must take a message for me back to the king, Idaeus. I swear to you, I would not ask you to do such a thing if it were not of the gravest importance.'

His eyes widened slightly.

'Tell King Priam,' I said, lowering my voice until it was almost a whisper, 'that the Greeks believe they have been given a prophecy from their gods that the city of Troy will fall. I hardly know whether or not to believe it, but . . . if it is true . . . the king should know of it.' I paused. 'Tell him also that there is a secret way into the Greek camp through the woods to the south, and that it seems the Greeks have decided to leave this path unprotected.' I thought of what Troilus had said of King Priam's order that he never speak to me again. 'Only – only do not tell the king that this information comes from me.'

'How do you know of the path?' Idaeus asked, with a frown.

I waved my hand. 'I overheard the Greeks talking about it in – in the camp.'

We were silent for a time.

'Why are you doing this, daughter of Polydamas?' Idaeus said at last. 'Do you know how much you risk if you are caught passing information to our side?'

I shot him a disbelieving look. 'Would you stand back and watch if you knew the city and the people you loved were in danger?'

He took this in. Then he crossed his arms and looked down at me, his face grave. 'You are full of surprises tonight, Krisayis. Is there anything else?'

'Nothing for now. Can you return?'

He considered. 'Perhaps in a few days. There is talk of a truce, and our king will need me to negotiate it if that is so.'

I gave him a swift smile. 'A few days should be plenty of time for me to gather more from King Agamemnon's war council.'

I forced myself to glance at Troilus' body lying at peace on the bier, and turned to pick up a rough cloth and a jar of spiced myrrh from the stool beside me, my hands trembling slightly, but certain in the knowledge that I was doing what was right.

'For now, however, we have work to do.'

Battle of the Gods

Mount Ida, Overlooking the Trojan Plain

It is just after the midday meal, and the gods are gathering in the assembly-place on Mount Ida, around the gap in the clouds above the Trojan plain. They are talking in low voices, wondering why Zeus has summoned them at such an unlikely hour. Perhaps he has had a message from the Fates.

Zeus waits until they have all settled themselves in their seats, then heaves himself up from his throne and turns to survey his council. 'Gods,' he says, spreading his arms wide. 'Sons. Daughters. We have a very important decision to make today.' He gazes around the gathered crowd.

When no one says anything, Zeus begins again: 'We saw a few weeks ago, on this very spot,' he bows his head to Athena, who is, of course, sitting upright and eager, 'my dear daughter go to war to help the hero, Ajax.'

Poseidon, who has been slumped against the back of his throne gazing up at the sky, jumps as Ares elbows him in the ribs. 'What?' he hisses at him, then sees Athena glowing with pride, and his face darkens. 'Talking about Cycnus again, are we?'

Zeus chuckles. 'Oh, brother,' he says, 'you mustn't always take things so personally.'

'What? Like when you got to rule the whole world and I was given the stinking sea?' Poseidon interrupts, under his breath, folding his arms. 'Like that, you mean?'

Zeus pretends he didn't hear.

'What I mean is,' Zeus says, reassuming his regal tone, 'we can't let that happen again.'

Athena jumps up from her seat in protest, the snakes on her breastplate hissing.

Zeus holds up his hand, and she sits down again sulkily.

Poseidon smirks with satisfaction.

'I'm not saying you did anything wrong,' Zeus continues, 'but we simply can't have squabbles like this interfering with the war. After all,' he beams around at the gods, most of whom are looking very disagreeable indeed, 'we are gods! We're meant to be setting an example!'

He chuckles feebly, but, when no one laughs, he turns it abruptly into a cough.

His wife Hera is staring coldly at him.

'Well,' he says, shifting slightly. 'Well – I suppose we could come up with some sort of compromise . . .'

'What kind of compromise?' Hera asks.

Zeus looks around him.

The gods are staring at him, stony-faced. The idea of not interfering in the war clearly has not gone down as well as he'd hoped. He sighs. He supposes he should have known better. They don't have many other pastimes than a bit of fun with the mortals, after all, and interfering in a war is usually the most fun of all.

He takes a deep breath. 'Well, we all know that Troy is going to fall. There's no argument about that. It's been agreed.'

He glances at Hera, and she gives him a small, tight nod of approval, her lips pursed.

Ares leaps to his feet. 'We know that,' he says, his deep voice echoing over the clouds, like thunder before a storm. 'But I'm the god of war. It's my job to determine how battles are fought and who dies when. You can't deny me that, Father.'

Athena jumps up again. 'And what about me?' she demands. 'It's not as if you're the only god of war, Ares. I have the right to interfere too, if I want.'

Zeus feels a mild sense of panic overcoming him. Things are getting more out of hand than he would like. The gods are all leaping up from their seats now, gesticulating and shouting the names of their sons and favourite heroes, facing off against each other and demanding their right to take part in the battle.

'All right!' Zeus thunders, and the gods fall silent. 'All right,' he says more calmly. 'Here's how it will be. Troy will fall. No,' he holds up his hand as Ares starts to interrupt again, 'listen to me. The outcome has been decided. If you agree that much, then we may be able to come to some arrangement.'

The gods nod, some more readily than others.

Hera and Athena are smiling triumphantly, the corners of their mouths turned up in a pronounced smirk.

'But,' Zeus interjects, 'if you really want to fight . . .'

The gods perk up.

'. . . then you'll have to decide here and now which side you're on so you can fight fair and square. No misunderstandings and,' he glances imperceptibly in the direction of his wife, 'no cheating either. The city will fall, but we have not yet decided who will live and who will die. You may try to save your favourites, and it'll all be out in the open. Nothing personal. All right?'

The gods raise a ragged cheer. Some even toast Zeus with their goblets of nectar by downing them in one.

He smiles in mild relief.

'Well, that's easy. We're with the Greeks.' The sharp sound of Hera's voice cuts through the cheers.

She and Athena are marching over to stand on the clouds above the Greek huts and tents pitched on the seashore. Both of them are still smiling.

Zeus hears a loud grunt from somewhere in the council. He turns to see Ares shifting in his seat, eyeing Athena with her spear poised over the Greek camp.

'In that case,' Ares says, in his deep voice, heaving himself up from his seat, 'it's only fair that I help the Trojans. After all, we can't have the two gods of war both fighting on the same side.' He moves over to stand above the walls of Troy, his armour clanking as he walks. There's a little sigh of admiration.

Zeus turns to the other side, and sees Aphrodite leaning towards Artemis, whispering very audibly about how handsome Ares looks in his armour and how brave it is of him to take the losing side. They giggle together, whisper a little more, and then, with Aphrodite leading the way, the two goddesses link arms and walk towards Ares, Aphrodite's hips sashaying invitingly.

All the gods' eyes follow her – almost involuntarily, it seems – until she reaches Ares' side.

Her husband, Hephaestus, looks a little puzzled. 'But – but I thought we've always been supporters of the Greeks,' he says uncertainly. 'Haven't we always supported the Greeks, dear?'

Aphrodite shrugs one creamy shoulder. 'I don't know,' she says, not bothering to look at him. 'You decide.'

Hephaestus' face brightens. 'I suppose it does make it fairer, if we split teams,' he says amiably. 'Good idea. So, I'll cover the Greek side, and you'll—'

But Aphrodite isn't listening. She's now talking in a low voice to Ares, with a delicious smile on her rosy lips.

Anyone who isn't Hephaestus would be able to see straight away that she has eyes only for Ares. But Hephaestus, it seems, is blissfully ignorant. He hobbles over to stand beside Athena and Hera, clearly very pleased with himself, and gives his wife a little wave from the opposite cloud.

She does not return it.

There are only two gods still sitting in the council now. Poseidon glowers at the two sides, torn between his enmity for the Trojans and his hatred for Athena. He heaves himself up from his throne, hesitates, and then, at last, makes his way towards the Greek camp.

'Don't read anything into this,' Poseidon growls at Athena, through gritted teeth, as he lopes towards her. 'This doesn't change anything between us.'

Athena brings her hand to her mouth to cover her smile.

Zeus rubs his hands together, pleased. 'Well, I think that's everybody.' He surveys the opposed gods, assembled above the Greek camp and the city of Troy. 'No – wait a minute. Where are Hermes and Apollo?'

The gods look around them, realizing that two of their number are missing. There is a moment of confusion as they mutter among themselves. Then—

'I believe,' Athena volunteers, her face contorted in a slight sneer, 'they were last seen chasing a wood nymph in the hills of Sicily.'

'Ah,' Zeus says brightly. 'Oh, well. Can't blame them. Very beautiful girls in Si—'

Hera glowers at him, and he stops mid-sentence.

An awkward silence falls over the gods.

'Aren't you forgetting someone else?' Hera asks cuttingly, into the silence.

Zeus looks at her blankly. 'Did I forget someone? Who?'

Her eyes spark. 'You, Zeus,' she hisses at him. 'You promised me Troy, remember? You're on the Greek side now.'

Zeus relaxes into a smile. 'My dear wife, I'm the ruler of the universe. I'm impartial.'

The snap in Hera's eyes would be enough to set the Underworld itself on fire. She places her hands on her ample hips. 'And I'm the ruler of our marriage bed,' she replies sharply. 'So, if you know what's good for you, you'd better get over here, Zeus, and fast.'

It is not a difficult decision to make. Zeus bows his head and shuffles over to stand beside his wife above the Greek ships. He wonders if there is any chance at all that the rest of the gods didn't hear that, and comes to the depressing conclusion that there probably is not. He shrugs his shoulders in a resigned sort of way, and thinks: When you are the father of the gods, your biggest problem isn't keeping the mortals happy. It is the mother of the gods you have to worry about.

The most powerful gods are now rallied opposite each other in heaven. The clouds darken beneath them as they survey each other. Who will make the first move? Who will dare to demonstrate their allegiance and make an attack for their chosen side?

It is Ares who throws his spear first. It crackles through the air, like a white bolt of lightning, and crashes into Athena's shield with a rumble, like thunder.

On the Trojan plain below, it begins to rain.

The battle of the gods has begun.

Dead Men

Χρυσηίς
Krisayis, Greek Camp

The Hour of Prayer
The Twenty-fifth Day of the Month of Threshing Wheat, 1250 BC

Several days after I first met with Idaeus, I was holding my arms overhead to try to shield my eyes from the sudden downpour that was slanting from the sky, but it was no use. Dark clouds had gathered over the sea and lightning was splitting the sky with bursts of light, like the clash of swords in battle. I ran across the sand from King Agamemnon's tent, glanced around me to check that no one was watching, then pushed open the door of the healer's hut and dashed inside.

A stooping figure with greying hair stood with his back to the door. He turned as I entered.

'Idaeus,' I gasped. 'I have only moments. King Agamemnon has left to visit Nestor, but he may return at any time.'

Idaeus strode towards me. 'You are dripping wet,' he said, with a frown, taking the warm woollen cloak from his shoulders and draping it over my own. 'Sit down.'

'Are we alone?'

He nodded. 'Yes.'

I lowered myself on to a stool, drawing the cloak closer around my shoulders. Idaeus and I had been meeting like this as often as we could since he had first come to the Greek camp. We had decided the healer's hut was the safest place: though Troilus had been buried in the black earth, as the Trojan custom was, Idaeus was constantly moving back and forth between the Greek camp and the city, delivering messages between the two kings, and the healer's hut was private enough that we could be sure we were not overheard. Machaon the healer, whose task it was supposed to be to heal the wounded and care for the dead, was a notorious drunkard and spent most of his days sleeping in his quarters at the Myrmidon camp.

'I have news.'

'Good or bad?'

I shrugged. 'Both. The council yesterday was discussing their warriors, assessing their strengths and weaknesses in battle. You should know that Opheltius is famed for his fighting from the two-horse chariot, but they were saying that he is notoriously weak in hand-to-hand combat. Our warriors should be able to take advantage of this.'

'I shall make sure to tell Prince Hector.'

I took a deep breath, frowning as I tried to remember all that had been said. 'Menelaus is famous for his loud voice, and is skilled in calling out to order the troops in times of trouble. You would do well to silence him. Diomedes is particularly skilled with the spear, and can kill a man at a distance of fifty paces. I have not yet heard how he is best defeated. And Teucer is a famed archer, but his right shoulder is injured and he cannot wield a sword at close range.'

'They should be fairly easy to deal with.' Idaeus grimaced at me. 'So what is the bad news?'

'Achilles,' I said, lowering my voice. I looked up at Idaeus. 'It seems he cannot be killed.'

Idaeus' brows drew together. 'No man lives for ever, not even the son of a god.'

'The warriors all say that Achilles was made invulnerable by his mother, the goddess Thetis.'

Idaeus let out a long breath. 'That is bad news indeed.'

'There is hope,' I said, 'though not much. Odysseus let slip a few nights ago that there is a single part of Achilles' body which the goddess unintentionally left vulnerable, where he can be killed, but nobody seems to know where that is. It appears that Achilles keeps it a most guarded secret.'

Idaeus was silent.

'The trouble is,' I said, standing up and pacing around the hut in frustration, then turning back to Idaeus, who was gazing up at me, his forehead furrowed, 'that if Achilles cannot be killed, how is Hector to stop him? How is Troy ever to be safe if the Greeks' greatest warrior cannot die?'

Idaeus shook his head. 'How indeed?' he said. 'How indeed?'

Βρισηίς
Briseis, Greek Camp

The Hour of the Evening Meal

The Twenty-fifth Day of the Month of Threshing Wheat, 1250 BC

The sounds of soldiers tramping back from another raid were echoing around the hut: the rhythmic stamp of a thousand feet on hard wet sand, the rattle of shields and spears, the sobs of prisoners being led into the camp, and over it all, the steady hammering of rain on the rush roof.

I was sitting on my small pallet, holding Achilles' lyre in my lap and plucking at the strings.

'You should not be playing that.' Patroclus was sitting on a stool, using his small bronze dagger to carve a wooden hawk out of driftwood. He was avoiding my eye, pretending he needed to focus on the woodwork.

'Why not?' I asked. 'Achilles is not here. He'll not know. Unless you tell him.'

Patroclus blushed slightly and did not look up from carving. 'Maybe I shall,' he said. 'In any case, I still do not think you should.'

I watched him as he chipped away at the wood. He seemed preoccupied, lost within his thoughts, his eyes distant. It was as if he hardly noticed what he was doing. As if he hardly cared.

'Why do you not fight, Patroclus?' I asked him suddenly. 'Why do you stay behind, when Achilles goes to war?'

He looked up at me, then down at his hands. It was a long time before he spoke. 'My father,' he said at last. 'My father made Achilles swear not to let me fight.'

'But you would like to? Fight, I mean?'

He continued chipping shavings of wood on to the floor. 'Who would not? War is where heroes are made. In Thessaly, my home, I am only Patroclus, son of Menoetius, companion of Achilles. Here I would have the chance to be something more.' The dagger hovered above the wood. 'Something different.'

'So you would wish to be with Achilles and his soldiers, raping and pillaging and burning the cities of the Troad?' I said bitterly. 'I see. And whose lives were they ruining today?'

He was avoiding my eye. Rain pattered upon the roof into the silence, and the fire sparked. 'I don't know,' he said. 'And do not be so harsh, Briseis. You know what war is like.'

'I know what men are like,' I said. 'I think Agamemnon has come to fill his overflowing coffers with Trojan gold. I think that most soldiers would do anything to bed a woman. And I *know* Achilles wishes for nothing other than to destroy and murder and burn as much as he can.'

'That is unfair,' said Patroclus, quietly. 'You do not know him at all, Briseis. You cannot talk about him like that.'

'Why can I not?' I said, growing heated. 'I may talk about him in any way I please. He's not here to defend himself.'

Patroclus returned to his wood carving, chipping away at the little bird, shavings of wood dropping on to the floor with growing insistence.

'You still have not told me where Achilles went.'

'I told you, I do not know,' he repeated. 'It is not your business.'

I stood up, my cheeks reddening with anger, my temper flaring after days spent cooped up in Achilles' hut with only Patroclus and my grief for company, letting the lyre fall on to the rushes on the floor. 'I do not understand it. How can you bear to stay at home and defend him while he is out murdering innocent men? How can you, Patroclus?'

'It's not so simple,' he said, frowning. 'Men kill because they have to.

Achilles is a man like any other. It is his job to kill. But he is capable of love, too—'

'Don't you *dare* talk of love!' I shouted, losing all self-control. 'Don't you dare try to excuse him! What does Achilles know of love? He killed my husband before my very eyes! My *husband* – the only man I ever loved. The only man who ever saw me for who I was, despite – despite everything that happened in Pedasus. Achilles did not even take the trouble to look as he stabbed him through the heart . . .' I collapsed on to a stool, shaking, my head in my hands. I could not even weep. That loss and that rage were beyond tears.

Patroclus did not know what to say. 'I am truly sorry,' he said. 'I—'

'I do not want your sympathy,' I said in a harsh tone, and my voice was steady. 'What is done is done, and he did it. I shall not forget.' I swallowed and lowered my voice. 'I shall never forgive him.'

Patroclus started to say something, but I spoke across him.

'So,' I said, straightening my face, pulling myself up, 'you know it all now. The worst is done. And you might be trying to hide it from me, but I know you know where he went. All I am asking is for you to tell me.'

Patroclus stood up slowly and walked towards the door. He pushed it open with both hands. Then he turned back to me, his eyes tortured with pain. 'Pedasus, Briseis,' he said, in a low voice. 'He went to Pedasus.'

Χρυσηίς
Krisayis, Greek Camp

The Hour of Evening

The Twenty-fifth Day of the Month of Threshing Wheat, 1250 BC

I slipped from the healer's hut into the damp air of the evening. The rain had stopped, leaving a mist that hung low over the rippling surface of the sea, fogging the deep gold of the sky, like the gods' breath on a bronze mirror. The shore was filled with captured slaves.

I felt my heart swell with indignation as I surveyed the crowds of women, their wrists tied to one another. I had seen this happen too many times already during my two weeks in the Greek camp. How much longer would the gods allow this suffering to go on?

A movement in the direction of one of the tents further down the shore caught my eye, and I gasped. The flap had just been drawn aside. Nestor and King Agamemnon were stepping out on to the shore, Nestor's white hair flashing in the low sunlight.

I gathered my tunic and started to run towards King Agamemnon's tent, darting between the groups of slaves gathered on the shoreline and hoping against hope that I would not be seen.

Βρισηίς
Briseis, Greek Camp

The Hour of the Setting Sun

The Twenty-fifth Day of the Month of Threshing Wheat, 1250 BC

I did not understand. The door was moving in the breeze, creaking on its heavy wooden hinges.

He had gone to Pedasus.

Pedasus.

He went to Pedasus. My home.

But what if he found my mother and father? What if he found my brothers, Rhenor, Aigion and Thersites?

How can I find out? Who would know?

Patroclus was my first thought. My throat tight, I ran towards the door and pushed it open, then dashed across the sand after him.

'Patroclus!' I shouted, but the wind whipped my voice out of my mouth and over the ocean. 'Patroclus – wait! Come back!'

But he was already lost in the maze of Greek huts and tents.

'*Patroclus!*'

I looked around desperately for someone to ask. Any man who could tell me what had happened to my family, if they were still alive or if they had passed into the kingdom of the Underworld from which no mortal ever returns, and all this while I had been making idle conversation with a Greek in the Greek camp.

And then something else caught my attention.

The whole beach was crowded with people, silent, still, bowed, their arms and legs bound. I looked again, carefully now, and my shout caught at the back of my throat.

They were all the women I had grown up with – all my slaves, young and old, all the noble ladies – arrayed in front of me, like some strange nightmare of Pedasus.

But there were no men.

I started to run towards the slaves, not looking where I was going, not caring who saw me.

'Have – have you seen Rhenor or Aigion?' I gasped, dashing between the rows of bent and broken women, searching for anyone who might be able to tell me where they were, any man among the crowd of smut-stained slaves.

'Did you see Prince Thersites, or the king? Do you know where they are?'

Eyes that were blank with despair were my only answer; sometimes, a look of pity.

'But they must be here somewhere,' I cried out. 'It's all right, you just have to tell me where they are. I am the princess! I'm here . . .'

Nothing. Just the soft breaking of the waves against the beach and the faint, mournful keening of seagulls.

'Please!' I sobbed, running in and out of the plaited chains of women, their faces blurred now. 'Please – they must be—'

'Princess Briseis?'

The voice was so familiar I felt as if I were in a dream.

I stopped running and faltered forwards a little, wiping the tears from my eyes, looking for the face that belonged to that voice . . .

'Princess!'

It was my nurse, Deiope. Her old face was creased with worry, but it was still her. I should have known that face anywhere, as if it were inscribed on the hardened clay of my heart.

'Deiope!' My voice cracked and I ran over to her. I unbound the ropes from around her wrists and ankles, and she folded me into her arms, stroking my hair and face. 'Is it you, Princess?' she asked, the tears running down her wrinkled old cheeks. 'Is it really you?'

'It's me,' I said unsteadily. 'It's me, Deiope. I am here. I am all right.'

She rocked me back and forth, cradling my head against her chest.

I felt the tears rush to my eyes more insistently than ever at the bittersweet pain of it, my love for her, the safety I felt, fleeting memories of a past that was gone and could never come back. The tears flooded out and on to her tunic, staining it dark.

'We did not know where you were!' she exclaimed, pressing me to her. 'We heard about Lyrnessus. We heard Prince Mynes had been killed and we thought they must have taken you, but we could not be sure if – if—'

'No,' I said quickly. 'No. I'm here. I'm a slave too. But – but that does not matter. Tell me, what happened? What happened to Pedasus? Do you know where my family is?'

Tears sparkled in her crinkled blue eyes. I had never seen her cry before. She took a deep breath. 'We did not stand a chance,' she whispered. 'He came like nothing I have ever seen – like fire. He . . .' she swallowed a sob '. . . he killed your father, the king. Not even your brothers could stop him, though they fought like heroes.'

He? I thought, flooded with dread. My heart was doing an odd kind of drumroll against my ribs. *No. Not him.*

Not him again.

'We were hiding in the women's quarters, all us slaves. Your mother the queen had already set out for her father's palace in Killa, disguised as a trader's daughter. The men had gone out to fight. Your brothers too. And the king had gone to the treasury with his guard to shore up the vaults. There wasn't anyone left to protect the palace.'

I could hear my heartbeat pounding in my ears.

'I looked out of the window, trying to see where they were, to check if we were safe, and I saw them. Your three brothers, down in the court, all fighting for their lives. And then *he* appeared, so suddenly you'd have thought he'd been transported there by a god – handsome, terrible, taller than Ares.' She lowered her voice to a whisper. 'Achilles. And he was so fast with his sword it looked like a dance – just a dance, like the ones we used to have on feast days, do you remember? His blade glinted in the sun. I looked away for a moment, blinded by the light. And when I looked again it was done . . . Our three sweet boys were lying in the dust . . .'

Her words melted into tears, and I held her close to me, my head on hers, trying to take in what she had just told me.

I could not weep now. I could not feel anything except shock. I could not believe they were gone: my father, my brothers, my family. It was too large, too much to take in that they, too, could be gone. That I would never see them again, or talk with them in the palace at Pedasus.

It cannot be true.

'Well, that's all done now,' Deiope said simply, crying herself to a last few sobs, then wiping her eyes on her smut-stained tunic. 'Zeus knows there's no sense bearing a grudge, even against those who deserve it, for the only harm we do is to ourselves. It'll all come right in the end, Princess – you'll see.'

Another memory flashed, unbidden, across my mind. Deiope, standing beside me in the chariot on the way to my wedding. Deiope, straightening my gold necklaces and earrings. Deiope, as I asked her about the prophecy, saying that all would come right.

And then, with the blinding force of lightning, it crashed over me. It was so obvious. *That was the prophecy. That's it.*

'Princess?' Deiope asked tentatively. 'Is – is something wrong?'

My mind seemed to be working faster than usual, images and memories flashing before my eyes.

He who seeks Briseis' bed shall then her brothers three behead.

He who seeks my bed. And we had always assumed it would be a suitor. And when Mynes had come and chosen me and all had been well, I had thought I was clear of the prophecy. *But it was not Mynes*, I thought feverishly. It was Achilles. Achilles had slain his way through the Great Hall of the Palace of Lyrnessus to get to me. He had killed my husband without even turning to look at him. It was Achilles who had killed my brothers, Rhenor, Aigion and Thersites.

And it was Achilles, the murderer of my husband, the slayer of my brothers, who wanted me in his bed.

I was rigid with shock. *The prophecy was right. It was Achilles, not Mynes, who killed my brothers and seeks my bed.* The words drilled through my head, over and over, like a chant to the gods.

Achilles. It was Achilles.

'The prophecy was right,' I whispered.

Deiope stopped stroking my hair and gave me an anxious look. 'The prophecy?' she said. 'You're not still worrying about that?'

I shook my head. 'Yes – no – I don't know . . .'

I felt as if the whole world was giving way beneath my feet. *Everyone I love, gone.* How could this have happened? How could the gods have done this to me?

What have I ever done to wrong them?

I gave a sob, and Deiope gathered me into her arms again. 'I don't know any more, Deiope.'

Someone pushed past me, their elbow burrowing into my ribs as they forced their way through the crowds of slaves. I stumbled back, tripped on my cloak and fell to the ground.

'What are you doing?' I exclaimed, pushing the hair out of my eyes.

A young woman of striking beauty stopped in her tracks and moved to lean over me. Her hair curled in loose golden waves over her shoulders, and her eyes were like honey. 'My apologies,' she said. 'I did not see . . .' She frowned. 'Wait.' She stared at the stamp of Achilles' family, a dolphin intertwined with a lion, sewn on to the corner of my slave's tunic. 'You are *Achilles'* girl?'

I felt a flash of pain at the sound of his name. 'You could say that.'

'Your name?'

'Briseis.' *No longer Briseis of Pedasus, or Lyrnessus.*

Just Briseis.

Deiope was glaring at the girl with her arms crossed, but the girl seemed not to notice as she moved closer and knelt by my side.

'Briseis,' she said, lowering her voice. 'I am Krisayis, the daughter of High Priest Polydamas of Troy, captured by the Greeks and now a slave in Agamemnon's tent. There is something I need to ask you.'

I felt numb, my mind still filled with despair and confusion. 'What is it?'

She took a deep breath. 'What do you know of Achilles?'

I gazed over the sea, unseeing. 'Much,' I said shortly. 'Much that I would not wish to know. He is a cold-hearted murderer. He pretends to grief at what he does, yet still he slays every man in the Troad, like a plague.' My voice broke, my throat thick with grief. 'He has destroyed everyone I ever loved.'

She considered me. 'He has not told you . . . He has not told you of any weakness?'

'He has not told me himself,' I said, distracted. 'But Patroclus says he has a weakness in his heel. He grew furious with me when I touched it once when bathing him . . .' I tried to think clearly through the fog that seemed to have settled upon my mind. 'Why do you ask?'

'No reason.'

But I thought, for a moment, that I saw her eyes brighten as if in triumph. In the next breath, however, it was gone, and she was peering down at me with concern. 'Here,' she said, holding a hand out towards me. 'Let me help you up.'

I stood, and looked into her face. She seemed honest, and her eyes were full of sympathy. 'Have you lost anyone?' I said. 'In the war? Is that why you are here, in the camp? Are you alone, too?'

She bowed her head. 'Yes.'

I clutched her arm. 'Tell me – this pain, this anger, does it stop?' I felt my legs sway slightly beneath me, and held on to her to steady myself. The world was swimming with tears as I gazed at her. I lowered my voice to a thread of sound. 'I don't think I can bear it. I don't think I can bear it any more.'

She looked at me for a long time, Deiope standing beside us, her hands on her hips now, her face creased in anxiety.

'No,' the girl said at last, leaning towards me, and her eyes seemed to have understanding in them. 'No, it does not stop.' She considered me. Then, inexplicably, she smiled. 'But there are other ways to fight your grief than with anger and despair.'

And, with that, she loosed herself from my grip and walked away across the beach towards King Agamemnon's tent, Deiope and I staring after her.

The Parting of the Ways

Χρυσηίς
Krisayis, Greek Camp

The Hour of the Setting Sun

The Twenty-fifth Day of the Month of Threshing Wheat, 1250 BC

I could hardly believe it. I had discovered Achilles' secret.

I knew how to save Troy.

I knew how to kill the greatest of the Greeks.

I almost ran back to King Agamemnon's tent, my heart skipping with excitement. I half wished I could turn back and tell Idaeus what I had just learnt, but I knew I could not risk any more delay. If the king noticed I had been missing . . .

I was rounding the corner of the hut of King Agamemnon's heralds, Talthybius and Eurybates, when I stopped short. There, ahead of me, standing before the heralds' driftwood shelter, was none other than my father, his grey beard damp with water and his white priest's robes flapping in the evening breeze.

'*Father!*'

I stared at him, hardly able to believe that he was real. But surely no apparition or invention of the mind could look so solid.

'Father?' I asked again, a little hesitant. 'It *is* you?'

He nodded.

I stepped forwards and knelt at his feet for his blessing, then felt the warmth of his hand touch my head. When he had finished, I stood up, looking into his old, lined face as if I would drink it in. 'What are you *doing* here?'

He smiled at me, and the corners of his eyes creased in the familiar way. I saw with embarrassment that there were tears, and pretended I had not noticed.

'My daughter,' he said, pulling me close to him. I inhaled the familiar scent of incense and smoke from his robes. 'Oh, my daughter. Thank the gods you are alive.'

A few soldiers passed nearby, talking between themselves and laughing. I let him hold me for a few moments, then pulled away, my mind flooded with a thousand questions. 'But why did you come?' I glanced over my shoulder at the warriors play-fighting beside the nearby huts, swords clashing on sharpened swords and spears burying themselves in targets of woven rushes with dull thuds. 'Are you safe? Does King Priam know? Did you—?'

My father held up his hands with a faint smile. 'Enough, daughter! Let me speak, and I will tell you all. I have come to deliver you from the Greeks. The herald Idaeus informed me that you were being held captive in the Greek camp, and I have brought with me a ransom with which to pay for your freedom. You are to go to Larisa, back to our home, where you will be safe.'

I felt my heart leap. No longer a slave. No more nightly torments in King Agamemnon's bed. I shivered with relief.

But then I remembered Idaeus.

There will be no one to pass Idaeus information from the Greek camp. I thought of the war council, and Odysseus' words echoed in my head: *Troy shall be yours.*

Troy shall be yours.

I felt the smile slide from my face.

'Daughter?' my father asked, a line appearing in his forehead.

I shook my head. There was a long pause. 'I cannot go.'

My father's frown deepened, and his eyes grew dark with anger. 'Krisayis, this is no time for disobedience.'

'I am not trying to disobey you, Father,' I said. 'But Troy needs me here.'

My father's eyes sparked. 'Troy,' he said, his voice rising in impatience, 'has been doing very well without you, daughter, and will do perfectly well when you are gone. You are to go to Larisa, where you will complete your apprenticeship to the Great God Apulunas in preparation for the advent of your sixteenth year.'

I stared at him. 'My – my apprenticeship? Surely you cannot still wish me to be a priestess. Not after all that has happened.'

He said gravely, 'After all that has happened, daughter, it is more imperative than ever that you serve the pure and virtuous gods and learn obedience from your fellow priestesses. You will reach your sixteenth year in ten days, and I am determined that you will be fully prepared for the initiation ceremony by then.' He took a deep breath. 'I am only trying to do what is best for you, Krisayis. The priesthood is the highest honour a woman in your position can hope for. You should be grateful for this chance to serve your city—'

At this I lost patience. 'By all the gods, don't you *see*?' I said, my voice rising uncontrollably. 'We are at *war*, Father! What use is it if you send me away to become a priestess when the fate of our country and our people is at stake? If we do not do something soon, there will be no city left to serve!'

I lowered my voice, struggling to keep myself from shouting. 'As a slave in Agamemnon's tent I can pass – I have *already* passed – important information to our heralds from the king's council of war. I have just this moment learnt the greatest, the most important piece of information of all. I can *help* with the war, Father. I can help Troy, if only you would give me the chance!'

My father's eyes were sharp as ice chips on dark rock. 'No,' he said.

I stared at him. 'No? That is all you have to say?'

'This is not your choice to make, daughter,' he said, his clipped tones conveying anger in every syllable. 'You are to go to Larisa, no matter what you think. I am still your father and your lord and *I say you shall go*.'

Βρισηίς
Briseis, Greek Camp

The Hour of the Stars

The Twenty-fifth Day of the Month of Threshing Wheat, 1250 BC

It was a long time before I returned to Achilles' hut. The stars were rising above the pool of the ocean and the curve of Atimite's moon was gazing at itself in the sea when I left Deiope's side at last and moved back towards my captor.

Achilles was there when I entered, alone, sitting on a three-legged stool by the hearth and playing his lyre. He seemed weary and careworn, frowning as he gazed down at the strings. I stopped when I saw him, then turned abruptly away.

'Wait – Briseis,' he said, setting down the lyre and striding towards me, catching me by the arm. 'Don't go.'

'Don't touch me!' I recoiled from him, pulling my arm from his grip as if from burning heat. 'Don't you *dare* touch me,' I said again, my voice low and trembling.

'Briseis,' Achilles said, as if he had not heard me. 'Patroclus has told me that you are the daughter of the King of Pedasus. I did not know. If I had, I swear I would not have—'

'Would not have *what*?' I cried, all my grief and rage bubbling to the surface until I could bear it no longer. 'You would not have slaughtered my father and brothers? Is that what you were going to say? You would not have killed my husband?'

'Briseis—'

'*No!*' I struck out at his face with my nails. I wanted to tear him apart. I wanted to destroy every inch of his flesh, to hurt him, if it might ease some of my pain. 'I will not hear you!'

I was beating his chest now, scratching, hammering at him, thrashing wildly like an animal in pain.

Achilles gripped my shoulders and still I thrashed out at him. He did not try to stop me.

'I did not know,' he said, in a soft voice, as I pummelled his chest with my fists, sobbing. 'I did not know, Briseis.'

I let out a cry. 'Is that your excuse? *You* killed them! No one forced you to be their executioner!'

His grip tightened upon my shoulders. 'I do what I have to,' he said, his voice tight. 'Whether because of the gods, or my fate, or the commands of my king – I must do it. From my earliest moments I have been trained to fight, told it is my duty and my destiny. I am a slave to my calling, Briseis, just as much as you are.'

I could feel myself weakening. I was so tired. My arms were feeble, my hands still beating upon his chest but hardly hurting him at all.

I looked up at him. His dark eyes were gazing down into mine.

And I did not see any hatred there. I did not see a killer.

All I saw was a man in pain.

I felt something shift in my heart – impalpable.

'I would never have wished to hurt you,' he said gently, leaning towards me, his voice straining with emotion. 'Never, Briseis. If I could take back what I did—'

'You cannot,' I whispered.

'But if I could . . . I would die to prove to you how much – how much I wish I had not—'

I felt like a spirit, drained by grief. His face was inches away from mine, his breath warm upon my face. Tears swam in my eyes.

'What I do, I have always done for greatness,' he said in a low voice. 'But perhaps there is another way.'

His hands slid from my shoulders to my waist.

As if I were in a dream, as if I were surrendering to some more-than-human force, I moved slowly towards him, all sounds silenced except the pulse of my blood in my ears. I felt the heat of him, his strong arms as they encircled me and pulled me closer. His hand was cupping the back of my head with easy strength, his lips were brushing mine, just as they had in my dream, my tears mingling upon our mouths, and then I was kissing him, insistently, desperately – because, despite everything, he was all I had left in the world. Because nothing else made sense, except the closeness of his body against mine, the warmth of his arms around me, and that we were together.

Because he was both my downfall and my destiny.

That night, I lay with Achilles.

Prayer to Apollo

Mount Ida, Overlooking the Trojan Plain

Night is falling in heaven. The storm is over, and now the heroines, queens and nymphs who make up the stars are taking up their positions, shining out in the dusk with a soft glow, like fireflies dotted over the clouds. The slopes of Mount Ida are quiet, and on the Trojan shore the only light is from the dying embers of the fires in the Greek camp and the torches of the watchmen.

All is peaceful.

Then a shout echoes across the clouds. 'Apollo! Hey, Apollo! Apparently there's a girl over here whose father thinks she's a perfect candidate to be your priestess.'

Hermes is doubled over, laughing, pointing through the gap in the clouds.

Apollo groans and tries to ignore him. He turns back to polishing his long silver bow, assiduously disregarding all Hermes' attempts to attract his attention.

The gods are lounging around Mount Ida – or some of them are, anyway. Ares, after all, is in the Trojan council drawing up the plan for the city's defences, and Aphrodite is busy keeping Paris and Helen entertained in their bedroom in Troy. The rest of the usual cast is here, though. Zeus and Hera are sitting side by side on their thrones, calm and serene, enjoying an evening drink. Apollo and his twin sister Artemis are off to the side, cleaning their bows and arrows with scrubby little bits of moonlit cloud. Athena is tending her pet owl with sips of nectar. And Hermes is perched on a tuft of cloud next to the gap that opens on to the Trojan plain, looking down and shaking with laughter.

Zeus turns to Hera.

'It's funny, isn't it,' he says in a conversational tone, 'how determined mortals are to believe that knowledge of the gods comes in a snap of the fingers? Why on earth do they think we give them such a long life, if it only took five seconds to work it all out?'

'Surely you would know,' she says shrewdly, 'since you made them so.'

Zeus looks stumped, and turns back to the gap in the clouds, in a magisterial, all-seeing way, to cover the awkward moment.

'She's very pretty, Apollo,' continues Hermes, wiping his eyes and still chuckling. 'Might be worth taking a look, even if you're not interested in the prayer.'

Athena's lip curls.

Apollo cannot pretend he hasn't been listening, as Hermes' voice is loud enough to carry all the way to the island of Lesbos if he wants it to. He looks up.

'Knew that'd get your attention.' Hermes chuckles. 'She's just your type too. Golden hair, good figure, great legs. Come over and see for yourself.'

At last, Apollo lays down the bow and gets to his feet, then walks over to the gap in the clouds and peers through. Among the tents and huts of the Greek camp, several hundred paces from the shore where the ships are drawn up, stand two small figures, outlined in the deepening shadows of night. One is an old man with a long grey beard and the white robes and headband of a priest. His hands are raised in the gesture of prayer, and he seems to be standing by an altar that is sending smoke up to heaven – his offering to the gods. The other is a beautiful young girl with curling golden hair that sends the light of the stars glinting back to Mount Ida, bronzed skin, and subtly suggestive curves beneath her tunic.

Apollo takes a good look. 'Who's the old man?' he asks, after a while. 'Not her husband?'

'Heavens, no,' says Hermes, leaning on a nearby cloud, glad – as always – to have got some attention and caused mischief into the bargain. 'Her father, I think, judging from what he's saying. I've been listening for a while – it's rather amusing, actually.'

'What's he asking for?' Apollo asks, still looking at the girl.

'To get her freed from the Greek camp. Apparently she's a Trojan, got captured or something. The old man,' he gestures down to the beach, where a leather pouch that must once have been full of gold coins is hanging limply by the old man's side, 'tried to ransom her from Agamemnon. Didn't work, though. Agamemnon took the gold off his hands, then refused to give the girl back.' Hermes rubs his chin gleefully and chuckles. 'Bet the old man didn't expect that. That girl must be pretty good in bed for Agamemnon to want to keep her.'

Apollo raises his eyebrows.

'Anyway,' Hermes continues, 'her father's determined to get her home to Larisa, so she can be initiated as your priestess. And that's what he's sacrificing to you for.'

Artemis walks over and interrupts them, peering down through the gap in the clouds. 'Isn't he a priest? The one who always makes those terribly long prayers?'

'You're right – he is,' says Apollo, in mild surprise. 'But he never mentioned he had a beautiful daughter.'

Hermes guffaws. 'Of course he didn't. He knew you'd be after her, like a hunting dog after a hare. But I guess,' he says, grinning, 'now he's in trouble he thinks it's worth the risk.'

Apollo frowns and doesn't say anything.

'So what's he asking for?' wonders Artemis, who has picked up her quiver again and is testing the sharpness of an arrow on the palm of her white hand.

'A plague on the Greeks for double-crossing him,' says Hermes, sitting back and twiddling his thumbs, his face plastered with a wide grin.

Apollo looks at him, eyebrows raised.

'Oh, you know – the usual display.' Hermes waves an indifferent hand. 'Disease. Death. Corpses piled up in heaps. He thinks that if the Greeks are punished with the plague, he'll make them realize that Agamemnon shouldn't have taken the ransom and kept his daughter, and they'll let her go free.'

'Sounds fair enough,' says Apollo, shrugging his shoulders.

Hermes grins.

Even Apollo permits himself a little smile.

'One thing, though,' says Hermes, glancing at Hera and Athena, who are both sitting bolt upright, and have clearly been listening to every word they've said. 'Just make sure you watch out for the dream team.' He jerks his head in the direction of the two goddesses. 'They won't take kindly to you sending a plague on their favourites. They're bound to interfere somehow. So watch your back, all right?'

Apollo doesn't reply. His eyes are still fixed on the golden-haired girl.

Hera and Athena are tensed, like hounds about to be set to the chase.

Then—

'Looks like we've got ourselves a job,' Apollo says finally, raising himself to stand, grasping his long silver bow and fitting an arrow to the string.

Hermes claps delightedly.

Zeus sits back and folds his hands to watch.

Hera and Athena narrow their eyes.

Artemis stands up, dips the tip of her arrow into a bowl filled with poison that has just materialized at her feet and pushes the razor-sharp arrowhead into the notch of her bow. They stand side by side at the edge of the gap in the clouds, brother and sister, and both aim their pointed arrows towards the Greek camp.

'So, brother,' Artemis asks, pulling the bowstring back to her ear, 'who first?'

Plague

Βρισηίς
Briseis, Greek Camp

The Hour of the Rising Sun

The Twenty-sixth Day of the Month of Threshing Wheat, 1250 BC

I opened my eyes. I was lying in Achilles' arms in his bed, the woollen covers tangled around our legs and a ray of early-morning sunlight falling across his chest. Patroclus' pallet was empty – he must have risen already. We were alone.

A wave of confused feelings broke over me as the memory of what we had done rushed back. Our passionate, frenzied love-making, the touch of a god on my skin. The look in Patroclus' eyes as he had told me about Pedasus. My despair; Deiope's familiar wrinkled face; the prophecy; the pain in Achilles' eyes; the relief I had felt as I fell into his arms.

I did not know what to think any more.

Was this always the way in a war?

'Briseis?'

Achilles was awake, his eyes half open.

I looked at him, my voice catching in my throat. 'Yes?'

In one swift movement he rolled over, took me into his arms and bent to kiss me, pressing down upon me. My back arched as he pulled me towards him, and I felt my spine tingle with new depths of desire, my body responding instinctively as my thoughts battled to make sense of what was happening.

'Last night,' he said, as we broke apart at last, 'last night was—'

The door to the hut banged open.

'My lord—'

Patroclus had burst into the hut, his face shining with sweat. He stopped short when he saw us together. Then his cheeks coloured scarlet. 'Oh.'

Achilles glanced at him. 'Can it wait, Patroclus?'

Patroclus shook his head. 'No,' he said tensely. 'It can't.'

Achilles leant over to kiss me, pushed back the covers and stood up. 'So what is it?' he asked, throwing a tunic over his head, striding to the clay wash-jug and splashing his face with water. 'Something important, I hope.'

'There has been an outbreak of plague in the camp,' Patroclus said. 'The soldiers are dying. Their bodies are heaped in piles on the beach, their skin marked all over with blistering red boils. They are burning them as fast as they can, but it is not fast enough. The healer Machaon says he has never seen a plague catch so quickly, and that it must have been sent by a god to cause so much destruction so fast.' He took a deep breath. 'It seems the whole army will go down if we cannot stop it soon, and you know as well as I that King Agamemnon will be more afraid for himself than for the men.'

Achilles stood up straight, linen towel in hand. 'The whole army?' he asked.

Patroclus capitalized on his advantage. 'Even you cannot sack Troy alone, and you know it,' he said. Achilles frowned slightly, but Patroclus pushed on: 'You need your men behind you. We must act, and quickly.'

Both were quiet for a moment. Then Achilles turned. 'You are right,' he said. 'Agamemnon is a coward, and if he will not act, I shall. I'll call the assembly. Patroclus, go to the heralds and tell them to summon the army.'

Patroclus strode to the door.

'Briseis.' He walked to the bed where I was still lying. 'I wish I did not have to leave you,' he said in a low voice.

'I will be here when you return.'

The corners of his mouth turned up as he kissed me again.

'Tell me one thing,' I said, as we broke apart. 'Before you go.'

He crouched beside me and took my hand. 'Anything.'

I took a deep breath. 'If you had known, would it have made any difference?'

He gazed at me, silent. He did not need to ask what I meant.

'Even if you had refused to go to Pedasus,' I continued slowly, 'Agamemnon would still have sent his troops. My husband and father and brothers,' I struggled to control my voice, 'would still have been killed.'

He bowed his head. 'That is true.'

'Why did you come to Troy?' I said, very softly.

Achilles was silent for a long time. 'I am a man, and the son of a lord of Greece,' he said at last. 'I was born to deeds of war. My destiny from the gods, and my orders from the king, have always been to fight.' He leant towards me and pressed my hand. 'You should know, Briseis,' he said, 'that if the scales of Zeus had landed another way, your father and brothers would have dealt the same fate to me.'

I looked into his face. I remembered the glint of war in Mynes' eyes the night that Lyrnessus had been sacked. I remembered my brothers playing with wooden swords in the sandy courtyard of Pedasus, taught to fight almost as soon as they had learnt to walk. My father had always been a warlike man, and I remembered how I had sat on his lap as a child and thrilled to hear his stories of armies marching over the plain with the dust rising at their feet, like a storm, and of warriors felled with sharp-tipped bronze.

But I had not thought that it could be real.

Now the realization that my father, my brothers, Mynes were warriors born – that, to some men, they had even been an *enemy*, as much as Achilles had been an enemy to them – crashed down upon me, like a wall of well-built stone.

And if things had been different, and the Trojans had invaded Greece, it would have been Greek mothers and wives mourning the men they loved, just as I mourned the men I had lost.

I gazed down at the coverlet, where a ray of sunlight was stitching the soft-woven wool with patches of gold. At last I thought I understood what Mynes had meant when he had made me promise to learn to live without him that fateful night.

We mortals were all the same: united by our anger and our grief, and, more than anything, our certainty that we were different.

But it did not have to be that way.

'Can you forgive me, Briseis?'

I looked up into the face of Achilles, and I felt the last shred of my hatred and doubt dissolve in his eyes, which reflected mine.

'Yes,' I said at last. 'Yes. I forgive you.'

Χρυσηίς
Krisayis, Greek Camp

The Hour of the Middle of the Day

The Twenty-sixth Day of the Month of Threshing Wheat, 1250 BC

I had spent the night begging my father to allow me to remain in the camp of the Greeks as the Trojans' spy; or, at the very least, first to return to Troy and tell the king myself what I had heard. Nothing had worked. My father had returned from King Agamemnon's theft of his ransom all the more determined to deliver me to the temple in Larisa.

As night fell and the stars rose in the heavens, watching my plight, he had forced me to stand beside him as he prayed to the gods and asked for a plague on the Greeks to force them to send me home.

So there I was, the following day, walking behind my father, like a convict to their judgement, into the assembly-place of the Greek camp.

Soldiers streamed around us into the open space, asking each other what was happening. Beneath the noise, I could make out from the huts and tents surrounding us the muffled shouts and cries of the victims of the terrible plague that had unexpectedly struck the camp that night, all – as my father had told me with a dreadful smile – on my own behalf. Healers and slaves were running across the assembly-place, carrying towels and hot water, and in the distance, on the other side of the camp, a large fire burnt to consume the dead. Even now the bodies of the victims of the plague were rattling past us, their skin pockmarked, their eyes wide and staring, heaped on the carts that had carried treasure from the cities the Greeks sacked.

A long, single trumpet call sounded over the noise of the gathering army, and my father stopped, holding my wrist with one hand, as if I would run away, forgetting that I had nowhere to run to.

One of the generals, sitting on a podium at the other end of the assembly to the right of King Agamemnon, who was, as usual, couched upon his throne, had raised himself from his seat. I could just make out a lean, muscled frame, long blond hair, and armour so brilliant it seemed to be the sun itself, not merely its reflection. The name rippled through the crowd, like the wind through the leaves of an oak tree: 'Achilles! It's Achilles!'

Achilles held out a hand, and the whispering died. All the soldiers were now gazing up at him with an expression of something approaching reverence on their scarred, leathery faces.

'Brothers,' he said, and everyone fell quiet. 'Last night a plague broke out in this camp.' He looked around the crowd, then to the carts that were trundling away from the assembly-place towards the fire. 'It has already taken many of our men. If we let it continue, our army will be gone before we have even left the gates of the camp to attack Troy. Are we to be struck down after our journey across the ocean, through wind and rain, after we evaded the curse of the gods at Aulis, only to die here because we are too afraid to supplicate the gods?'

The men were shaking their heads and muttering. Some called, 'We're not cowards!' or, 'Tell us what to do, Achilles, we'll stand by your side!'

Most, however, were less convinced. 'What if the gods are against us?' I heard some ask. 'Troy cannot be sacked, and here's the proof!'

Achilles smiled in a self-assured way and waved his hand again for silence. 'Men,' he said reprovingly, 'brothers! Do not fear the gods!' He spread his arms wide. 'The gods favour the Greeks,' he said. 'They favour their chosen sons. What we need,' and he scanned the crowd, 'is a priest, skilled in the arts of reading dreams, who can tell us why Apollo sent this plague upon us. Then, once we know what we have done to offend him, we can make a sacrifice and win his favour again. Do not be afraid, brothers: I, of all people, understand the gods.'

I frowned. Here was that Apollo again, the one Odysseus had talked of. Yet what kind of god was this? Why would the Greeks' own god, the one they seemed to worship as a prophecy-giver, punish them, and with such a terrible plague, when they did not even know what they had done wrong? I glanced at my father to see if he had noticed, but he was looking straight ahead.

'One small error corrected,' Achilles continued, 'whatever that error may be, and you will be back, fighting for Troy and all her treasures. And it is written in the stars that the city *will* fall – and that *you* will be the ones to take it!'

The men roared. They were shouting his name now in a rhythmic chant, shaking their spears up and down in the air.

Achilles was standing as still as a monument, holding his spear up against the sky.

Agamemnon, on the other hand, wore an expression of pure distaste. It seemed he was not enjoying himself as much as Achilles was.

But then something terrible happened. My father – my own father, who should have known that this was the last thing in all the world that I wished him to do – shouted over the crowd, his white priest's robes conspicuous amid the dark leather and bronze of the soldiers' armour and shields.

'I am the High Priest of the Great God Apulunas, god of the Trojans and protector of Troy. And it is the anger of our gods, the true gods of Ida, not yours, that has brought this plague upon you,' he called, his voice loud and clear. Everyone ceased their shouting and turned to look at him.

I could feel my face burning with anger by his side. How could he be doing this? How *could* he?

'You must consider, before I speak,' my father went on, in a ringing voice, 'that what I say may not be pleasing to all who hear it. I may anger a powerful ruler, and a king's anger is worse than that of a lesser man, since he has the power to fulfil his threats. Promise, then, that you will protect me, if I tell the secrets of our gods.'

Achilles bowed. 'I will, old priest,' he said. 'No one will lay his hands on you while I live – not even Agamemnon.'

My father bowed back, ignoring the glare of mixed rage and contempt that King Agamemnon was giving him. 'Know, then, that the reason the Great God has sent this plague upon you is not for any error on your part or that of the army. It is because Agamemnon, King of the Greeks, dishonoured me.'

I buried my face in my hands, wishing I could shout aloud or weep – which, I did not know. I could not listen. I could not be forced to watch my father destroy my future and Troy's last hope before my very eyes.

'You all must know,' he continued, into the hushed silence of the assembly, as the soldiers around him backed away from us, making a space around us in the crowd, 'that I serve King Priam of Troy. There was a reason I came to the Greek camp last night with King Priam's ambassadors. It is my daughter.'

I flushed even more deeply and did not remove my hands from my face.

'My daughter was captured by your men at the same time as they killed Prince Troilus. When I found out that she was still alive, naturally I wished to protect her. I therefore came to the Greek camp with twice her worth in gold, and offered it to King Agamemnon in exchange for her safety, and in the name of the Great God Apulunas, mightiest of our gods, whose priestess my daughter is destined to be. Your king took the gold but now refuses my daughter her freedom. In so doing he insults me and my god.'

I was looking into the darkness behind my fingers, trying to pretend this was not happening, but, still, my father's words bored into my ears, like a hoe digging into freshly ploughed earth.

'And now you wonder that the Great God has sent a plague on your army,' my father finished in the confident tone that I knew so well. 'He heard my appeal against the disrespect shown by your king for the proper dealings between kings and men. And he will continue to send his arrows down on the Greek camp until you right Agamemnon's wrong. Send my daughter back to her home in Larisa and make there a sacrifice of a hundred oxen in honour of our god. There is no other way to appease him.'

He finished speaking and there was silence around us. I peered from behind my hands, and saw King Agamemnon rise from his seat. 'You speak, Polydamas, as if it were a great gift to the Greeks that you came to us with your pouch of paltry gold,' he sneered, as he paced around the podium. 'But I do not see the benefit for us.' He waved his hand to the crowd. 'And certainly,' he said, approaching the front of the podium, 'I do not need to be accused by a jumped-up Trojan like you.'

My father's mouth was set in a firm line.

'Now, as for your daughter, Krisayis,' King Agamemnon leered, 'now that I understand. She's a pretty little thing. I've enjoyed having her with me. Enjoyed her even more than my wife Clytemnestra, in fact – if you know what I mean.'

The men guffawed and nudged each other, winking.

I stared hard at my feet, trying to ignore the men pointing at me, laughing.

'But,' Agamemnon said, in a loud voice, holding up his hand to stop the men's whistles and cheers, 'I have resolved to give her back, in spite of this. I will fit out a ship to escort her to her home in Larisa this very day. I will even,' he said, giving a mock bow to my father, 'grant you safe passage back to Troy with my heralds, priest, to ensure you come to no harm. Let none of you say that Agamemnon is not a magnanimous king. I have one condition, however.' He paused and looked around at the gathered men before him. 'It simply would not be right for me to be deprived of *my* prize when you all have yours,' he said, and his voice was as smooth as the finest first-pressed oil. 'After all, I am your king.'

Most of the men in the crowd nodded. It was a simple equation. Kings had to have more because more things meant more glory, and glory was the stronghold of power. And the men knew they needed a powerful king if they were to succeed.

'So my condition is this: find a suitable prize for me in return, and I will gladly send the girl back to her home, make the sacrifice this priest demands and end this plague.'

He settled back in his seat with an air of self-satisfaction.

But then Achilles leapt to his feet. 'And how are we to find a prize for you, glorious son of Atreus, when the prizes from the pillage of the cities have already been handed out?' he asked. 'Why do you not, for once, listen to sense rather than your greed? You know that there is not a single prize left from the sack of the cities of the Troad. The men have been given their reward, and we cannot take it back. Send this girl back in obedience to the god's command, and I promise you, when we sack

Troy – which we *will* do – you shall receive three and four times the amount we could ever give you now.'

The men began to cheer again, but Agamemnon stood up, laughing, and raised his hand for silence. They were instantly quelled.

'Oh, Achilles,' he said, pretending to wipe away a tear, 'you really do amuse me. Did you honestly think that would work?' He clapped Achilles on the shoulder. 'Do you intend to sit here by the ships enjoying your lovely prize, the beautiful Briseis, while I give up mine?' He laughed again and shook his head. 'No, no – we cannot have that. In fact,' he said, stroking his beard and walking over to the other end of the podium, then turning to look back at Achilles, 'I have just had an idea – an inspiration from the gods, let us say. What better way to prove your loyalty to your king and your devotion to this cause than to give up *your* prize?'

He paced back around the platform and smiled mockingly at Achilles. 'Since the gods are taking lovely Krisayis away from me, I shall make a visit to your hut, Achilles, and have *your* prize, the beautiful Briseis, for myself.'

With a single movement, Achilles drew his sword. Before anyone had seen what he was doing, and before the king's bodyguards could run up on to the stage to protect him, he had placed the tip of his gleaming blade at Agamemnon's throat. His face pressed right up against Agamemnon's, he hissed, in a deadly whisper, 'Say that again, Agamemnon, and you will feel my sword in your throat before you've had time to curse the gods that you were ever *born*.'

Agamemnon had gone pale.

His bodyguards had frozen, none of them a match for the great Achilles.

The two men stood there, motionless: Agamemnon, his face twisted with terror, and Achilles, his sword-tip held to the king's neck, the blade glinting in the sunlight.

There was a long pause as everyone stared at Achilles' blade, and Achilles stared into Agamemnon's frightened eyes.

Then I gasped. The air around Achilles had begun to shimmer. It was as if heat were rising from the ground, blurring the air, and as the air moved and turned solid it made a sound – an unearthly sound, like wind blowing through water or singing against stone.

'A god!' I heard the soldiers around me whisper, some of them touching their fingers together in the sign of the gods, others gazing up at the sky. 'Olympus save us, it must be a god!'

I felt a shiver run through me as Achilles paused, as if listening to the strange music that was coming from the air. Then, slowly, he sheathed his sword and stepped away from Agamemnon, breathing hard, his hand still on the hilt, like a threat.

The air ceased to shimmer.

My heart was hammering in my chest.

'You're a coward, Agamemnon,' Achilles spat. 'A damned, drunken coward. I detest you. Was it for this you came to Troy – to sit comfortably in your tent, too afraid to fight, risking the lives of your men in battle and, when they return from the fight, to steal their prizes for yourself? Is this what you call war? Because it sounds to me like plain, simple *thievery*!'

Agamemnon was visibly shaking with a mixture of rage and fear.

'This is what I'll tell you,' Achilles said, stepping closer and taking him by the scruff of his tunic, 'and you had better listen closely if you wish to see the light tomorrow. Since you are foolish enough to take Briseis away from me, hear the cost of what you've done.'

He let Agamemnon go. The king stumbled, gasping and clutching at his throat. 'You can take the girl,' Achilles spat. 'I shall not prevent it, nor will you die at my hand this day, since the goddess Athena herself has only now told me I must release her to you, and I should be a fool to disobey the gods' commands. But if you think I am going to fight for you after this insult, then *you* are grossly mistaken.'

Achilles turned to face the army. 'I have no quarrel with the Trojans – what have they done to wrong me? No, Agamemnon. My quarrel is with you, for taking away my prize, simply to satisfy your greed.' He was bellowing now, his voice cracking with the strain of his emotion.

He drew his sword again and held it up to the sky, his huge hand shaking in his anger. 'And I swear by this sword and by almighty Zeus, who governs the heavens and upholds the rights of the leaders of men, that some day soon, when the sons of the Greeks are laid low at Hector's hands, you will have need of me. And then, Agamemnon, you will regret that you took away my woman, my prize and my honour.'

As he finished speaking, Achilles dashed his sword to the ground, so hard that the blade drove through the platform and into the sand, its hilt quivering violently. Then he leapt from the stage and stormed through the crowd, which parted in silence to let him go.

A low murmur broke out as soon as Achilles had left the assembly-place.

King Agamemnon was straightening his tunic and trying to regain his composure, and the crowd began to disperse to their various huts.

I stared at my father, hardly able to take in all that had happened. *Achilles . . . a god . . . And I am to go to Larisa . . .*

'Come,' my father said firmly. 'Come, Krisayis. We must find a ship to take you home.'

Taking Leave

Βρισηίς
Briseis, Greek Camp

The Hour of Offerings

The Twenty-sixth Day of the Month of Threshing Wheat, 1250 BC

Several hours later and I was still lying on Achilles' bed, thinking back to what had happened.

I lay with him, I thought. *I lay with Achilles.*

The words did not sound strange. They sounded as they were: the making and unmaking of my fate.

And what of my family – my father, my brothers? A small voice said, in the back of my mind, *What of Mynes?*

My heart beat a little faster as I put the question to myself.

Have I done wrong?

Have I forgotten them?

There was a moment as I lay there, testing the words upon myself.

But then I shook my head.

No. Mynes will always be there. But I promised him that I would forget what I could never get back until we can be together again. I promised to protect myself and not to grieve.

In that, I have done what he asked of me.

And Mynes would be waiting for me in the Underworld. He would wait until I joined him and we could be together always.

But not yet. Not yet.

Suddenly the door to the hut crashed open so loudly that I started, clutching at the covers. I saw Achilles enter, closely followed by Patroclus.

'You must calm yourself,' Patroclus was saying, in a tense voice. 'It is not—'

But Achilles was not listening. He had picked up the rough wood table, complete with the dishes from last night's meal and, with a single movement, hurled it against the fir-beams. It gave a sickening crunch and fell to the floor in splinters.

Patroclus approached him. 'Achilles, wait—'

But Achilles was in a worse rage than I had ever seen him. He seemed hardly capable of listening. Lifting the gorgeous lyre, he threw it, too, across the room, shattering it with an ear-splitting twang of wood and string. The chairs went next, the chest of clothes, the oil-lamps – anything he could lay his hands on.

I froze rigid to the bed, watching in terror as Achilles destroyed everything in the hut with a single touch.

'Achilles – you must see reason—'

Achilles turned on Patroclus with a furious glare that would have made a lesser man quake. 'Reason?' he thundered, so loudly that I could feel his words vibrating in my chest. 'You talk *reason* – to me? Try talking reason to that thieving, back-stabbing, cowardly *dog* of a king!'

He seized a nearby helmet by the crest and slung it against the door, which smashed shut, making the stakes of the walls shudder.

'What happened?' I asked, my eyes wide.

Achilles did not answer. He was standing still now in the centre of the room, his chest heaving with rage, his dark eyes burning, looking around for something else to vent his anger on.

'King Agamemnon is demanding that Achilles hand you over to him,' Patroclus said, in an undertone, keeping his eyes fixed on Achilles.

I stared. 'Why?'

Patroclus kept his voice even. 'Because Apollo's terms for ending the plague is the surrender of Agamemnon's prize – another Trojan slave-girl, by the name of Krisayis. King Agamemnon seemed to feel he needed compensation, and, well, he is resolved on you. Achilles claims,' he glanced over at Achilles, 'that the goddess Athena appeared to him in the assembly to warn him against angering Agamemnon and so, he says, he is forbidden to refuse Agamemnon's demand.'

I paused to take in what he had just said. 'I have to *leave*?' I asked.

Patroclus nodded.

'I must leave Achilles, and go to Agamemnon?'

Patroclus nodded again.

I felt a torrent of despair rush through me, like a mountain river in spate. 'But I cannot go!' I exclaimed in horror. 'I cannot leave you – not now! Achilles, tell him I cannot go!'

Achilles hardly heard me. He was pacing the hut, blind with fury, his fists clenched, the pulse racing at his temple.

'How dare that spineless swine try to teach me a lesson? How dare he?' Achilles roared, swinging a fist into the wash-jug and sending it flying to the ground. 'Who does he think he is? Zeus himself? To have the nerve to try to tell *me* what to do! I am the son of Thetis! I am the greatest fighter in the whole Greek army – the greatest there has ever been! And he thinks he can humiliate me – in front of everyone! He thinks he can take away the only –' his voice grew thick and harsh, and he took a spear that was lying on the ground and threw it, fast as a bolt of lightning, into one of the fir-beams where it lodged deep, shaft quivering '– the only woman I've ever—' He broke off, breathing heavily. 'I swear it, if it were not for Athena's command, I should cut out his coward's heart and feed it to the dogs!'

I slipped from the bed, wrapped a fine-spun robe around my shoulders and walked over to Achilles. 'Do you have to obey the gods?' I said. 'Did you not tell me that you make your fate yourself?'

Achilles groaned. 'My mother told me this would happen. She said that you would be taken from me, and that I should let it happen, for it would be the gods' will and the command of Zeus.' He ran his hands through his hair. 'Why?' he shouted, towards the sky. 'Why must I choose?'

There was a silence. Then, distantly, but growing ever clearer, the faint sound of voices floated to us on the breeze.

'Agamemnon's heralds,' Patroclus said. 'They are coming.'

I felt the panic rising in my chest. 'Don't leave me, Achilles. I cannot bear to be alone again.'

He drew me towards him and held me to him. 'You will never be alone,' he said passionately. 'You will never be alone, Briseis.'

He bent to turn my chin up to him. 'I will send Patroclus to you,' he said. 'He will make sure that swine of a king is treating you well. You can trust him to send messages to me.'

A single tear rolled down my cheek. 'Achilles, I – I don't think I can stand—'

'Talthybius and Eurybates are outside, Achilles,' Patroclus said abruptly, and he pushed open the door.

The sound of voices was louder now, and accompanied by the crunching of sandals on sand.

Without warning, Achilles pulled me towards him and kissed me, deeply, urgently, one hand against the small of my back, pressing me into his body, his mouth so hard on mine that I could hardly breathe.

Then he let go and turned away without a word.

Agamemnon's two heralds were standing outside on the seashore, each of them carrying the golden messenger's rod and looking distinctly uncomfortable.

There was a tense silence as Achilles stepped out of the hut.

'There is no need to be afraid, Talthybius,' I heard Achilles say shortly. 'I do not blame you – it is Agamemnon who shall have to answer for this, not his heralds.'

They took a tentative step forwards, clearly still afraid of Achilles and what he might do.

'Hand her over, Patroclus,' Achilles said, and his voice broke. He turned away as Patroclus led me through the door and over to the heralds.

I glanced at Achilles, my eyes brimming with tears, my mouth framing a plea, a protest, but his back was to me.

Patroclus handed me to them, then stepped back. He was still avoiding my gaze.

'Well – if that is all – we shall not trouble you any further, Achilles,' Eurybates said awkwardly.

They turned to lead me away to Agamemnon's tent.

I looked back. Patroclus and Achilles were standing before the hut,

Patroclus watching me with a strange expression on his face, Achilles turned aside, looking out towards the sea.

It was the last time I saw Patroclus and Achilles together alive.

Χρυσηίς
Krisayis, Greek Camp

The Hour of Prayer

The Twenty-sixth Day of the Month of Threshing Wheat, 1250 BC

I was following my father to the beaked ships of the Greeks, two guards flanking me on either side, my thoughts filled with despair, when I saw her. Dark-haired and pale-skinned, Briseis was being led from Achilles' hut by the heralds of the Greeks, and they were approaching us, not twenty paces away. My heart leapt.

Perhaps there was one last chance for Troy, after all.

I stopped where I was.

'What are you doing?' one of the guards beside me asked roughly. 'We're meant to be going to the ships. No stopping on the way. That's the king's order.'

I pointed down to my feet. 'My sandal has come untied.'

The guard exchanged a look with his companion.

The other guard shrugged his shoulders. 'Women . . .'

I took this as assent and crouched to the ground. As the guards turned away to talk to each other, I risked glancing up. In a single, heart-stopping moment I saw that Briseis was only feet away from me.

The heralds who were leading her had stopped to talk to my guards. Reaching out, I caught at her cloak and pulled at it with all my strength.

The clasp broke and the cloak fell to the ground at Briseis' heels. She turned. 'What—'

I placed a finger to my lips, and her eyes widened as she caught sight of me.

'You!' she whispered, bending down as if to pick up the cloak. 'What are you doing here? I was told you were on a ship, on your way home!'

I spoke quickly, my voice low. 'I will be soon. Briseis, I have to warn you before I leave. The Greeks have been given a prophecy that Troy will fall. I do not know if it is true or not, but if it is . . . you are the only one left in the Greek camp who can help to prevent it.' I paused, gazing into her eyes, which were round with fear. 'You have to be the one to kill Achilles. You and I are the only ones who know his secret, and when I am sent to Larisa—'

'Krisayis?'

It was my father's voice, and it was biting with impatience.

'Promise me,' I said in a rush. 'Promise me you will do your utmost to ensure Achilles dies so that Troy is saved.'

Her face was oddly pale. She shook her head. 'No.' She took a deep breath. 'No. I cannot.'

'*Krisayis!*'

'But—'

Hands grasped at my shoulders and pulled me up to stand. 'That's enough. No more delays.'

I turned and stared back at the girl as the guards half marched, half dragged me away towards the line of the breaking sea, but she did not meet my eyes. I watched with a sense of desperation as she straightened her back, then began to walk towards King Agamemnon's tent, like a soldier marching to battle, the heralds at her sides.

My last hope, gone.

I stared at her. How could I trust her to come to her senses and do what she had to for Troy? And why – *why* – had she suddenly changed her mind? Had she not said that Achilles had killed those she loved most? Why, by all the gods, did she not wish him destroyed?

Then I forced myself to look away. There was only one more thing I could do.

'Father?'

I tried to get free so I could talk to him, but the guards tightened their grip upon my shoulders as we walked.

'I am allowed to talk to my own father,' I said pointedly.

They did not release me.

'Father, I have something I must tell you. In private.'

My father did not turn. 'Whatever you have to say can wait until I come to see you in Larisa.'

I struggled against the guards, but their grip was like metal against my skin. 'It cannot wait!' I gasped, as one of the guards dug his fingers into my collarbone and pain ripped across my chest. 'It is about the fall of Troy!' I shouted to him, throwing caution to the winds. 'I must return to the city and tell the king myself!'

At last, my father turned to me, his eyes fixed upon mine, his expression unreadable. 'King Priam has given orders that you are not to return to Troy. He is most displeased at the death of his son in defiance of his command, and he holds you in part accountable for it.'

I gasped. 'No! He cannot!'

We had reached the ships now, their prows soaring high into the sky above us, like immense trees in a forest, their hulls creaking with the ebb and flow of the waves. Our eyes locked, and I tried to beg him, without words, to listen to what I was trying to tell him.

'Farewell, daughter,' my father said, turning from me, his head bowed.

'No!' I kicked and struggled against the guards, but they pushed me easily on to the ladder that leant against the ship's hull and almost lifted me up it and on to the deck. 'No! Father—'

But my words were drowned in the snapping of the sail as it unfurled into the wind, and my father did not hear me.

Goddesses

Mount Ida, Overlooking the Trojan Plain

At least someone is smiling as Krisayis is dragged away from the shores of Troy. In the skies above, seated on the peak of Mount Ida, Hera and Athena are watching the scene with undisguised pleasure. It is a clear afternoon – Hera has made sure of that – and the sun moving to the horizon in the west is a pale gold, setting the sea glimmering in tones of yellow and green-blue, and glinting off Krisayis' golden hair.

They both watch as the sails of the ship are hoisted, white like a bird's wings upon the sea, and the prow ploughs into the furrow of the sea. Soon the vessel is rounding the headland of the Trojan bay.

It is Athena who breaks the silence at last. 'It worked,' she says, with a smile.

Hera nods. 'Yes. It did.'

They exchange a knowing look. 'Of course, I expected Agamemnon to steal the treasure,' Athena continues, in a conversational tone. 'He probably would have done it without my help. But who would have thought Krisayis would be so easy to get rid of after that?'

Hera smiles and leans back on her throne. 'Apollo played right into our hands,' she says, with smug satisfaction. 'What fools he and his sister are. I imagine they didn't consider for a second that we might actually want her gone, what with all the trouble she was causing, passing information to the Trojans.' She turns to Athena with approval. 'You played your part well last night.'

Athena shrugs her shoulders. 'It wasn't hard to pretend to be annoyed with them. Hermes is getting my back up half the time anyway.'

Hera gives a sympathetic sigh. 'Yes, I know. He does tend to do that.' She turns to the south, towards the little town of Larisa. 'The question is,' she continues, with a slight frown, 'how we are going to keep Krisayis there, once she arrives.'

'You think she won't stay?'

Hera gives a grim laugh. 'No. She will do everything she can to escape, so she can tell the Trojans what she has found out about Achilles. And we can't have that – can we?'

Athena shakes her head. 'No. We can't.'

Hera taps her fingers against her olive-skinned thigh. 'I've been thinking,' she says at last. 'You saw how taken Apollo was with her last night, I'm sure.'

'Has there ever been a time he has not been after some mortal or other?'

'Well, quite.' Hera smiles. 'I was thinking, however, that perhaps this time we might want to encourage his suit. Give him a little nudge in the right direction. To keep Krisayis distracted, so to speak.'

Athena frowns slightly. 'What about Cassandra?'

Hera waves a hand in a regal gesture. 'She was a princess. When did you last hear of a priest's daughter refusing a god?'

'Well, if you're sure . . .' Athena turns to gaze at the little temple of Apollo in Larisa, set by the shining azure shore of the sea, the blue smoke of sacrifice curling up to the sky from its altar. She looks back at Hera. 'So, which of us should be the one to do it?'

The corners of Hera's mouth turn up in a smile. 'Me, I think,' she says. 'Apollo would never listen to you.'

Athena gives a wry smirk. 'I'll take that as a compliment.'

And with that, Hera stands gracefully from her throne and wafts away towards Apollo's palace.

PART III

Changing Camps

Βρισηίς
Briseis, Greek Camp

The Hour of the Evening Meal

The Twenty-sixth Day of the Month of Threshing Wheat, 1250 BC

The walk to Agamemnon's tent was short enough, though every step I took away from Achilles' hut felt like a thousand paces across the world, an interminable distance, and every grain of sand along the shore was marked by one of my tears.

Talthybius drew aside the flap and made me a mock bow. 'After you, Princess,' he said, pushing me inside.

Agamemnon was sitting in his chamber on a throne covered with richly woven cloth and so laden with cushions that there was hardly room for him. Others of the Greek leaders were lying on couches beside him or sitting on carved stools around a large, circular table, laughing and pulling at half-naked Trojan slave-girls. Agamemnon was drinking deep from a gem-encrusted goblet as we came in, and hardly noticed us amid all the noise until Eurybates cleared his throat loudly.

'Ah, Eurybates!' he said, smacking his lips, his words slurring into each other slightly. He hiccuped. 'And Talthybius. You've brought the girl. Excellent.'

Talthybius prodded me in the back with one bony finger and hissed in my ear, 'Bow to the king!'

As I inclined my head, Agamemnon let out a low chuckle and shifted himself slowly forwards on his throne. He peered at me, short-sighted little eyes squinting in the flesh of his once-handsome face, now turned old and flaccid by too much drink and too little fighting. The foul smell of him wafted over me.

'She *is* pretty,' he said, with a belch, and patted his bulging stomach as the Greek lords around him tittered. 'I'll give Achilles that – she's damned pretty. Well, it looks like we did a good bit of business today, did we not, men?'

The lords – those who were not out cold on the floor with drink, or occupied with the Trojan girls – cheered and held up their goblets. 'To King Agamemnon – leader of men!' one shouted, and he raised his goblet, slopping wine all over the floor as he did so.

'King Agamemnon!' the others mumbled, and the room was quiet as the men drank deeply.

'Well,' said Agamemnon, heaving himself up from his seat with difficulty, 'I think I shall retire to bed. At least I'll have a new companion to keep me warm tonight – not like Achilles.' He grinned around at his generals, lapping up their sycophantic laughter, like an overfed dog.

'He only has Patroclus now!' shouted one of the lords, and the others dissolved into howls of laughter and jeers.

'I've always wondered what they got up to, shut away in their hut!'

One of the lords guffawed. 'Why else d'you think he brought him to Troy?'

'And why d'you think he doesn't let Patroclus fight?' another cut across him. 'Scared of losing his pretty-boy, isn't he?'

'*Enough!*' A white-haired lord had stood up, his aged limbs trembling with silent anger. His bright blue eyes seemed to spark with rage. 'That is *enough*. How are we ever to win this god-forsaken war if we cannot refrain from tearing apart our own army with slander?'

But the men were not listening. The old lord looked at Agamemnon in outraged appeal.

Agamemnon's lips still twitched as he held up his hand. 'You heard Nestor. Settle down. It's not our business what Achilles and Patroclus get up to in that hut of his.' He smirked, and several of the lords snorted into their goblets.

Nestor looked as if he wished to say more, but knew better than to try.

'And now,' Agamemnon said, lifting up his long tunic and stepping down from the platform, 'to bed.'

He held out his hand, heavy with rings, to me, and I took it, eyes downcast, trying not to look at his flaccid face and thick lips.

His grin widened.

Agamemnon lifted the curtain to his sleeping chamber and stepped inside, grunting as he heaved his massive rear on to the pile of cushions and woven blankets that was his bed.

I moved slowly in behind him. The room was large and spacious, filled with rich tapestries and carved tables beside the bed bearing golden goblets with the dregs of wine. I hesitated by the entrance.

'Come,' the king said, leering at me and patting the covers beside him. 'Come, join me.'

He was untying the silver-studded belt around his fat paunch as he spoke.

I caught another waft of the sour smell of him as he pulled his tunic up and over his head, revealing a pale flabby chest and a belly like the gut of an old pig.

I clenched my fists. 'I would rather not, my lord.'

His leer disappeared, and his small eyes narrowed. 'It does not matter what you want, girl, it matters what *I* want. I order you to come here.'

I held my ground. 'Believe me, if you knew what it would cost you, you would think differently.'

His eyes narrowed further until they were small slits in his face. 'What are you talking about, slave?' he snapped. 'You are my property, you belong to me. You are mine to do with as I please.'

I bowed my head. 'I am your slave now.' I paused, fingers trembling. I *would* not lie with this foul king of the Greeks, no matter what it cost me. 'But I was also the slave of Achilles.'

He sneered at me. 'Not any more.'

I nodded, praying that I was saying the right thing. 'But Achilles seems not to think so. He still seems to think I belong to him by right of conquest, though he has been forced to give me up.'

'And why would I care?'

I took a deep breath. 'Do you think Achilles is a man who is used to sharing? What do you think he will do when I tell him that you lay with me, the slave he still believes is his property, and his alone?' I swallowed. 'Do you truly think he will hold back from killing you this time?'

I let the words hang in the air. Agamemnon's eyes widened in surprise, then narrowed again in anger.

Moments passed. I could almost see the emotions flickering across Agamemnon's face – fear, defiance, then fear again – as he considered what I had said.

'Very well,' he said at last, flicking his ringed fingers at me in a dismissive gesture, his face a mask of calm, though I could see his chest trembling with the petulant anger of a king unaccustomed to denial. 'Very well. Get out of my chambers, slave.' He sneered the word as he heaved himself on to the bed. 'And tell the guards to have Diomedes send in the girl from Thebe he was playing with.' He turned away from me. 'I do not want a woman Achilles enjoyed dirtying my bed, in any case.'

I bowed my head and backed from the room as quickly as I could. 'Yes, my lord.'

Χρυσηΐς
Krisayis, Larisa

The Hour of Daybreak

The Twenty-seventh Day of the Month of Threshing Wheat, 1250 BC

The journey to Larisa took half a day. We had arrived just as the sun disappeared behind the horizon to dip into the sea and the evening breeze was blowing gently through the leaves of the olive trees. Lycaon, the priest who tended the temple of Apulunas at Larisa in my father's place, had welcomed me and taken me to our old stone hut by the sanctuary to sleep.

But I could not sleep.

I was needed in Troy. And now I was at least half a day's ride from the city with only nine days remaining until my initiation, by which time Achilles might already have killed Prince Hector and sacked Troy.

As Night began to pull her dark cloak from the sky and Dawn brushed her rosy fingertips over the trees in the forest outside, I drew back the rugs and fleeces on my bed and crept around the hut in the half-darkness, gathering my robes. I had made my decision. I could not let my father stop me, even though I knew he meant well, that he wanted to save me. Not when the fate of our people was at stake.

I would escape to Troy and tell King Priam myself how to kill Achilles.

It did not take me long to gather my few possessions. I swung my travelling cloak around my shoulders, glanced back at the small room, then opened the door and moved quietly outside.

Birds were calling to each other in the trees, and I was glad of their chatter as it covered the sound of my footsteps on the dried pine needles that lay scattered on the forest floor. I did not know how early Lycaon would rise from his bed, and I could not afford to be heard. The temple grounds seemed quiet, however, the sounds of birdsong mingling with the faint lapping of the sea against the shore of the bay.

I let out a breath as I reached the beaten-earth path that wound through the trees. I had known of this hunter's track to Lycaon's farmhouse since my childhood – how many times had I visited Lycaon and his wife, Eurycleia? – but it had been five years since I had been in Larisa.

Fortunately, someone – one of the hunters, no doubt – had been keeping the path clear, for the ferns and brambles were beaten back neatly at the edges, and the branches of trees that had fallen across the path had been cut to allow passage. I was lucky that it was still passable, for much of the forest seemed to have become more overgrown in the time I had been in Troy.

Smiling to myself, I lengthened my stride.

Lycaon's farm was a straggling cluster of buildings made of dark grey stone, set on top of a small hill that looked out over the still-dark sea to the west. Pigs grubbed around in a pen by the gate to the farm, and Lycaon's hunting dog, Dromas, was sleeping on the porch. His black fur was patched with white around the jaws now, and he opened a sleepy eye at me as I undid the latch on the picket gate as slowly and quietly as I could.

'Hush, Dromas,' I said, refastening the gate and hurrying over to scratch him behind the ears. 'Hush, it's me, Krisayis. You remember me, don't you?'

The dog sniffed at the hem of my robes, considering me. He gave a soft sigh as I started to scratch him in his favourite place under his muzzle, then closed his eyes again and laid his head back on his greying paws to sleep.

I breathed a sigh of relief and straightened. The stables were around the other side of the farm, towards the sea. Gathering my cloak around me, I retraced my steps back from the porch and followed the cart tracks around the side of the farmhouse. I looked up. The window to the room where Lycaon and Eurycleia usually slept was still dark.

'Krisayis?'

I almost groaned aloud. Turning as slowly as I could, I saw Lycaon walking towards me from the beehives by the outhouses, carrying a clay pot filled to the brim with dark honey. His eyebrows were furrowed and his expression was grim.

'What, by all the gods of Ida, do you think you are doing here?'

Lycaon summoned two young farmhands from the fields to march me back to the hut. They smelt strongly of grass and goat dung, and I tried not to flinch as they stepped close to me and placed heavy hands on my shoulders, forcing me forwards. We trudged down the path into the forest and away from the farmhouse, Lycaon leading the way with Dromas, the farmhands flanking me at the rear.

'I've told you,' I said, as Lycaon asked me for the tenth time what I had been doing so far from the sanctuary. 'It is years since I have been in Larisa. I wanted to see everything again.'

Lycaon muttered something under his breath. 'And since when has my home been one of the sights of Larisa?'

I tried to shrug my shoulders. 'I have memories of going there as a child.'

'That still doesn't explain why you were up and out of the temple grounds at the first light of dawn.'

I hesitated. 'I couldn't sleep.' At least that much was true.

Lycaon sighed and bent down to pick up a stick to throw for Dromas. 'I don't know, Krisayis,' he said, hurling the stick into the trees. 'Your father sent a messenger ahead a few days ago to say you might be coming, and he warned us you might try to escape. It is hard for me to understand *why* exactly you would wish to run away in the midst of the war but, then, I am also having difficulty explaining why you were skulking around my stables by yourself at daybreak.' He paused and gave me a direct, penetrating look. '*Were* you trying to escape?'

I said nothing.

He sighed. 'I thought so.'

We continued through the undergrowth in silence. The path was narrow, and the farmhands either side of me had to wade through knee-high ferns and brambles so our progress was slow. At last – it felt much longer than before – the trees began to thin and I caught sight of the stone walls of the sanctuary up ahead. I turned to the left on instinct, to make my way towards the small stone hut, but Lycaon shook his head. 'We're going to the temple.'

I almost stopped in surprise, but the farmhands' heavy palms on my shoulders pushed me on. 'Why? I'm not allowed to enter the temple until my sixteenth year.'

Lycaon nodded slowly. 'You are not. But I'm afraid Eurycleia and I cannot risk you trying to escape again, Krisayis. You are too dear to your father – too dear to us to lose.' He turned to me, his expression unusually grave. 'There is a war out there on the plain. Your father has already put his life in danger once to rescue you from the enemy. We cannot tempt the Fates again.'

I frowned at him. 'But then why are you taking me to see the temple?'

He did not reply.

We had reached the edge of the precinct now, a high stone wall that ringed the sacred buildings, a smaller imitation of the great sanctuary in Troy.

Lycaon whistled to Dromas to lie down beneath a fig tree and told the farmhands to wait for him there. He nodded to the guard who stood at the gates to the precinct and pushed them open.

I was growing more and more confused, but I could not help also being a little curious. My father had always been adamant that no one but an initiate could enter the sacred precinct of the god. Why was Lycaon revoking this rule now, only a few days before I was to become a priestess?

Lycaon started to climb the steps to the temple, his wooden walking stick clattering against the stone.

'What are we doing?'

Lycaon did not answer but halted at the top, a little breathless, waiting for me to catch up. Two slaves were standing in the shade of the portico beside the large bronze doors, which were wide open, letting in the heat of the summer morning.

I caught a glimpse of a large dark stone slab that towered up to the roof of the temple, polished and shining, with a face carved upon it – the holy image of Apulunas. I turned to Lycaon. 'Why have you . . . ?'

Lycaon placed his hands upon my shoulders, but it was a gentle gesture. 'It pains me deeply to have to do this, Krisayis,' he said, his bushy eyebrows knitting together on his forehead. 'But it is for your own safety. I hope you will understand that one day.'

'Do – do what?' I asked, alarmed now. 'Lycaon, what do you have to do?'

At that moment I heard the slaves step forward and felt their hands under my arms, digging into my ribs.

'Wait – no!'

But they acted as if they could not hear me. In one swift movement they lifted me up and dragged me through the huge bronze doors of the temple.

'Lycaon!' I called back in terror. 'Lycaon, what are you doing?'

The slaves dropped me on the hard stone floor. I caught a glimpse of Lycaon's pained expression as they returned to his side, and a last flash of sunlight on bronze, before the doors swung shut with a shuddering crash and the heavy wooden bolt scraped across them, throwing me into darkness.

I was trapped.

Fateful Words

Βρισηίς
Briseis, Greek Camp

The Hour of the Middle of the Day

The First Day of the Month of the Grape Harvest, 1250 BC

Several days later I was making my way down to the sea with the peelings from King Agamemnon's midday meal. The plague had gone as swiftly as it had come, lifting its poisonous mantle from over the camp like a mist rising before dawn, and the army had left to fight upon the plain that morning. I had spent the last hours trying to shield my ears from the sounds of battle that floated towards us on the breeze, the faint clashing of metal upon metal and the cries of wounded men. The sun, Apulunas' chariot, was at the height of its journey across the sky, and its rays beat down hard upon my head. I tried to loosen my tunic at my throat, feeling the sweat trickle down my spine.

I dropped the peelings into the shallows and turned to walk back up the dunes towards the tent, trying to keep my mind away from the battle beyond the palisade and the sounds of the warriors dying beyond the gates, to stop the memories of Lyrnessus that kept flashing across my thoughts. Then another noise caught my attention – the sharp, clear clash of metal upon metal from the other end of the shore, echoing over the water. I glanced over, shielding my eyes against the glare of the sun.

Achilles was standing on the beach by the line of the breaking sea before his hut, encircled by at least forty men – and he was fighting as no mortal could ever fight. Sword glinting in the light and moving so fast it was a blur of sharp-edged bronze. Tunic swirling around him like a storm-cloud as he parried, thrust, lunged, dived, all the warriors attacking him at once.

I drew a breath sharply.

Had Agamemnon sent those soldiers to kill Achilles while the army went to war?

I wondered if I should run for help, if I would be in time before they killed him. I glanced back to the tent, to the guards who stood at either side of the entrance. They were watching me, spears planted in the sand behind them, eyes narrowed beneath their helmets.

I looked back at Achilles. Even in the midst of my fear, I could not help but marvel at him. It was as if he knew where the swords would go before the warriors themselves did, anticipating every movement, every thrust, so that he escaped the cutting blades again and again, diving and twisting, the sweat shining upon his skin. Two warriors advanced and he parried them swiftly, knocking their swords to the ground, then turned and blocked the attacks of three more men with his shield, varying power and deadliness, swift and strong when he needed to be.

A young warrior attacked, and within a moment Achilles had disarmed him and thrown him to the ground, his foot upon his neck. There was a moment as I watched, half terrified, half fascinated, waiting for the blow to fall, for the sword-blade to sever the young man's neck.

But it did not come. Achilles reached down, pulled the man up by his hand. And then the fighting started again.

I stared.

And then I realized.

These were not men sent by Agamemnon to kill Achilles. These were Achilles' own men. He was playing with them, practising, leading them in a dance, while the rest of the Greeks fought and died beyond the camp walls.

It was at that moment I knew that, without Achilles, the Greeks could never win the war.

'Briseis!'

I looked over my shoulder. A solitary figure wrapped in a brown cloak was striding across the beach towards me. I raised my hand to shield my eyes as he approached, the smell of salt strong on the wind. 'Patroclus!'

He quickened his stride. He looked tired, I thought.

'Patroclus!' I said again, as he came nearer, and I held out my hand to him. 'I am glad to see you.'

His face coloured as he took my hand in his, a brief gesture. 'I am sorry I could not come before,' he said. 'I— It was very—'

He stopped, his ears turning red.

He loosed my hand and I started to walk along the shore in the opposite direction, past King Agamemnon's tent, ignoring his confusion. 'Tell me, how is Achilles?'

He lowered his voice as he moved to walk beside me. 'Achilles is well. Angry with King Agamemnon, and frustrated not to be at war.' He gave a half-glance back over his shoulder. 'He is taunting the king,' he said. 'He wants Agamemnon to see that he wastes his strength here while out there our comrades die upon the plain.'

I nodded, glancing at the dust billowing over the camp palisade from the battle on the plain and the faint sounds of battle-cries and clashing weapons. 'Has he spoken of me at all?'

Patroclus shrugged his shoulders. 'Perhaps. But there are more important things to talk about than you, Briseis.'

'What things?'

'The war,' he said simply. 'A war that King Agamemnon is losing, now that Achilles has left the fight. The Greeks have not been able to sack a single city since Pedasus.'

I frowned at him. 'And you expect me to commiserate with you?'

He seemed to shake himself. 'No. No, of course not. I'm sorry.'

We walked on in silence for a while.

'Has King Agamemnon been treating you well?'

'He leaves me to my own devices, for the most part. I see him only at the evening meal.'

'What? He does not . . . You do not . . .'

'Lie with him?' The corners of my mouth went up in a small smile. 'No. I managed to persuade him otherwise.'

Patroclus accepted this in silence. 'You know,' he said at last, 'there has been a rumour that the king is planning to send an embassy to Achilles.'

I stopped and faced him. 'An embassy? Why?'

Patroclus looked away quickly, as if he regretted what he had said. 'It is probably nothing. But the rumour is that the king will try to persuade Achilles back to war, and that he will offer to return you to him as a bribe.'

'I could be returned to Achilles? I could go back to him?'

'I said it was only a rumour.'

I turned towards Agamemnon's tent, a little way down the shore now to the west. 'And if Achilles took me and he went back to war . . .'

I stopped, thinking of Achilles surrounded by forty warriors, and the fear I had felt at the thought that he might be killed. 'Would Achilles be safe? If he went back to fight?'

He raised his eyebrows at me.

'I don't want anyone else to die because of me,' I said fiercely.

Patroclus let out a careless laugh. 'Achilles is the Greeks' greatest warrior! You have seen him fight. It is his enemies who should tremble for their safety. And besides,' he smiled, 'Achilles has his mother's protection. He cannot die.'

'His mother's . . .'

Patroclus lengthened his stride. 'Thetis. She took him to the Underworld when he was a child and dipped him in the life-giving waters of the River Styx. His body is immortal where it touched the water. Except, of course, for his heel.'

There was a moment as I took in what he had said. 'His – his heel?' I repeated slowly. 'You mean . . . when I touched his heel all those weeks ago and he flew into a rage . . . and you told me it was his only weakness . . .'

'It's the only place Achilles can be killed.' He frowned at me. 'But I thought you understood that?'

I felt a sudden rush of horror sweep through my body, like a storm wave on the open sea.

I had told the Trojan slave girl, Krisayis, only a few days ago.

And then, when she left, she had spoken of Achilles' 'secret'. She had asked me to ensure that he was killed.

She knew. *She knew.*

And she wanted Achilles dead.

'No,' I said, stammering in my fear. My skin was suddenly cold, my palms clammy. 'No, it can't be.' Then I rounded on Patroclus. 'Why didn't you tell me? If I had only known . . .'

'I thought you did.'

'I did not,' I said, my voice rising in panic. 'I did not.' I started pacing up and down before him.

Patroclus was staring at me in suspicion and surprise. 'What—'

'Patroclus,' I said, turning around, 'if King Agamemnon does indeed send the embassy to persuade Achilles back to war, you must make sure that he refuses it.'

His eyebrows rose even higher. 'Refuse? But I thought you wanted to return to Achilles.'

'Achilles must be kept from the war.' I took a deep breath. 'At any cost. Even if I do not see him again.'

Patroclus gave me a suspicious look. 'Why?'

'It does not matter why. But if you care about keeping him alive –'

'More than my own life,' Patroclus said.

'– then he must not go to war. Do you understand me?'

Patroclus stared at me for a few long moments. 'Why are you so eager to save Achilles, after all that he has done?' he said at last. 'Why not let him die, if you are so certain he will be killed, when he destroyed the people of Pedasus, *your* people?'

'Have you ever been in love, Patroclus?'

His eyes dropped to the ground, swiftly, so I could not catch their expression. 'Yes,' he said, his voice even.

'Then you know that if you lost the one you loved – if you saw them killed before your eyes – then there is nothing, *nothing*, you would not do to prevent it happening again.'

Patroclus stayed still for a long time. Then he gave an almost imperceptible nod. 'Yes,' he said, turning to walk on. 'Yes, I know that.'

The Gods Prepare

Mount Ida, Overlooking the Trojan Plain

'Do you think this wreath goes with my hair?' Apollo asks Hermes, ruffling his perfect golden locks into a rakish quiff.

Reluctantly Hermes takes his eyes off Aphrodite as she bends over to pick up a stray ivory hairpin and glances at Apollo. 'Wouldn't make much difference if it did,' Hermes says, taking a big bite from a bunch of golden ambrosia and crunching it. 'You've got Aphrodite looking after you. I'll tell you one thing: no one will notice your hair when she's done with you.'

Aphrodite leans over Apollo, and her scent – something like all the flowers in the world distilled into a single perfume – wafts over him.

'Stay still,' she says, tapping his hand away from his hair as she rearranges the wreath of laurel leaves on his head. A couple of cupids flutter around her, carrying armfuls of olive-oil jugs, bottles of scented perfume and hairpins. As she stands back to check her handiwork they give an admiring sigh.

Hermes cocks his head to look at Apollo. 'I have to say,' he says, through a mouthful of ambrosia, 'I'm surprised how encouraging Hera was. She normally disapproves of our little adventures. Well,' he smirks, 'the ones she hears about, anyway. But she seemed quite pleased about you and what's-her-name.'

Apollo tries to nod but can't, as Aphrodite has his head in a firm grip. 'I know,' he says. 'I was, too. But perhaps she's come around to me at last.' He grins. 'Maybe she was impressed by the plague. It was quite spectacular, even if it did take down some of her beloved Greeks.'

At this precise moment, Athena wanders on to the cloud, her pet owl perched on her shoulder. She stiffens like a statue when she sees Aphrodite – she still has not forgiven her for winning Paris' contest – but when she spots Apollo sitting on a billow of cloud, having his hair arranged by Aphrodite, she relaxes into an easy smile.

'What are you doing?' she asks, in a teasing voice.

'Nothing,' Apollo says nonchalantly, trying unsuccessfully to keep his eyes from Aphrodite's voluptuous bosom as she leans over his shoulder to position a lock of hair. 'Can't a god get dressed in peace?'

Athena opens her mouth to say something, but Hermes interrupts. 'Oh, leave him alone, Athena,' he says, taking another loud bite. 'Just because you don't wear make-up doesn't mean the rest of us can't indulge in a bit of a beauty routine once in a while.'

Athena gives him a smile that is sweeter than ambrosia. 'I wasn't going to say he shouldn't,' she says. 'In fact, Apollo, you're looking rather dashing. That wreath suits you. It goes with your hair.' She pauses as the two gods exchange surprised looks. 'So what's going on, then?' she asks, walking around Aphrodite, eyeing her perfume-filled bottles and ivory combs. 'Why are you two up here canoodling with Aphrodite and her flying midgets?'

'No reason,' Apollo says. 'Just wanted a—'

'Apollo's set his sights on someone,' Hermes interrupts, in a loud stage-whisper, winking at him.

'What, again?' Athena asks, with an unusually indulgent smile. Hermes hushes her, and she lowers her voice. 'Who is it this time?'

Hermes glances around him, as if checking for eavesdroppers. 'Another Trojan,' he says.

'Another?' she asks, as if she does not already know. 'What is it with these Trojan women? If they're all so beautiful, why did Paris go all the way to Greece to get Helen?'

'Good point,' says Hermes.

At this moment, Aphrodite claps her hands. 'Done!' she says, stepping back to eye the results. The cupids applaud.

'Hermes – Athena – what do you think?' Apollo asks, with self-satisfaction,

toying with his laurel wreath and gazing down into the ocean to check his reflection.

Athena smiles and nods in approval.

Hermes claps him on the shoulder. For a moment, the three gods gaze down at a small temple far, far below, set on the water's edge to the south of Troy.

'You're the most attractive god on Olympus,' Hermes says, grinning. 'Trust me, brother. Nothing will go wrong this time.'

Embassy

Χρυσηίς
Krisayis, Larisa

The Hour of the Setting Sun

The Third Day of the Month of the Grape Harvest, 1250 BC

I spent the next few hours pacing up and down the temple in a barely concealed rage. I could not believe what Lycaon had done. How could he be such a fool? How *could* he have locked me up when I was the only one who knew how to win the war? And how *could* my father have sent me here, of all places? Did they want Troy to fall?

I would *make* Lycaon let me go. When he found out what I knew, he surely would not keep me here.

I refused to sleep in case Lycaon or the slaves came in. From time to time, baskets of food and watered-down wine were pushed in through a hatch in the west wall, but as soon as I ran to the hatch to demand to talk to Lycaon, whoever had brought them was gone.

For the rest, I was alone.

After what felt like several days spent shouting, pacing, cursing and pounding on the bronze doors with my fists, I had to give up. My bones were aching with tiredness, and my knuckles were bruised. A few torches had been lit in the brackets on the columns that supported the roof when I had first been shut in there. They were guttering now, at the very end of their use, and I lay down in the flickering pool of light beneath one, curled up on the cold stone floor, trying to rub some warmth into my fingers.

When I awoke, I had no idea what time it was. The heavy bronze doors did not let in any light, so I could not tell the time of day, and there were no windows. Someone must have come in while I was sleeping, because a large basket filled with food had been placed right beside me, and the guttering torches had been replaced with fresh ones. I leapt to my feet, then winced at the pain in my back and neck, stiff from sleeping on the hard stone, and ran to the doors. I pounded upon them. The worked bronze reverberated with a dull, ringing sound.

Still no reply.

I turned away in frustration, muttering under my breath a curse to the gods that I should have slept when Lycaon came, and started back towards the basket of food.

Then I stopped absolutely still. The light of the torches spread through the temple with a faint yellow-orange glow. But where it had used to reflect the dark glint of polished stone, there was nothing.

The statue of Apulunas had gone.

Βρισηίς
Briseis, Greek Camp

The Hour of the Stars

The Third Day of the Month of the Grape Harvest, 1250 BC

Two days later Patroclus returned as the stars were beginning to scatter the sky with silver dust. He found me at the back of the tent, folding the woollen blankets and linen for storing in the drying racks behind the kitchen where the heat of the fire could keep them warm and dry away from the sea-wind.

'Briseis. Talthybius said I might find you here.'

Patroclus was standing by the tied-back curtain that served as the entrance to the drying cupboard. His brown cloak was around his shoulders, and his arms were crossed over his chest, his face pale.

I set down the linen that I was holding and moved closer to him, frowning. 'Are you all right?'

He nodded tightly. 'There is much I have to talk to you about.'

I followed him out of the tent and towards the sea, as we had done before. It was a cool evening, and the breeze brushed the skin of my bare arms as we walked. The waves were curling on to the shore one after another, and clouds were blotting out the light of the stars in patches across the sky, the full moon shining out, like the open eye of the gods, watching us. It was almost peaceful, with the sea rolling towards us wave after wave, and the cool, calm air of night settling upon us was tinged with salt.

Patroclus waited until we had walked a good hundred paces

before he spoke. 'King Agamemnon sent the embassy,' he said.

I stared at him. 'And?'

He picked up a stone and threw it at the tumbling surface of the sea. 'Achilles refused him.'

I let out a breath of relief.

'He refused,' I said, closing my eyes. 'He is safe. He trusted me more than I would have thought.'

Patroclus stopped to send another stone skittering over the surface of the sea. 'Oh, of course he does.' His voice was ironic, bitter.

I turned to look at him. He was wearing an ugly expression on his face, his mouth twisted with pain, his usually kind eyes narrowed. 'What – what do you mean?' I faltered.

He gave a bitter laugh. 'Of course you would not understand,' he said. 'You, with your beauty, whom every man you ever wanted has desired, and even the ones you did not.' He picked up another stone and hurled it out to sea. 'I suppose *you* cannot imagine how it feels to watch the one you love spurn you. How it feels to see the desire on their face, which should be for you, given to someone else.'

'What? You . . . you . . . but you always . . . but you never . . .' I stopped and tried to gather my thoughts. 'You are in love with *me*?'

Patroclus stared at me. Then, inexplicably, he started to laugh. Not as if he were mocking me, though. More the laugh of someone who had thought he was acting in a comedy, only to find out it has been a tragedy all the time. 'You think I am in love – with *you*?'

I frowned. 'Well, yes,' I said. 'Who else could it be?'

The look he was giving me was one of pure disbelief.

'Briseis,' he said, and his voice cracked slightly. There was a long pause as we gazed at each other. 'Briseis, I am in love with Achilles.'

I stared at him.

The silence stretched between us.

'I am sorry if it shocks you,' Patroclus said stiffly, into the silence. 'I know that Achilles fancies himself in love with you. But I have loved him far longer,' he said, and he walked on, across the line of the sea. 'You had no right to tear us apart. At least now that he has refused the embassy, you will not be returning, and we can be as we always were.'

I felt my temper rising as I hurried after him. 'Tear you apart? I did no such thing! Achilles fell in love with *me*, Patroclus!'

'Oh, really?' he said, his voice louder and his strides longer. 'If he loves you as much as you say, then why did he refuse to take you back?'

The heat rushed to my cheeks. 'He listened to my advice!'

'I did not tell him!' Patroclus rounded on me. 'I did not tell him what you said! There! I have said it!'

He looked like a man in torment. His eyes were wide and his fists clenched, the knuckles white.

I glared at him, anger still pulsing in my ears.

'It is no wonder that Achilles does not love you, Patroclus, if you are a man of so little honour!' I shouted at him. 'How do you think a warrior such as Achilles could love a coward who spends all his time hiding behind the camp walls? He told me so, Patroclus! He told me so himself! He thinks you are a *coward*!'

Patroclus' face whitened in the moonlight. Then he turned away. 'Did he say that?' he said, his voice very quiet.

At once I regretted what I had said.

'I am sorry, Patroclus,' I said. 'I was angry, I only said it to upset you—'

But Patroclus held up his hand to silence me. 'I should leave,' he said abruptly. 'Achilles will be missing his cowardly companion.'

'Patroclus, no . . . I—' I tried to reach out to catch his shoulder, but he was already walking briskly away across the moonlit sand.

'Patroclus!' I shouted after him.

But there was no reply.

Χρυσηίς
Krisayis, Larisa

The Hours of Night

The Third Day of the Month of the Grape Harvest, 1250 BC

A searing white light blinded me, and I fell to the floor, shielding my eyes.

The glare dimmed to a warm golden colour. I took my hands away from my eyes.

A young man was standing in the centre of the temple before me, where Apulunas' holy stone should have been – a man so handsome that my breath caught in my chest and I almost choked. His whole body and skin seemed to be made from a fine golden light, as if he were not wholly real but just a spirit, a being of light made from the rays of the sun. His fair hair had threads of gold in it and his perfectly muscled body was like the image of a carved statue, a golden cloth wrapped around his waist, the skin chiselled into soft ridges over his bare chest. His eyes were deep and golden, like pools of sunlight, and the hint of a delicious scent, like all the flowers of the world distilled into a single perfume, wafted from his hair and skin, the very scent of desire.

'Sorry about that,' he said, leaning on a thin golden sceptre.

The air around him seemed to shimmer, as if he were radiating heat or light – I could not tell which.

'I always forget how fragile you mortals are.'

'Mortals?' I asked weakly. 'What – what do you mean? Where is the stone? Who are you?'

He gave a laugh, like the sound of golden bells tinkling on the breeze. 'I'm a god, Krisayis,' he said, curling a perfect lock of hair around one finger. He smiled. 'I'm Apollo.'

There was a long silence. Then I put my hands on the ground and pushed myself to stand. 'I don't understand,' I said.

'Apollo,' he repeated, bending down to examine his reflection in the white marble pool that lay before where the sacred stone would normally stand, then turned to me. 'Oh, I see,' he said. 'Apulunas? Maybe Apaliunas?' He rubbed his forehead. 'I lose track of all the names. Surely you must have heard of me.'

I felt my knees go weak beneath me. *Apulunas?* 'Of – of course I've heard of you! But – but my father said that the gods only appear to their chosen priests! W-why would you appear to me? I'm not even your priestess yet!'

I almost said, *Neither did I ever want to be*. But if this really was the god ... if it truly was the Great God himself ... I pinched myself, hard, on my forearm. It hurt a great deal, tears springing to my eyes. *This cannot be true.* 'Am – am I dreaming?'

He smiled again, that divinely handsome smile. 'Fortunately for you, no,' he said. 'I know it is much more convenient for you mortals to commune with the gods while you sleep. But, well, from time to time we like to *talk* to someone. In fact,' he said, his smile widening, 'I have an offer for you, beautiful Krisayis.'

I swallowed. 'An offer? What kind of offer?'

He chuckled. 'Perhaps we should discuss it over some wine.' He gestured towards the aisle of the temple, behind the thick limestone pillars. In an instant plump cushions materialized upon the floor, low cedar-wood tables piled with roasted meat, dried fruits, almonds and wine, and burnished bronze lamps hung from tall slender stands.

I gasped. 'How ...'

He held out a hand as if to lead me over, but I noticed, as I reached out to take it, that I could not touch his skin. It was as if there were an invisible barrier between my fingers and the golden shimmering outline of the god's image. I stared at him.

He shrugged his shoulders. 'One of the downsides of being divine. We cannot touch anything of earth. You know, food, drink, and . . .' he flashed me a sly grin '. . . a few other things besides.'

My eyes widened even further. Then I shook my head. *Surely – surely I am dreaming. This cannot be real.*

'Sit,' he said again, gesturing towards the cushions.

I moved over slowly and sat down, half expecting not to be able to touch those either, but I sank easily into their comforting warmth, so different from the hard stone I had slept upon. I reached for a honeyed apricot, a thick slice of roast venison and a goblet of deep red wine, realizing suddenly how very hungry I was after so many hours without proper food.

Apulunas – if, indeed, it *was* Apulunas, and not some apparition of my imagining – settled himself on one of the cushions, too, and watched me as I ate, with a curious expression – was it longing? – on his face.

When I had eaten my fill, he leant forwards. 'So, Krisayis. As I said, I have an offer to make you.'

I did not reply.

'I know your heart's desire, Krisayis.'

He had startled me. 'My heart's desire?' I lowered my voice. 'How could you possibly know that?'

Apulunas laughed, and his golden outline glowed a little more brightly. 'I am a god,' he said. 'I know everything. I know, for example, how much you *long* to be a princess of Troy.'

I stared at him.

He grinned, and settled himself a little more comfortably on the cushions. 'I know how you wish you could be the equal of your friend Cassandra, how neglected and overshadowed you feel when you are by her side, however well you try to hide it. I know how you detest being a mere priest's daughter, and how the very idea of being a priestess and serving me in this temple for the rest of your life, as your father demands, appals you.' He paused. 'I can give you the chance to make a difference. I can give you the power to choose your fate, to rule the city you love, to help the people of Troy.'

Apulunas dropped his voice, whispering now, so I had to lean forwards to catch his words, the golden light of his skin glowing even more brightly. 'I can make you,' he breathed, 'the queen of queens.'

The words rang in the still, musty air of the temple, like a drop of golden oil on water. I gazed at him, all thoughts of food forgotten. 'You can?' I murmured, the words catching in my throat, my face very warm.

'Of course.' Apulunas leant back, resting his head on his arm and smiling easily at me. 'All you have to do is consent to come to Mount Ida with me and become the lover of a god, and I will give you everything you have ever dreamt of and more.'

My heart was racing as I considered his words. *All you have to do is consent to come to Mount Ida with me and become the lover of a god. I will give you everything you have ever dreamt of and more.*

I tried to force myself to think. But the image of myself as a queen, the equal of Cassandra at last, no longer the daughter of a priest, no longer afraid or overruled but free to choose my destiny, kept floating into my mind, and I could not concentrate. To make a difference at last . . . not to be ordered around by my father and Lycaon but to be free to choose my own destiny and to change the fate of Troy . . . I could do so many things. I could help so many people. What did it matter if I gave myself to a god, and the handsome, immortal sun-god at that, if I could save my city?

'Wait,' I said, frowning slightly. 'There are some things I don't understand.'

Apulunas raised his eyebrows. 'And what are they?'

I tried to clear my thoughts and decide which to ask first of the multitude of questions that seemed to have flooded my mind from the moment he had uttered those fateful words: *I am a god.*

'My father,' I said slowly. 'My father has served you all his life, yet you have never once appeared to him. If you are the god Apulunas, as you declare, then why have you chosen me? Why not appear to my father instead, if you truly wish to help us and our city?'

He laughed aloud, a laugh like sunlight upon a flowing stream, but he said nothing in reply.

'And,' I pressed on, 'when you say I must come with you to Mount Ida, you – you said you cannot touch anything of earth,' I said, my cheeks reddening slightly as I looked Apulunas full in the face. 'Besides, my father has told me always that the gods are pure and chaste. That the gods do not have desires as we mortals do. Why would you wish to take me with you, if that is so?'

Apulunas smiled, and I felt myself shiver with pleasure at the beauty of him. 'If a mortal consents to come with us to our mountain home then, yes, we can touch them,' he said. 'But they must come willingly. My father Zeus is annoyingly firm on free will.' He rolled his eyes. 'And as for pure and chaste, would you really expect us to live alone for eternity?' He grinned at me. 'Surely that is a little harsh, Krisayis.'

I thought this over. 'And I can return, can't I – afterwards? I can go back to Troy?'

Apulunas laughed easily. 'Of course. As soon as you and I have, let us say, enjoyed each other's company a little more – you will be returned to the city.'

'I have your word on that?'

He smiled. 'Do you need the word of a god? I am divine, Krisayis. You can trust me.'

I frowned at him.

Apulunas leant closer, the ambrosial scent of him wafting over me. 'When you return, you will be the most powerful queen in the world.'

There was another pause as I took this in. 'But – but that's another thing,' I said slowly. 'When I was in the Greek camp I heard them talk of their gods, that they had given them a prophecy that Troy would fall. They said that their gods protected them. But that cannot be true, can it? I mean, the only gods are ours – I mean you – the true gods, Troy's protectors. How could the Greeks have thought they had heard a prophecy from the gods?'

He waved his hand. 'A mistake,' he said, in an airy tone. 'These prophets, one can never rely on what they say. And, besides, there are so many prophecies flying around. They often catch the wrong ones. And if you lie with me, Krisayis,' he said, as if in a flash of inspiration, 'you will have all my power at your disposal to give to Troy.'

'But then . . .' I was thinking hard '. . . but then if power was all that was needed to save Troy, why haven't you already helped us? You have all the power in the world to save my home, the people you say you protect and love. And yet we have been fighting for weeks. Why not help us now to win the war?'

A flicker of irritation crossed his face, but in a moment it was gone. 'You are a mortal, you would not understand such things.' He gave me a patronizing smile. 'You humans are always so distracted by your love for your families and your homes. You cannot understand that it is far, far more complicated than that.'

There was something very strange in what he was saying – *as if*, I thought suddenly, *as if he is trying to avoid telling me the truth.* 'I do not see what is complicated about not wanting those you love destroyed.'

Suddenly, unbidden, another image came before my eyes. Troilus, looking up at me from his bed with love in his eyes. Cassandra, laughing with me in our shared chambers, giggling at our shared secrets. The warmth of the hand of the Trojan bard in the Greek camp, when his palm had touched mine.

And it was then, out of nowhere, I realized that perhaps Apulunas did not know my heart's desire at all – because I had not known it myself.

I struggled with this new feeling erupting inside me, this sudden certainty, as strong and unfamiliar as the first taste of new wine in spring. I looked up at the golden outline of Apulunas.

Our eyes met, and I knew what I had to do. 'I cannot accept your offer,' I said.

Apulunas' forehead creased, very slightly, in a golden frown. Then, unexpectedly, the corners of his mouth turned up in a gently mocking smile. 'You don't know what you're saying,' he said, his voice dripping condescension. 'Poor Krisayis. You've seen a god for the first time and he wants to lie with you. You're overwhelmed. I understand.'

'No,' I said again, my temper rising. 'No, you do not understand. I cannot accept. I – I *will* not accept.'

There was a long silence.

'You *will* not?' Apulunas repeated, his smile vanishing.

'No.'

There was a moment as I looked at Apulunas and he looked at me.

Then there was another flash of white light and, without warning, the cushions, tables and food disappeared, sending me plummeting on to the hard stone floor.

Apulunas leapt to his feet. 'You choose to deny the attentions of a god, like your foolish friend Cassandra?' he asked. His skin was glowing a deep, fiery red now. He was no longer handsome: he looked angry and petulant, his sensitive mouth sneering.

I almost collapsed as a wave of shock flooded over me. Cassandra must have been telling the truth. But I held my ground. 'Yes.'

'You choose to deny me, when I have promised you all the influence and power you could ever wish for?'

'Yes,' I said.

Without warning, he let out a long laugh. 'What fools you mortals are!' He began to circle around me. 'Don't you see, Krisayis? The gods you Trojans worship to protect you, and the gods the Greeks invoke, you think we care for you at all? You think we protect one side more than the other? You truly think *I* will help the Trojans win the war when I know that they will lose? You think Athena,' his eyes glittered, 'or, as you call her, *Atana*, will not turn her eyes from the Greeks the moment they offend her? The god of war, the goddess of love, the god of lightning – are you such a fool that you cannot see we are the *same*?'

I stared at him. I was remembering that day in the Greek camp, when my father released me to Larisa and Achilles said he had been visited by Athena. And Odysseus, saying that Apollo had given them the prophecy about the fall of Troy . . . How had I not seen it?

He gave me a terrible smile. 'We are *divine*, Krisayis. Every mortal upon the earth worships us in different names. How many gods do you think heaven can hold? The Greeks,' his smile broadened, 'even use similar names to yours . . . I would have thought at least some of you would have worked *that* out . . . eventually.' His eyes glittered. 'But, then, perhaps it is a good thing my father Zeus gave you so little intellect. Imagine how few wars there would be if you knew the truth.'

I shook my head numbly. 'And everyone thinks you are the protector of Troy . . .'

Apulunas laughed. 'Troy has been fated to fall since before the Greeks even came to your shores, and a thousand years before! Even as I built the city with my own hands, even as I made the temple where you foolish mortals worship me as your protector, I knew that it was destined to be destroyed, a city founded for burning and pillaging and looting. And Hera has had her sights set on it ever since Paris gave the golden apple to Aphrodite.' He flicked his forefinger against his thumb with a shrug of his shoulders. 'And you, who think you are so important, are nothing but dust, a mortal who takes a breath of air and is gone for ever. What does it matter if the people of Troy die because their city is destined to fall? It is *we* who remain.'

I almost staggered. 'No . . .'

His smile broadened into a grin. 'Ah, poor foolish mortal. You thought that you would change the fate of Troy?'

'You are lying,' I breathed, my voice harsh. 'You are lying.'

'You will see soon enough which of us is all-knowing and which of us is a fool,' he said. 'But you should know that it is not about power, or love, or even beauty – only what we gods want.' He tilted his head. 'Speaking of which, I need to give you a reminder of my visit. You cannot defy a god without consequences, Krisayis. You, of all people, should know that.' He paused.

'What do you mean?'

'I cursed your friend with being doubted though she speaks the truth, for her insolence in denying me. From you, I shall take the only thing you have left.'

I stared defiantly at him, though in truth my knees felt as weak as water. 'And what is that?'

He leant towards me. 'Your beauty.'

The Camp Sacked

Βρισηίς
Briseis, Greek Camp

The Hours of Night

The Third Day of the Month of the Grape Harvest, 1250 BC

Back on my pallet in the slave quarters of Agamemnon's tent, I could not sleep. The memory of Patroclus' white face kept surfacing in my mind. If only I had not said anything! Patroclus had always been kind to me. I should not have taunted him. But I had been shocked and angry, upset. If he had not goaded me in the first place . . .

I turned on to my side, trying to find a comfortable place to lie on the hard straw. The thought that had been haunting me all night came back to me with the force that all our deepest fears possess.

What if Patroclus was right?

What if Achilles did not care for me after all?

I closed my eyes. *No. Don't think it. It isn't true. He only said it to upset you.*

But if Patroclus was telling the truth and he had not told Achilles what I had said, why *had* Achilles refused the embassy? Did he not want me back? Was I not the reason he had left the war?

I turned over to the other side, pulling the thin linen sheet flat over the straw. One of the slaves beside me opened her eyes at the noise and hushed me irritably.

I tucked my knees up to my chest for some warmth and tried to let go of my fear. I would find Patroclus tomorrow and apologize. I would wait for him all day on the shore if I had to, and tell him that I had not meant what I had said, and that I was sorry for it.

And then, surely then, he would tell me that he, too, had spoken in anger.

That Achilles cared for me still.

Χρυσηίς
Krisayis, Larisa

The Hours of Night

The Third Day of the Month of the Grape Harvest, 1250 BC

I looked up from where I lay. All I could remember was a burst of white light and a blast of cold air, then blackness as my head had hit the ground. The dark temple around me flickered, then swam into view. The torches in the brackets on the columns had been snuffed out, but a cool, silver-white light was suffusing the floor around me.

Moonlight.

I looked up quickly. The doors were hanging open on their hinges, swinging in the cold breeze from the sea, as if they had been pushed apart by some unnatural force. Outside, the stars were glittering in the dark sky, and a full moon was shining with a pale white glow.

I pressed my hands against the cold stones of the floor and pushed myself up unsteadily to stand. The force that had knocked me unconscious . . . the doors . . .

I spun around, the memory of what had happened suddenly returning. Heart beating very fast, I stared into the shadows of the temple, looking for any movement, any sign that someone was there. But I was alone.

Apulunas was gone.

I gathered my cloak around me and set out for the open doors, my legs still weak but my stride determined and quick. It was more important now than ever that I return to Troy. If what Apulunas had said was true, my city was in greater danger than any of us could ever have imagined.

I had to get to Prince Hector and tell him what I knew.

The walk through the woods felt interminably long. My head ached from where it had hit the floor and I felt exhausted from lack of sleep, but I refused to allow myself to rest. The moonlight pooled in patches of pale light on the forest floor, guiding me to the rough-beaten path to Lycaon's farm and turning the leaves of the olive trees and pine needles to silver.

At last I emerged from the forest. Dromas did not even raise his head as I crept around the side of the farmhouse to the stables. Three heavy chestnut horses and a grey mare stood stabled in the yard, their dark eyes regarding me sleepily. I walked up to the mare and stroked her soft, warm nose, then lifted a leather bridle and bronze bit from a hook on the stable wall nearby and fastened it to her mouth. She snuffled as I took the reins and led her, as quietly as I could, to the mounting block. The stable yard was quiet, and it would be many hours before Lycaon woke and saw that I had taken his mare. I drew a deep breath, then climbed on to her back and took the reins into my hands. Turning her, I urged her into a walk, then a trot through the northern entrance to the yard and into the moonlit fields. Then I dug my heels into her sides, and we were out on the plains, my hair flying behind my back as we galloped north, following the twisting line of the coast to Troy.

Βρισηίς
Briseis, Greek Camp

The Hour of Daybreak

The Fourth Day of the Month of the Grape Harvest, 1250 BC

The next morning I awoke abruptly in the same position I had fallen asleep, back stiff and my feet as cold as blocks of ice. The sun was rising, bleak and pale through the linen of the tent. The sound of soldiers shouting and screaming slaves was on the wind all around me.

I could smell smoke.

It was like the sack of Lyrnessus all over again.

The odour of burning grew stronger, bitter.

I sat up. Slaves all over the tent were waking, their expressions puzzled. The curtain to the quarters parted and one of the kitchen slaves appeared, her face a picture of terror. 'Get out!' she shouted. 'All of you, get out! The Trojans are sacking the camp! It's going up in flames!'

In a moment I had grasped my cloak and leapt from the bed. The room was a confusion of panicked voices, slaves running in all directions, and the distant sounds of battle. I darted through the kitchens to the camp outside.

The air around me was filled with a thundering drum of noise. Soldiers were shouting, women screaming, bronze-tipped arrows hammering against wood. A large hole had been smashed in the wooden palisade near the camp's south gate, and a company of Trojan soldiers was pouring through the gap, shouting and rattling their spears against their shields. A group of them had managed to set fire to one of the ships and it was already blazing, a bright orange-red stain on the sky and dark smoke billowing over the camp.

'A larger force approaches!' one of the lookouts called down from the rampart. 'The entire Trojan army is gathering for the attack! Sound the alarm!'

A cacophony of trumpets was added to the noise, shrieking to the sky a warning to the Greeks. I turned in horror to look back at the upper city of Troy, set high on its rock over the bay. Would the Trojans recognize me? Or – I shuddered – would they kill me before I had the chance to tell them who I was?

I looked around desperately, my skin cold with terror, searching for someone, anyone, who might save me.

But this time I was alone. I had no Mynes to protect me.

'Briseis!' a voice close by me shouted, and I felt my wrist locked in a strong grip, pulling me upright. Before I knew where I was, I was being dragged across the sand, half pulled, half running.

'Patroclus!' I gasped. 'What are you doing here? Why—'

'No time for questions!' he shouted, pushing his way through the crowds of Greek soldiers arming themselves, still holding my wrist. He had a rough beaten-bronze shield on the other arm and held it over our heads to protect us from the fire arrows that were now showering down from the sky, setting aflame anything they hit. I ran through them, shaking with fear, my free hand held over my head.

'This way!' Patroclus gestured to me, leading me along the edge of the open assembly-place. Soldiers were running in every direction, some in groups hurriedly arming for battle, testing their spear-tips or tightening their breastplates and greaves, others dashing to the palisade to man the battlements, hurriedly pushing bronze helmets on to their heads and clutching only a shield for protection.

'In here!' Patroclus swung to the side and pushed me into a large shelter filled with spears, swords and round bossed shields: the weapons storehouse, guarded by four thick-set warriors with bronze breastplates. At least thirty slave-girls were already gathered inside, their faces white with fear, tunics smut-stained. Patroclus followed me and leant against a wooden beam, panting and out of breath, his shield limp on his arm. His left hand was bleeding where an arrow had grazed it.

'You should be safe here,' he said briefly, and turned to leave.

I caught him by the arm, and when I spoke, my voice was quiet. 'Patroclus,' I said. 'You saved my life. I thank you for it.'

He shrugged his shoulders. 'I could not leave you unprotected. If only because of Achilles' love for you.'

Again he turned to go, but I held on to his arm. 'Wait,' I said. 'I have to tell you. What I said last night – it was wrong of me. I did not mean it, it was not true. I only said it out of anger.'

Still he did not look at me. 'Briseis, I must go,' he said.

'Very well. But you do believe me, don't you?'

He looked away. 'Guards!'

The door swung open.

'Farewell, Briseis,' he said. And then there was nothing but the sound of the storm of arrows and the flaming ships before the door closed again, and Patroclus was gone.

Χρυσηίς
Krisayis, Troy

The Hour of the Rising Sun

The Fourth Day of the Month of the Grape Harvest, 1250 BC

My thighs were aching from holding myself upright on the horse and my back was throbbing with pain by the time the sun was rising through the trees. The path I had found several hours before wound back and forth through the dense sun-dappled woods that carpeted the plain all the way to Troy along the course of the River Scamander. I was close to exhaustion, but it was good to feel the warmth of the sun on my face. It was easier to stay awake now that the sky was growing brighter, the faintest tinge of rose brushing the tips of the trees.

Suddenly I saw a flash of pale stone on the horizon, between the close-set branches of the oaks. I stopped the horse. If I squinted, I could almost make out . . .

I urged the mare into a canter, and we raced along the path through the woods, all thoughts of fatigue forgotten. There was no mistaking it now. Those familiar well-hewn stones, the towers ringing the high walls, the gentle slope of the plain down towards the sea . . .

It was Troy.

I felt my heart leap with excitement. As we neared the city and the walls loomed overhead, I slowed the mare to a walk, gazing up at the towers and trying to see where I had come out. I spotted a stone marker of the god Apulunas close by the walls, planted into the ground, and then I saw them. The South Gates, huge as ever, soaring up into the sky.

I dismounted from the mare and tied her reins around the trunk of an olive tree. I was thinking fast now. The guards would never allow an escaped prisoner of the Greeks into the city without interrogation, and the battlements were bristling with Trojan bowmen. And what would happen if more Greek soldiers were scouting the forest, or there were Greeks upon the plain?

I leant against an old oak tree nearby, nursing my sore muscles and peering desperately around the thick trunk towards the gates. A large group of peasants was emerging from the wide forest path that led from Mount Ida to the city, dragging a couple of ox-wagons full of barley husks, mud-covered onions and green sprigs of bitter vetch. It was my best hope.

Pulling the hood of my travelling cloak over my head, I hurried along the edge of the forest towards them, careful to keep to the shade of the trees, looking around me all the time for the first sign of Greek warriors. The peasants were walking quickly, their faces set in grim determination, scanning the plain with quick, darting, fearful glances, their children running alongside them, whispering to each other. As I approached, the tallest man saw me and drew the wagons to a halt. 'Who's there?' he called, his voice full of fear as he drew out a cudgel. 'Stop! Don't come any closer!'

Slowly, very carefully, I took a step towards them. 'Please, I mean you no harm,' I said.

The man raised his eyebrows and looked at the others.

'A woman! And a Trojan!' he said, in a thick country accent. He peered at me. 'What are you doing here, out on the plain, alone? Don't you know how dangerous it is, lady?'

'I have been travelling and I – I lost my way. I need to get into Troy.'

The other peasants started muttering to each other.

The man frowned at me. 'We're the only ones allowed into the city by express permission of the king's son, Prince Aeneas. No one's been through the gates in or out for weeks now – not since Prince Troilus, the gods bless him, was killed.'

I tried not to betray a flicker of emotion. 'And you? Why are you allowed in, then?'

He rubbed his chin. 'Prince Aeneas sent word to us farmers to come, as the city's running out of food. The Greek camp is under attack, and no one knows when there'll be another chance to travel safely across the plain.'

'Will you let me come into the city with you?'

The peasants exchanged looks between themselves.

'I don't know, girl. How do we know you aren't a Greek spy?'

'How many Greeks do you think speak with a Trojan accent?' I asked, a little impatiently. We were losing time, and the longer we stayed upon the plain the more chance the Greeks would have of finding and capturing us.

The farmer shrugged. 'They might.'

I sighed. Slowly, I reached up and lowered my hood. My golden hair tumbled out over my shoulders, and I swept aside my cloak to show the white robes of a priestess-initiate that I had been made to wear in Larisa. 'I am the daughter of the High Priest of Apulunas, Polydamas, and companion to the Princess Cassandra. And I have a horse.' I gestured to the shadowy olive tree a hundred paces away where the grey mare was tied. 'You are welcome to her on your return. I shall not need her.' I looked him directly in the eyes. 'I beg of you, sir, in the name of the King and Queen of Troy, will you let me accompany you?'

The farmer considered me. Then he made a gruff sound in his throat. 'We've heard of Polydamas.' He exchanged a glance with a woman who stood beside him – she must have been his wife. 'And a horse tamed on the Trojan plain will sell well with the Mysians. All right, girl. We'll take you into Troy.'

I let out a sigh of relief. 'My thanks to you,' I said. I pulled my hood back over my head and moved into the group of peasants, trying to ignore the children who were staring at me, mouths open.

The oxen swayed and plodded across the plain, the peasants striding alongside them. As we approached the gates, I gathered my cloak closer around me.

'Business?' shouted the sentry from the tower.

The tall man squinted up. 'Farmers from Mount Ida,' he called back quickly, clearly anxious to leave the plain. 'Bringing more supplies to the city as the Prince Aeneas ordered.'

The sentry consulted with an official standing next to him,

who pulled out a bundle of clay tablets. 'Names?' barked the official.

'Mesthles of Gargarus, and this here is my wife, Phegea, and my brothers, Biantes and Gyrtios,' said the farmer.

'And those?' called the official, pointing.

'My children,' the farmer said, without turning.

There was a long silence as the sentry scanned the official records. My mouth was dry, my heart beating a drumroll on my ribs.

'You may enter,' said the sentry, and gave the signal to his fellow guards.

The gates to the city of Troy swung open.

As soon as the wagons were inside, I darted out from among the peasants with a quick word of thanks, and ran up the road, mingling with the crowds of Trojans going about their daily business. I dashed up the cobbled streets that I had run through just a few months ago with Cassandra, before everything had happened.

The marketplace was empty of stalls now. Instead, a long line of slaves wound through the open space to the door of the king's granaries, where it seemed the palace was handing out clay pots filled with barley meal and vetch that smelt something like a mixture between boiled greens and damp clothes. I darted up the steps to the upper city, two at a time, through the Dardanian Gate, with its flanked pairs of stone lions, and—

'Cassandra!'

I had run full tilt into a slim girl with a cloud of bright auburn hair. She stared at me in my travelling cloak, her eyes wide, as if she were seeing a ghost. '*Krisayis!* What – what are you doing here? I thought your father ransomed you from the Greek camp to go to Larisa!' She stared at me. 'What has *happened* to you?'

I began to answer her, but she waved her hands at me. 'Wait,' she said, 'it doesn't matter. You can explain later. You have to come with me to the lookout tower, now!' She paused, breathless with excitement, her eyes shining. 'The Greek camp has been taken, Krisayis!'

I took a deep breath. 'So I heard.'

'Come and see!' She started away, but I pulled her back.

'What if my father sees me, or the king?' I whispered. 'They will send me back to Larisa!'

She waved a hand impatiently. 'Your father has gone to Didyma to consult the oracle about the outcome of the war. He won't be back for another month at least, and *I* shall deal with my father. I shall tell him that you were not to blame for Troilus' death.'

I glanced at her, hesitating. 'You will? You – you truly believe I was not to blame, then?'

She smiled, her blue eyes sparkling. 'Krisayis, how could you doubt it? Of *course* I believe you! I heard the messenger from Troilus summon you to the South Gates! When I heard what had happened – the best horses from the stables, gone – I knew at once what my brother must have done. He was always hot-headed, and you never were.' She laid her hand upon my arm. 'You have nothing to be sorry for. And I shall tell my father so myself.'

I smiled back at her, and it felt like the first time I had done so in weeks.

'Come,' she said, and she held out her hand towards me. 'Come *on*!'

We ran up the paved road into the familiar shade of the palace with its smoothly worked stone and brightly painted walls, through the winding corridors and myriad rooms I knew so well. We climbed the circling stair up to the top of the tower in the walls, breathless now.

And there we were once more, as we had been when Paris had brought Helen to Troy. I turned to look out towards the plain and, beyond it, the sea.

The Greek camp was on fire. One of the ships was burning, like a beacon, on the water, sending towering flames leaping up into the sky and a column of thick, dark smoke that drifted towards us.

Trojan soldiers were pouring from the Scaean Gates beneath us, west on to the plain, moving like a parade of small black ants to the Greek camp and swarming over it, climbing the wooden palisade, burning huts and tents.

Cassandra took my hand. 'Shall we watch?'

I nodded.

Together, then, we walked over to the edge of the tower to watch the battle that would determine our fate.

Change of Plans

Mount Ida, Overlooking the Trojan Plain

Zeus is sitting on his throne on the very topmost peak of Mount Ida, chin on fist, brooding as he looks through the gap in the clouds on to the Trojan plain and watches the smoking Greek camp.

Then he rubs his tired eyes. He's finding it hard to concentrate on the Trojans. Family problems, as ever, are getting in the way of work. Today Zeus is dealing with a wayward son, who fancies his chances a little too much with the ladies. He saw him again, last night, trying it on with another mortal girl.

Zeus sighs as he remembers how upset Apollo was when he got back to Mount Ida, then is distracted as the image of the girl's radiant golden hair and perfect figure rises unbidden in his mind. He catches himself and shakes his head, trying to get rid of the thought.

A shower of rain falls over the island of Tenedos.

The worst of it all, he thinks, is that if Apollo keeps going like this he will turn out exactly like his father.

'*Zeus, darling?*'

Zeus doesn't turn. It's Hera, and she's probably just here to tell him off again for letting the Trojans have even the slightest hint of a victory. He frowns more deeply and buries his chin stubbornly in his fist.

'*Zeus?*'

Her tone is oddly sweet, honey-like. He sighs. He can't pretend to ignore her for ever. He turns around.

His jaw drops.

She smiles at him. 'Is something wrong, husband?'

Zeus tries to glance down at the Greek camp, which is now burning profusely, but his attention is drawn to his wife, like a hound on the scent, and his eyes swivel back to her. 'No – I mean – no,' he splutters. 'Absolutely not.' He waves a hand at her, gulping and mouthing soundlessly. 'You – you look – beautiful.'

It's true. Hera's skin is shining, like the sun, her eyes are sparkling, and there are no fewer than three glistening teardrop diamonds shimmering in her ears. To Zeus, she is nothing less than a vision of perfection. And a hint of a perfume that smells like all the flowers of the world hangs around her hair.

She sallies over to him, swinging her hips, which are somehow curvier and more inviting than they were yesterday.

Zeus is still gaping at her as she sits on the throne next to him and starts to stroke his hair and beard. 'How are you, husband?'

He goggles at her and doesn't say anything.

She laughs, a tinkling laugh, like a bell, that sets the diamonds at her ears sparkling and sends a rainbow dancing down from the top of Mount Ida into the sea. She caresses his neck and starts to kiss it, softly.

'Hera,' he croons, smiling, 'what's come over you?'

She starts to kiss his lips, his hair, more passionately now. 'Aren't I allowed to want to lie with my husband from time to time?' she asks, kissing him deeply and climbing on to his lap. As one, they roll from the throne on to the grass, and purple hyacinths, crocuses and lotus-flowers spring up beneath them, sending fragrance into the air as they are crushed beneath the bodies of the gods.

Zeus is kissing her fiercely, holding her head in his hands, his eyes growing dark with desire.

'Oh – just a moment,' he says, stopping mid-kiss and letting go of her hair. He whirls his hand around them, and a golden cloud, the colour of the setting sun, wraps itself about the two lovers. He leans back in to kiss her again. 'Just so the others don't see.'

*

An hour later, Zeus is asleep. His snores shake Mount Ida and cause several flocks of birds to rise indignantly from the forests into the air, flapping their wings and squawking.

Hera is sitting beside her husband, smiling with satisfaction as she looks down at the mass of god beside her, deep in sleep. It'll be another few hours until he wakes, and that should be enough. She stands, stretches, and looks down through the gap in the clouds towards the Greek camp.

It's time to get Achilles back in the game.

Duel

Χρυσηίς
Krisayis, Troy

The Hour of Prayer

The Fourth Day of the Month of the Grape Harvest, 1250 BC

We were standing there on the walls, Cassandra and I, talking in low voices to each other as we leant over the parapet, looking towards the Greek camp. Our soldiers were pouring through a gap in the camp fortifications and slowly, relentlessly, pushing the Greek forces back through the huts towards the sea.

The Greeks were trapped. Our victory was within sight.

Then Cassandra gasped. She stared at me. 'I – I don't believe it,' she said, her voice hushed. 'It can't be. Krisayis . . .' Cassandra gazed at me, her eyes round with fear '. . . it's – it's *Achilles*.'

'*What?*'

She pointed out to the plain. 'It's Achilles,' she repeated, her voice trembling.

I stared down towards the camp. I blinked. Achilles was running out on to the plain from the Greek camp. His bronze breastplate was so bright in the afternoon sun that it shone out like a star, a dazzling golden white. He was racing over the sand, spear held high in the air, and behind him the Greek troops were gathering, rushing together from all corners of the camp, swarming in his wake. It was as if they had been inspired with courage, like the breath of life, shouting Achilles' name in a rhythmic beat as they punched, stabbed and sliced at our troops with a sudden terrible energy.

Our men had clearly been taken by surprise as they were falling over each other in their haste to escape, running and stumbling away from the fortifications of the camp, barely able to fight as they were pushed back over the plain by the wave of Greeks falling on them, like a glittering bronze storm.

The echo of their shout, *A-chil-les, A-chil-les*, washed over the walls and rang in my ears.

'But – but Achilles swore to leave the war!' I gasped, horrified. 'I saw him, Cassandra, when I was in the Greek camp – he swore by the gods he wouldn't come back when King Agamemnon took his girl instead of me! Why would he fight now?'

She shook her head, eyes wide and scared. 'I don't know,' she said fearfully. 'This is the first time he's ever fought around the city, against Troy itself. I mean – we've heard terrible stories of what happened when he sacked the towns of the Troad, and . . .' She trailed off.

'. . . they were razed to the ground,' I finished in a whisper. 'All the men were killed and the women captured. I saw them.'

She nodded. 'And my brother is somewhere down there,' she said. 'What will happen to Hector?'

My heart filled with dread. *He doesn't know how to kill Achilles.*

A crowd was gathering on the battlements now. More and more of the Trojan nobles were bursting out of the tower staircase, pointing over the plain and repeating the ominous name of Achilles to each other; awestruck, terrified, hardly able to believe that what their eyes were showing them was true – that Achilles, godlike Achilles, had joined the war on Troy at last.

Achilles was running towards the city, his armour shining brighter and brighter, his outline clearer.

Our army was stampeding back towards the gates, running for their lives amid the cloud of dust that was rising under their feet, horses whinnying and falling under the confused mass of infantry.

'Where is my son?'

Queen Hecuba had appeared on the walls, followed closely by King Priam and her other sons.

King Priam seated himself in the canopied throne across the crowded tower, but the queen ran over to the battlements and leant over the edge, scanning the breaking wave of the Trojan retreat. I turned quickly away so she would not see me, but she had eyes only for her son. 'Have you seen him?' she asked Cassandra, her voice thick with emotion. 'Is my Hector alive?'

'I don't know, my lady Mother,' Cassandra said. 'I saw him a while ago, fighting around the Greek camp – but I don't know where he is now.'

'If Achilles—' Queen Hecuba broke off, clearly unable to finish the thought.

Achilles was two hundred paces from the city walls now.

Our army was pinned against the fortifications, a trail of corpses scattered in their wake across the plain, the Greeks still clashing their spears against their shields and shouting Achilles' name in a deafening roar.

The gates were closed, and our men could not risk opening them for fear that the Greeks would break into the city.

There was nowhere for the Trojans to go.

And then – inexplicably – silence fell over the two armies.

It was hard at first to see what was happening. The Trojans seemed to be melting to one side, the Greeks drawing back on to the plain.

'What is happening?' I whispered to Cassandra. 'What are the Greeks doing?'

'I don't know,' she said, her eyes wide, staring down over the walls.

And then Achilles moved into the space that had been cleared by the armies, and I knew what was happening.

There was going to be a duel.

But Achilles cannot die.

'Hector!' Queen Hecuba gasped, as a tall, broad-chested Trojan with a gold-plumed helmet stepped out of the Trojan ranks and faced the figure of Achilles. 'Oh, my boy, my boy!' She started to rock back and forth, arms clasped to her chest, moaning. 'Why could you not stay at home, like your other brothers, and let our men fight for you?'

A voice cut across her: 'Have I missed it? Have I missed the battle?'

The gorgeous slim figure of Prince Paris stepped delicately out of the tower door, holding Helen by the hand. Once again, despite all the tension and fear for Prince Hector below the walls, I felt that peculiar sensation of desire and fascination as I watched Helen walk towards the battlements, her long hair swinging behind her, like liquid silver, her grey-blue eyes like smoky pools of mercury, trailing behind her that musky scent of roses and jasmine.

'Missed the war, I should say,' Prince Aeneas said loudly, from beside King Priam's throne. 'Our thanks for leaving your boudoir to come and see your brother die, though. Very gracious of you.'

Paris went white. 'Is – is Hector down there?' he asked faintly.

Helen leant over the walls, and when she spoke her voice was low, rich and musical. 'Yes, he is, and he's with – but—' She turned to Paris, her lovely forehead creased. 'I don't believe it. It looks like – *Achilles*.'

All the remaining colour drained from Paris' cheeks.

The warriors were circling each other, like wild beasts. They were testing each other, one darting forwards and making a light jab with his spear, then retreating. Strangely, it looked as if Hector was the stronger as he lunged powerfully back and forth, but Achilles was fast on his feet and dodged out of the way, dancing around him light as an acrobat.

'You need to attack before he wears you out, my son,' I heard King Priam mutter, under his breath.

I looked around in spite of myself. The king was leaning on the arm of his throne, fists clenched so hard that his knuckles were white. 'Throw it – *now*!'

As if he had heard his father's voice, Hector leant back, his whole body arching, like a bent bow, weighing the spear lightly up and down in his hand. He took a few running steps, then shot the spear away from his body. It arrowed out of his hand in a perfectly straight line, the deadly point hissing through the air as it went.

In a heartbeat, Achilles crouched low to the ground, shield held close over his head.

The spearhead glanced off the bronze boss and whistled over him.

Hector had missed.

King Priam covered his face with his hands and groaned.

Queen Hecuba was still rocking back and forth, muttering silent prayers to the gods, her eyes turned up to the sky and tears pouring down her cheeks.

I looked back down to the plain, my fists clenched at my sides, my nails digging into my palms.

Hector had darted forwards and, while Achilles got back to his feet, had seized his spear from where it was buried, tip down, in the sand.

The Greeks were laughing and jeering at him, whistling and making rude gestures.

And then the same thing happened again – but this time it was Achilles who was arching his body back, Achilles running over the sand and flinging his huge ash spear with all his strength, watching, head craned up to the sky, to see if his aim was true.

I covered my eyes with my hands, half wishing I could not watch, but peering through my fingers all the same, desperate to see what would happen to our prince.

But the cast was too low and Hector easily lowered his shield to block it. The tip of bronze crumpled against the hide layers of the tall oval shield and the spear rattled back with a loud ringing sound, clattering on to the plain, like a dropped stick.

Hector started to move in towards him.

But Achilles did not give up. He reached down and, with a sharp scrape of metal on metal, drew a sword from his belt and charged towards the greatest warrior of Troy.

If Hector died now, Troy would be lost.

I tightened my grip on Cassandra's hand.

Hector was running faster than I had ever seen him. In one swift movement, he drew his left arm tighter towards his body to cover his body with his shield, then swung his right arm back and, with lightning speed, raised his spear above his head. The point glittered in the sun and then, as he let it go, flashed like a shooting star towards his opponent.

There was a moment, when Achilles simply stood still, mid-run, his sword still held high above his head as the spear point buried itself in the soft part of his neck, just above his collarbone, tunnelling its way through to the other side. Then he stumbled forwards a little. Blood gushed from his neck and gurgled through his throat, almost like a voice, a curse.

He fell to his knees, and then collapsed, face-forwards, on to the ground.

I held my breath, excitement and incredulity fighting for my attention in equal measure.

I looked around. No one could believe what had just happened. I could not believe it.

Achilles is dead!

But – how is that possible? He was hit in the neck, not the heel, he—

I heard the whisper around the parapet, heard it echoed like a breeze through the trees by the army below the walls.

Achilles, the greatest of the Greeks and son of a god, is dead!

The whisper grew louder, swelled into a rumble and then a roar.

'Achilles is dead! Achilles, the greatest of the Greeks, is dead!'

The nobles on the tower were celebrating, laughing and clapping. Even King Priam was smiling.

I turned to Cassandra and laughed aloud. She threw herself into my arms and embraced me.

The Trojans on the plain were shaking their spears in the air, roaring Hector's name. The Greeks stood silent and petrified, as if they had been turned into statues of bronze.

Slowly, Hector walked over to the dead body, crouched beside it and turned it on its back. With an enormous wrench, he pulled the spear from Achilles' throat. Then he took Achilles' helmet in both hands, and pulled it off.

Then, suddenly, all at once, the Greeks were shoving and pushing at each other, pressing forwards in a great mass to look at the body.

And now it was the Trojans who were stock still and silent, staring.

'Why aren't they moving?' Prince Aeneas asked impatiently, from beside his father's throne. 'My brother just killed Achilles. They should be counter-attacking, the fools!'

It was Helen who answered him. She drew her veil slowly back from her face and gazed down from the walls, her lovely face impassive. Then—

'It's not Achilles,' she said quietly.

'Not Achilles?' King Priam said loudly, astounded, and I heard his words repeated through the crowd in a low, breathless murmur. I felt my breath catch in the back of my throat. *How could it not be Achilles?* And then I remembered again what Briseis had said about his heel, and my heart dropped. 'But – but that is impossible! That is Achilles' armour. I am sure of it!'

Helen took a deep breath, still looking down at the body lying limp and bloody below the walls. 'It's Patroclus.'

Βρισηίς
Briseis, Greek Camp

The Hour of the Setting Sun

The Fourth Day of the Month of the Grape Harvest, 1250 BC

We could hear the army tramping from the plain as I huddled in the armoury with the other slaves. The shower of missiles upon the roof had ceased almost an hour ago, but we had been too frightened to leave our sanctuary. We had heard the muffled shouting, too confused to make anything out, then the distant sounds of weapons clashing upon the plain.

And silence.

Now the army was returning – but whether in victory or defeat, we did not know.

Neither did we know any more which side we wanted to win.

At last, unable to bear the tense silence inside the armoury, I decided to leave. I pushed open the door.

The guards that had stood outside when Patroclus had brought me there were gone. The camp was eerily quiet. Bronze-edged shields and broken spears littered the shore, and here and there wild dogs shuffled through the huts, noses to the ground. I picked my way around arrows lodged in the sand and bits of charred wood that had fallen from the burning ships towards the assembly-place.

And then I heard a cry of unearthly grief, a long, piercing moan, like the howl of a wounded animal.

My heart froze. I had recognized it before I had even had time to think. I would know that voice anywhere.

It was Achilles.

I gathered my tunic in one hand and started to run, darting between collapsed tents and fallen door-posts, my only thought to get to Achilles. The sound had come from the assembly-place.

I quickened my pace, avoided a discarded spear, darted past a soldier fallen upon his side and groaning in pain, ran around the side of Agamemnon's tent to the clearing . . .

And saw something that made me feel as if the ground were shifting beneath my feet, like the sea in a storm.

Patroclus, lying on a funerary bier raised upon a mound of earth, his brown eyes closed in death, his body clothed in the simple brown tunic, now stained with blood, that warriors wore beneath their breastplates. The soldiers standing by, respectful, sorrowful. As I gazed upon his body lying there in death, I saw Mynes' body, unburied, lying in the ruins of Lyrnessus. The bodies of my brothers, my father – everyone I had ever loved.

I held my arms out to each side of me and staggered through the crowded Greek warriors to the centre of the assembly-place.

A group of helmeted generals was clustered in the centre, and I pushed my way towards them, the soldiers buffeting me on each side. I could see Agamemnon in the middle, Odysseus, Menelaus . . .

And then I reached them, and found Patroclus. His body, his young, honest body, mangled, just as Mynes' had been, just as Rhenor's, Aigion's and Thersites' had been when they died . . . I let out a strangled cry and fell to my knees by his side, sobbing.

One of Agamemnon's bodyguards came up to me and caught me by one shoulder. 'What do you think you are doing, girl?' he asked roughly, pulling me away from Patroclus' body. 'You have no right to be here with the generals.'

I screamed and struggled against him, kicking and shouting Patroclus' name in sobs and gasps.

'Wait,' I heard Odysseus' brusque voice say, and the soldier stopped at once. 'Leave the girl here, Thoas. We may need her.'

He let go of me, and I fell to the ground, crawling through the dust back to Patroclus' side.

'Briseis?' said a voice. 'Briseis – is that you?'

It was Achilles. Close to, he seemed wild, desperate, possessed. His hair was fouled with dust, his face smeared with ashes and streaked with tears. He dropped to his knees beside Patroclus' bier.

I groped my way towards him. 'What happened?' I asked him, my voice breaking. 'What happened?'

Achilles shook his head. He could not speak.

Odysseus looked down at the pair of us, a curious expression on his face, then took a long, deep breath. 'Patroclus led the army out to Troy. He managed to push the Trojans back from the camp to the walls. There was a duel and . . .' he exhaled slowly '. . . Hector killed him.'

Achilles started to howl.

'Does anyone actually know *why* he went to war in the first place?' Nestor asked, his brow furrowed.

Odysseus shrugged his shoulders. 'We do not. It is clear, at any rate,' he glanced down at the huge, collapsed figure of Achilles beside me, 'that he was not ordered out.'

A slow terror was filling me. The echo of the words I had spoken in anger rang through my head.

How do you think a warrior such as Achilles could love a coward who spends all his time hiding behind the camp walls?

I felt a shiver run down my spine, and tears trickled down my cheeks.

Oh, Patroclus. Why did you go to war? Did you listen to what I said, foolish words that meant nothing? I tried to tell you! I tried to tell you they were not true . . .

'But what about the armour?' Diomedes asked, his face creased in a frown. 'We all saw him fighting in Achilles' armour. Why was he wearing it? Where is it?'

Odysseus swallowed and glanced at Achilles again. 'We do not know why Patroclus took it,' he said shortly. 'But I assume he thought – quite rightly, it turns out – that it was the only way he would be allowed to fight, as everyone knew Achilles had sworn not to permit it.' His tone became business-like. 'In any case, we lost the armour. Hector took it before Menelaus and I could get to the body. There was nothing we could do.'

Achilles was running his hands distractedly through his hair, groaning and weeping.

'Achilles,' Odysseus said abruptly, turning to him, 'you may have lost Patroclus, and Zeus knows I'm sorry for it, but we need you now – more than ever.' The other generals were nodding.

My ears were ringing. All thoughts of Patroclus left me as I realized what Odysseus was about to say.

'No!' I shouted. 'No, Achilles – you cannot go to war!'

The bodyguard, Thoas, kicked me in the ribs and I reeled, gasping for breath.

Odysseus ignored me. 'You saw how close we were to having our camp burnt to the ground, and if we had not mistaken Patroclus for you and thought you were there, leading us . . . If you could just lay aside your quarrel with King Agamemnon and come back and fight, I am sure,' he looked at the king, who gave a small nod, 'that Agamemnon will be more than happy to give you everything he offered before—'

Achilles had stood up. 'The quarrel does not matter any more.'

'What?'

'You heard me, Odysseus. The quarrel does not matter. I have lost Patroclus. I have lost my honour. I have failed in my oath to Menoetius.' His eyes glittered darkly, dangerously, and though his voice was quiet it was full of a suppressed rage. 'Hector will pay for this.' He paused ominously. 'Even if it costs me my life, *Hector will pay*.'

My vision blurred. My throat was so dry I could hardly utter a sound, only weep and shake my head.

Agamemnon rubbed his hands together. 'Well, that's settled, then,' he said. 'And, Achilles, if I was a little harsh earlier – well, you know how it is when Zeus decides to send down the goddess Delusion on us mortals—'

Odysseus interrupted him: 'We can pass over the excuses,' he said drily. 'What Achilles needs to know, Agamemnon,' and he fixed him with a hard stare, 'is if you will return the girl you took from him.' He pointed at me.

'Oh,' said Agamemnon, caught in mid-speech. 'That.' He glanced at me, his face blank. 'Yes,' he said easily. 'You can have her, Achilles, and my oath, by all the gods of Olympus, that I didn't take her to my bed.'

'No,' I moaned. 'Achilles, no . . . Please . . . *don't fight*.'

Achilles ignored me, and his eyes met Agamemnon's. There was a long silence as the two men, the king and the warrior hero, gazed at each other.

The entire army seemed to hold its breath.

Then Achilles gave a small, curt nod, and my world collapsed.

Agamemnon roared his approval.

Achilles gazed at the silent sea of soldiers and bronze-helmeted generals, his eyes blazing, face grim, jaw set. Slowly, deliberately, he drew his sword from the scabbard and raised it into the air. The blade flashed gold in the light of the setting sun, like a beacon on the shore. All at once, the men burst into an explosion of sound, cheering and stamping and shouting, clapping each other on the back, chanting Achilles' name and rattling their spears and shields.

Achilles was going to war.

And there was nothing I could do.

Appeal to the Prince

Χρυσηίς
Krisayis, Troy

The Hour of the Stars

The Fourth Day of the Month of the Grape Harvest, 1250 BC

That evening King Priam held a feast in Hector's honour. It seemed the king and queen were determined to celebrate the sacking of the Greek camp and Hector's defeat of Patroclus. No one, it seemed, cared very much that it had not been Achilles. One Greek dead was better than none, after all, and King Priam and Queen Hecuba were simply glad that their son was still alive.

But Hector had to know how to kill Achilles when he faced him: if he did not, then Troy would be destroyed.

'Where are you going?'

Cassandra and I were preparing for the feast in her high-roofed, cedar-scented chambers. I had told her the whole story: my capture and Troilus' death, the prophecy of the fall of Troy, the secrets I had smuggled from the Greek camp, being sent to Larisa and Apulunas' awful revelation and curse. When I had reached this part of the story, she had let out a deep breath.

'You were lucky.'

I gave her a rueful smile. 'Lucky? I shall never be noticed by a man again.'

Cassandra shrugged her shoulders thoughtfully.

'It could have been worse. Look,' she said, and she handed me the same small bronze hand-mirror.

I took it and held it up to my face, my fingers trembling, wondering what I would see there.

At first I did not notice any difference. My honey-brown eyes stared back at me, round and slightly fearful; my golden hair curled down over my shoulders, my full mouth was the same. And then, gradually, I saw it.

I was still me, and yet I was no longer myself. There was nothing memorable there any more. The spark in my eye, the colour in my cheeks were gone, as if I were a pale ghost – beautiful, but imperceptible. The eyes of any man would slide over me, as they would over a lack-lustre spirit. Apulunas had not made me ugly. He had made me completely and utterly unremarkable.

'Beauty has to be seen,' I breathed, my fingers trembling slightly as I handed the mirror back to her. 'He has all but made me invisible.'

Now I turned back to her from the door. She was sitting before her dressing-table, her long red hair spread out over her shoulders, still holding the bronze mirror. 'I must tell Hector how to kill Achilles.'

She sighed. 'Yes. I have been thinking that too.'

I looked at her in surprise. 'You have?'

She nodded. 'Ever since you told me what Briseis said to you in the Greek camp.' I made to speak, but she shooed me away, smiling slightly. 'Be on your way, Krisayis, or Hector will have left the feast and you will have no chance to fight with Fate this night.'

I smiled and pushed the door open, then walked quickly through my old chambers, out into the corridors towards the courtyard and the Great Hall. The sour smell of barley meal drifted towards me on the breeze as I crossed the courtyard, and the stars twinkled overhead, like bright oil-lamps flickering in the blackness of the sky. I remembered the last time I had stood before those doors in my golden dress, so sure of my beauty and of Troilus' love. And now I would never know either of those things again.

But that was in the past. There was no use regretting it now. There were more important things to be done.

I took a deep breath and pushed the doors open.

Hector was easy to find. The royals sat, as they always did, on the stone-carved thrones to the right of the hearth, and on that night Hector was the recipient of every toast, the subject of every prayer to the gods and every song sung by the bard on his three-legged stool by the fire. The Trojans were rejoicing as if they had won the war, not simply a battle and a duel.

I glanced around the hall and breathed a sigh of relief. The king and queen were busy greeting the nobles on the other side of the Great Hall. If I was quick I might escape the notice of the king. I made my way over to Prince Hector and bowed very low. 'My congratulations to you on your victory, Prince.'

He looked over from his conversation with his brother, Paris. It felt strange not to see the flicker of appreciation upon their faces at my beauty. Most of the princes seemed hardly to have noticed I was there.

'Krisayis,' Hector said, with a slight frown. 'I thought you had been forbidden from the city by my father.'

I bowed my head further. 'I was. I would not have returned, had I not been convinced that our city is in grave danger and that I might be of service to it.'

There was a short pause.

'I beg you to listen to me,' I said, careful to keep my voice low. 'We have known each other since we were young, have we not, Hector? I must speak with you immediately, before your father the king sees I am here. What I have to say concerns the fate of Troy.' I looked up at Paris. 'Perhaps we might speak in private?'

Hector considered me. 'The fate of Troy?' he asked, in a low voice. He leant forwards, lowering his voice even further. 'The herald Idaeus informed me, in confidence, that you passed us information of great import from the camp of the Greeks. He thought it best not to reveal to my father and mother, the king and queen, that it was you who was the spy, for they might not have taken kindly to it after Troilus' death. But I know that it took great bravery on your part to spy for us among the Greeks, and for that I thank you. Do you bring me more news yourself?'

I nodded, keeping my eyes down.

Hector stood from his throne then and drew me to a corner of the hall, Paris watching us warily.

When I was sure we could not be heard over the loud cheers and laughter of the feast, I turned to Hector. 'You know that they say Achilles cannot be killed,' I said, without preamble. 'They are right. But he has a weakness.' Hector frowned, but I continued, determined to give him the news I had waited so long to tell. 'His mother, whom the Greeks call the goddess Thetis, made him immortal in all his body but his heel.' I took a deep breath. 'This is the only part in which he can be killed,' I said. 'You must strike him in his heel and destroy our greatest enemy while Troy still stands.'

Hector had been silent while I spoke. Now, to my utter confusion, he was smiling. 'Oh, my dear Krisayis,' he said gently. 'You are right to say that we played together and grew up together here in the palace. You are as a sister to me, as Cassandra is, and as a brother, I honour your words. Yet you surely cannot still expect me to believe such stories. These are tales for children, not grown men and warriors. If I believed all the tales I heard I should have to run my sword through every inch of Achilles' body.'

My eyebrows knotted in a frown as I took in what he had said. 'You – you do not believe me?'

He placed his hands on my shoulders. 'My wife, Andromache – she, too, thinks that she can direct the orders of battle from her loom. I know it must be hard for you to sit here in the city while we fight upon the plain but, Krisayis, you must understand that I am far better versed in matters of battle. I have a council of war. I have been advised and trained in matters of the battlefield since before I could speak or write. I do not blame you for believing such a tale but,' he patted my shoulder, 'you should not concern yourself with it.'

I could hardly believe what I was hearing. 'Hector, you must listen to—'

But the prince had already turned away from me and was walking back to the royal thrones. As he reached his place and sat down to the feast again, I could clearly hear him retelling the tale of Achilles' heel with a smile, and Paris' shouts of laughter in response.

I sank down the smooth plaster of the wall to the floor, watching Hector and Paris laugh together with a sense of gathering frustration and dread. Would no one believe me except Cassandra? Did my words count for nothing, simply because I had been born the daughter of a priest and a woman? Would *no one* listen to what I had to say?

And if they did not, how could Troy survive?

PART IV

Death of a Hero

Mount Ida, Overlooking the Trojan Plain

Many weeks have passed. Achilles has returned to the war, as he promised he would, and the tides of battle have turned. The Trojan plain is unrecognizable, a blackened field of dust, littered with the dead, constantly ploughed by the feet of Greek and Trojan soldiers in the never-ending strife of war.

But the greatest loss of all is that of Hector. Hector, King Priam's son, his heir, his protector; Hector, tamer of horses, the greatest of the Trojans, father of the next Trojan king. He was killed at the hands of Achilles in the fury of his revenge. He ran the length of the walls of Troy before Achilles' deadly spear severed his throat and his life-blood ran into the earth. Achilles trussed up his corpse behind his chariot and dragged it through the dust of the Trojan plain, fouling his dark hair with dirt and blood. Hector's wife fainted when she heard the news. His mother cried. His sister prophesied in vain. Even the father of the gods mourned his passing, for with his death, the city of Troy must also fall.

But there is one more man who must die before that.

The gods are sitting on Mount Ida, watching the battle. All of them, that is, except Hermes.

'I'll take a bet on the next one to go,' Hermes whispers, into Apollo's ear, from his seat in the back row of the council of the gods. 'Ajax versus Aeneas. I'll give you good odds.' He looks slyly at Apollo. 'Seven to one Aeneas wins.'

Apollo tries to pretend he's concentrating on the battle below, but the temptation is too much. He never could resist a good gamble, and Hermes knows it. 'Seven to one? Against Ajax? He's the best Greek warrior, after Achilles.' He snorts under his breath. 'Try ten to one, then I'll start listening.'

Hermes considers. 'All right, ten to one, but if you lose, I get that water nymph we met last night.'

Apollo is about to protest, but Athena turns from the row in front and gives them a severe look. The pair falls silent for a while.

'All right,' Apollo whispers, almost imperceptibly, out of the corner of his mouth. 'Ten to one and the water nymph into the bargain, and count yourself lucky.'

Hermes settles back in his seat and crosses his arms in satisfaction.

Silence falls again as Hermes and Apollo watch the war, now eagerly following the progress of their two warriors. Ajax has come into Aeneas' range – they could be fighting at any minute.

'Come on,' Apollo mutters, to the small red-plumed figure that is Aeneas. 'Come on – just a little bit to the left . . .'

But then, unexpectedly, another hero – Odysseus, to judge from his distinctive boar's tusk helmet – veers into Aeneas' path, and the two engage in a lengthy duel.

Ajax moves off to the left and away from Aeneas.

Apollo slumps back in his seat and turns to Hermes. 'This is boring.'

Hermes nods. Apollo is right. Nothing has happened for days except a few skirmishes. They haven't had something even vaguely exciting, like the death of a hero, to liven up the action.

He turns from the war to survey the rest of the gods instead.

Athena and Hera, of course, are sitting smugly side by side, watching the success of their Greek protégés with evident pride. But all the other gods, he notices, are distinctly uninterested. Hephaestus is playing croquet with his walking stick and a bit of cloud. Ares is tapping his fingers impatiently on one burly thigh and keeps glancing back towards Aphrodite, who is sitting just behind him, looking ravishing.

'I don't know why you're keeping us here, Father,' Ares says to Zeus, in a low growl.

Hermes smiles to himself. Ares is clearly itching to get away. No doubt

Aphrodite has promised him another secret rendezvous in her bedroom. He glances at Hephaestus, who is, it seems, still completely in the dark, poor fellow. Look at him, *Hermes thinks,* playing with his croquet set. It's almost enough to make one feel sorry for him.

And yet he can't blame Ares for feeling frustrated. Hermes taps his foot irritably on the clouds, his brief moment of amusement gone. He can't stand the way Zeus always waits for the Fates to sort things out. What happened to being the all-powerful king of the gods? What was the point of being endowed with immortality and all kinds of fantastic powers if you weren't using them?

Hermes has had enough of sitting around. And, in a moment, he's made up his mind. There's one god on Olympus who still has enough initiative left in him to make things happen. 'Psst,' he hisses at Apollo, who's nodding off. His head is bouncing against his chest, curly gold locks waving gently as his breath rises and falls.

Hermes nudges him in the ribs. 'Psst. Sleeping Beauty.'

Apollo starts and grunts loudly as he wakes up.

Athena turns again, incredulous and disapproving, to give both of them a prolonged stare, which Apollo returns with interest.

'I've had an idea,' Hermes whispers, pulling Apollo away from his staring match with Athena.

Apollo turns his attention to Hermes. 'What?'

'Something to liven things up.'

Apollo rolls his eyes. 'At last,' he says, under his breath, cricking his neck. 'How long is it they've been fighting? A year? Two?'

'More like ten,' Hermes says, with a yawn. He leans closer to Apollo. 'I think,' he says, lowering his voice, 'it's time we caused some trouble.'

A slow grin spreads over Apollo's face. Hermes always knows how to cheer him up. Together, they get up from their seats, trying not to make a sound as they walk slowly away from the council, although most of the other gods are either asleep or watching Hephaestus' croquet game. The pair goes around the back of a particularly large cloud, and the council disappears out of sight.

'So,' Apollo asks eagerly, as soon as they are far enough away not to be overheard, 'what's your idea?'

Hermes grins mischievously at him. 'I think Athena deserves a bit of trouble, don't you?' he asks, flicking at bits of cloud so they float on the air, like dandelion fluff. 'The Greeks are so predictably successful. All those victories, one after another.' He yawns to illustrate the point. 'It's not like we don't know what's going to happen in the end. But,' he says, grinning, 'Athena and Hera are so smug. And we wouldn't want to make things too easy for the dream team, would we?' He leans over to whisper in Apollo's ear.

Apollo's eyes widen. Very slowly, a smile spreads over his face. The two gods exchange a look of pure mischief. They understand each other perfectly.

'So who d'you think should do it?' Apollo sniggers in a very un-godlike way. 'Who'd annoy Athena the most?'

Hermes considers the question, like a connoisseur assessing the value of a piece of jewellery. He gazes down at the plain to give himself time to think. The armies are still clashing beneath the walls of Troy. His eye is caught by a figure standing on the battlements. It's holding a bow and arrow, and is firing left, right and centre with no sense of aim whatsoever, arrows exploding from the bow, like water bubbling out of a burst pipe. Most telling of all, perhaps, is the leopard skin slung over one of the figure's bronzed and perfectly oiled shoulders.

'Ah.' Hermes raises a hand to his chin, captivated. 'Paris. The perfect match.'

Apollo raises his eyebrows. 'Paris? That prince can't aim a bow to save his life. He never spent as much time training for war as Hector – he's an utter coward! Just look at him!' He gestures to the walls, where Paris has just let fly another arrow. It arcs up into the air and then, spinning out of control, plummets towards the ground some fifty feet west of the Greek line. 'How's he going to hit anything except a passing bird?'

Hermes saunters up to Apollo and places an arm around his shoulders. 'That's why it's so much fun.' He grins. 'And why we need you, brother. After all, aren't you meant to be the god of archery? Or,' he asks innocently, 'is that just another story the mortals tell?'

Apollo's chest puffs with wounded pride. 'You know I'm the best shot on Olympus.'

'Well, then,' replies Hermes, his eyes twinkling, 'I think you should go and

give this young Trojan a lesson in using that bow of his before it's too late.'

They exchange a last grin. Then Hermes winks at Apollo, and Apollo straps his bow and arrows to his back and leaps from the cloud with the grace of a bird.

He sees the little island of Tenedos far on the horizon, set like a green jewel in the glittering ocean, and the coastline of the Troad, curving out before it in a white line. He sees the thin blue lines of the two rivers of Troy, and the patchwork of green fields, olive and tamarisk trees, and the oak forest stretching to the south. Now he's getting closer, and he can make out the dust from the battlefield, the ships of the Greeks pulled up on the sand with their high, curving prows, and above it all, the towers of Troy rising into the sky . . .

And then, light as a leaf blown on the wind, he lands on the walls.

He's standing next to a young man who, he assumes, from the drench of scent that wafts towards him on the breeze, must be Paris. He looks up and catches Hermes' ironic wave from behind one of the clouds. His grin widens as he imagines Athena and the rest of the gods up there, watching the war with no idea of what he's about to do.

But not even the virgin goddess will be fast enough to stop him now.

The young Trojan is still firing arrows all over the place, his hands clammy and his face covered with sweat.

Apollo comes to stand right beside him, invisible and silent as a whisper of wind. 'Hello,' he says in his ear.

Paris jumps.

'Who— What—?' he splutters. He's looking wildly around as if he has been visited by a spirit from the Underworld. 'Hector?' he whispers fearfully. 'Is – is that you?'

Apollo laughs. He knows the young man can't see him, but it never stops being fun, watching the way the mortals act so surprised.

'Not Hector,' he says. 'A god. I have a job for you, Trojan.'

Paris quakes. 'What kind of job?' he asks, and his voice rises uncontrollably. 'You're not going to kill me, are you?'

'Kill you?' Apollo asks, leaning back against the battlements and winking up at Hermes. 'Heavens, no. In fact, I want you to do the killing for me.'

Paris looks down at the battlefield. 'I'm not going down there, if that's what you want,' he says, with a stab at defiance, but his trembling lip gives him away. 'I'm no good at fighting.'

'You don't have to be,' Apollo says. 'What's that you have there in your hand?'

Paris looks down. 'A bow,' he says doubtfully. 'But I can't shoot to save my—'

'Oh yes you can,' Apollo interrupts. 'You forget who's helping you, Paris.'

The young prince gulps and glances around him, as if hoping he's imagining things.

Apollo moves closer. 'Do it,' he whispers, breathing courage into the young man's ear. 'Nothing could be easier. Do it.'

Slowly, as if he's moving in a dream, Paris raises the bow and stretches the string tight to his ear. The tip of the arrow is shaking badly in his fingers.

'That's it,' Apollo says, and he guides the bow down, so that the arrow is pointing straight towards the plain. 'Now – let go!'

Paris does as he is told. The arrow jumps from the bowstring, like a bird, and flies through the air with deadly force.

Apollo leaps with it. Twisting and spiralling around the arrow, he shapes the wind to guide it closer, ever closer to his target. He's searching for a single warrior, the warrior whose name Hermes whispered in his ear.

The plain looms dangerously close. Suddenly shields and blood and swinging axes are all around, and still the god and the arrow spin down together as one.

Fighting men leap and thrust, bend and fall in the dance of war, but the arrow passes clean through, whistling through the gaps between shields and under raised arms as if the movements of the warriors had been choreographed around it in some savage dance. A chariot charges across their path, horses whinnying and manes thrashing in the battle-din. A sword swings within a hair's breadth, singing as it grazes the edge of the arrowhead. All around there is a confused mass of fighting men, Greek and Trojan, man and boy, the living, the dying and the dead melding into each other, shifting shapes in the confusion of war . . .

And then, at last, the god spots his target.

A long mane of blond hair. Glittering black eyes. Strength that no other mortal can match.

The arrow dives towards the ground, guided by the wind of the god, spinning and flashing in the evening sun.

Achilles is whirling, like a storm, upon the battlefield, flattening men, crumpling them to their knees as he comes upon them in the full fury of his battle-rage. His spear catches a Trojan in the back as he runs and brings him face down into the dirt. His sword is a blur of bronze and blood. He lunges to deal a deadly blow, whirls on his heel, dives under a thrown spear. He draws his sword and brings it high into the air to split a Trojan skull.

As he moves, for a brief moment, his feet can be seen clearly through the dust.

His heel is exposed.

With deadly precision the arrow makes contact. Sharpened bronze meets flesh.

Before Achilles can so much as turn to look at what has happened, the arrowhead buries itself in the ankle, punching through cartilage, splitting tendons and bone. It tunnels through the flesh, bursts out the other side and lodges itself in the plain. Blood – dark blood – leaks out into the dust in a slow pool.

Achilles stops.

Everyone around him stops.

They fall deathly silent as they stare at the spreading pool of Achilles' blood, the arrow sticking incongruously from his heel like a third limb. No one except Apollo notices the flash of brilliant white light from the sky, announcing that the goddess Athena has seen what has happened and is coming to her favourite's aid.

But she will be too late.

Achilles is on his knees now. The sounds of battle are muffled to his ears. The life-force is leaking out of him into the ground with his blood. He inches forwards, gasping. He wavers. Then he falls.

The veil of death covers his eyes.

Achilles, the best of the Greeks, is no more.

Final Acts

Βρισηίς
Briseis, Greek Camp

The Hour of the Evening Meal

The Seventeenth Day of the Month of Ploughing, 1250 BC

I was sitting in Achilles' hut, tending the small altar to Apollo – a bronze brazier for burning incense – when I heard the sound of the army marching back through the camp. I knew at once, from the silence, that something was wrong.

My fingers went cold. I dropped the incense and stood, walked over and pushed open the door.

The soldiers were returning to their huts, unlacing their bloodied breastplates and dropping their spears and swords, their shoulders bent, eyes turned to the ground as if they would not look each other in the face and see the recognition of what had happened there.

'What – what is it?' I asked, my voice high and unnatural in the silence that had fallen over the camp, like a dense mist. 'Did we lose?'

They would not look at me, any of them. I saw Ajax push open the door to his hut and disappear behind it into the darkness.

'What happened?' I said again.

A soldier nearby – young, from his unlined brow and the light beard upon his chin, though his eyes spoke of years beyond his age – met my eyes at last. 'Achilles,' he said, his voice hoarse. 'He's—'

'No,' I whispered. 'No . . .'

'He's dead,' the soldier said, and he turned away.

I looked around at the men, the men he had served with and led, whose lives depended on him. 'It's not possible,' I mumbled. 'He couldn't die. He wasn't meant to die.'

But the soldiers were wrapped in concern for their own lives, their own loss, and they did not listen.

I turned back towards the hut, numb. The deep, desperate ache inside me was more than grief. It was emptiness, desolation, as if Death surrounded me on all sides, encircling me with his dark, spreading wings, waiting, waiting to take all those I loved, and in the centre of it all, I stood on the shore, watching them fall away, waiting for when he would take me too.

The hut was dark and empty when I opened the door. On Achilles' bed, the blankets were still tumbled over the fleeces as he had left them that morning when he went out to war. We had not lain together since that first night, the night before the plague came and I was taken to Agamemnon's tent. Indeed, since I had returned, Achilles had hardly looked at me, or I at him. Patroclus' death had changed us both. He had become like a man possessed, a man without thought for anything but war and killing and blood-fury. Could I still have seen in him the man who had told me that he, too, was a slave to his fate?

No. Not any more.

That man had gone. He had been destroyed, like a ripe crop of wheat flattened in a summer storm, when he had laid eyes upon Patroclus' dead body. As something within me, too, had broken that day. We were, neither of us, what we had been.

I felt the tears start in my eyes and leant against the doorpost, brushing them away fiercely with the linen of my tunic. I looked around the deserted hut, at Patroclus' empty pallet, Achilles' empty bed.

Mynes.

Patroclus.

Achilles.

I said their names only in my thoughts: husband, friend, lover. All of them in the shadowy caverns of the Land of the Dead.

I let out a sob and cradled my head in my hands, the tears leaking through my fingers.

I could not believe that he, too, was gone.

That I was alone in the world of men once more.

Χρυσηίς
Krisayis, Troy

The Hour of the Setting Sun

The Seventeenth Day of the Month of Ploughing, 1250 BC

Many weeks after Hector's death had rocked Troy to its foundations, Cassandra and I were in the herb garden, gathering fragrant lavender and marjoram leaves with the women of her chambers. My father had not yet returned from Didyma, and I had kept to Cassandra's rooms as much as I could, hiding myself from the king among the many serving women and slaves of the women's quarters. Cassandra was pale and quiet, and I often saw tears glinting in the corners of her eyes. I, on the other hand, could not grieve. I felt empty, betrayed. If only Hector had *listened* to me . . . If only . . .

I felt the frustration of it all building up inside me until it became almost unbearable.

'Oh, what does it *matter*?' I burst out. I dashed the neat handfuls of marjoram to the ground, scattering them over the lines of ordered herbs, their names carefully marked on small chips of wood. 'What does it matter, when nothing we do makes any *difference*?'

Cassandra set down her basket of lavender, her eyes wide. 'Krisayis . . .'

'No!' I shouted. It was too much to bear, after all I had done, that Hector should still have died. That he had refused to listen to me. That Cassandra had lost her brother and Troy its greatest protector, and that everything I had tried to do had not prevented it. 'How can you suffer it? How can you bear that no one listens to you, that you cannot make any difference to the world but simply pass through it like a shadow, a slave to the passions of men and gods?'

I was pacing around the rows of plants now, my feet treading indiscriminately on paved gravel and fragrant green leaves. 'I told you what Apulunas said, Cassandra! He told me that the war is nothing but a game to the gods!'

I turned to face her.

'If Apulunas was telling the truth, and the gods are the same for us and for the Greeks, why should they care any more for us than they do for them? Cassandra – what if the gods have decided that Troy shall fall, and there is nothing we can do?'

'Nothing you can do?' Cassandra said fiercely, taking me by the shoulders, her blue eyes blazing. 'You risked your life in the Greek camp to pass information back to Troy. This is not nothing, Krisayis! Or do you think that the lives of even a few Trojans are not worth saving?' She glared at me, her fingers tight against my shoulders.

I held her gaze defiantly. Then I let out my breath and dropped my eyes. 'No – you are right, Cassandra. One man returned alive to his wife and home is worth – is worth all that I have done. It is just that—'

There was a sound of running feet in the corridor beyond the herb garden. We both turned, our breath catching in our throats. What new calamity had now befallen us?

'Princess Cassandra!' a voice called. A messenger was coming into view between the pillars that separated the garden from the corridor beyond. He was breathing hard, his face red and alight with excitement. 'News from your father! You are to come to the walls immediately. Achilles has been killed!'

I turned to stare at Cassandra, and found her gazing back at me. 'Killed?' I asked, my pulse racing at my throat. 'How?'

The messenger was hopping on the spot in his excitement and barely looked at me as he said, 'Prince Paris shot an arrow through his heel.'

I stared at him, then laughed aloud.

Cassandra took me by the arms and we whirled each other around.

'He is dead! Achilles is dead, at last!'

We came to a stop, dizzy and panting, breathless with laughter and giddy with the sudden happiness of the news.

The messenger was still hesitating by the colonnade, clearly anxious to be gone. 'Shall I escort you to the tower, Princess?'

Cassandra shook her head, smiling, still breathing hard. 'Tell my father we shall be there in a moment.'

The messenger left.

Cassandra's eyes were shining. 'Krisayis – Paris must have heard what you told Hector!'

I nodded. 'He must have! No, wait – he *did*! Prince Hector told him! And I didn't even think . . . didn't think . . .' I trailed off into silence. An idea had come into my head. Others had suggested it before . . . but with what I knew, it might just be possible . . .

And if it works . . .

'Krisayis?' Cassandra asked tentatively. 'What – what's wrong?'

I hit myself on the forehead. 'Of course! Why didn't I think of it before?'

Cassandra was utterly puzzled. 'Think of what?'

I was pacing up and down the gravel paths now, thinking hard. 'Yes,' I muttered to myself. 'Yes, it's perfect.' I turned to Cassandra. 'Cassandra – there *is* something I can do!'

She looked at me, stunned. 'What?'

But I had already caught her arm and turned towards the arch into the corridor. 'Come,' I said, pulling her towards it. 'Come. We must go to the tower. I have to see King Priam.'

'But what about my father's orders against your return?'

'That doesn't matter now. There is one last piece of information I think he needs.'

King Priam and Queen Hecuba were sitting on their carved wooden thrones with the blue glass dolphins, surrounded by their sons and advisers, as Cassandra and I climbed out of the staircase on to the tower. The queen turned at the sound of the door closing, and Cassandra walked over for her blessing.

'Stand, Cassandra,' King Priam said, as she moved to kneel before him. His old face was alight with a smile. 'Stand, and see for yourself, my dear daughter, that Achilles is dead. Our greatest foe has been defeated. Do you doubt, now, that Troy shall stand for a thousand years and more?'

I saw Cassandra's pale cheeks flush slightly.

'Ah, daughter,' the king said, taking her hand, 'I was only jesting. You take your prophecies seriously, I know. And yet I cannot help but defy them, when I see Achilles lying down there on the plain, his knees loosened by your own brother's arrow!'

Cassandra did not say anything in reply. Instead she turned to me where I was standing, still by the tower door. 'My lady mother, my lord father,' she said. 'Krisayis has something she would tell you.'

The king and queen turned towards me, seeing me for the first time as I walked across the tower towards them and knelt down.

'*Her!*' Queen Hecuba exclaimed.

King Priam's forehead had deepened into a frown. 'How dare you return to the city, daughter of Polydamas?' he asked, in a low, rumbling voice. 'How dare you look upon me, when my son died because of your unworthy seduction?'

I moved to stand, my hands cold with fear but determined to say what I must, and opened my mouth to speak, but Cassandra spoke before me.

'She was not to blame,' she said, in a high, clear voice.

King Priam stared at his daughter, disapproval etched all over his face.

'Troilus asked her to meet him by the South Gates,' Cassandra continued. 'I heard the messenger who delivered his request to her. Troilus wanted to run with her from Troy and had horses brought for the purpose. I have already asked the groom and Axion, the guard of the gate, and they informed me that this was entirely Troilus' plan. Ask them, my lord, and they will tell you. Krisayis had nothing to do with Troilus' death. In fact, she tried to stop him.'

Cassandra's eyes were bright as she turned to me. I smiled at her, overcome with gratitude. Then I turned towards the thrones. 'My king,' I said, my heart beating very fast, 'when I was in the Greek camp, I believe the herald Idaeus was bringing you information from the tent of King Agamemnon, or as much as I was able to pass him.'

The king's expression sharpened. '*You* were the spy among the Greeks?'

I nodded. 'Yes.'

Queen Hecuba took a breath in, glancing over at her husband. 'You took such a great risk, for us?'

I nodded again. 'For Troy – yes.' There was a long pause, and I felt the eyes of the king and queen upon me, distrust and astonishment radiating from them in equal measure. 'There is more,' I said quickly. 'When I was with Prince Troilus in the woods outside the walls, we overheard the Greeks.' I swallowed, my throat dry. 'They said that they had decided not to post guards within the woods, for fear that our bowmen might torch the trees. I told Idaeus as much. But it is of far greater consequence now than I thought it was when I first heard it.'

'And why is that?' Queen Hecuba asked, her voice sharp with disapproval.

I looked directly at her. 'My queen,' I said, 'I know that Achilles' death makes our victory seem near. But I, too, have seen and spoken to the god Apulunas, and he has told me that Troy is fated to fall. And it is coming soon. We must do all we can to save the city.'

The king and queen exchanged glances that were heavy with suspicion.

'You saw the Great God Apulunas?' Queen Hecuba asked, glancing from Cassandra back to me. 'You saw him, too?'

I bowed my head. 'Yes, my queen. It is happening. The city is about to fall. Indeed, the god Apulunas told me it has been fated to fall since before the Greek ships sailed.'

The king leant forwards upon his throne. 'Daughter of Polydamas,' he said, and I was surprised to see that he was smiling, 'Troy has not been captured for a thousand years. Our walls are the strongest in all the world. Our greatest enemy is dead. What makes you think that I should believe the foolish imaginings you and my daughter have conjured together in her chambers, when everything tells me that we can and *will* win this war?'

'I do not ask that you believe me,' I said steadily. 'All I ask is that you take precautions. I have seen how captives are treated in the Greek camp. The men are killed without mercy, the women enslaved in the beds of their lords or sent to work the silver mines in Thrace. My king, should we lose –'

King Priam shook his head in disbelief.

'– *should* we lose,' I continued firmly, 'the men and women who make the city of Troy what it is must be saved. For Troy is far more than its buildings and its walls. It is its *people*.'

The frown had returned to King Priam's face, but I would not be stopped.

'It is the women who lay clothes to dry on the rooftops of Troy,' I continued. 'It is the fishermen who catch the silver fish in the bay,' I gestured out over the plain towards the sea, sparkling blue in the sunlight, 'and sell them on the stalls of the marketplace. It is the princes who live in the palaces on the windy heights of the city, and the slaves who draw water from the wells. This, my king – *this* is Troy. And if we act now, we may still be able to save our city before it is too late.'

King Priam shook his head again. 'I have heard that King Agamemnon treats his prisoners without clemency,' he said, 'but we shall have no need of his mercy when we win.'

'Father,' a voice said. Prince Aeneas, King Priam's third son, had stepped forwards. 'If I may speak.'

King Priam bowed his head.

Aeneas cleared his throat. 'What you say is right and just, as it should be from the mouth of a sceptre-bearing king. But I am bound to remind you that we are drawing on our last supplies from the granaries, and that even now the last of the barley meal, millet and vetch are being sent to the poor of the city. The harvest has not been gathered, as the farms were left untended when the Trojans came to the shelter of the city, so the stores of wheat have not been replenished. Hardly any merchants or farmers have been allowed in or out since, upon your orders. When did we last see shellfish from the bay upon our plates? Or fresh meat hunted from the hills?' He took a deep breath. 'I fear that, if we do not remove the poor and the sick and those unable to fight from the city soon, we shall have nothing left with which to feed our army. And if our soldiers do not eat, then how shall we ever win the war?'

King Priam's brows knitted. Then he turned to his adviser. 'Is this true, Dryops?'

Dryops bowed his head. 'It is, my king. The overseers of the granaries estimate that we have but a few weeks' supply of barley remaining, with so many additional mouths to feed, and barely a week's worth of vetch.'

The king tapped his fingers upon the arm of his throne, thinking.

I held my breath, hardly daring to hope.

At last, King Priam turned back to me. 'Very well, daughter of Polydamas,' he said, his words clipped. 'We shall send the women, slaves and children and those who are old or injured from the city, as my son suggests. Dryops, you will send an edict to the heralds, to be proclaimed throughout the city, that all who are unfit to fight are to leave the city. We must preserve food supplies for our warriors and nobles. You will give our people assurances that they will return to Troy as soon as we have driven the Greeks from our shores.'

Dryops nodded briskly. 'Yes, my king.'

'Daughter of Polydamas, you will aid Dryops in organizing their removal through the woods, if, as you say, they have been left unguarded. My spies inform me that it is the custom of the Greeks to engage in funeral games and feasts until the twelfth night, when they light the pyre and burn their dead. We shall have the people leave the city on that night, while the Greeks are burning Achilles.' He gave me a shrewd look. 'Do you think you can manage it?'

I nodded, my heart racing. *Twelve days . . .*

'Then,' he continued, 'our people should be taken to the fortified towns beyond the mountains in the south, on the border with the Maeonians, where they can await our victory and then return.'

I glanced at Cassandra, and saw my own happiness and disbelief reflected in her face. Then I knelt before the king and queen, gazing up into the faces of the last of the dynasty of Laomedon, who held it in their hands to determine the fate of the city I loved most. 'I shall begin immediately, my king,' I promised.

Βρισηίς
Briseis, Greek Camp

The Hour of the Stars

The Twenty-ninth Day of the Month of Ploughing, 1250 BC

I had been sent to Agamemnon's tent the day Achilles died, though still the king did not dare to lie with me, fearing the vengeance of the spirits of the dead if he took me before Achilles' body was consumed upon the flames.

Now, after twelve days of mourning, gifts and funeral games, they were burning Achilles on his pyre. From where I stood on the platform around the wooden palisade to the east, I could see the flames flickering against the dark night sky in a shower of sparks that melted into the stars.

I could not bear to be with everyone else. I could not bear to see the false grief on Agamemnon's face. I could not endure watching the generals and the soldiers weep for a man they had never truly known. The gnawing pain inside me, the emptiness of loneliness and loss, was almost more than I could tolerate. When I had heard that Achilles was dead, that Paris had struck him in the heel as he fought around Troy, that I would be leaving Achilles' hut for the tent of the king once more, I had felt as if a part of me had been lost that I would never find. As if Mynes had taken with him to the Underworld more than half of what I was, and Patroclus and Achilles together had taken the small part that remained.

I turned away from the sight of the pyre, but its orange glow was still imprinted against my eyelids. Nearby, the sound of the eastern lookouts laughing and playing dice echoed hollowly in my ears. I could not understand how anyone in the world could laugh any more, now that Achilles, too, was dead.

Troy lay on the horizon, still and quiet in the evening air. A few watch-fires glimmered on the walls, but apart from the flickering fire of the torches, there was no movement.

Or was there?

I narrowed my eyes. On the horizon, barely visible, a strange ripple seemed to be crossing the short span of the plain between the southern gates of the city and the forests that spread south to the lower slopes of Mount Ida, many, many thousands of paces distant. I stared at it. The movement was constant, but so faint that I might almost have missed it. It was as if a river were crossing the plain where I knew that there was none . . . a river . . .

A river of *people.*

My eyes widened in shock.

It was the Trojans.

They were escaping from the city.

I tried to make out if the lookouts had seen what I had. There were only two of them, for there was no gate on this side of the camp and most of the guards were placed along the southern part of the palisade where the settlement was most vulnerable to attack. And, from their laughter and the rattle of dice as they hit the table, the lookouts had noticed nothing.

But, still, if they saw the Trojans leaving the city . . .

I made up my mind. Gathering my tunic in my hands, I hurried back along the wooden rampart, then down the ladder to the camp as fast as I could. The huts were deserted – all the soldiers were watching Achilles' body burn – and my way was unimpeded as I dashed through the tents and huts, one hand held to the ache in my side, the other hitching my tunic up from under my feet.

At last I saw it. The healer's hut. Without pausing, I pushed the door open and slipped inside. I had been there only once before, sent by Agamemnon's healer for some cures, and it was dark, one old terracotta oil-lamp burning in the corner. My fingers fumbling in my fear, I picked up the lamp and held it up to the clay pots, one after another, trying to make out in the flickering light the writing scrawled upon them in black glaze.

Heliotrope ... common fumitory ... mallow ... rock-rose ... stoneseed ...

And there it was. In a large jar sealed with wax: *juice of the poppy*. My hand shook as I lifted it from the shelf and carried it to a table, where a jar of red wine – stolen, no doubt, from the stores of Pedasus or Lyrnessus – and a goblet, still half full, stood beside a bundle of tablets that the healer had clearly been reading before he had left to watch Achilles' pyre. Pulling the wax stopper from the pot of poppy juice, I tipped it slightly and poured several drops into the jar of red wine, enough, as Deiope had told me when I was young, to invoke a deep and instant sleep.

I had to walk more slowly back to the palisade to stop the wine spilling. The lookouts were still playing dice. I could hear their shouts to the gods to bless them with luck, their laughter and curses growing louder, as I climbed slowly, careful not to spill a drop, up the ladder on to the rampart. They hardly noticed as I approached them, their eyes fixed on the game.

'Brave guards,' I said, doing everything I could to keep my voice steady. One looked up, then nudged the other in the ribs. He grunted.

'I bring you wine from King Agamemnon himself,' I continued, holding out the jar and gripping my fingers to keep them from trembling. 'He wishes you to pour a libation to the gods in honour of the great Achilles. He sends you this good wine as a token of his thanks for your watch this night.'

The lookouts' faces mirrored greedy grins.

'Give it here, then,' the first one said. He grabbed it from me and poured a few drops to the ground before sloshing the rest into their goblets. His breath stank of wine already, and the jar swayed in his hand as he poured. 'To the great Achilles!'

They raised their goblets and drained them in one.

There were a few moments as they looked at each other, still grinning, the dice upon the table showing two ones: the losing throw. Then, slowly, their faces relaxed. Their eyelids drooped.

As one, the two men slumped on their stools.

They were asleep.

I let out a long, low breath and glanced towards Troy. A steady stream of people still rippled out from the South Gates into the darkness, heading for the black line of the trees of the forest. It would be several hours at least before the guards woke, and when they did, they would know at once what I had done.

And King Agamemnon would not allow me to live for it. He would come after me and ensure that I was punished for my treachery.

I turned again towards the line of Trojans escaping to their freedom.

But when he does, I shall be ready.

Χρυσηίς
Krisayis, Troy

The Hours of Night

The Twenty-ninth Day of the Month of Ploughing, 1250 BC

'I won't leave you behind.'

I took Cassandra's hand and squeezed it. Though I could not see her face in the shadows of the night I knew that she was weeping.

We were standing by the South Gates, Cassandra's slave Lysianassa beside us, and the last of the Trojan men, women and children huddled around each other for warmth close to the great double gates as they awaited their turn in the line to escape from the city. The past twelve days had been a blur of checking names against the heralds' lists, packing belongings, finding guides to lead the way to the mountains, persuading the reluctant Trojans that they must leave their city and their possessions under royal decree. Cassandra and I had not slept for many nights. Now, on the twelfth night after Achilles' death, the Trojans were at last escaping from the city under the darkness of a new moon, hoping against hope that the Greeks would be too occupied with their mourning to notice the line of people streaming across the plain to the unguarded paths of the forest and the hills in the south.

I turned to Cassandra, my eyes heavy with fatigue. 'You have to, Cassandra! I will follow tomorrow with your brother Aeneas' wife as soon as her child is born, as we agreed. It is far better that I risk taking them alone tomorrow than that we delay the escape.'

'Please, let me stay with you. I'll leave the city when you do, I promise.'

I smiled at her in the darkness. 'A princess of Troy is far more valuable than I am. You must get yourself to safety now with the rest of the Trojans, for King Priam and Queen Hecuba, if for no one else.'

She hesitated for a moment, then, at last, I saw the silhouette of her head nod. She reached for my other hand and bent forwards to whisper, 'Troy owes you much, Krisayis.' She squeezed my hand. 'Because of you, our people will survive.'

There was a pause.

'It seems you did manage to trick the gods, after all,' she said in a low voice, and I could tell that she was smiling.

I smiled too. 'Perhaps I did.' I embraced my friend.

As we broke apart, a man stepped forwards from the shadows, a young shepherd from the hills with a plain-spun tunic and broad cheekbones. 'We should leave now, Princess.' He indicated the line of Trojans, which was even now dwindling and disappearing beneath the towering shadows of the walls. 'There is much distance to be made and there are only a few hours before daybreak.'

I nodded. 'Yes. My thanks to you, Iapyx. Make sure these last of the men, women and children reach the mountains beyond the forest before dawn.'

He looked up at the sky, then down at me. 'With the gods' will, my lady.'

I glanced at Cassandra, and she gave me a sidelong smile.

'Keep your wits about you, Iapyx,' I said, 'and we may not need the help of the gods.'

The Last Song

Βρισηίς
Briseis, Greek Camp

The Hour of Music

The Thirtieth Day of the Month of Ploughing, 1250 BC

I did not sleep that night. The slaves around me slept soundly in the quarters of King Agamemnon's tent, their dreams filled with ordinary cares. I, too, was untroubled in a way. I had never felt as clear as I had that night on the starry shores of Troy.

At last, at the very last, I knew what I must do.

Since Death had chosen to take from me the men I loved, I would join them in the Underworld myself and make my destiny at last.

The next morning, the sun rose to a clear sky, the clouds tinted with gold at the edges and the horizon a clear pale pink, like the inside of a shell – oddly beautiful, this dawn, as if the goddess knew it was the last time I would see her fingertips creeping over the horizon. I made my way between the slave women, already busying to prepare the king's morning meal, towards King Agamemnon's council chamber.

The lords were gathering for their usual morning meeting with the king, and a young slave – she could not have been more than twelve years of age – stood by the entrance, a pitcher of wine in her hands, her face pale and her eyes rimmed with dark circles of fatigue.

'Let me take that,' I said, moving to stand beside her. 'You go and get some more sleep.'

She gave me a swift, grateful glance. 'Are you sure?'

I nodded. She handed me the pitcher and slipped back into the slaves' quarters without another word.

The lords had assembled now. They sat where they always did, on juniper-wood stools set around the large circular table beside Agamemnon's throne.

'We have gathered,' Nestor rumbled, 'to discuss our tactics for the coming battles, now that Achilles is dead.'

One by one, the lords fell silent. I felt my fingers grip the clay pitcher in my hands at the sound of his name. But I would not allow myself to be distracted.

Not today. I was waiting, waiting for the sound that would announce the camp guards had discovered what I had done.

'Clearly, we no longer have any chance of taking the city by force,' the king said. He was glowering, his mouth narrowed to a thin line, and it was plain he felt nothing but anger at the loss of Achilles. 'No matter how stubborn he was, with Achilles gone we might as well be attacking the best-fortified city of the Aegean with a group of girls armed with shuttles and looms.'

Ajax leapt to his feet. 'Now wait just one moment—'

But Odysseus interrupted him. He had stood up, too, and had placed his hand on Ajax's shoulder. 'Come, Ajax,' he said. 'Be seated. I have a suggestion to make, my king, if you will hear it. One that . . .' he smiled '. . . does not require force of arms at all.'

'Another of your magic tricks, no doubt,' the king growled. It was evident he would not be easily impressed today.

Odysseus inclined his head. 'Indeed.'

He reached into his cloak and drew out a scroll of papyrus. Bending forwards, he spread it before the seated lords and proceeded to explain in a low voice something I could not hear. The other lords were pointing and muttering, and King Agamemnon's expression was shifting slowly from scepticism to incredulity, then excitement as I watched.

I squinted to see what they were looking at, but it was impossible from where I stood, and I dared not move.

Not yet.

At last the king thumped his fist on the arm of his throne. 'It's perfect!' he shouted, his belly wobbling with delight. 'Odysseus, you son of a trickster, you are Hermes reborn!' He spread his arms wide. 'My lords, soon we will break into the city of Troy, and you will bed its women!'

The lords cheered and raised their goblets to the sky.

'And I,' Agamemnon continued smoothly, 'shall have Achilles' slave girl at last.' He wetted his fat lips with his tongue. 'Good practice for the Trojan women we shall soon have, do you not agree?'

The lords laughed. The king's eyes swept the tent and found me, standing by the entrance. His eyes narrowed.

At that very moment, the tent flap was swept open and two men came running in, their armour clanking, helmets under their arms, to kneel at Agamemnon's feet.

I clenched my hands, fingers white. *There is no way back now.* I felt my hands shake slightly at my sides and tightened them harder, determined no one would see I was afraid, Agamemnon least of all.

It was almost time.

'My king!' one gasped, rising to stand. 'We have news of the gravest kind – of treason in your camp!'

King Agamemnon shifted in his throne, his face alert. 'Treason? By whom?'

The other drew a long breath. 'A slave – a slave girl. She drugged us with her wine!'

King Agamemnon's gaze shifted, slowly, towards me.

The lookouts turned and saw me.

'Her!' the first man shouted, pointing at me. 'It was her, my king!'

King Agamemnon's eyes were slits in his face. 'You tried to poison my guards?'

I shook my head. 'No.'

Diomedes laughed. 'But of course she would say that. She is a Trojan and a slave. These Trojans are all dirty, lying thieves.'

The lords laughed nastily.

I felt a strange ringing in my ears, courage rising in my chest now that the final moment was here. Perhaps this was how Achilles and Mynes had felt when they prepared to go to war.

At last, my time had come.

I set down the pitcher upon the table, carefully, and moved a few paces so that I stood facing the council of war. The lords were eyeing me as they would an untamed horse, fear and derision in their faces in equal measure.

'Get back to your place, slave,' Ajax called. 'What right have you to come near the true-born sons of Greece?'

But King Agamemnon's lips twisted into a humourless smile. 'Let us see what she has to say,' he said, his eyes boring into me. 'Let us see if she thinks she has anything worth saying, before she dies.'

I looked into the faces of the Greek lords – Odysseus, Ajax, Nestor, Diomedes, Agamemnon, all my captors – and took a deep breath.

'You have underestimated me, Greeks,' I said quietly.

There was a cry of rage and disbelief from the gathered lords.

'How dare she speak to us in such a way?' Diomedes shouted. 'It is an insult!'

King Agamemnon's expression had changed from pretended humour to anger, his eyebrows lowering upon his forehead like Zeus' thunderbolts upon the clouds.

'You have always thought that slaves and women were worth nothing,' I continued, my voice rising over the tumult, 'but, because of a slave, the greatest of the Greeks is dead. Because of a slave, you will never have the Troy you think to gain. And, Agamemnon,' I turned to gaze at the king, my voice gaining strength with my courage, 'you will *never* have me.'

I did it before they had a chance to guess what was in my mind. In a breath I was at the entrance and out of the tent, past the guards before they could see me and running, running across the shore, running through the assembly-place to the huge flaming pyre that lay in its centre, still piled high and burning strongly as was the custom until the eve of the twelfth day.

I heard a shout from behind me, '*Stop her!*', but I would not be stopped.

At last, after all that I had endured, I would make my own fate, as both the men I had lain with in love had told me that I would.

Achilles' pyre was burning hot as I reached it, the air around it shimmering, the flames lapping up to the impossibly blue sky. Faggots of new dry wood were piled up on the mound of packed earth, crackling invitingly, like the hearth Patroclus had tended in Achilles' hut. A makeshift ladder was still propped against the soil, where someone had been throwing driftwood onto the blazing fire.

In a single breath I scaled the ladder and threw myself on to the flames. My thoughts turned to Achilles as the haze of black smoke surrounded me, the way he had held me that night upon the shore, the heat of his arms, each of us the downfall of the other. I thought of Patroclus, dragging me through the Greek camp in a hail of arrows, whittling away at a wooden bird; Patroclus, his brown eyes open and staring. And I thought of Mynes, the husband I had loved, the sound of the rain pattering upon the olive tree as we embraced each other, the taste of the wine he had brought me on our wedding night upon my lips.

'No! Stop her! *Stop her!* She is *mine* to kill!'

But it was too late. I was already halfway to the Land of the Dead and the mist-covered banks of the Styx. The sound of the waves lapping against the shores of Troy, and the confused shouting of the Greek guards – those were the last things I heard. I focused my eyes on the sky, the blue shifting palely to white, and then to the brightest, sheerest, most shimmering light.

Wait for me in the Underworld.

Wait for me, Mynes, my love.

I will be there soon.

Wait for me.

Wait for me.

Χρυσηίς
Krisayis, Troy

The Hour of the Setting Sun

The Thirtieth Day of the Month of Ploughing, 1250 BC

All of the ordinary people of Troy were gone from the city, now. Only the warriors remained, a few of their most loyal slaves, and those of the royal princes and nobles, who had chosen to stay behind to guard their homes and their riches as their wives had fled. My father had come back from Didyma, only to refuse to leave his beloved temple again, no matter what I said to try to persuade him otherwise. And King Priam and Queen Hecuba had sworn to stay with their city, their nobles and their warriors, convinced of the thickness of their walls, the height of their towers and their inevitable victory to the very last.

That evening the palace was empty as I made my way from Cassandra's deserted chambers to my last feast in Troy. I was due to leave the city that very night under cover of darkness, as the final escort from the city for Princess Creusa, who had that very morning given birth to a little baby boy, Ascanius. There was a ghostlike quality to the echoing chambers and long, empty corridors, as if I could almost sense the ruins they would become: the deep trenches and low stone walls and piles of rubble, insufficient tribute to the living, breathing soul of Troy that had once been its people. The high-roofed scented chambers of young lovers, the gardens where beautiful girls had once walked and the wide roads that wound through the bustling city, full of loud-mouthed foreign merchants and dark-skinned slaves: all of them nothing, without the people who had made them live.

I slipped into the Great Hall and moved towards my usual seat near the window, far from the royal thrones, not wishing to talk, wanting to savour every last moment I had. The hall, the last stronghold of the rich and noble, was still populated with its usual boasting warriors and lords – though now it was small beer they drank, not wine, and boiled vetch and barley upon their platters. It was as if they would pretend, and go on pretending, that this was the feast of a city rich in wheat and wine and figs, not a starving city's last meal, in spite of the grey barley upon their plates and the thick, tasteless beer: for in their determined ignorance lay their hope.

When the tables were cleared of what little food remained and the wine-pourers were serving the last of the small beer, the bard struck up his lyre, first tuning the four-stringed shell so that it sang like a swallow in spring.

I glanced over at him, wondering why he had not left Troy with the others. He was young, dark-haired and tanned by the sun, with brown muscled arms and an honest, open face. His eyes were closed as if he were listening intently to the music pouring from his instrument. His song told of the gods, as the tales of bards often did: this one the story of Are and Arinniti, and their scandalous love-affair. He sang of how Arinniti's husband, Haphaistios, when he caught the two gods in his bed, bound them there with an ingenious set of chains, and summoned all the other gods to see. And how much mirth there was in heaven when the gods caught Are and Arinniti in the middle of their love-making, naked as the day they were born!

King Priam and Queen Hecuba, the warriors and gathered nobles were laughing as the singing came to an end and the slaves entered the hall. The nobles got to their feet, some unfastening silver pins from their cloak-clasps – the only treasures they had left – and placing them by the bard's leather pouch, gifts for his performance, as they walked to the large painted doors that led out to the courtyard.

The Great Hall was empty now. The bard was packing away his lyre and putting the gifts of silver into his pouch. I noticed how tall he was when he stood, and my heart beat a little faster.

'You sing well,' I said, my voice echoing across the empty hall.

He did not turn, but continued to fill his pouch.

'I said, you sing well,' I said more loudly.

Still he did not turn, and the silence stretched. He was fastening the straps now and lifting the lyre on to his back.

'Can you not hear me?' I asked again. 'I said—'

'I heard you, Krisayis,' he said, and his voice was clear and sweet.

I blushed. 'Oh.' I paused. 'Wait – how do you know my name?'

He did not answer. I stared at his back as he fastened the lyre, thinking. A memory had stirred unexpectedly in the back of my mind: the Greek camp, a tent, a voice; a sweet, clear voice, saying my name.

A sudden realization came over me.

'It was *you*!' I exclaimed. 'It was you, in the Greek camp! You recognized me there, too!'

He nodded slightly, still not turning, gazing out through one of the arches of the colonnade that faced the olive grove.

'But – but how did you know it was me?' I asked. 'We never even saw each other, and I'm sure I've never seen you before.'

'I have a talent with voices,' he said simply, bending to pick his leather pouch from the floor. 'And every young man in the Troad knows the name of the most beautiful girl in Troy.'

I blushed more deeply, then searched for something matter-of-fact to say. 'I liked your song,' I said.

He bowed. 'Thank you.'

He moved to leave.

'Wait,' I said, not quite sure what I was going to say. 'Where did the song come from? I – I should very much like to learn it.'

'I invented it,' he said. 'I enjoy telling stories.' He moved towards the doors.

I was thinking back to what he had said. *Every young man in the Troad knows the name of the most beautiful girl in Troy.* I blushed and smiled. *Beautiful. He called me beautiful.*

'Wait!' I called after him. 'You think I'm beautiful! Isn't that what you said?'

Slowly, he stopped.

'You think I'm beautiful!' I repeated, my heart racing. *Could it be that*

Apulunas' curse had not worked after all? 'You can see me, can you not?'

He hesitated, then, very slowly, shook his head.

'No, Krisayis,' he said. 'I may not be deaf, but I am . . .' he turned and pointed to his eyes, which were white and slightly glassy '. . . blind.'

My heart fell. 'Oh. I – I'm sorry.'

He smiled, then walked towards me and reached for my hand. The same warmth flooded my body that I had felt that day in the Greek camp. 'But I do not have to see you to know how beautiful you are. After all, there is more to it than simply seeing.'

Suddenly, there was the sound of something hard and heavy rolling across the floor towards us. The bard let go of my hand and bent down deftly to pick it up. He held it out to me.

'Is this yours?'

It was a golden apple. I took it from him, turning it over to look at the soft gold sheen of its skin. There was an inscription on it in elegant slanting writing, and I held it up to the fading light.

For the Most Beautiful.

I looked at it, thinking.

Then I walked over to the arch of the colonnade, reached back and threw it up, up into the sky. It went spinning through the air, glittering in the evening sun.

And then it was gone.

Epilogue

'So there you have it,' Hermes says to the cupids. They are gazing up at him, their little mouths open, entranced. Even the older ones have forgotten their duties and are lying, chins propped on fists, staring at Hermes. 'The story of the Trojan War, the real story, told the way it happened by the people it happened to, and me, Hermes, the god who watched it all.

'It wasn't too long after our story ends that King Agamemnon decided to make use of Odysseus' plan, and the Wooden Horse, filled with Greek soldiers, was welcomed inside the walls, like a gift from us gods. When the city was silent and the sky above Troy was dark, the Greeks came out from the horse's belly and opened the gates to the army. The city was burned to a crisp, its well-built walls shattered, its towers toppled.

'Cassandra's prophecy was, at last, fulfilled, and the loveliest city in the Aegean was left smoking on the horizon as the Greek ships sailed away, Helen standing at the stern of Menelaus' vessel, watching the ruins of Troy slip over the edge of the earth.

'Yes,' Hermes continues, as the cupids gaze at him, 'the Greeks won the Trojan War, and so, as it always goes, they and their poets were the ones who sang the tales of their victory. But what the Greeks and the Muses did not tell you,' he permits himself a smile, 'was that, when the Greeks entered the city, they found only the warriors and nobles, their king and queen. There were no women to rape, no children to murder and enslave, no ordinary folk to put to the sword or slaves to steal and sell for gold. All the other citizens and slaves of Troy were gone – escaped to Mount Ida far to the south and beyond, where

they lived and thrived and then, when many years had passed and their children were grown, returned across the rocky ridges of the mountains and north towards the Trojan plain to settle Troy once more. And so, in the end, the people of Troy were saved.'

He points down from the clouds, and the cupids peer over the edge, as if they can almost see the crowds of Trojans walking together – children on mothers' hips, husbands leading aged fathers by the hand – over the mountains' sloping flanks and north to Troy.

'But Briseis did not leave,' Hermes continues. 'She found her end on the Trojan shore, consumed by fire and her love, thereby eluding a fate that would have seen her tortured and killed for treason at the hands of her captor Agamemnon. She was reunited at last in the Underworld with Mynes, the man she had loved most; and they will spend eternity there together, as they could not on this earth.

'As for Krisayis,' he says, 'she escaped Troy with her bard that very night, before the Greeks sacked the city. And, now I think of it, I may as well claim credit for that last little incident while I have the chance. Who else, after all, would have thought to steal the golden apple from Aphrodite's dressing-table all that time ago? Who else would have been clever enough to think of a way around Apollo's curse? And who else would have dreamt of playing a trick on my dear brother by sending a blind bard to fall in love with his unfortunate paramour?

'Sometimes I'm just too clever for my own good.'

The cupids giggle, and some applaud.

Hermes grins. 'I must admit, Apollo wasn't amused when he found out, but he's got over it now. And he's managed to find other ways, and other women, to console himself.

'So Krisayis and her bard are travelling the country somewhere to the south of Troy, blissfully unknown to the gods, not famous enough to tell stories about, but happy enough to last them both a lifetime. And more, I shouldn't doubt.

'It's the memories that really count, you see.

'After all,' he says, 'isn't that what stories are?'

Author's Note

The book you have just read is inspired by a 2,500-year-old poem called the *Iliad*, an epic narrative composed in ancient Greek by a blind poet called Homer, who lived in the islands off the coast of modern Turkey around 750 BC. It is the story of Achilles, the most famous warrior of the ancient world: his anger at King Agamemnon, his grief at the death of Patroclus, and the duel with Hector that ultimately sets the seal upon his fate. It is a story about war and the choices that men have to make in war. It is a tale of blood and guts and death, and the fight to win Helen and the city of Troy.

But there is another – hidden – side to the *Iliad*, the part of the story that Homer left more or less untold, and that is the story of its women. I have always been fascinated by the female characters of the *Iliad*, who hide behind the scenes, behind the walls of Troy or in the huts of the Greek camp. When they make their brief appearances in the poem, they can be loving and sensitive, like Hector's wife, Princess Andromache. They can be guilty temptresses or remorseful victims of Fate, like Helen. They can be warm and caring mothers, like Queen Hecuba, anxious mothers, like Thetis; they can be daughters, sisters, friends and wives.

But the two women I was always most fascinated by were Briseis and Chryseis/Krisayis.[1] Why them? Well, in the *Iliad*, it is these two women who set the whole plot in motion. The poem opens with the events described in this book: the outbreak of plague in the Greek camp, and

1 Krisayis' Greek name, *Χρυσηις*, is normally transliterated into English as Chryseis. I chose to spell her name differently (though the transliteration Krisayis is, in fact, equally true to the Greek), both in order to maintain a more Anatolian presence in the text ('ch' and 'ei' are particularly Greek sounds), and to avoid confusion between Briseis and Chryseis' names.

Achilles calling the assembly. It is at this assembly in the first book of the *Iliad* that Krisayis' father forces King Agamemnon to give her up, and that Agamemnon, in turn, takes Briseis away from Achilles. Achilles leaves the war in outrage – and the stage is set for the story of the *Iliad*. One could even say that if it weren't for these two women the story of the *Iliad* – one of the greatest works of world literature – would never have happened. And yet, despite their vital role in setting up the plot, Briseis and Krisayis are subsequently rarely mentioned. Krisayis is shipped off the scene only a few lines after the assembly has finished, and Briseis remains in the poem to make one-line appearances and a single brief speech to mourn the death of Patroclus.

It is when you start to pay attention to these two fascinating women, however, piecing together the bits and pieces of evidence scattered throughout the *Iliad* and other literary works about their past lives and their experience of the war, that you start to appreciate just how rich and exciting their stories are in their own right – quite capable of rivalling even Achilles' tale.

This, then, was where I got interested. Sifting through the clues the *Iliad* gave me, I discovered Briseis' harrowing tale – married to Prince Mynes of Lyrnessus, losing her husband and three brothers at the hands of Achilles, then forced to be a slave in his bed. Reading the *Iliad* alongside subsequent retellings of the Trojan War story – including Shakespeare's *Troilus and Cressida* – I discovered the ancient tradition of Troilus' love for Krisayis, her capture by the Greeks and her release to Larisa.[2]

Those stories were enough to have me hooked. They were just waiting to be told.

But it is not simply that Briseis and Krisayis' lives make good stories. Their experiences make us think about the *Iliad*, and war more generally, in an entirely different way. When we imagine what the female prisoners of war in the Greek camp must have gone through, what it must have been like to lose your husband, your father, your brothers, and be forced into slavery to the man who killed them; all of this makes us reflect on the experience of war for everyone involved, not

2 Krisayis' hometown is called Chryse in the *Iliad*, but is altered here to the name of a nearby Homeric town to avoid confusion with her Greek name.

just the people fighting on the battlefield. It makes us understand the cost to families, households, whole ways of life, not only to the young men who tragically lose their lives in the fighting. It makes us realize, fundamentally, just what is at stake in a war. But it also shows us the things that men and women alike can fight for, even in times of deepest trouble – the qualities of love, beauty and, in the very end, peace.

You might be wondering at this point how much of the story I have told above is actually true. Well, that is a twofold question. On the one hand, you might ask how true it is to historical fact. Was Achilles a real person? Did Troy exist? But you could also ask how close it is to the legendary story of the *Iliad*, which inspired this book in the first place. The simple answer is that all the main events and facts come directly from the *Iliad*. The arc of the story from the plague onwards – Krisayis' journey to Larisa (Chryse), Briseis' transfer to Agamemnon's tent, Achilles' refusal of the embassy, the death of Patroclus and of Hector – are all integral to the narrative of the *Iliad*. What I have added are the motivations, thoughts and feelings of my characters; their reactions to an unfair world in which they have very little or no power to affect the events they are caught up in. My aim, ultimately, is to provide a fresh look on the timeless legend of the *Iliad*, and to put the reader, if just for a moment, into the shoes of two of the key actors behind the scenes.

And so to the first question: is the *Iliad* really just a legend? You might think it is simply a good story, and that is what people did think, for thousands of years. But in 1876 the palaces of Agamemnon, Nestor and Menelaus were discovered in mainland Greece, strikingly similar to their Homeric descriptions. And in 1871 the city of Troy itself was rediscovered by Frank Calvert and Heinrich Schliemann on the shores of the Dardanelles in Turkey, exactly where Homer had placed it. The archaeological site provides a compelling insight into the piecemeal construction of history, with cities built in layers one on top of another from 3000 BC (Troy I) right up to 500 AD (Troy IX). Indeed, it is particularly interesting that the city which has been identified as Homer's Troy – labelled by the archaeologists as Troy VI/VIIa – was built over and reoccupied again and again on the same site for several hundred years after the so-called 'fall' of Troy around 1250 BC, right up until well into the period of the Roman empire. Who knows? Perhaps, despite what Homer would have us believe, the people of Troy really did survive to rebuild their city.

The world of the women and heroes of Troy is fascinating and – as with all history (which is one of the wonderful things about it) – there is always more to learn. If you want to find out more, take a look through the suggestions for further reading, and visit my website at www.emilyhauser.com.

Bronze Age Calendar

We now know that Ancient Troy looked much more to Anatolian customs from the Hittite empire in the east than it did to those of the Greeks. In terms of time, however, we have very little evidence from Troy itself as to how they measured the passing of hours, months and seasons, so I have had to turn instead to Mycenaean Greece. The evidence from ancient Mycenaean Greek tablets for the calendar is fragmentary and difficult to piece together, but various different words have been found that seem to apply to months of the year. Thus we have *wodewijo* – the 'month of roses'; *emesijo* – the 'month of wheat'; *metuwo newo* – the 'month of new wine'; *ploistos* – the 'sailing month'; and so on. Although we have no further clues as to which months these referred to, by matching them to the farming calendar in Hesiod's *Works and Days*, as well as the seasonal growth of plants and crops in north-western Turkey, I have amassed the following Bronze Age calendar, which is followed throughout the text (ellipses (. . .) and question marks indicate names and translations that are uncertain):

dios	The Month of Zeus	January
metuwo newo	The Month of New Wine	February
deukijo	The Month of Deukios (?)	March
ploistos	The Month of Sailing	April
amakoto(s)	The Month of the Harvest	May
wodewijo	The Month of Roses	June
emesijo	The Month of Threshing Wheat	July

amakoto(s)	The Month of the Grape Harvest	August
. . .	The Month of Ploughing	September
lapatos	. . .	October
karaerijo	. . .	November
diwijo	The Month of the Goddess	December

The ancient Greeks of the later period split the hours of daylight into twelve, no matter the time of year – meaning that these so-called 'hours' were longer in summer and shorter in winter. Each hour was named after one of the twelve *Horai*, goddesses of time. Taking the hours of daylight on the summer solstice at the site of Troy (15.05 hours), I have divided them in twelve to create an approximation of the hours of the *Horai* below:

Augé	The Hour of Daybreak	05:29
Anatolé	The Hour of the Rising Sun	06:44
Mousiké	The Hour of Music	07:59
Gymnastiké	The Hour of Athletics	09:14
Nymphé	The Hour of the Bath	10:29
Mesémbria	The Hour of the Middle of the Day	11:44
Spondé	The Hour of Offerings	12:59
Életé	The Hour of Prayer	14:14
Akté	The Hour of the Evening Meal	15:29
Hesperis	The Hour of Evening	16:44
Dusis	The Hour of the Setting Sun	17:59
Arktos	The Hour of the Stars	19:14
. . .	The Hours of Night	20:32 until dawn

Glossary of Characters

Most of the characters in this book come from the real legends and poems of the ancient Greeks; names of the Trojan gods are taken either from the Hittite texts (in the case of Arinniti, Apulunas and Zayu), or from the ancient Mycenaean Linear B tablets. Mortals are indicated in **bold**, and immortals in ***bold italics.*** Characters I have invented for the purposes of the story are marked with a star (*).

Achilles – The son of Thetis and Peleus, Achilles is the greatest warrior to fight on the Greek side against Troy in the Trojan War. He was raised on the slopes of Mount Pelion with his friend and mentor Patroclus, who accompanies him to Troy.

Aeneas – A member of the Trojan royal family and (in this story) son of King Priam; husband of Creusa and father of Ascanius. After the events of this book, he will be the leader of the escape from the sack of Troy and the founder of the city of Rome.

Agamemnon – King of the Greeks and ruler of Mycenae, King Agamemnon leads the expedition against Troy along with his brother Menelaus. Having incurred Athena's wrath, he returns to Greece after the war only to be killed by his wife and his cousin in their plot to overthrow him on the throne of Mycenae.

***Aigion** – The second of Briseis' brothers in Pedasus.

Ajax – One of the Greek warriors and lord of Salamis. After the Trojan War, when Athena becomes angered with the Greeks, she drives him mad and he commits suicide in shame.

Andromache – Princess of Thebe and daughter of King Eëtion, later wife of Hector. After the fall of Troy, she is taken prisoner by the Greeks and becomes a concubine of Achilles' son, Neoptolemus.

Aphrodite – Goddess of love and sex, and winner of the beauty contest administered by Paris.

Apollo – God of archery, medicine, the sun and poetry, Apollo is often to be found in the company of his half-brother, Hermes. Apollo appears in the Hittite texts under the guise Apulunas or Apaliunas in a treaty with King Aleksandros of Wilusa, an ancient king of Troy.

***Ardys** – King of Lyrnessus, husband of Queen Hesione and father of Prince Mynes.

Ares – The god of war.

Artemis – Goddess of hunting, the moon, childbirth and virginity; twin sister of Apollo.

Athena – Goddess of wisdom and war, Athena sides with the Greeks and will do anything to help them win.

***Bias** – Father of Princess Briseis and husband of Queen Laodice.

Briseis – One of the two main narrators of our story, Briseis is the princess of Pedasus.

Cassandra – Daughter of King Priam and Queen Hecuba of Troy, and Krisayis' closest friend.

Cycnus – Son of Poseidon and king of Colonae, just south of Troy.

***Deiope** – The nurse of Briseis in Pedasus.

Deiphobus – The second of King Priam's sons and husband of Helen after Paris dies.

Diomedes – One of the Greek heroes and lord of Argos.

Eurybates – One of the two heralds of King Agamemnon.

Fates, the – Three goddesses whose job it is to spin the thread of human life.

Hector – Eldest son of King Priam of Troy and husband of Andromache. He is the best fighter in Troy and the leader of the Trojan troops.

Hecuba – Wife of King Priam of Troy and mother of Hector, Deiphobus, Aeneas, Paris, Troilus and Cassandra. After the fall of Troy, she is captured by Odysseus and taken to Greece as a slave.

Helen – 'The face that launched a thousand ships', Helen is said to be the most beautiful woman in the world, and was originally married to Lord Menelaus of Sparta. When Aphrodite wins the beauty contest she promises Helen to Paris of Troy. After the Greeks sack Troy, she is captured by her cuckolded husband Menelaus who, though he intends to kill her, cannot do so when faced with her beauty. They return to Greece together instead.

Hephaestus – The lame craftsman god and husband of Aphrodite.

Hera – Queen of the gods and wife of Zeus, Hera is a strong supporter of the Greeks in the Trojan War and wants nothing more than to destroy the city of Troy.

Hermes – The son of Zeus and Maia, Hermes is the messenger god and god of tricks and thievery.

***Hesione** – Queen of Lyrnessus, wife of King Ardys and mother of Mynes.

Homer – The name of the poet who wrote the *Iliad*. He is believed to have lived around the eighth century BC. The ancient Greeks thought that he was blind, and that he lived on the island of Chios, just off the western coast of modern-day Turkey.

Krisayis – One of the two main narrators of our story, Krisayis is the daughter of the High Priest of Troy, Polydamas.

***Laodice** – Mother of Princess Briseis and wife of King Bias.

***Lycaon** – Priest at Larisa during the absence of High Priest Polydamas.

Menelaus – Lord of Sparta and brother of King Agamemnon of Mycenae. Menelaus was originally married to Helen before she left for Troy with Paris, and sails back to Sparta with Helen after the capture of Troy.

Menoetius – The father of Patroclus. When Odysseus came to summon Achilles and Patroclus to war, Menoetius made Achilles swear not to let Patroclus fight.

Muses, the – The nine goddesses of poetry and song, daughters of Apollo and the goddess Memory.

Mynes – Prince of Lyrnessus and husband of Briseis.

Nestor – A Greek noble and lord of Pylos, Nestor is an old man and a venerable orator.

nymphs – Female spirits of the natural world, nymphs inhabit forests, rivers, mountains and the sea.

Odysseus – Lord of Ithaca and husband of Penelope, known for his cunning. He endures a ten-year journey by sea back to Ithaca because of the wrath of Poseidon.

Paris – A son of King Priam and Queen Hecuba, Paris was chosen by Zeus to judge the beauty contest over the golden apple. He was sent soon after on the embassy to Lord Menelaus of Sparta, along with his elder brother, Hector, where he promptly stole Menelaus' wife Helen and took her back to Troy with him.

Patroclus – Patroclus is Achilles' friend and mentor, and son of Menoetius.

***Polydamas** – High Priest of Apulunas in Troy and father of Krisayis.

Poseidon – God of the ocean and brother of Zeus.

Priam – The king of Troy, husband of Hecuba and father of Hector, Deiphobus, Aeneas, Paris, Troilus and Cassandra. He is killed during the sack of Troy by Achilles' son, Neoptolemus.

***Rhenor** – Eldest brother of Briseis and prince of Pedasus.

Talthybius – One of the heralds of King Agamemnon.

Thetis – Sea-nymph and mother of Achilles.

***Thersites** – Youngest brother of Briseis.

Troilus – The youngest son of King Priam of Troy.

Tyndareus – Lord of Sparta and father of Helen.

Zeus – King of the gods, Zeus is the god of thunder and husband of Hera.

Glossary of Places

Aegean (Sea), the – The part of the Mediterranean Sea that separates the mainland of Greece from what is now the mainland of Turkey.

Argos – A city in Ancient Greece and capital of one of the states of Greece, ruled over by Diomedes.

Aulis – A town in northern Greece (modern *Avlida*) where the Greek fleet gathered to set off to Troy.

Black Sea, the – A sea in the north-eastern Mediterranean almost entirely surrounded by land and connected to the Mediterranean by the narrow strait of the Hellespont (now called the Dardanelles).

Colonae – A town in the Troad just south of Troy, ruled over by Poseidon's son Cycnus.

Cranae – A small island off the Laconian coast in Greece, where Paris and Helen were said to have spent their first night together.

Dardanian Plain – The plain around Troy, so called after Dardanos, a legendary king of Troy.

Egypt – One of the most powerful ancient civilizations of the Mediterranean, builders of the famous pyramids and a key player in Bronze Age politics and trade, the Egyptian pharaohs exported grain, paper, gold and linen around the Mediterranean.

Ethiopia – A distant and mythical land in Homer, located at the end of the earth. The gods often go to feast with the Ethiopians, who are noble and godly people.

Gargarus – The topmost peak of Mount Ida.

Greece – Homeland of the Greeks, comprising the city states of Argos, Ithaca, Mycenae, Phthia, Pylos and Sparta, among others.

Hades – Both the god of the Underworld and the name of the Underworld itself, where the ancients believed that the spirits of the dead went to spend eternity. It was reached by crossing the River Styx in a boat ferried by a man called Charon. There were several different parts to the Underworld: Tartarus, where the wicked were punished, the Elysian Fields, where the heroes went, and the Isles of the Blessed, the ultimate destination and eternal paradise.

Ida, Mount – The largest mountain on the Trojan plain and the home of the gods.

Ithaca – A rocky island to the west of mainland Greece ruled over by Odysseus.

Larisa – The hometown of Polydamas and Krisayis, called Chryse in the *Iliad* but changed in this book to avoid confusion with Krisayis' name. Although the exact location of the ancient city of Chryse is unknown, it is most often identified with the site of a Hellenistic temple to Apollo on the south-west coast of the Troad, near the modern village of Gülpinar.

Lemnos – An island to the west of Troy.

Lesbos – A large island to the south-west of the Troad.

Lycia – An ancient Anatolian civilization in what is now south-western Turkey. It is ruled over by Sarpedon, king of the Lycians and a Trojan ally, who brings his troops to Troy to help with the war.

Lyrnessus – The town ruled over by Prince Mynes and his parents, King Ardys and Queen Hesione, and the later home of Briseis. Although the location of the city is unknown, Lyrnessus clearly lay between Pedasus and Thebe in Homer's description of the geography of the

Troad. It is now thought to have occupied the hill of Antandros in modern Altınoluk, on the southern coast of the Troad a few miles south of the slopes of Mount Ida.

Maeonia – A region to the south of the Troad.

Mycenae – A city in the Peloponnese, one of the largest in the ancient Greek Bronze Age world. It was ruled over by King Agamemnon and was rediscovered by Heinrich Schliemann in 1876. The ruins of the impressive palace can be seen today. Mycenae was famous for its gold: Homer calls it 'rich in gold'.

Mysia – A region to the east of the Troad.

Ocean – The ancient Greeks believed that the ocean encircled the whole world like a river around a flat disc of land. The sun and moon were thought to rise and set from the waters of the ocean.

Olympus, Mount – A mountain in northern Greece and the home of the Olympian gods.

Pedasus – The hometown of Briseis on the southern shore of the Troad. It is usually identified with modern Assos.

Scaean Gates – The western gates of the upper city of Troy, and the main gates leading towards the seashore and the battleground.

Scamander, the – One of the two rivers that runs across the Trojan plain. It was believed that the river was also a god: Homer describes him fighting on the side of the Trojans against Achilles in the war.

Sparta – A city in the south of Greece ruled by Menelaus and Helen and the later home of the famous Spartan warriors.

Styx, the – The river that formed the boundary between earth and the Underworld; to enter the Underworld the ferryman Charon had to be paid to take the dead across. It was seen as sacred by the gods: they would often swear oaths by the River Styx. Its waters were thought to confer immortality, and it is into the River Styx that Thetis dips her son Achilles in the hope of making him immortal.

Taygetus, Mount – A mountain range in the Peloponnese, the southern peninsula of Greece, near Sparta.

Tenedos – A small island just off the coast of Troy.

Thebe – City of Andromache, Hector's wife, and ruled over by King Eëtion. The exact location of Thebe is uncertain, but most scholars identify it with the modern town of Edremit, on the coast south of Mount Ida.

Thrace – The mountainous region to the north of Thessaly in Greece.

Troad, the – The peninsula in the north-western part of Turkey on which the city of Troy was built, today called the Biga Peninsula. It includes the cities of Troy, Larisa, Chryse, Pedasus, Lyrnessus and Thebe among others, as well as Mount Ida.

Troy – The ancient city of King Priam, which was besieged by the Greek forces of King Agamemnon around the twelfth century BC. It was rediscovered by Heinrich Schliemann in 1871 on the hill of Hisarlık in north-western Turkey. Its ruins can be visited today.

Underworld, the – Also called Hades, this was where the ancients believed that the spirits of the dead went to spend eternity. It was reached by crossing the River Styx in a boat ferried by Charon. There were several different parts to the Underworld: Tartarus, where the wicked were punished, the Elysian Fields, where the heroes went, and the Isles of the Blessed, the eternal paradise.

Further Reading

The *Iliad*

Translations from the Ancient Greek

Fagles, Robert. *The Iliad*. London: Penguin, 1991.

Fitzgerald, Robert. *The Iliad*. Oxford: Oxford University Press, 2008.

Lattimore, Richmond. *The Iliad*. Chicago: University of Chicago Press, 2011.

Lombardo, Stanley. *The Iliad*. Indiana: Hackett, 1997.

Secondary Reading

Silk, Michael. *Homer: The Iliad*. Cambridge: Cambridge University Press, 2004.

Schein, Seth. *The Mortal Hero: An Introduction to Homer's Iliad*. Berkeley: University of California Press, 1984.

Homer

Fowler, Robert (ed.) *The Cambridge Companion to Homer*. Cambridge: Cambridge Press, 2004.

Griffin, Jasper. *Homer*. Oxford: Oxford University Press, 1980.

Kirk, Geoffrey. *Homer and the Epic*. Cambridge: Cambridge University Press, 1965.

The Trojan War

Strauss, Barry. *The Trojan War: A New History*. London: Hutchinson, 2007.

Thomas, Carol and Craig Conant. *The Trojan War*. Westport: Greenwood Press, 2005.

Wood, Michael. *In Search of the Trojan War*. (dir. Bill Lyons) BBC, 1985.

The Bronze Age World

Mylonas, George. *Mycenae and the Mycenaean Age*. Princeton: Princeton University Press, 1966.

Osborne, Robin. *Homer's Society*, in *The Cambridge Companion to Homer*, Robert Fowler (ed.), 206–219. Cambridge: Cambridge University Press, 2004.